CITY ∽ OF ∾ SPELLS...

Sometimes, it's hard to remember everything that's happened in a series so far! That's why we've got a handy recap to remind you of everything that went down in *Into the Crooked Place*, so you're refreshed and ready to dive into the magic of *City of Spells*. Enjoy!

TAVIA, WESLEY, SAXONY, AND KARAM make their money in magic. But when the deadly Loj elixir sweeps the streets of Creije, they realize their Kingpin is off the rails. The elixir is mind control and Ashwood's using it to usurp their political leaders and create a realm of dark magic. And he's got Crafters (original magic creators who are all *supposed* to be dead)!

The gang decides to stop him, but they each have their own agenda: Tavia thinks the magic is connected to her mother's death. Wesley wants to replace Ashwood as Kingpin. Karam's part of an ancient order that protects Crafters (besides, even if she and Saxony broke up she's NOT letting her go off alone with a couple of crooks). And Saxony wants revenge. Turns out, *she's* a Crafter and Ashwood has taken her sister!

Together, they flee Creije and take a train across the world to Karam's home of Wrenyal to find allies. When they get there, Karam is reunited with her childhood friend Arjun and the leader of his ~~~~~~ (im~~~~~~antly) imbue

Wesley with magic, and then Arjun and a bunch of others join their fight. Along the journey, Karam and Saxony rekindle their romance (finally!) and things seem to be going well. Until a messenger bat tells them that Asees and the Crafters they left behind have all been killed by Ashwood.

Also, Creije is being toppled as more people fall under the thrall of the Loj. Uh-oh! But the gang has a plan! They're going to use time bombs to magically freeze Ashwood's armies, so they can be easily killed. Let's see him escape *that*.

They face a bunch of trials to get past Ashwood's magical defenses, like reliving their worst memories. Wesley sees the Crafter girl he betrayed years ago to rise higher in Ashwood's ranks and feels really crappy about his past choices. Also, Tavia and Wesley almost kiss! But then Tavia decides Wesley is too much of a bad influence. Damn!

When they finally get to the Kingpin's island, they're shocked to see Saxony's sister, Zekia, is there willingly. And *she* created the Loj elixir. What?! Turns out, she's also the girl Wesley gave up to the Kingpin, and so he feels responsible for her corruption. Oops.

A deadly fight breaks out and Wesley wounds Ashwood, making him flee through a magical gateway. Then staves— ancient Crafter markings—appear on Wesley's skin and Saxony realizes he's a true Crafter! His magic was hidden, even from him. Zekia then uses mind control to masquerade as Tavia and convince Wesley to leave with her. They escape through the gateway, leaving the *real* Tavia heartbroken.

Meanwhile, Karam and Arjun have set off the time barrels, freezing the Kingpin's army and defeating his forces, including a living, if mind-controlled, Asees. Yay! Only, then the island starts to crumble and sink into the sea. Not so yay. BUT the gang manages to escape just in time, and they set off to assemble a bigger army of Crafters and criminals from across the world to defeat Ashwood. And Tavia vows to rescue Wesley!

CITY OF SPELLS

Also by Alexandra Christo

To Kill a Kingdom

Into the Crooked Place

CITY OF SPELLS

ALEXANDRA CHRISTO

HOT
KEY
BOOKS

First published in Great Britain in 2021 by
HOT KEY BOOKS
An imprint of Bonnier Books UK
80–81 Wimpole St, London W1G 9RE
Owned by Bonnier Books
Sveavägen 56, Stockholm, Sweden
www.hotkeybooks.com

Text copyright © Alexandra Christo, 2021
Illustrations copyright © Patrick Knowles, 2019, 2021

A CIP catalogue record for this book is available from the British Library.

Paperback ISBN: 978-1-4714-0843-4
Hardback ISBN: 978-1-4714-1066-6
Also available as an ebook

1

Printed and bound by Clays Ltd, Elcograf S.p.A.

Hot Key Books is an imprint of Bonnier Books UK
www.bonnierbooks.co.uk

To all the magic you bring into the world every day.
Even when you don't realize.

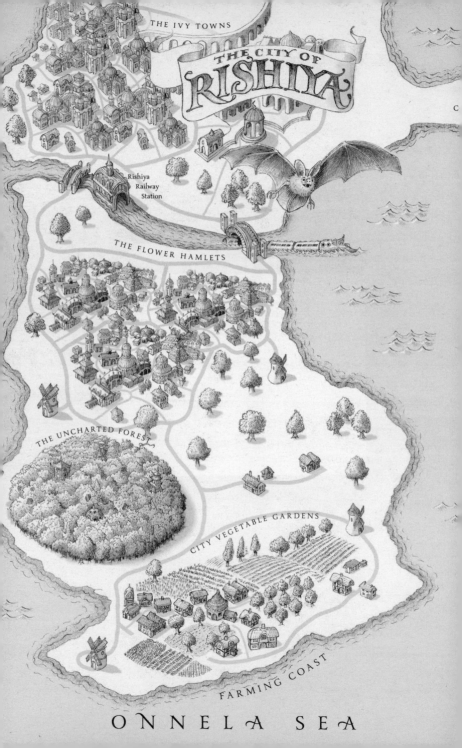

THE IVY TOWNS

THE CITY OF RISHIYA

Rishiya
Railway
Station

THE FLOWER HAMLETS

THE UNCHARTED FOREST

CITY VEGETABLE GARDENS

FARMING COAST

ONNELA SEA

THE STEADY MOUNTAINS

THE CITY OF
CREIJE

Creije Railway
Station

OSSING

The Crook

Central Bridge

CREIJE CITY OUTSKIRTS

CITY CROSSING

THE LOOMING VALLEY

THE BARREN WOODS

TISVGEN

Tisvgen Railway
Station

CEMETERY SHORE

PROLOGUE

Vea

Vea Akintola didn't want to die, but people hardly ever got a choice in that.

Death was a monster in a world of magic, and unlike other monsters, it didn't lurk in the shadows or hide where you never thought to check. It stood out in the open, where you could always see it.

It let you know that it was there, that it was waiting, and that it would come for you.

Vea cradled Malik in her arms and let his tiny fingers wrap around hers. He held on to her like she was a secret he wanted to keep for himself.

"It's time," her mother said.

Vea nodded. Her mother was always prompt, even when it came to killing her.

"Are you ready?" Vea's mother asked, swooping her hair into a long graying braid that trailed down the staves on her arms.

Her curls flicked at the ends, refusing to be properly tamed, escaping wherever possible.

Vea's mother had a magic in her that was hard to pinpoint. It was in every part of her, from her white eyes to the scars that looked like puzzles across her familiar face. She looked gentle and harsh, brave and fearful, and very much like a mother, in that she stared at Vea like she'd *better get a move on*, lest she be late to her own funeral.

"I'm ready," Vea said, at the same time that Malik said, "Here we goooooo."

"Will there be magic?" he asked.

Malik was only five and so often didn't understand what was going on.

"Lots and lots," Vea said, tickling his stomach until his laughter carried into the wind.

She didn't tell him that afterward the magic would disappear and he would be left empty.

Hollow, but safe.

She focused on the *safe* part and chose not to think too much about what it might be like for him to grow up not knowing anything about all the little parts of himself and why they ticked and tocked the way that they did.

Vea's mother opened the door to the tree house and they stepped inside. Vea caught sight of her eldest daughter, Saxony, in the forest, and clutched on to Malik tighter, as if hugging him would be the same as hugging her.

She hadn't had the chance to say goodbye.

Not even to her husband, Bastian, who she loved dearly and who loved her back just as much—maybe twice as much—and so definitely couldn't be trusted to kill her.

Vea's mother was different.

Mothers could do things nobody else could, like predict the future, or tell truths from lies, or find all manner of lost things even in the places that everybody had surely already looked. It was their job to do the impossible and the unthinkable. For instance, Vea's mother would kill her so that the realms would be safe. And Vea would let her so that Malik would be safe.

Vea placed her son onto the small table in the center of the room, while her mother drew symbols on the floor and hummed an old song.

"Don't you know anything less sad?" Vea asked. "Sing happy birthday to Malik or something. You sound like you're at a funeral."

Her mother shot her a look, like she wanted to say, *This is a funeral*, but what she actually said was, "We've already sung that to him and he'll be spoiled if we do it twice."

"It's not like he'll remember," Vea said.

"Then there's definitely no point in doing it," her mother said back.

Alongside the predictions and the lie detection and the finding of lost things, mothers were also very good at having the last word. The dead never got the last word. They never got to say much at all, only the words others put in their mouth for years after they were buried.

The dead left their legacy to the living and the living often changed it entirely.

"It's going to hurt," her mother said, and for the first time her voice broke.

Vea stroked Malik's hair from his face.

Whatever pain she felt would be worth it. It was the only way to stop all the evil in the world from snatching at her son. So many predictions, and in each of them his magic would bring only war and death.

It was her job to make sure that never happened.

To save him from himself.

"I love you," her mother said.

Vea swallowed.

She kept looking at Malik.

"I love you," he said, parroting his amja. "I love you and Daddy and Saxony and Zekia and magic."

He said Saxony like *Safony* and magic like *magik!!*

Vea kissed him on the head and took in a deep breath to steady herself and take in his scent one last time. Like grass and river salt.

"I love you to the shadow moon," she said.

Malik's deep brown eyes blinked up at her and his staves shone like starlight over his dark skin. She felt a pang in her heart, deep in the center, knowing that he'd never be able to use the gifts the Many Gods had given him. He'd never become Liege and never lead their Kin into a world of wonder.

She was going to steal it all from him. His future and his past. And the secret of why would live deep inside of him, in a place so hidden that even he wouldn't be able to find it.

Vea looked to her mother. "Start the spell."

Her mother nodded and began humming again, though this time the words were a curse and they floated through the air and into Vea's ears like a fire stick. They burned and scratched, and when Malik started crying—which he never, ever did, even when he broke his toe or chipped his tooth chasing Saxony around the Uncharted Forest—she knew that the curse was reaching into his heart and clawing out all of those ticks and tocks.

He screamed.

The world turned to dark and smoke.

There was a loud bang and the windows of the tree house burst like tears and Vea's mother was thrown into the forest. The fire was black, like shadows. They burned against Vea's skin and she couldn't move to run.

She stared at Malik, who cried, but remained untouched by the flames of his own magic. Vea tried to tell him that she loved him one last time, but she couldn't. So instead she watched as he cried, as he blinked up at her with those dark eyes, and then finally disappeared.

Only once he was gone could Vea close her eyes.

Only once he was gone did the flames swallow her whole.

1

Tavia

Tavia stroked her knife, waiting.

The moon was like a beam, casting far too much light on the uneven streets, forcing the shadows to retreat and leaving little space for anyone who might want to hide.

And these days, people needed all the hiding places they could get.

The street was empty, save for Tavia, and too quiet for it to be anything other than purposeful. She pulled up her hood.

This was the place.

Tavia knew a lie when she heard one—after all, she'd worked for the infamous Wesley Thornton Walcott, who was probably the best liar out there—and that skittish little Rishiyat busker hadn't been lying when Tavia held a mirror doll to the skies and scraped her knife against its carved face. He hadn't been lying when that same cut appeared across his own cheek and when his eyes widened as Tavia moved the knife to the doll's neck.

And he certainly hadn't been lying when she punched him in the face.

This was the spot.

Tavia wiped at her forehead.

The winds of Rishiya were too warm for her taste. She missed the biting edge of Creijen winter. Rishiya was a garden of buildings, with flowers falling from rooftops and vines curling around windows. The streets were filled with crisp leaves and smooth tree roots that coiled across the city and around the narrow rivers that hosted modest floating railways, the banks of which were amassed in purple holly and wildflowers.

And the ivy towns—where she had stolen her share of wallets while tightening her plan earlier that day—were bright and beautiful in a way that made Tavia feel just how rough her edges were.

But she wasn't in Creije anymore and she could never go back.

The Kingpin had seen to that.

Tavia checked her timepiece as the busker approached.

He was tall and stocky, with a wide jaw and dark eyes. His face matched the description, and the way he walked toward her, untouchable, and so similarly to the way Tavia knew she had walked the streets of Creije, told her this was her guy.

Nolan Kane.

Tavia smiled as he got closer.

Exactly two hours after sundown, just like her source had promised. Rishiya's best busker was prompt—he liked routine.

What a moron.

Keep them guessing. Don't do what's expected. Never let yourself get predictable.

Wesley had taught her the most important lesson a busker could know: how to be invisible.

"If you're not looking for me, then you should be," Nolan said, all bright teeth and smarmy eyebrows. "I'm about to give you a wild night."

Definitely not invisible.

"So what's your poison?"

"My poison," Tavia repeated, as though she was pondering it. "I'm a little particular. What have you got?"

"Anything," Nolan said. "Everything."

"That's a big promise to make."

Nolan took off his backpack and held it up like a trophy.

"There's not a single piece of magic in all of Rishiya that I ain't got tucked away. Any charm or trick you want, for the right price."

"So much magic in such a little bag," Tavia said. "You sure seem confident."

"Ever heard of a relativity charm?" Nolan asked. He tapped his backpack twice. "This baby can hold three times what it should."

Moron. Moron. Moron.

"You have any time magic in there?"

"Sure do. Looking to undo the last few days?" Nolan asked.

Which was silly, because you could barely rewind a few minutes with the best time charms out there. Tavia didn't want to erase the past: She wanted to disrupt it.

Time will be carried in strange hands,
across the realms and through stranger lands.
What is done will be undone,
a battle lost is a battle won.

That was the prediction she had heard from the fortune orb Wesley helped her create, and though Tavia didn't care much for prophecy, she could hardly ignore it. After all, the time barrels they had built to freeze the Kingpin's army had jolted something inside the old man, too.

Impossibly, it had hurt him.

They had made him *run*, and even if Tavia didn't put much stock in prophecy, she sure as shit put stock in people running away.

Whether Karam or the others agreed with her, it didn't matter.

Tavia knew what she was doing and she knew what they needed.

"I've got a memory serum," Nolan said. "Want to erase days or years? I've got it all. Whether it's you who wants to forget, or if you've got someone else's mind to play with."

Tavia pretended to look bored at the thought and let her eyes scan the streets as if she was looking for another busker.

Give up the goods, Nolan, she thought. *You know you want to.*

"Or maybe you know someone who misses the glory years," Nolan said, inching closer to her, desperate not to lose a sale.

Tavia understood that urge better than most.

"I've got something that can make people young as we are, younger even. Turn back their body clock for a whole day. And it can be all yours," Nolan said.

Tavia offered him a coy smile. "All mine?" she asked. "By the gods?"

"As long as you have money to spend," Nolan said. "You do have money to spend, don't you? I ain't got patience for time wasters."

Tavia reached into her pocket.

She had money all right. And though it wasn't hers—a technicality at best—she was ready to spend it.

Just not on this guy and his magic.

Tavia pulled out her gun.

"Great sales pitch," she said. "I think you've inspired me to take the lot as a contribution to our war effort."

Nolan's face shifted, eyes narrowing as Tavia gripped the bone gun tighter, taking aim.

Wesley's gun still felt odd in her hand, more delicate than she was used to and shaped in a way that didn't quite fit her grasp. Maybe it had been made for him or, even if it hadn't, it had carved itself around him, taking the shape Wesley wanted and molding itself to whatever he needed.

Wesley had that kind of effect.

"You're one of the people trying to go against the Kingpin," Nolan said. His mouth twisted into a sneer. "Haven't you heard? Dante Ashwood is fixing to tear down anyone who gets in the way of his new realm. Doyen Schulze can't stop him. You're on the wrong side and you don't have what it takes to win."

"We'll see about that," she said. "Now hand over your backpack while I'm being nice enough to let you live."

Nolan laughed and stepped forward so the gun was pressed

right to his chest. "How about *you* run along while I'm being nice enough to let you live," he said. "You don't have the stones to kill me. I can see it in your eyes."

He wasn't exactly wrong.

Shooting people wasn't Tavia's style, and killing a busker on the streets to steal his magic seemed excessive. She'd hoped the gun would scare him into submission, since she wasn't sure she could take him on in a fight. Tavia had always been better with magic than her fists, but the last thing she wanted was to waste good magic trying to rob him. They needed all the charms they could get these days.

"So that's a no to being robbed at gunpoint, then?" she asked. "Fair enough. I'll admit it was a bit much. Luckily, I have a Plan B."

Tavia took a step back—because she was not about to let this amateur snatch her weapon—and reached into her pocket with her free hand, keeping her eyes on Nolan to make sure he didn't try anything. Tavia was still as alert and quick as Wesley had taught her to be.

She may have spent the last week in a forest, but she wasn't rusty enough to let her guard down.

"A Plan B," Nolan repeated. "To shooting me?"

"A girl has to have her options," she said.

She squeezed the charm in her fingers, letting the magic wash over her with a familiar warmth. At first, it felt like it was pulling at her insides, tugging the skin from her bones and the nails from her fingertips. Her hands shook, her joints locked, and Tavia's eyes flickered until all she could see was pure, blinding white.

When the realms finally shifted back into color, Tavia was not alone.

She was surrounded by six more versions of herself.

All the Tavias stood with their black hair carving across their chins, gray eyes daring as they pulled knives from their pockets and guns from their belts and ran fingers over brightly polished knuckle dusters.

They circled Nolan with that same slow smile.

Tavia could feel them each at the corners of her mind, taking a small piece of her for themselves. She didn't need to think about what she wanted them to do because they were already inside her mind, predicting her actions and readying to do what she needed.

Duplicate charms were a real party and just the latest in a line of new magic the Crafters in their camp had created.

Tavia could get used to the power amp.

"Guess you're outnumbered now," Tavia said. "And maybe I couldn't take you alone in a fight, but I bet the seven of us could kick the crap out of you no problem."

Nolan's eyes were wide, his voice breathy with disbelief. "What in the name of the Many Gods is this?"

"Magic," Tavia said.

And with enough force to make even Karam crack a smile, she hit Nolan square across the jaw.

He went down in an instant, his backpack dropping onto the ground beside him.

"You're going to pay for that," he said, clutching his jaw. "My underboss taught me how to—"

"Let me tell you about *my* underboss," Tavia said.

She knelt down beside him and her many selves smiled onward in encouragement.

"His name was Wesley Thornton Walcott, and do you want to know what he taught me?"

Nolan flinched.

It was enough of an answer. Wesley's name was legend in the realm and synonymous with awful things Tavia preferred not to think about.

She snatched Nolan's backpack from the ground and stood.

"This is the part where I thank you for your donation to our war effort," Tavia said, tapping the backpack just like Nolan had. "All the tricks and charms of Rishiya. All the magic I could ever hope for. What a steal."

"Laugh all you want for now," Nolan said. "But when the Kingpin tears apart your city and burns everyone in it, I'll be there. I'll be by his side with the loyal buskers, and not even your big bad underboss will be able to stop the fire-gates from raining down on you and everyone you love."

Tavia swallowed.

She didn't want his words to hit close to home, but they did.

Dante Ashwood was already attacking districts within Creije and ripping apart everything about the city that Tavia had fallen in love with.

It was her home.

Wesley's home.

And right now she was powerless to save it.

Without her ruthless underboss to lead the buskers, Tavia was the only one left to fill the shoes of leadership among the crooks they had gathered, and yet she couldn't even put a bullet in a guy like Nolan.

Wesley wouldn't have hesitated. He wouldn't have stopped to chat and trade blows.

"Save your breath," Tavia said, trying to paint on her old smile. "You're going to need it for the long walk back to your underboss. I doubt he'll be happy that you got boosted on your own territory. Looks like you're in for a heap of trouble from dear old Casim."

She hitched the backpack onto her shoulder and turned from Nolan, her many selves following the action in a perfect reflection.

Only, there were now a dozen Rishiyat buskers standing in front of her, armed to the teeth with magic and guns. And not a one of them looked happy to see her.

"You need a hand, Nolan?" one of them asked.

From behind Tavia, the busker's laugh echoed.

"Now who's outnumbered?" Nolan said.

And then his friends charged at her.

For a moment Tavia had almost forgotten that she wasn't alone, before the six other versions of herself jumped in the way. They met Nolan's friends with fists and knives, taking on two or three each and creating a blockade between the buskers and Tavia.

Her many selves may not have had magic of their own, but they could throw a better punch than she could.

Tavia smiled onward at them, feeling an odd sense of pride, but she had only a few seconds to live in that moment before she felt herself being pulled violently back.

Nolan was yanking at her hair, keeping Tavia pressed against him. She wriggled against his grip, but the bastard was strong and the more she struggled, the more he pulled. The more his chest seemed to bounce with laughter.

"You're not so cocky now, are you?" he whispered in her ear.

His breath was warm and damp, and Tavia flinched away.

Nolan pushed his knife to her throat, pressing it with enough force that Tavia felt the blade draw a small line of blood across her neck. It dripped down to her chest.

At that, her duplicate selves paused slightly, twitched, as though the blade had touched them, too.

Tavia cursed.

She needed focus for them to work properly. She needed to not be distracted by a blade at her damn throat.

"Any last words?" Nolan asked.

"Yeah," Tavia said. The blade nicked her again as she spoke. "Never get this close to an enemy."

She threw her head back, skull cracking into Nolan's lip. His teeth dug into her and she felt the moment his blood sprayed outward onto the back of her neck.

Nolan screamed and fell to the ground, and Tavia didn't hesitate before she grabbed the backpack from where it had fallen beside him.

"You stupid little b—"

Tavia didn't wait to hear the end of that sentence.

She ran, faster than she'd ever run before.

She could still hear her six duplicate selves struggling to fight off the attackers, their grunts growing fainter with each step she took.

Djnfj.

It was not the best situation she had ever put herself in.

Especially since duplicate charms didn't last long and once the Rishiyat buskers had destroyed her magic selves, they were going to haul ass to catch up with her and tear her a new one.

Tavia almost regretted going at this alone. Karam had warned her that leaving camp *unsupervised* would be dangerous. Bringing a busker or two along for the ride would've been the smart play, but Tavia had to show them that she could get things sorted alone. That they could rely on her to do whatever needed to be done. She couldn't lead people if she was always relying on them to help her.

Anyway, there were worse things than being killed, and one of them was knowing that Karam was right.

Tavia rounded a corner, breathless.

She wasn't sure how much longer she could keep running, and she really didn't want to resort to using her newly stolen magic to escape.

She needed it.

Their army needed it.

Not just the time charms, but the rest, too. Every new busker they recruited needed new magic to protect themselves against Ashwood's army of Crafters and Loj-infected civilians, and there was only so much magic that their own Crafters could generate. Apparently, spinning new spells into charms took more time than she had originally thought.

What Tavia needed now was a hiding place.

She turned another corner and the sound of music echoed over. In the curve of the street, caught between an alley and a tree that reached for the night sky, was just the thing she needed.

The Last Hope.

When she'd scouted the bar as a place to lie low in case anything went wrong, she hadn't actually expected—or wanted—to use it. Rishiya didn't have much in terms of a nightlife, especially to someone who'd grown up on the streets of Creije, and this place was famous for boring booze and big bouncers.

It also, apparently, didn't take kindly to buskers. Which made it pretty perfect for wanting to escape Nolan and his band of bastards.

Tavia ran past the small queue and straight to the man guarding the door, who she'd already slipped a whole load of coin earlier that day. She flashed him her best smile and with a quick nod, he moved to push her through, something Karam—who took her job as a guard pretty seriously—would have frowned upon.

With one last cursory look to check she wasn't being followed, Tavia headed quickly inside.

She slowly edged past the flurry of people discussing politics with their liquor glasses poised by their lips, and found a quiet booth in the corner where she could keep her eyes on the doors in case Nolan and his friends made an appearance.

"Can I get you something?" a waiter asked, offering Tavia a menu.

She shook her head.

"We have the best drinks in town," he said. "Anything you want."

Cloverye, Tavia thought. *Just leave the bottle.*

But "I'm fine" was what she actually said. "Really. *Tek*."

The waiter nodded and walked away, though he left the menu, and if Tavia hadn't been waiting out a horde of buskers, she would have called him back for that bottle of Cloverye and a straw.

As she looked around at the bar, she thought about how the Last Hope really was aptly named, because Tavia couldn't imagine anyone who enjoyed fun making it a frequent choice. The music was low and far too smooth, forgetting to toe that gentle line between being quiet enough for people to order drinks but upbeat enough to let any worries fade away. It didn't have the same violent charm as the Crook.

"Fancy meeting you here."

Tavia closed her eyes in a sigh.

"Small world," she said, turning on the stool. "One might say it was suffocating."

Nolan did not look impressed, and Tavia suspected that it wasn't just because of his new black eye, or the blood on his mouth, or the various scrapes her duplicate selves had been good enough to give him.

Behind him, ten of his busker friends glared in perfect unison.

At the very least, she was happy that the other Tavias had managed to take down two of his crew, but eleven against one was still crappy odds, and she kicked herself for spending so long watching the front entrance to the Last Hope and turning her attention from the back.

Rookie mistake.

Something Wesley would have never let happen.

Except, try as hard as she could, Tavia wasn't Wesley. She was fast, but not fast enough. She could scout an escape and throw magic at her enemies, but she couldn't have eyes in the back of her head like he always seemed to.

She was good, but still not good enough.

"Just tell me that you weren't able to follow me," Tavia said. "I might be having some bad luck, but I swear you weren't on my tail. Save me some pride here."

"There's a tracking charm in the backpack," Nolan said. "Might have been good for you to check your stolen merchandise."

Tavia cursed, loud enough for him to raise an eyebrow. She'd have to remember to take that out after she kicked his ass. Tavia couldn't risk Nolan following her back to the forest.

"You have something of mine," Nolan said.

"And you have something of mine." Tavia gestured to his black eye. "Though you can keep that. How about I keep the backpack too and we'll call it even?"

"You're hilarious," Nolan deadpanned.

"Thanks," she said. "Most people don't appreciate how hard humor can be in the face of death."

"At least you know that you're going to die." Nolan took a menacing step toward her. "I hope you're prepared for how slow I'm going to make it. Maybe I'll even bring your head to my underboss. I'm sure Casim would appreciate one of Wesley's little goons as a trophy."

"Wow." Tavia grimaced. "That's really graphic. I think you offended my friend's delicate sensibilities."

She gestured with a nod behind him and when Nolan finally turned, he came face-to-face with Karam: Creije's most deadly fighter and the woman who was currently teaching Tavia how to kill someone in a dozen different ways.

Karam stepped forward, her skillfully embroidered clothes cascading down to her ankles in a way that was almost delicate, and so very much the opposite of Karam. Even from where Tavia stood, she could smell the peppermint salve on her friend's sliced knuckles, something the fighters in Creije loved to use to soothe their injuries and that Karam wore every day, just in case.

"I thought we agreed that you were going to stop being stupid," Karam said, Wrenyi accent thick on her tongue.

"I didn't agree to anything," Tavia said. "Did you *follow* me here?"

Karam crossed her arms over her chest. "Are you complaining about me saving you?"

"I don't need saving." Tavia leaned back in the booth. "I'm a busker, not a damsel."

Nolan looked between them with a disbelieving scoff. "Are you two finished?" he asked. "Because we were about to kill her."

For the first time, Karam looked at him, as if she had only just realized—or cared—that he was there.

"We have not been introduced," she said.

"No," Nolan said. "We haven't."

Karam held out a hand. "Hello," she said.

And then she used that hand to grab ahold of Nolan's shoulder and pull him toward her.

Without warning, Karam cracked her head against his.

The buskers broke into a frenzy as Nolan stumbled back, clutching his bloody nose. Quickly, Karam landed a kick to one of the others.

Tavia jumped up from the booth just as Nolan regained his footing, smashing a glass from a nearby table over his head. She shifted the backpack on her shoulder and slammed her foot against another busker's knee.

He went down with a yelp.

"This is why I had to follow you," Karam said.

She kicked a busker in the chest and as he bent over to catch his breath, she rolled across his back and punched another clean in the face.

"You are so *reckless*."

Tavia sighed at the lecture, which was becoming Karam's specialty these days.

"If you were so worried about my safety, then you could have helped me take Nolan down back in the streets before his buddies showed up," Tavia said.

She swung her fist into the air, catching the cheek of a nearby busker, just the way Karam had taught her.

Karam took out her knife and threw it into the shoulder of another. "I thought you did not need saving," she said.

Tavia rolled her eyes and kneed one of Nolan's friends in the groin.

"Forget making it slow!" Nolan yelled, pulling out a knife. "I'm going to gut you where you stand."

Tavia shook her head. "He really does like being graphic," she said to Karam.

She reached into her pocket for a pair of mirrored glasses and slipped them onto her nose, like she had seen Wesley do a dozen times.

"Here," she said to Karam. "Put these on."

Karam wrinkled her face and looked at Tavia like she was starting to lose her mind, but when she saw Tavia's hands go to her pocket for a second time, it seemed Karam knew better than to argue.

"What in the Many Gods are those for?" Nolan asked, wiping the blood from his nose.

Tavia clutched the charm in her hand, its jagged edge spiking into her palm like tiny needles.

"A way to show that if there's one thing I have," she said, "it's style."

She threw the charm down onto the floor and it exploded into a blinding light. Nolan and the others clutched at their eyes, screaming loud enough to drown out the bar's music altogether.

"Come on!" Tavia yelled. "We need to go!"

She pulled Karam toward the door, where the customers were now blindly running and screaming as their vision temporarily disappeared.

They spilled back out onto the streets of Rishiya and Karam ripped the glasses from her face.

"Have you considered trying *not* to get yourself killed every now and again?" she asked as they darted through the city.

"Not really," Tavia said, struggling to keep up with her pace. "I think I'd find it boring."

She didn't need to look at Karam to know that she was rolling her eyes, but Tavia felt invigorated. She had the magic she'd come for, so all in all the trip to the city had been a roaring success. And with the warm breeze on her neck and fire of victory in her belly, Tavia felt like maybe all hope wasn't quite lost.

Karam could call her reckless and the Crafters in the camp could call her a danger, but Tavia had a job to do. She had buskers to lead, and she was going to win this war and save Wesley, whether people approved of her methods or not.

2

Zekia

Zekia had a gun.

She'd never had one before and she wasn't even sure if she'd use it. She didn't like how large it looked in her small hands, or how heavy it felt for something that held only six bullets. Six lives that could be ruined. Zekia's hands were far smaller and could ruin far more than that.

Still, she had a gun.

It was best to have a gun when Wesley Thornton Walcott was conscious. Zekia had learned that the hard way.

The former underboss of Creije was handcuffed beside her, at the head of their army, eyes like charcoal as he stared into the bloody wreck of the district. The handcuffs were as unnecessary as Zekia's gun, because everyone—even the people they were about to kill, who should have been too busy to notice—knew that Wesley could slip them in a moment.

The best the cuffs could do was slow him down, but if

slowing Wesley down was an option, then Zekia would take it. He had fast hands and kept using them to try to kill members of their army. Though in fairness, Zekia had been using hers to do a lot worse, but his anger was never directed at her.

Of all the people he'd tried to kill, she was never one of them.

Maybe he was starting to understand that they were supposed to be by the Kingpin's side together, as family.

Wesley was bruised but not broken, and he watched with unblinking eyes as they tore through Creije, a piece at a time. This was the first district they would take from the capital and it wouldn't be the last.

One down, six to go.

It was dark out, and the once affluent High Town was now littered with soldiers, ash from the burnt-down houses of Creije's wealthy elite smoldering behind them. Zekia could see the busker dormitories from here, where Wesley had made his name. The windows stretched in high arches, colored glass like rainbows across the building so that it almost looked like a place of worship. She imagined him growing up there, practicing tricks while the moon watched patiently above.

She liked this part of Creije, which mixed people rich in gold with orphans like Wesley who did what they could to survive. Two sides of the world, so close to each other. Living in perfect contrast, like the array of colors on the dormitory windows.

"You won't kill me," the man in front of her said.

Zekia looked down at him.

They had captured him all too easily a few hours ago, not long after they'd stepped off the floating railways and into High Town.

There had been a lot of blood since then and a lot of screaming that Zekia hoped quickly to forget. But the moment they'd approached the district barricade and thrown this man to the ground, there had been an impasse.

He was on his knees and looking at Zekia's new gun with a narrow glare. She didn't know why—the gun wasn't originally meant for him. Still, he glared, and the way his fellow soldiers paused and held their breath made Zekia wonder just how important his life was in all of this.

Was he a general?

Did he command them while Doyen Fenna Schulze ran and gave orders from the safety of her hideout in Yejlath?

"Killing you doesn't matter," Zekia said. "The future is what matters, and I'm going to fix it."

The man spat on the ground by her feet. "You won't win. *Frjl* will always prevail."

The idea of freedom seemed funny to Zekia now. It was a dangerous thing to have and to be. Were these soldiers free as they followed orders to risk their lives and go against Dante Ashwood? Was Zekia free, trying to save the realms from a vision that had almost killed her?

If you knew the consequences of something, were you ever really free to choose what your heart desired?

"Creije will never fall."

"You're wrong," Zekia said.

Conquering Creije would be hard, but not impossible, and once it fell, the other cities wouldn't be far away. They looked to their capital as a beacon, following its example or trying to measure up to what it stood for.

If they took Creije, the rest of the Uskhanyan realm would come easy. Zekia was sure.

Almost.

As an Intuitcrafter, she should have had foresight, but now there were always far too many visions screaming in her head to make sense of. Too many futures that could come true and too many paths people could take. These days, guessing was the most accurate thing she could do.

She'd tried to focus and make sense of all the possibilities once, but she'd lost herself somewhere along the way, and now pasts and futures and their in-betweens swam through her veins like hungry fish.

It didn't matter, though. Ashwood had shown her the only future that mattered.

He'd shown her how to fix everything.

Zekia raised the gun to the man's head.

She'd never shot someone before. She'd never needed to.

She wondered if it would feel different to destroy a person without magic.

She heard the shuffle as the soldiers behind the barricade gritted their teeth and adjusted their weapons. She was standing in the center, between her army and theirs, and if she killed this man, they'd fire their guns and her Crafters would fire their magic.

More of the dead screaming through her mind.

Zekia closed her eyes. Her finger squeezed against the trigger and—

"Don't."

Wesley was a shadow over her.

"Kid," he said, placing his cuffed hand on top of hers. "Don't."

Zekia looked up at Wesley.

He was a little skinnier than when they'd first taken him, with hollowed cheeks and a chin she pictured cutting her finger on. He was also very tall, especially when Zekia was standing side by side with him like this. Then again, Wesley was also a good few years older than her and Zekia suspected that when she got to be his age, she'd be just as big.

Wesley still wore a suit, but it was stained with his blood. And his eyes, stamped purple as the sleeplessness mixed into bruising, held pupils that were nothing but large black circles stealing all the color from him.

He had been stubborn and he had been punished for it, because sometimes hurting people was the only way to save them. Dante Ashwood had taught her that lesson well. And once she finally got Wesley to give in, he would be so proud of her strength.

When she finally got Wesley to give in, everything would be okay.

They would be a family.

Zekia just had to try a little harder.

"Will you join us if I let him go?" Zekia asked Wesley. "Will you join us now that Creije is on the line?"

In an ideal world, Wesley would have said yes.

He would have taken her hand and said he'd be her big brother.

He would have told Zekia that he liked the view from his high horse very much, but that he liked the view from a throne a lot more.

Instead, Wesley lifted his hand from hers and said, "I wouldn't join you if my life was on the line."

"Don't you think it is already?"

Wesley laughed and Zekia didn't mind, even if it was the bitter, horrible kind of laugh that was meant to make her feel like killing him, just so she wouldn't be able to use him.

She liked it when Wesley laughed. She liked seeing him happy. She thought it was good that she made him smile every now and again, because the rest of the time all she did was make him scream.

"I'm not afraid of you, kid," Wesley said. "If you were going to kill me, then you would have done it already. And Creije isn't on the line. One district won't break my city. I built it to be strong and when this is all over, it'll still be standing."

Zekia could see why people found Wesley frightening. Even now, when he was hungry and cold and looking like he was about ready to fall over, he still looked formidable. He still looked like an underboss.

"The city may be standing, but the people will be on their knees."

It was Dante Ashwood who spoke then, and Zekia couldn't help but think how his voice sounded like a whisper in the wind and a storm in the dead of night all the same.

Dante Ashwood, Kingpin of Uskhanya and future Doyen of the realm, had shadows swarming him like fireflies to offer a shield of protection. Zekia thought they smelled like dark, burnt magic, as if Ashwood had seared their power to him, and sometimes she held her breath when they neared, just in case they tried to burn her from the inside out, stealing the parts of her mind that had not yet gone.

Zekia took one of Wesley's cuffed hands in her own.

His fingers were cold and limp, and he stared blankly ahead as if she hadn't touched him at all. When Zekia squeezed his hand, his jaw ticked.

Wesley looked like he was trying very hard not to kill her.

The moon acted as a torch as they eyed the barricade.

The fort was erected by the amityguards, with guns and charms holding their positions steady. There were hundreds and hundreds of them, but Zekia wasn't worried. Her army had what these soldiers never could: vision. The hope of a new realm, ruled by magic, with Crafters ready for a glorious future, filled with peace and light and no more pain.

They just had to kill a few people first.

But it was worth it. Ashwood had told her so.

Sometimes you have to hurt people to save them.

Ashwood approached the man on the ground and placed his large hands around the prisoner's head.

"Surrender," Ashwood said.

From behind the barricade, a voice cracked through a speaker. "We don't take orders from crooks."

Wesley snorted. Zekia squeezed his hand tighter.

Just surrender, she thought. *If you surrender, then I won't have to do anything bad.*

"Nobody needs to die today," Ashwood said.

"You sure as fire-gates do," the voice shot back.

Ashwood sighed, and in a last attempt to stay the bloodshed, he said, "Lay down your weapons and join me. Or keep them and die."

There was a pause.

Utter and complete silence.

The capital city of Uskhanya was alive every second, from dawn to dusk before the cycle started over, and usually a scream could barely be heard above the bastardized magic and laughter of criminals. But now Zekia could hear the birds crying out in warning and, if someone had a pin, she'd probably hear that drop too.

The speaker crackled again.

The man on the other end took a breath.

"*Djefil*," he said. "Go fuck yourself."

Ashwood sighed. He turned to Zekia. She caught a glimpse of that ghost smile somewhere in his face, and swallowed.

"We can save you."

Zekia said it quietly, almost a whisper, but then Ashwood twisted his hand around their prisoner's neck and Zekia felt the snap shoot through her.

There was a wave of anger from the amityguards and in mere seconds bullets spat out from behind the barricade. They stopped inches from Zekia's face, hitting the shield her Crafters conjured. Crashing against the force field, they sounded like raindrops on a tin roof.

Zekia turned to Wesley, whose hand was still limp in hers. He stared ahead, barely blinking his black eyes as the shots continued.

When he swallowed, Zekia heard it over the gunfire.

Wesley knew what was coming.

He knew the future without needing mind magic.

He knew what Dante Ashwood was going to say, because

he knew the man just as well as Zekia did, and he knew what it took to achieve greatness. The sacrifices that needed to be made for a better future.

"Kill them all," Ashwood said.

And so they did.

One district down. Six more to go.

3

Saxony

SAXONY WAS NOT IN charge and it was really starting to get on her nerves.

"My answer is final," Amja said. "We're not talking about this any longer and I'm finished going around in circles with you."

Saxony's amja, her long steel hair grazing her clasped hands, sat on the wooden chair next to Saxony's father, Bastian. Amja had a look in her eyes that told Saxony to stand down, designed to make her feel regret at challenging her authority, or shame at not trusting in her wisdom. Only, it didn't work so well anymore. Now all it did was make Saxony want to yell about how wrong her family was.

Saxony had seen war. She had seen what Ashwood was capable of firsthand, especially with her little sister at his side. She knew this was not the time to back down or run scared.

"You're right," Saxony said. "No more talking. What we need

is action. We have to summon the other Crafter Lieges from across the realms. Ashwood has an army of Crafters and that's exactly what we need."

Amja did not even look at Saxony when she spoke next.

"I am the Liege of this Kin now," she said. "And I will not endanger any more of our people."

She said it as though that was final and Saxony was a child who needed to know her place. Saxony had never thought that she'd want help from Wesley Thornton bloody Walcott, but at times like this, with her amja refusing to see sense, Saxony almost missed the underboss's penchant for convincing people to do things they didn't want to. Not to mention that Wesley had named Saxony temporary leader of the Crafters, and without him here to back her up—with Amja acting as Liege to her Kin in Zekia's place, and Asees and Arjun sectioning their people off to the other side of camp—Saxony was starting to feel like she'd been demoted in some way.

Like nothing she said mattered anymore.

And boy did it *suck*.

"I do not want more strange Crafters in our camp," Amja said. "Or more buskers from the other cities. You've already brought in an army of misfits to roam around our village. Now you want to fill it with more people we don't know or trust? You want to start another War of Ages?"

"The war has already started!" Saxony said, failing to contain her frustration. "If I could contact the other Crafters myself, then I would. But only a Liege has that power, Amja, and since you're standing in Zekia's place, it's your responsibility to help protect us."

"I'm protecting us by staying far from this war and waiting for Zekia to return home."

Saxony rubbed her temples to keep the growing headache at bay.

Amja was scared, she knew that. She was one of the few Crafters who had survived the War of Ages and now, fifty years onward, she bore those scars inside and out. But hiding wasn't going to help them, and neither was the delusion that Zekia would run back into their arms the same as she was the day she'd left.

Saxony had seen her sister standing beside Ashwood. She had felt her power when Zekia tried to kill her and then stole Wesley away. She knew that if she wanted her little sister back, then they were going to have to drag her kicking and screaming.

"Father," Saxony said, turning to Bastian. "Please, make her see reason."

He sighed and pushed aside a strand of hair that had strayed from his braid into his face. He swallowed, and those piercing brown eyes that Saxony had looked up into for so many years dimmed. He was a large man, but at this moment she couldn't help but think he looked so very small.

"We've lost too much already," Bastian said. "I won't lose the only child I have left."

"Zekia is not lost," Saxony said, with enough force that her father almost moved back in surprise.

She could get her sister back.

Even if Zekia had done terrible things and even if she had created that awful elixir. Zekia might not be able to lead their Kin anymore, but she was still Saxony's sister.

She could still be saved.

"You don't want to lose another child," Saxony said. "But I don't want to lose another sibling. I was too young to protect Malik when he died, but I can rescue Zekia if we do this."

Her father stayed silent, but Saxony didn't miss the way his frown twitched when she mentioned her brother's name. They rarely ever spoke of Malik, like not saying his name out loud made the pain go away, but looking at her father now, Saxony could see the agony in his eyes. The grief at losing a wife and a son all at once.

"We know what is best for our people and it's not another war," Amja said. "You must trust this wisdom."

Saxony wished that she could, but she had already seen what monsters lurked in the shadows and now those monsters were stepping into the light, and if someone didn't do something—if *she* didn't do something—then they would swallow the world.

"You're making a mistake," Saxony said. "And we'll all suffer for it."

She turned from them, the family she had been born into, who she'd once trusted more than anything, and left the room wondering how in the name of the Many Gods she was supposed to win a war with hardly any damned soldiers.

Saxony all but ripped open the door of the tree house to the outside world, bottling the scream in her throat. Outside, Karam stood with her arms crossed at her chest and a knife hitched to her belt, just in case.

Around them, the forest cooed. A poor attempt to calm Saxony.

Karam's smile tilted. "Does that look mean your family went

along with everything you said with a happy smile?" she asked. "Because you do seem happy."

"It's like you're a mind reader," Saxony said. "Really, you've got a lot of talent. Sure you're not an Intuitcrafter?"

Karam smirked and held out her hand for Saxony's. The moment their fingers locked, all of the anger that she had felt dissipated.

Well, not all of it, because Karam wasn't a miracle worker and Saxony was truly pissed off, but enough that she felt like she could breathe a little easier.

"I feel like there's no point in even trying anymore," Saxony said as they made their way down the branched staircase. "I'm only ever hitting dead ends."

And, really, there were so many other things she'd much rather be doing than trying to break through to her amja. War aside, Saxony wanted little more than to spend an uninterrupted evening with Karam. In her arms. In her bed. She wanted more than just the few stolen moments and kisses they had been afforded over the past few days.

But there was no rest in the fight against the wicked, especially with Dante Ashwood attacking districts in Creije.

"You will get through to them," Karam said. "It is in your blood to lead."

She squeezed Saxony's hand a little harder.

"I appreciate the faith," Saxony said. "But it's like talking to a busker about the law. Totally pointless. Won't change their minds no matter what."

"Tell that to Tavia," Karam said, as their feet touched the soil.

She gestured across the way, to where Saxony's old friend

was sitting by the campfire, sorting magic into piles, alongside a group of buskers.

"She changed from wanting to run from Creije and its criminals, to fighting to save it and organize her comrades into an army."

"Yeah," Saxony said. "Because Wesley convinced her to, not me. Right now I don't think she'd listen to me telling her to run from a fire."

Tavia was great at holding grudges, and ever since the battle on the Kingpin's island, she'd been clutching on to this one tighter than ever. Yes, Saxony had sent messenger bats that nearly got them killed. And, yes, she had even planned on killing Wesley way back when, but that was before he saved her life and before she knew her sister was Ashwood's puppet.

It wasn't Saxony's fault that Zekia had taken him.

Despite what Tavia believed, Saxony didn't want Wesley in Ashwood's clutches any more than she did. He was dangerous at the best of times, let alone when he was in the Kingpin's pocket.

Besides, she owed him a life debt.

"You will have to talk to Tavia eventually," Karam said. "Preferably before you are on the battlefield together."

Saxony slumped down onto a nearby log, kicking at the dirt. "It's not like I haven't tried," she said. "But I've developed a magical new ability to walk into a room and somehow make Tavia walk straight out of it."

Karam sat beside her and sighed in that way she always did when she thought Saxony was feeling sorry for herself.

"Yes," Karam said. "She is so stubborn. It is strange how you were ever friends with someone who could hold such a grudge."

She looked at Saxony with her eyebrows raised.

"Subtle," Saxony said. "I get it. We both need to sort out our issues, but can't I just indulge in my misery for a while? You could comfort me. I'll take anything you can give."

She waggled her eyebrows suggestively and Karam gave her a stern look, which only made Saxony smile more.

It felt like these days the only comfort Saxony had was Karam. Their relationship was unyielding, a part of herself that she knew would never waver or change, even in the face of war. Everything else seemed to have shifted irreparably, from Saxony's leadership to Tavia's friendship to the Uncharted Forest itself.

Saxony had grown up among these trees, and yet they seemed the strangest of all to her now. It was still beautiful and Saxony still felt a certain peace when she looked into the skies and saw the leaves curling into the clouds, shielding them just enough to let the warm orange sun through but to act as a barrier to most of the rain.

Yet it felt like a place from her past rather than her future.

She remembered running from one tree to another as a child, skipping across their branches like she was flying, the moss under her feet and the sky in her large curls, looking down on the boat-filled waterways that glistened like jewels. She would close her eyes and listen to the song of the forest, the music of its branches and how the tune changed with her mood.

Now all she could think about was Creije, falling victim to Ashwood.

That was the city she had fallen in love in.

The city she'd met her best friend in.

The city in which they'd started this quest.

And they were primed to lose it.

"You're my constant," Saxony said.

She pressed her forehead to Karam's, placing her hand to feel the steady drumbeat of her warrior's heart.

"Coming back here hasn't felt much like home at all these past few days, except for when I'm with you. With you everything makes sense."

"Yes," Karam said. Her breath tickled Saxony's lips. "I am really quite amazing."

Saxony scoffed, but she didn't argue. She simply closed her eyes and inhaled the sound of Karam's half laugh, memorizing the melody of it before she finally pressed her lips to hers and let the rest of the world fall away.

4

Tavia

THE FOREST WAS LIKE a fancy cell. If cells had birds that woke you up before sunrise.

Not that Tavia hated it. The Uncharted Forest was beautiful, but she couldn't get comfortable. Tavia was used to shadowed streets and a cautious moon, with bright-eyed tourists and endless possibilities of magic and mayhem.

There was none of that here.

Not to mention that they had been in the Rishiyat camp for over a week and the only real progress made in their war against Dante Ashwood, Kingpin of all that was unholy and bastard-like, was that they hadn't gotten themselves killed.

Yet.

The forest was pretty, but it didn't seem to be helping them. As it was, their army had a grand total of eighty Crafters, including the sixty they had rescued from the Kingpin's island. Some followed Saxony's amja, some followed Asees, but most of them just looked like they wanted to go home. Wherever home was.

They weren't in good shape, even with the forty buskers Tavia had wrangled into staying on their side without Wesley to lead them. And if Wesley were here, then he'd probably tell her—*when. When* Wesley got here—he'd tell her what a piss-poor job she was doing at managing everything while he was away.

"You don't have the authority for this, busker."

Casim, underboss of Rishiya, stared down at Tavia like she was a fly he quite fancied swatting. A specter of his face, tired but youthful, hovered over the open fire like a cloud. His mouth was stern, eyes faded and just as wicked as Tavia had always pictured them.

It had taken her days to secure this meeting, and robbing Casim's buskers—arrogant little gits like Nolan included—hadn't exactly helped to put her in the underboss's good graces. Still, it had gotten his attention, and after a few *delg* bats and a lot of wishful thinking, Casim had agreed to meet. Or, more precisely, sent her a charm that melted into the open flames and then sprouted his uppity little face from the embers.

"I have the authority," Tavia said. "The buskers in this rebellion follow me now."

"And you want me to send more buskers to your cause," Casim said. "Risking my own neck in the process."

"It's not like Ashwood is going to let you keep your neck once his power trip comes to an end. He's preaching Crafters as the new, superior race. You think just because we use magic, we'll be any better off than the regular folks he's going to exterminate or enslave?" Tavia almost laughed. "We'll either be next, or be regulated to his guard dogs, watching over the prisons and jumping when he tells us how high."

Casim's entire face twitched at that.

Like any underboss, he was not the sort of person who liked taking orders. Underbosses were charged with ruling entire cities, with the Kingpin trusting them to keep the trades going, and usually Ashwood's only concern was how much magic they sold, or what charms they should push. Tavia could see that the thought of Ashwood breathing down his neck and imposing his every whim on Casim's city was not his idea of a bright future.

"You think he controls you now?" Tavia asked, pressing the nerve. "Just wait and see what happens if he wins."

"And you think us teaming up will save it all?"

"I think that you can convince the other underbosses to join forces and *that* might just save us all."

"Doubtful," Casim said. "When it comes to the Kingpin, they're all a bunch of damn chickenshits."

Tavia kept her chin high, and her stare hardened. "You can convince them. There are nine underbosses in this realm and I know for a fact that each of them values what you have to say."

Which was a lie. Technically, Casim was part of the inner circle. Part of the four underbosses who thought themselves superior enough to dictate to the other five—Casim, Stelios, Ilaria. And Wesley. Casim was by no means the most powerful or the most respected, but, with Wesley gone, he was the best she was going to get. She doubted the others would even give her the time of day.

Casim was the easiest link to pull from the chain.

"What do you know of the other underbosses?" he asked. "You're just one in a sea of replaceable buskers that Wesley took under his wing."

Tavia shook her head.

He didn't know how wrong he was.

Wesley had kept Tavia versed on every other underboss in the realm. *Just in case*, he'd said to her. *You never know when they'll crawl from their shadows.*

Tavia knew their wants and their ways. She knew their limits and their lies. She knew each and every one of the underbosses by name and she knew that all of them would turn against Dante Ashwood for a better offer. If crooks could be trusted to do one thing, then it was to not be at all trustworthy.

"Are you saying that you're not powerful enough to convince the others to help?" Tavia asked. "Maybe I should be talking to Ilaria or Stelios instead."

She would have done it in the first place, except that Casim was not only their closest ally, being underboss of the city they were hiding in, but he was also one of the most scared when it came to Wesley's name.

Casim's snarl grew.

"Watch yourself, busker. Don't think that just because you were under Wesley's protection before that it affords you any mercy now that the Kingpin has him."

Tavia wondered if someone's teeth could break from gritting them so hard, because if so, then hers were fit to bursting. Just the mention of Wesley's absence set her off-kilter and brought her hand to his bone gun, which was nestled

~ 44 ~

in her belt loop, where she always kept it these days.

It gave her the smallest of comforts, but it was all she had left of him.

"Wesley is where he needs to be for the moment," Tavia said, the bluff heavy on her lips. "And you're a fool to threaten me. Wesley named me the best busker in all of Creije."

"But he's not there with you," Casim said, sounding uncertain. He craned his neck, searching the shadows with grim reluctance, as if Wesley might just appear around the corner.

And there it was.

Maybe there were those who might have feared Casim.

But Casim feared Wesley.

And Tavia could use that.

"Wesley isn't here," she said. "For now. But do you really think that the Kingpin can hold him for long, or that he's not exactly where he wants to be? Dante Ashwood is powerful, but Wesley is Wesley, and when he gets back, he'll come to me asking for a report on who was too scared to do what had to be done. He'll want to know his enemies."

Casim's eyes widened a fraction, but he kept his game face on for the most part, which Tavia had to give him credit for. Still, the fear was there and she had seen the slip of it. She had been the one to cause it.

Wesley would be proud of her for that, wouldn't he?

"Fine," Casim said. "I'll send you my buskers and I'll talk to the other underbosses about where their loyalties lie. Maybe I can convince some of them to help without getting myself killed for treason. But if I'm going to risk my life, then I want something in return."

Tavia didn't like where this was going. Deals with underbosses never went well and it was always better to stick to threats instead. That's what Wesley would have done.

"I want Wesley himself to give me his protection," Casim said. "I want his promise that he'll ensure my safety and reward me for my loyalty after all is said and done."

Tavia felt a headache coming on.

She couldn't ensure Casim's safety any more than she could ensure her own, or that of her friends. The plan had always been for Wesley to take Ashwood's place, because he was the one who could make real change and Tavia knew that everything he'd do, even the awful stuff she'd hate, would be in the best interests of Creije and the rest of the realm. But when he came back, though he'd stand by Tavia and the others, the last priority on his list would be ensuring the safety of another underboss.

Casim didn't need to hear that right now though. He needed to hear that he was safe.

"Of course you'll have protection," Tavia said. "By Wesley himself. It goes without saying."

She pictured Wesley's face when he got back and heard about what she'd done. Whether he'd be mad, or just laugh at the idea of being a bodyguard.

Casim smiled. "I'll be in touch. Look out for my truce."

And then he disappeared, into the fire and into the wind, leaving only the stale stench of their alliance in the air.

"What are you doing?"

Saxony's voice was unmistakable.

Tavia turned to see her friend, brows knotted together, and Karam by her side, surveying the fire with a neutral look, like she was still deciding what the right reaction should be.

"Was that who I think it was?" Saxony asked, walking into the clearing. "Did you just make some kind of a deal with an underboss?"

Tavia didn't like how scolding Saxony's voice sounded, like Tavia was a kid in need of punishing for going against what the grown-ups wanted.

"You're making a deal with Ashwood's henchmen now? Tavia, you can't trust them."

"I know what I'm doing," Tavia said. "Creije is on the line, Ashwood is conquering districts, and I'm not going to let my home fall to ashes. We need to start thinking of a plan to get Wesley some help before it's too late."

"So this is less about Creije and more about your boyfriend," Saxony said.

Tavia's eyes narrowed.

It was about all the people the alliance could save. She didn't contact Casim just for Wesley; she did it because every night all she could picture were the innocents in her city, injected with the Loj over and over until Ashwood had sunk his claws in deep enough to leave marks that would never fade.

She pictured her mother, whispering at shadows as the magic slowly ate away her mind.

Can you see them now, ciolo? she always whispered. *My ghosts.*

"Saxony," Karam said, stepping in between them like she could sense a battle on the horizon. "Perhaps we should talk about this another time. You two are both—"

"You might not like Wesley," Tavia interrupted. "But you should know that having him as an enemy would be a mistake."

"I can handle Wesley," Saxony said.

"You'll *handle* him? He's on our side."

"Speaking of our side, if we're all on the same team, then why are you going behind my back?"

Tavia all but scoffed. "Weird how much that hurts, isn't it?"

Saxony's jaw clenched and the air between them grew thick with the rising sun.

"You both must take a breath and remember our mission," Karam said. "We cannot tear ourselves apart when our foes are waiting to do just that."

Tavia looked to Karam. She wasn't sure when the warrior had become the peacemaker, tying Tavia to her old friend in an awful, obligatory way that she still couldn't get used to.

"We need to come together to find a solution to this war," Karam said. "Tavia is right in saying that Wesley is an asset and that the underboss of Rishiya can provide us with more soldiers."

"I know that," Saxony said. "But we need Crafters to win this war and we can't do it without my amja's help. I just need time to convince her. And once I do, we can fight the Kingpin and save Zekia and—"

"So Zekia is worth saving, but not Wesley," Tavia said. "She can be redeemed, but anyone you don't care about can go straight to the fire-gates?"

Saxony's eyes tensed and Tavia didn't miss the flicker of hurt that crossed her friend's face. "That isn't what I said."

The wind breezed warmer on Tavia's cheeks and she knew that the change in the air wasn't just from the sun anymore, but from Saxony's magic. Her Crafter powers were like a wildfire, buried skin-deep, ready to rise at any moment.

"What you say and do are two different things," Tavia said. "Who's to say which side of your personality we can trust today?"

Saxony didn't say anything in response, and whether that was because there was nothing she *could* say, or because she knew Tavia wouldn't listen anyway, it didn't matter. Saxony turned without another word and headed back into the camp in the space of a few blinks, leaving Tavia alone with Karam.

"You need to stop punishing her," Karam said. "We are not enemies here."

Tavia wasn't so sure.

She could forgive a lot of things, but Saxony's actions had nearly gotten them killed at the train station when they tried to escape Creije. Her family had attacked them in Granka, and Saxony's letters had led the Kingpin straight to Asees and Arjun's Kin. And then there was that whole matter of Saxony's little sister kidnapping Wesley from right under their noses.

It wasn't enough that Ashwood had murdered Tavia's mother with magical experiments, but now he'd taken the one person she had left who—

Tavia swallowed.

It's okay, ciolo, her mother's voice whispered.

Tavia had thought that as an orphan she knew what it was to be alone, but she was wrong. In the span of no time at all, she had lost her underboss, her home, and her best friend. Wesley had always been there for her to rely on, even if she never wanted it, and Saxony had always been a source of light and friendship in a city she took for granted.

Now both were gone.

Now everything seemed wrong.

"Keep acting like this and you will push everyone away," Karam continued.

"There are more important things than Saxony's feelings or my popularity," Tavia said. "If we don't stop Ashwood from destroying Creije, he'll trample the other eight cities too, and then spread the Loj elixir across Uskhanya. And after our realm is gone, he won't stop there. Maybe he'll go for your realm next."

"So you team up with any crook you can?"

"Casim isn't just a crook, Karam, he's an underboss. Buskers across the city will listen to him and he could even convince the other underbosses to give us buskers from their cities. Then we'll have the numbers to really give Ashwood a run for his money."

"And you can save Wesley," Karam said.

Tavia didn't deny it.

What was so wrong with wanting to save her oldest friend and the only home either of them had ever known? It didn't make her a bad person, just because every motive she had wasn't selfless.

"I understand that you want him back," Karam said. "But the way that you are doing things is—"

"Saving Wesley saves the city. It's as simple as that. And if you and Saxony have a problem, then maybe you're the ones doing things wrong."

Truth be told, Tavia was tired of justifying every action she took, or making excuses so it seemed like she wasn't overstepping boundaries everyone else had created around her.

She was a busker.

She was the *best* busker that the capital city of Uskhanya had and maybe Saxony's people were too scared or too unwilling to get their hands dirty, but Tavia wasn't. Her people weren't. They were going to do whatever it took to get the job done, even if it meant aligning with monsters.

5

Wesley

WESLEY THORNTON WALCOTT DIDN'T CRY.

In the list of terrible things he'd done in his life—and Wesley liked to keep track of things like that—he was sure crying had never been one. He knew that memories were fickle, of course, but he trusted his mind to keep hold of important stuff like that.

Those were the things that needed to be remembered if he was going to hold a grudge properly, and if there was one thing Wesley Thornton Walcott did well, it was hold a grudge.

Wesley didn't cry in the face of death.

He didn't cry because he had only half a family—the half that gave him a house but not a home, that protected him but did not love him, that stared at him like he was something so very *other* in a realm of strange magic and monsters.

He didn't cry when he crossed lines and burned bridges.

He didn't cry when he threw away friendship for leadership.

And he didn't cry when Zekia clawed through his mind, or

when her shadow demon clawed through his body. They could try to break Wesley into a thousand pieces, but he wouldn't give them that. He'd fought his way up from the streets of Creije and there was no way he was going to go down without a fight.

"Fighting is hard," Tavia said. "Sometimes the bravest thing you can do is just give in."

She sat beside Wesley in the cell, her grin sly as ever, while the low glow of night filtered from the cracked window, reflecting the sky in the pool of Wesley's blood.

"Don't you ever just want to give up?" she asked.

She shuffled closer to Wesley and squeezed his hand.

"It's okay if you do."

Wesley held on to the sound of her voice, like a cliff's edge, even though he knew it wasn't really her voice at all.

He'd learned that by now.

He knew better.

He turned to Tavia and pushed a flick of black hair from her eyes in a way he had never dared to before. It was damp with sweat and clinging to her cheeks like seaweed, making her look young and restless.

"Get the hell out of my mind, kid," he said.

And then he pushed Tavia's head back so hard that it cracked against the surface of the cell wall. There wasn't blood this time, but Wesley winced like there had been.

He heard a sigh and then Tavia's newly limp body disappeared into smoke, and from across the room Zekia stepped out of the shadows.

"You're getting quicker," she said. "The first time it took you ages to figure it out."

"Maybe you're just getting sloppy."

Though truth was, most of Zekia's illusions had been perfect from the start, and if there was one thing she excelled at, it was making Wesley doubt every second of his life was real.

Still, she could never get Tavia right.

The first time she'd tried, Wesley was too out of it to see the small discrepancies, but it was the easiest thing to spot now. A conjured Tavia made Wesley feel cold and uncertain. She was always missing the bite to her words and the tilted smile that could never quite be replicated. She was missing the glint in her eye that told Wesley he was awful and she would forgive him for it anyway.

Zekia could try all she wanted, but she'd be hard-pressed to create an illusion as damn irritating and wonderful as the real thing.

"Want to give it another whirl?" Wesley asked. "I think I've still got some sanity left in me today."

Zekia let out a great huff of breath, like she was frustrated that Wesley had stolen her favorite toy. Beside her, a shadow demon growled, its eyes like pure darkness. It looked at Wesley in a way that said, *Yes. Again. Let me taste the blood this time.*

"No," Zekia said. "Enough for today."

Thank the Many Gods, Wesley thought, and then hoped she hadn't heard.

Though it was impossible to be sure, and being unsure was something Wesley hated. Even more than the fact that he knew he looked like utter trash and had to turn away from any reflection he caught sight of. His suit was always stellar—one thing Zekia was good at in between the torture was keeping

Wesley dressed very much like himself—but the sharp edges in his eyes that he'd carefully cultivated over the years looked more rounded and dull.

Maybe it was the lack of food.

Maybe it was the lack of sun.

Or maybe he just didn't adjust well to being tortured.

Either way, Wesley didn't plan on sticking around to get used to it.

The shadow demon bared its teeth, talons rising, and Wesley couldn't help but grimace. Not because he was scared—he'd never show that so easily—but because he could smell the demon's breath from across the room.

There was torture and then there was just plain nasty.

"Down, boy," Zekia said, clicking her fingers in the air.

The shadow demon howled, the sound like the whistle of a boiling teapot, or an old steam train that couldn't slow down. It cozied up to her side and Zekia smiled. She didn't need to kneel down to stroke it, because Zekia was only fourteen and the shadow demon was nearly the size of a grown man. Perhaps twice that when it was on its hind legs.

It was weird to watch it obey her, like she was a leader and not just a kid who didn't know she needed help.

"Do you know why a shadow demon can't be killed?" Zekia asked.

Wesley was not in the mood for a quiz.

"It's because they're not born of blood and bone like us."

The demon cawed by her side, like it approved of this lesson about its history.

"They're made from the darkness left behind by the cursed

spells. Spells that steal a mind, spells that steal a soul, and spells that steal a heart."

When Zekia stroked the shadow demon, half of her hand grazed its spine and the other half fell into the abyss of its ghostly body.

"You can't kill shadow demons because they're made from magic and magic can never die," she said. "In the end, magic always wins. It's forever. It's a gift from the Many Gods and we have to protect it."

Wesley kept his breath steady.

"Is this part of the torture?" he said. "You didn't break me with your mind magic or your shadow demon, so you want to bore me with a history lesson?"

Zekia laughed.

She laughed a lot when Wesley spoke, even though half of what he said really wasn't that funny. Torture had dampened his sense of humor.

Still, she always laughed, like she thought that if Wesley knew she liked him, he might just forgive her for everything. And the thing was, he did. Wesley missed the little kid he'd befriended, who, despite everything, he couldn't bring himself to hate.

"You're too stubborn and Ashwood will get mad soon," Zekia said. "You're ruining everything, Wesley. The future is so dark and I can't make it light without you, don't you see?"

She pushed her long black braids from her face, her bracelets clinking together.

"If you're looking for light, I'm the wrong person," Wesley said. "Just because Asees and Arjun gave me a magical loan, it doesn't mean I know anything about your Crafter dreams. I'm not like you, kid. I never was."

Zekia played with the hem of her dress.

"You know that's not true," she said quietly. "You know that you're not a vessel for someone else's power."

Wesley sat up against the wall in a way that made his ribs hurt a little less.

"Wesley," she said, her voice a mix of nerves and joy. "Don't you feel it? Your magic isn't borrowed or stolen. It's *awakened*."

"I'm not falling for any more of your mind games."

Zekia shook her head and took three quick steps toward him, almost excited. She bent down, her dress pooling into his blood.

"You're a true Crafter, Wesley," she said. "You're one of us. I knew it the second I got into your mind. I've been wanting to tell you for days, but you've been pretty mad and I didn't know how to say it."

Wesley shook his head. "Bullshit."

"It's not," Zekia promised. "I swear it on the Many Gods and on my life and on everything else in the realms. You're not like the other buskers and crooks. You're like us, Wesley. You're just like *me*."

An Intuitcrafter.

Wesley wanted to tell her she was even more crazy than he'd thought, but the more he looked at the earnestness in her face and the more he tried to rack his mind, the more nothing else made sense.

A true Crafter.

As the thought raced through his mind, the magic inside of him sparked.

Yes, it whispered, after so long silent. *Yes.*

Was that why magic had always felt like home to him?

Not just a skill Wesley needed to learn and master, but a part of his soul that had always been missing. When Ashwood first took him from the streets and taught him to be a busker, it was like a fire inside of Wesley started to burn too hot and fierce to ever dissipate.

He touched the silver staves running up his arm, so similar to the ones Zekia had.

They had appeared during the shadow moon, when his power felt infinite and wondrous. He'd been so worried they would disappear one day and that he'd become that empty shell again, but they hadn't. They'd stayed and the power inside of him hadn't left either.

You're like us.

You're one of us.

Wesley had never belonged to anything or anyone.

He'd never had anything he hadn't stolen or taken with blood. Except for magic.

Magic had always felt so very much his, even when it was just a trick bag or a charm he kept in his back pocket. Each and every one felt like air in his lungs.

Now he finally knew why.

"I know you think we're wrong," Zekia said. "But we just want the Crafters to be okay again. Like before the war. Like better than before. You have to want that too, now you know you're like us. Don't you?"

Wesley wasn't sure what he wanted right now, except to get out of this place and take her with him. He needed to see the sun and feel the air on his face and have Tavia glare at him like he was a huge bastard.

It was the only way to get any kind of damn clarity.

"Kid," he said. "Let me get you out of here. I can take you back to your family and we can fix all of this. We can go to the forest and—"

"Be quiet!" Zekia snapped. "You can't talk about that place here."

"Then let's go and talk about it somewhere far away from here," he said.

Zekia's smile faded and she stood up slowly from the floor, the damp dripping from her dress.

"You're not going anywhere," she said.

"Kid—"

"No!" she yelled, shaking her head wildly. "You can't go. I won't let you leave."

Wesley sighed.

Thing was, he already knew how to escape. He'd been planning it since the moment they took him, going over every possible scenario. The problem had never been that he couldn't go, but that he didn't want to go without Zekia.

The chains weren't keeping Wesley prisoner; she was.

Even now, she was still the ghost inside his mind, making him second-guess every decision.

She was like this because of him.

She was with Ashwood because of him.

Wesley couldn't leave her behind again, like he had done all those years ago, when he'd thought being an underboss was worth any sacrifice.

He couldn't go back to Tavia and Saxony and Karam without her.

Zekia deserved a chance.

At the very least, Wesley owed her that.

At the very least, he had to try.

6

Karam

KARAM WIPED THE BLOOD from her knife.

"Again," she said.

Tavia opened her mouth in outrage, nursing the minor flesh wound on her shoulder. She really was very dramatic at times.

"You're enjoying this way too much," Tavia said.

Karam pocketed her knife as a show of peace. "Believe me, I take little pleasure in trying to school someone with no athletic skill."

Tavia's eyes narrowed in the beginnings of a glare, though there wasn't much heart behind it. "I think I'm offended," she said. "I'll have you know that I once scaled a building."

"Which you got pushed out of."

"I stole a backpack full of magic from Rishiya's best busker."

"And then got chased by his friends so I had to rescue you."

"I faced Dante Ashwood and survived," Tavia said, grinning proudly, her chin aloft.

Karam raised an eyebrow, unimpressed. "We all did that."

Tavia's glare reappeared and Karam couldn't help but laugh at her outrage.

"You've got something on your face," Tavia said, her voice a stale monotone.

Karam stopped smiling.

"There." Tavia crossed her arms over her chest in satisfaction. "All gone."

"Guard up," Karam said. "Or I may stab you for real this time."

"No, you're way too fond of me now. We're practically best—"

"We are not friends," Karam interrupted.

Though mostly she said it out of habit rather than truth. Like a game between the two of them, insults a common currency of affection. Tavia had a knack for being simultaneously very unlikable and very, very endearing.

If only she had the same knack for being good with her fists.

As it was, when it came to teaching Tavia how to fight, Karam had her work cut out for her. It wasn't that the busker had no skills whatsoever, just that none of her skills were the right ones, and so Karam spent half her time sighing in despair and the other half trying not to punch Tavia in the face.

"After this, we're moving on to magic lessons," Tavia said. "That Nolan bastard had some damn good charms that I've been waiting to try out. I'll be teaching you how to turn your enemies into literal dust in no time."

Karam grimaced.

Not because of the violence, but because using magic still

made her skin itch. She preferred her fists and being able to feel her enemies' bones rattle. There was a strange comfort that came with a good old-fashioned brawl. It was simple and certain.

Magic was like a question with no answer, or an answer with no question. It was there one moment and gone the next, in all things and part of nothing, existing entirely outside of the world and yet responsible for each and every particle of it.

Karam's most dreaded days were when her lessons with Tavia finished and Tavia's lessons with her began.

"Don't give me that look," Tavia said. "This was the trade-off. You teach me how to be a stealth assassin and I teach you how to be a damn fine trickster. If we're going to survive this war, we need magic and fists to work together."

"A very inspiring speech," Karam said.

"Not as good as the one you gave about how to poke someone's eyes out. I still have nightmares about that."

Karam merely shrugged. "I am a firm believer that every woman should know how to blind her enemies."

Tavia laughed, loud and unabashed one moment, only for it to be cut short with jarring finality the next.

She stared ahead, to a space beyond Karam, all the joy gone from her face.

Across the way, Saxony was talking to a group of Crafters in her Kin, and Tavia watched her with all the curiosity of a hunter watching prey.

"Do you think she's trying to rally them to her side?"

"They follow her amja," Karam said simply.

"A woman too scared to lead properly." Tavia pocketed her

knife, a sign she was done with the lesson. "Saxony should just take the reins from her and become Liege already."

Saxony gestured with her arms wide and one of the Crafters, a man a little shorter than she was, shook his head.

"I do not think it is that simple," Karam said, watching their interaction. "They will not follow Saxony because she asks them to. I believe she has to show them that she is the right choice. She has to earn it."

"And the way to do that is by standing around with her thumb up her ass?"

Karam didn't bother turning to glare at Tavia.

She kept her eyes on Saxony, who looked up to the sky with a defeated exhale. Karam almost felt like she could hear the sigh from where she stood across the camp. And then, as though she could sense Karam's focus, Saxony turned to look at her.

She gave her a small, secret smile and Karam's heart pounded furiously.

Even now. Even still.

Everything Saxony did made her pulse quicken.

Probably because the moments they spent together were so fleeting and nearly constantly interrupted, leaving Karam to grasp at the smallest things for satisfaction and building a thirst for Saxony that could never quite be quenched.

When Saxony began to walk over to them, Tavia cleared her throat like she was preparing for an onslaught.

"Good conversation?" Tavia asked. "You looked like you were really getting through to them."

"They're just as scared as my amja is," Saxony said. "And they won't go against an acting Liege."

"I guess that means I'm the only one pulling my weight in this war, then," Tavia said.

This time, Karam did glare at her. Not because she disagreed that the steps the busker had taken were necessary, but because she was getting a little tired of having to play peacemaker and diplomat in this newly fractured group.

Karam was a warrior. A guard. A soldier. She was not a mediator and it seemed she spent too much time these days ignoring her strengths in favor of fixing other people's weaknesses. Sometimes, she couldn't help but feel that she'd be better used somewhere else in this war, doing something that really mattered.

She would have said as much if a *delg* bat hadn't then swooped down from the sky, cutting through the trees. It circled overhead, around the three of them, squeaking mercilessly as it awaited the code word it needed to land.

"Who would be sending bats to us?" Karam asked. "Everyone we know is here, in this camp."

Everyone except for Wesley, of course. Though none of them would draw attention to that if they could help it.

"Relax," Tavia said, and then, looking up toward the sky, she called, "*Truce.*"

The messenger bat darted downward and landed on Tavia's outstretched hand with all the speed that it took for Karam to blink. Tavia stroked its head and the creature nestled into her fingertip. Karam had always thought they were awful things, not because of their appearance but because they could find anyone, anywhere, delivering a message even to the spirits. It seemed too much power for one thing to hold.

And then, of course, there was how they delivered their messages, with someone else's voice trapped in their throats. It made Karam shudder to think of.

"Speak to me, little guy," Tavia said.

The bat seemed to nod, and stretched out its wings like a curtain. It opened its mouth and Karam braced herself for the transformation of its voice.

"I have kept my promise," the bat said in a croak.

Karam recognized its tone as belonging to the underboss she had heard Tavia dealing with before.

Casim.

"I have four dozen buskers ready to send your way," it said. "I'm talking to the other underbosses, but you'll understand it takes time and I must be careful. Once we have your location, my forces will be with you within the week. Give Wesley my regards and let him know that I've put my faith in him."

"Good job," Tavia whispered into the creature's ear.

A few dozen more buskers wasn't something to scoff at with their armies so depleted, and so Karam clapped Tavia on the back in a way she hoped said that she was pleased.

"I have to tell Casim where we are so he can send the buskers," Tavia said. "But I promise that he's too scared of Wesley to betray us."

Saxony seemed to think this over, and Karam wondered whether she would have to referee another fight between them, as Saxony refused to trust an underboss.

To her surprise, Saxony nodded.

"Do it," she said. "Send the bat back. You were right to contact him."

"I was right?" Tavia repeated the words slowly, like they were the last ones she had expected.

"You were," Saxony said. "And it's time I did something to help our armies too. I'm done trying to convince my amja to help me summon the other Lieges. I've got a new idea."

"We are not killing your amja, are we?" Karam asked. "I think perhaps that is an overreaction."

"That's Plan C," Saxony said. "Plan B is going to someone else for help, like Tavia did."

"You are going to the next Liege you know with the power of summoning," Karam said as the understanding dawned on her. "Asees."

Saxony nodded. "And your friendship with Arjun won't hurt to convince her." She smiled tightly. "If you don't mind me wagering your connections, that is."

"Of course," Karam said. "But once Asees helps you to summon the other Lieges, what will we do next?"

"We kill Ashwood."

Karam liked that plan.

"But I want to find a way of killing him without hurting anyone in his army," Saxony said. "I've been thinking about it a lot. We know that not everyone follows him willingly. Some people are just civilians infected with the Loj."

Tavia crossed her arms over her chest with a sigh. "They're innocent," she said.

But Karam shook her head. "There are no innocents in war."

Though truly she thought the opposite.

Everyone was innocent in war, doing whatever they thought was best, even if it was convoluted and evil to everyone else.

No soldier set out to be the bad guy. Every villain was the hero of their own story. War was built on innocence corrupted and lost. That was the thing battle stole from people, before it took their souls.

"I'm going to figure out a way," Saxony said. "But we need a real army before we talk about how to storm the gates of Creije."

"You mean save Creije," Tavia said. "You have to make sure that the other Lieges you contact know that's the plan. They can't just be out for blood and revenge. We need to save the city."

Karam knew that by *city*, Tavia also meant *Wesley*, since the two had always been very much one and the same. Karam couldn't help but agree with her, because it was Wesley who had seen the promise in a young Wrenyi runaway and offered her the means to become the warrior she needed to be. She owed him so much—too much—and abandoning him now, after he'd saved them all in one way or another, was not the way forward.

"We must find out if Wesley is still himself," Karam said. "If the Kingpin is inside his mind, then—"

"Zekia's mind is the one we should be worried about," Tavia said. "Since she's clearly lost it."

Karam agreed, but she could also never forget that Zekia was Saxony's little sister, and in Karam's mind that afforded her a certain unfair immunity for her crimes.

"She is just a child," Karam said.

Tavia's eyes turned severe. "That stops being an excuse when you become a mass murderer."

Karam supposed she had a point, but she had to wonder where they drew this invisible line of morality. They had all killed someone at some point, or played a part in the deaths of strangers and foes alike.

None of them were free from sin, with clean hands unstained by blood. They were soldiers and warriors, and Karam couldn't quite work out how they had made the distinction between fighter and killer.

She wasn't sure what side of the line she fell on. For Zekia and the Crafters who believed in the Kingpin's new world, weren't Karam and the others just villains who were trying to steal it from them?

"Wesley has killed people too," Saxony said. "He handed Zekia over to Ashwood once before. Maybe my sister is too far gone, but you need to think about the possibility that Wesley might also be beyond saving."

"I have," Tavia said, but there was no change in her eyes.

She had been threatening to give up on Wesley for years, but her inaction spoke volumes that her vows could not. Threats were nothing if they didn't carry weight, and Tavia's words were as light as air, flying from her lips and across the wind into nothing.

She couldn't give up on Wesley, even if she tried. Karam could see that. Just like Karam would never give up on Saxony, or choose a side that didn't have her on it.

If the years of Wesley being a crook and a total bastard hadn't changed Tavia's heart, then Ashwood's influence wouldn't. This war wouldn't. She'd try to save him until the end, even if that put her on the opposite side from her friends.

Karam clutched her pehta's pendant, threaded around her neck and falling perfectly beside her thumping heart.

She wondered what side he would be on, or if he would counsel the absence of such a choice, trying to bring their armies together instead of preparing for them to fall apart. Or perhaps he would still have preached peace and given them a solution that offered no bloodshed or trampled loyalties.

Karam wished he were still alive to ask, but it was useless to hope for such things, because her father was gone, as so many others soon would be.

Life and loyalty were constantly in flux and Karam knew that sooner or later every bond on this side of the Onnela Sea would be tested.

She and Saxony and Tavia would fight this war on whatever side it took to save the people closest to them. Karam could only hope that those sides stayed the same for as long as possible.

⁓

ASEES LOOKED between Karam and Saxony, as though she were trying to decide who was more senseless. She finally settled on Saxony.

"You want me to go against the leader of your Kin? The woman who is allowing us safe stay in this place?" Asees asked her.

Though Asees and Karam had grown to respect one another, their mutual love for Arjun like a bond between them, she often looked at Saxony in a way that was far from endeared. Nobody could blame her, given everything that had happened between the two of them.

Asees resented Saxony for the *delg* bat that Ashwood had intercepted, leading so many of her Kin to be killed and for

Asees herself to be inflicted with the Loj elixir. While Saxony resented Asees for trying to kill her while infected.

It didn't make for a sturdy partnership.

"Saxony was the one who brought you here, to that safety," Karam said. "And she also helped to save you when Ashwood had you under his thrall. She could have easily killed you to protect herself."

From beside Asees, Arjun folded his arms across his chest to indicate how stubborn he planned on being, as though the way he stood as a shield beside Asees wasn't enough of a clue.

"Both Asees and I helped to save Saxony's people from that island and grant her underboss the magic he needed to help," he said.

Karam cared for him as a brother, but that didn't mean she wouldn't smack some sense into him when he needed it. "I believe we are all even with saving each other's lives," she said. "But does the Indescribable God not teach us to also think of the rest of the realms?"

Asees let out a long breath. Karam knew that using their god as a bargaining chip was a low blow, but that didn't make it any less true. Being selfish was not the same as being right.

Asees stared at Karam.

She wasn't a tall woman, especially compared to Saxony, but she had a way of sizing people up to make them feel smaller than her, despite her stature. It was the job of a Liege to be wary of everyone who might be a danger to their people. Right now, Karam fell reluctantly into that category.

"It is an ancient spell," Asees said. "And it has not been used in an age."

"That is only because Crafters keep to themselves now," Karam said.

"We have *always* kept to ourselves."

Asees shook her head so that her dark hair swayed against her stave-covered arms.

"Asees is right," Arjun said, because of course he took her side in most things.

The last time he hadn't, their Kin had nearly been destroyed. Karam knew he still carried that guilt with him each day.

"Traditions are sacred and varied," he said. "We have never even agreed on where our powers come from. Saxony's realm believes one thing, ours another. And even among realms, the Kins were always separate."

"That did a lot of good when the war came," Karam said. "*Hei reb. Heb mina kori ak maku.*"

Karam hadn't planned on calling him an idiot, but she also hadn't thought he'd be acting like one.

"Times change," Saxony said. "We can't do what we've always done just because it's all we've known. We have to make a change to see one."

Arjun shuffled and looked to Asees, his eyes filled with conflict. "I agree that more magic would help in the war, and we have seen firsthand what happens when we try to escape fighting."

They were all picturing the attack on Asees and Arjun's Kin back in their homeland of Granka. Ashwood had slaughtered so many of their people, and the rest he'd taken and forced to do his bidding under the Loj elixir. If they had joined Karam and the others back then, rather than staying behind, then maybe that blood wouldn't have been spilled. Karam didn't want them to make that same mistake again and she trusted Saxony's judgment on this.

"War is not something you can hide from, or pretend is not happening just because it is not yet on your doorstep," Karam said.

It would get there eventually, it always did. And even if it didn't, even if the forest kept them safe for the time being, how could any of them live with themselves if they stood by and watched others die in their place? The good of their people wasn't more important than the good of the world, and Karam would bring dishonor to her family and to the order of the Rekhi d'Rihsni her grandparents had died for if she let them choose their people over everyone else.

"The summoning spell is dangerous and it has only been used a handful of times since the beginning of the realms," Asees said. "The last time anyone thought to try it was during the War of Ages."

When the Crafters were stolen from their beds and used like commodities rather than people.

"We brought magic into this world," Saxony said. "Let's use it for good."

"You truly believe calling strangers to help us is best?" Asees asked.

"We cannot look at everyone we do not know as a stranger who is not important," Karam said. "Strangers are not strange to their own families or the people who love them and mourn for them. They have lives and they deserve a chance to live those lives. We can help them do that, with your magic."

The silence that followed those words was tense, and Karam dreaded the thought that maybe they had burned a fragile bridge, or alienated another leader. With Saxony's grandma refusing to help, Asees was the only Crafter left with the power they needed to make a real change.

"I left last time to follow these people," Arjun said. "But I will not leave your side again, Asees. I will follow you and your decision in this. Whatever it will be."

"But if I say no, then you will think I am wrong," Asees said, with a small grimace.

Arjun's silence was enough of an answer.

"You trust her with your life?" Asees was looking at Karam now. "You love this woman, but you are of *our* people, Karam. So I ask you now, once more, is this the right choice?"

"There is only one choice," Karam said. "One side and one war for one enemy. Dante Ashwood has to be stopped."

Asees nodded. "Thank you," she said, and looked to Saxony with large, firm eyes. "I will help you. I will not run from this and make the mistakes of my past again. We will call the Lieges of the realms to come to our aid."

Saxony's smile was like magic in itself. "Thank you," she said. "I promise, doing this will change everything for us."

Saxony was finally taking the steps she needed to help her people, and though Karam was proud of her, it also made her wonder if she should start doing the same.

Karam's hands were tied here and even if she couldn't bear the thought of leaving Saxony, her beautiful Crafter seemed finally ready to go at things. She was starting to become strong enough to do this without Karam by her side, and that meant that it was nearly time for Karam to go.

There were things she had to take care of, things she knew nobody else could, and she'd been putting it off for too long.

Karam threaded her hand through Saxony's, knowing that this was both the start of something and the end of something.

7

Saxony

SAXONY WAS ALONE WITH Asees, her stomach tied in knots as the Liege explained the ritual and the fact that she was going to be greeted with fear and hesitance. Lieges didn't often speak among themselves and Crafter Kins almost never came together in harmony. They stuck to their own, hiding from the world and from each other.

"Are you ready?" Asees asked.

She held out her hand.

"I've been ready for a while now," Saxony said.

She tried to hide her joy, but as she took Asees's hand to form the summoning circle, Saxony couldn't help but let her lips tilt upward into a smile. Tavia was right: She had spent too long trying to pander to her own family, or waiting for the other shoe to drop.

She needed to get something done, just like her old friend had.

Now was that moment.

She and Karam had convinced Asees—the Crafter Liege of another Kin, of another *realm*—to join hands for the first time in decades. It felt good to have them on her side, trusting her judgment. They believed in Saxony, and that was something she hadn't felt for a while.

All that was left was for the rest of the magical world to follow.

"We're going to save everyone," Saxony said. "Together."

The moment the words left her lips, their magic ignited.

Though they both spoke the summoning command—Saxony in Uskhanyan and Asees in her native Wrenyi—the words were not what mattered. They rarely were. It was the intention, and magic could always read that well enough.

Saxony focused on the wish inside of herself and let her mind reach out like a talon to those she needed. Her skin warmed with her Energycrafter magic, the fire in her veins blazed as it propelled her mind onward, but Asees's grip didn't lessen in her own. She didn't flinch or rip her hand from Saxony's. She only squeezed tighter, until Saxony could feel the woman's Spiritcrafter magic tingling against her fingertips.

The power of a Liege, feeding Saxony's magic with her own and imbuing the spell with the sacred power it needed.

Any person could use a *delg* bat, any Crafter could contact a blood relative with the help of a crystal ball, but only a Liege, someone trusted to lead the ancient power of their Kin, could call another Liege.

And Asees was calling them all.

Help us fight for peace.

The Kins scattered across the realm of Uskhanya that Saxony called home.

The Kins revered in Asees's home realm of Wrenyal.

Those hiding in Volo, or blending in on the streets of Naustrio.

Every Liege in the four realms, however many or few there were, would hear this call.

Help us destroy the man who would destroy us.

The air hummed and crackled and burned.

Saxony pushed harder.

She felt Asees push harder.

And then, like a wave bursting from the ocean, Saxony heard the voices of her people echoing back to her.

Crafters, across the realms.

Lieges.

Saxony squeezed her eyes shut tighter and their shouts grew louder and louder until finally, after her head began to pound with them, they escaped her mind and traveled into the air. When Saxony opened her eyes, ghostly figments of the Crafter Lieges from the four realms stood in front of her.

They were seventeen altogether.

Saxony swallowed.

Nearly all of them had answered.

This was it.

The time for waiting was over. They wouldn't stand around in fear that the Kingpin might attack and disrupt their sanctuary. They would strike him first. They would be the ones to wage war and Dante Ashwood would cower before them.

Asees smiled and let go of Saxony's hand, nodding in a bow to their new guests. Her dark hair swayed against her stave-covered arms. They were not silver, like Saxony's and her Kin's, but a deep gold that made Asees look almost royal.

She felt royal. She was a Liege, as Zekia was once destined to be, as Amja was now acting, as the summoned Crafters in front of her were.

As Saxony could only ever hope to be.

"Thank you for answering our call," Asees said. "Are we all happy to speak in the Uskhanyan tongue?"

"We all have translation charms, Asees," a man, whose accent she thought might be Volen, said. "Continue as you plan. Like everyone, I am eager to hear what is to be said."

"There is much to discuss, Lionus," Asees replied. "But though I had the power to bring you here, the idea was not mine. You should speak to the woman whose plan I believe we should follow. Her wisdom has taught me many things."

Asees turned to Saxony, and for a moment Saxony almost froze under the pressure.

Asees nudged her firmly forward.

"Hello, my name is Saxony Akintola of the Rishiyat Kin."

Her voice was too small. Too fumbling. She cleared her throat and tried again.

"We called you here to talk about Dante Ashwood, the Kingpin of Uskhanya," Saxony said.

Louder, firmer, like a leader would.

There was a murmur among the Lieges. They had all heard his name, whether they were from this realm or not. Ashwood had been a driving force in the War of Ages and so there was not a Crafter alive today who didn't know the shadow man.

"He has a new magic," Saxony said. "He calls it the Loj elixir. It's something he has been trying to perfect for many years, which caused the magic sickness across our realm.

Now it's finally perfected and he's using it to build an army."

"We've heard whispers," a Liege said—a woman, whose accent was familiar. "I am Theodora of the Kythnu Kin. My people have heard of Creije's battle and since their Liege hasn't joined us today, I'm assuming that means their Kin has fallen? Do you have word of this?"

"Fallen?" the Volen man—Lionus—asked. "I cannot believe that's true. What is this magic that could take a whole Kin? How did Dante Ashwood create it?"

Saxony wondered if she should lie to them about Zekia, because telling a room full of powerful Crafters that her sister had helped to invent a magic that had started a new war wouldn't make the best impression.

Even so, she didn't want to begin this alliance with lies.

She didn't want to hide things from them, when now more than ever they needed to come together as a team.

They had to trust her.

"It's mind control," Saxony said. "And my sister, who was taken by Ashwood, helped him to create it."

She saw the twitch in their eyes.

How Lionus in particular had to bite down on his lip to keep it from curling into a snarl.

These Lieges weren't going to be sympathetic to a girl who'd lost her sister. They were angry with a Crafter who had betrayed her kind. As though Zekia's actions made Saxony an enemy too.

"I don't know the Creijen Liege," Saxony said quickly, before they had time to voice their doubts on her intentions. "I never met anyone from their Kin while I lived in the city and I've heard no word from them since Ashwood started attacking districts."

"They were small," Theodora said. "Only six of them. Their old Liege and his entire family were killed by buskers in their home twelve years ago. Creije's magic trade makes it unsafe for many Crafters to gather there."

The trade that Tavia and Wesley had been a part of and that, even by extension, Saxony and Karam had joined. They had buskers in their army, and Theodora's revelation meant that didn't bode well for an alliance.

"Your sister," Lionus asked. "She has joined Ashwood?"

"Zekia was supposed to be our Liege," Saxony said. "Until he stole her and used her powers for his evil. Now the Loj elixir is creating soldiers out of civilians. It's infecting Crafters and non–magic users alike."

"What does Ashwood want?" Lionus asked.

"To kill us all," Theodora said.

"Actually, it's worse," Saxony said. "He wants to create a world where everyone without magic is a slave and he becomes king of everything. A world where even Crafters will be subject to his brutality."

It was the seven Uskhanyan Lieges, those of Saxony's own realm, who looked most troubled by this. It was their home, after all, that was in the most immediate danger.

"I think we can all agree that would be bad," Saxony said. "He's attacking the capital city of Uskhanya as we speak and it's only a matter of time before Creije is under his command."

"What is it that you want from us?" Lionus asked.

"Help," Saxony said. "I want you to send members of your Kins to help us fight Ashwood's army."

"You want us to turn against our own kind?" he asked,

clearly conflicted at the thought of Crafters fighting Crafters.

She hadn't seen what Saxony had seen. Lionus didn't know how the Loj could change a person.

"The Crafters with the Kingpin must be saved," Saxony said. "Either from the Loj, or themselves. I don't want to hurt them."

"Then how will you save them?" Lionus asked.

"I'm still working on that," she said honestly. "But I can't do it without your help."

"I am the Liege of the only city in Naustrio with a Kin," one of the women said. "Our realm is not a magic one and I decline to join a war that could destroy the few Crafters we have left. May the Scholarly Goddess be with you in battle."

The woman bowed and then her image dispersed into smoke.

"I decline too," another said.

"I will not risk my people for a battle that hasn't touched our shores," another agreed.

"We wish you luck from the Lonely Goddess," a fourth said.

They dispersed as the only Naustrios woman had, leaving just eleven remaining. Two Volen, two Wrenyi—Asees included—and all seven of the Uskhanyans. Or eight, Saxony supposed, if she counted herself.

"I think I speak for all of Uskhanya when I say that those lot can go to the fire-gates," Theodora said. "This war belongs to us all and we'll fight it."

"Hear, hear!" the other Uskhanyans yelled out.

Some muttered *cowards* under their breaths and though Saxony tried to keep her face neutral—though she understood the fear of those who had left—she couldn't help but secretly agree with the sentiment.

"The Uskhanyan Lieges amongst us can join you," Lionus said. "But why should the rest of us? I do not wish to be callous, but Ashwood exists in your realm. If we join you, it will make us a target."

"We are already targets, Lionus," Asees said.

She stepped to Saxony's side and Saxony felt oddly strengthened by that small act of solidarity.

"Ashwood attacked my Kin in the realm of Wrenyal. In the holy city of Granka."

Lionus blinked. "He came for the holy city?" he asked. "Why were we not told of such things?"

"I was busy trying not to be killed," Asees said, adopting Karam's sarcastic monotone. "He slaughtered many of my people and took the rest of us as puppets. Myself included."

Asees swallowed and Saxony could feel her grief like a fist. If Ashwood hadn't intercepted her letter to her family, then maybe Asees's Kin would have been safe. There was no limit to the guilt she would carry for that.

"If it weren't for Saxony's Kin and a group of buskers, I would not have survived," Asees said. "I understand your hesitance. I was the same when they first asked for my help, and it cost me my people."

"Ashwood doesn't care about borders and realms," Saxony said. "Nobody will be safe, just like we weren't safe the last time war came for us."

"An army of Crafters has never been done before," Lionus said. "We would be the first to create our own resistance to the world."

"And change it for the better," Saxony said. "It's not just

about defeating Ashwood, but creating true peace in the world. Right now, I even have buskers from across the realm—crooks and criminals who I thought were the most untrustworthy of all—pledge themselves to this army and this cause. We're uniting against a common enemy to create an uncommon future."

A silence followed as they considered her words and the prospect of working with buskers, who sold magic rather than protected it. Saxony could see them weighing up her call to arms with their lives. It wasn't an easy decision to make, but whether they acted or not, the lives of their people would still be on the line. At least with Saxony, they'd have a chance at surviving.

"You are not a Liege," Lionus said, looking at Saxony like she was a strange creature.

I know, Saxony thought. *I'll never be one of you.*

It was the bane of her recent days and made her thirst for the time when it was just her, Karam, Tavia, and Wesley, and she had some kind of authority.

"You are not a Liege," Lionus said again. "But you speak as one."

Saxony didn't dare to breathe.

"I will follow you," Lionus said. "I will send members of my Kin in Volo to help you create this vision of peace and fight our common enemy."

"I will follow too," the other Volen Liege said.

And then the Wrenyi Liege. And then each of the Uskhanyans, again and again until all eleven of them had pledged themselves.

It would mean dozens, maybe a hundred more Crafters on their side.

Saxony bowed her head in thanks. There were no words to describe the way her heart pounded with gratitude in that moment, knowing that these leaders of magic had put their faith in her. She was giving them something to fight for. She was giving them the chance of a new age where they would never have to be scared again. She was giving them hope and they took it gladly.

Dante Ashwood was trying to build a new world, but now Saxony could build a world of her own. One where her people could truly be united, truly be safe, and truly be free.

8

Wesley

CREIJE WAS TURNING TO ASH.

The tall rainbow-stretched buildings still stood, the streets still gleamed in a glorious sun-flooded maze, and the sky remained bright and endless in the day, while shadowed in misdeed whenever the moon hit the air.

It looked very much the same, but so much that the once-great capital had stood for was disappearing. All that it was and hoped to be, every dream the tourists brought to the city or from it, seemed to be chipping away.

In this district, the fourth they had taken, the floating railways that once coiled through the cobblestone were now desolate and empty, the thrum of jugglers and street performers giving way to a silence that made Wesley's toes curl. The city was dying in every way that counted.

Only three more districts stood.

Creije was more than halfway to falling and the Kingpin

wasted no time in taking the people from the streets and trains and homes and shadows that gave them temporary refuge. He plucked them one by one, like ripe fruit, and lined them in pretty little rows, ready to devour them whole.

And he made Wesley watch.

Everything Wesley had built was crumbling. Those miraculous novelties that he'd weaved into the city, the parts of himself—blood and soul—that had gone into making it great, were like smoke in the air.

Little by little.

Step by step.

One by one.

Wesley could smell the Loj elixir in the wind.

He could see it drip down the sides of people's faces, as those already enthralled held the new victims to the ground and force-fed it to them. He could hear it gargle in their throats as they tried desperately to keep from swallowing the magic. And Wesley could feel the moment the air turned and their hearts gave way to the Kingpin's power. Their eyes as black as the endless night that had stained his, their resolve withering like dying flowers.

One by one.

Wesley looked at Zekia with every harsh angle he had left. Staying here was getting to be too much and Wesley wasn't sure how much longer he could do nothing while his world burned.

"Why don't you just shove your little mind control elixir down my throat?" he asked. "Then I wouldn't care about any of this."

Zekia's eyes glistened with an odd kind of sadness. Wesley

couldn't believe the girl he had once cared for had been the cause of this pain. He couldn't believe the person in front of him was the same child who wanted so desperately to prove there was good inside of him.

He couldn't believe that he had turned her into this.

"It never works on you," she said. "I'd do it if I could, but we've tried too many times and it only makes you angrier."

Wesley leaned back against the brick wall and slumped slowly to the floor. He tried to shut out the screaming of his people outside, but it was sharper than any knife he had used to cut through his enemies.

Zekia was right. She had tried to give Wesley the elixir before, but it had barely made him blink. Wesley wasn't sure whether it was because his magic had finally found its way back home inside his heart, taking root so deep that it couldn't bear to be lost again to numbness, or if he really was just a stubborn bastard. Perhaps his mind refused to be conquered so easily.

"We'll find another way to bring you to our side," Zekia said. "And you won't have to listen to these people anymore. We're moving to another city soon and there will be wind and water and you'll get some fresh air."

She tugged on the thin thread wrapped around Wesley's hands like a leash. The magical string glowed bright silver under the moon, like a row of stars tethering him to his captor. Wesley missed the handcuffs, but he'd slipped them enough times that now the thread of magic was the only thing they trusted to secure him.

Not that it would stop him. Not that anything could.

"After that you'll come to us the old-fashioned way," Zekia

said. "I'll make sure of it. *Pure grit*, like you always told me."

"And if that doesn't work, then we will carve him up piece by piece until the only parts left are the loyal ones."

Wesley jerked his eyes up as Dante Ashwood approached. The shadow man who had made him into one of the most powerful people in the realms. Wesley should have been used to being Ashwood's slave, since an underboss was basically a glorified skivvy, but he hated the fact that he was on the ground while the Kingpin towered over him, as though he may as well have been on his knees.

Part of the ruse, Wesley thought. *Let him think I'm breaking*.

"Just make sure you don't touch my smile," Wesley said. "It's far too charming to be cut to pieces."

Ashwood made a sound that was almost a laugh, but also very nearly a scream.

"Do you know what makes you different from the rest of the people in this forsaken city?" he asked.

Wesley rested his chin on his knees. "My sunny disposition?"

"Your loyalty," Ashwood said, unaffected by his wry tone. "These people can be bought and bargained for. They can be swayed and subdued. They can be changed by magic and madness. Soldiers are easy to come by, my boy, but family must be earned."

Wesley's gut twisted at the mention of *family*. Right now, the only family he wanted was far across the realm, a lifetime away.

"I will earn your loyalty once more, Wesley. Just like I earned your sister's."

Wesley spat out a laugh. "We're not a family," he said. "And if we were, then it would make me proud to be an orphan."

Ashwood's shadows did not flinch around his hidden face.

He took a step closer to Wesley, until his magic felt like oil in the air. "I chose you," he said. "When you were young and unaware of your power. I nurtured all of the sparks inside of you and soon you'll repay me for that. Soon you'll see that I'm the only family you've ever had. I'm the only one who understands the things inside your heart."

Wesley's jaw clenched, teeth grinding together with such force that he felt like his bones were shaking. The fact that a man like Ashwood saw kinship in Wesley made him want to be sick, and the worst part was Wesley had nobody to blame but himself, because he had fed into that, carefully nurturing his reputation as an evil bastard and doing whatever it took to rise to the top and stay in the Kingpin's good graces.

Including sacrificing Zekia.

But that was then and this was now.

Now, despite what the Kingpin wanted, Wesley wasn't scared that one day his promises would sound too pretty to ignore and all the horrors that had happened would start to look like a means to an end. That without Tavia, or even the likes of Saxony and Karam, to balance Wesley out, the worst parts of him would rise to the surface.

Maybe once, it would have been possible.

Maybe in another lifetime, or if everything Wesley loved wasn't hanging in the balance. But now, here, in this place, Wesley could never side with someone like Dante Ashwood. Not when he could see the city he loved withering in the cold dead of night.

Wesley had only stuck around this long to see if he could

pull Zekia from the old man's clutches, but he knew now that it was too late. Too much had happened, and Wesley being here only made her want to stay more.

It was time to go and if Zekia wouldn't come, then he'd do what he had done all those years ago.

Wesley would leave her behind to rot.

9

Tavia

THE MOON WAS HIGH and there were monsters lurking beyond the forest.

Tavia had seen her fair share of evil and heard her fair share of whispers, but there was something different in the wind tonight, and as it swayed through the tree branches it almost sounded like a croon. It sounded like death.

She patrolled a lot, mostly out of habit from nights spent wandering the streets as a busker in search of people to sell the Kingpin's darkest magic to. Tavia was restless and she wasn't used to sitting still, or standing around doing nothing.

Especially at night.

Nobody else was interested in the patrols the way she was. The Crafters in the Rishiyat camp were either too confident in their power, or too complacent in their hidden sanctuary, but either way none of them thought to search the trees for intruders. Even Karam seemed to be spending most nights focused on pillow talk with Saxony, instead of hunting for enemies.

Maybe Tavia was just the mad one who needed to stop looking for danger where there was none and enjoy the small solace they had found while it lasted. She'd thought about that a lot over the past few days as she searched the woods alone and found nothing but crisp leaves and, once, a small snake that didn't even take the time to hiss at her before slithering away. She thought about it tonight as the moon stared down at her in judgment and begged her to just *go to sleep already*.

And then she heard the crack of those crisp leaves—a sound that could only be footprints on the dirt—and she felt the whispering trees gasp, and suddenly Tavia didn't feel like she was mad anymore.

She hid behind a mossy trunk, her hand on her knife hilt as Nolan Kane, the cocky little bastard she had bested back in the city center, sighed, unzipped his pants, and started to piss on a nearby tree root.

Tavia resisted the urge to look away, just in case he spotted her and tried to pull something, but the wincing couldn't be helped.

How in the fire-gates did he find this place? And what in the name of the Many Gods is he doing here alone?

Alone.

Tavia focused on that, just as she focused on the backpack by his feet. More magic, ready for the taking.

Nolan didn't look like he had company. In fact, as he swayed and pressed a hand to a tree trunk for balance while he carried on with his business, he looked a little drunk, his eyes bloodshot under the light of the stars.

Drunk and alone, with a heap of magic at his side.

Now that was interesting.

Tavia stepped from the shadows and the trees rustled in warning. Perhaps for her to run and turn back, or perhaps to alert the others that someone was so close to their camp.

Tavia ignored the trees and focused on the magic by Nolan's feet. She could take on one drunk busker, and his backpack looked too good to resist.

How funny it would be to rob the same guy twice in just a matter of weeks.

How hilarious it would be when she told Karam about it later.

"Fancy meeting you here," Tavia said.

Nolan looked up at her in a squint.

Slowly, he zipped his pants back up.

"Are you following me?" he asked in a slur.

"No," Tavia said. "Are you alone?"

"No," he said, but it was clearly a lie.

"Did you just . . . wander into the Uncharted Forest?"

Tavia was beginning to doubt the intelligence of Rishiya's supposed best busker.

Nolan swallowed and it seemed to make him stagger a little. "I was in the Flower Hamlets having a drink and got tailed by some amityguards," he said. "I needed somewhere I could lie low and they weren't gonna check this place. It's *uncharted* for a reason. It's haunted."

Tavia laughed, unable to help it. Getting chased by amityguards seemed like a lifetime ago and it was reassuring to know that Doyen Fenna Schulze still had control of the other cities in Uskhanya, even if Creije was falling.

"I hate to break it to you," Tavia said, "but you haven't exactly found safe haven. Now, how about you hand over that backpack without a fuss, for old times' sake?"

Nolan grabbed the backpack from the ground and hugged it protectively to his chest.

"No way," he said, blinking as though to sharpen his vision. "You get away."

Tavia laughed and reached into her pocket, pulling out the small marble that she had stolen from this very bastard back in the city. It was a deep, unyielding blue, and when she tossed it up and down in her hand, she thought it looked a little like holding the ocean.

"So instead of coming with me willingly, you fancy putting up a fight?" she asked. "I could do with a little exercise tonight, I suppose."

"No need to get violent," Nolan said. "I'm unarmed. Lost my knife back in the Hamlets."

He raised his hands high in the air in surrender, backpack included, and gave Tavia what she thought was supposed to be a charming smile. Nolan stepped forward, stumbling a little on the uneven ground, and then his hand shot to his pocket and he threw a trick bag at her before Tavia could even think to dive out of the way.

The pouch landed at her feet.

And blew her straight back onto her ass.

A jolt of what felt like lightning zapped through Tavia's toes and propelled her to the forest floor. Nolan ran, sprinting through the forest without looking back.

Tavia groaned.

"Curse your mother and the train she rode in on!" she yelled.

She pulled herself to her feet and chased after him, winding through the trees she had spent the last few weeks hiding among.

"May the Many Gods spit in your father's beard," Tavia yelled as Nolan jumped over a small creak. "And chop his balls right—"

Nolan tripped.

His foot caught in a large tree root and he fell with a loud thud straight onto the forest floor, the wet dirt splashing up like water around him. He tried to get back up, but his drunken arms collapsed underneath him and so eventually he just lay there, rolled onto his back, and murmured a curse that made Tavia raise her eyebrows.

"If this is the best that Rishiya has to offer," she said, "then I don't know why I was so worried."

"Get back!" Nolan said.

He kept the backpack clutched to him and reached inside to pull something out. Tavia's hand lingered by Wesley's gun, just in case, only when Nolan pulled the first piece of magic he seemed to find, it was a far greater weapon than the one she had.

The purple liquid swam inside the vial, lighting the ground and banishing the moon's glow from that patch of the forest.

The Loj elixir.

"Where did you get that?" Tavia asked.

"Get back," Nolan said again, still flat on the ground. "I'll use it, I swear. It'll knock you into a haze!"

"It would do more than that," she said.

Tavia stepped toward him and drew Wesley's gun.

"Drop it," she told him.

And, as if there was something in her eyes he had never expected to see—something she had never expected to feel—Nolan did as he was told.

The Loj elixir was outside of Creije, in the very city Tavia and her friends had hidden themselves. She didn't know how it had gotten here, but if it wasn't contained anymore, then that meant that it could be anywhere.

It meant that they had been wrong, thinking Dante Ashwood wanted Creije first.

He wasn't taking on Uskhanya a city at a time, starting with their home before making his way across the realm.

He was doing it all, everywhere, right now.

———

LESS THAN ten minutes later, Tavia pushed Nolan onto the ground.

Around her, the two dozen buskers she had woken from their night's sleep for backup smiled in that same slow and deadly way that Wesley had taught them.

The way only a Creijen could.

She didn't wake Saxony or Karam. She didn't want them to be here to see the side of her that she needed to show.

"Shall we kill him?" one busker asked.

"Nah," said another. "Let's just cut out his tongue so he can't talk."

Nolan tried to sit up a little more, but it looked like the dizziness from all the alcohol was getting to him. So instead he slumped back onto his elbows and glared like he didn't fear death half as much as he feared losing.

"You," he said to Tavia, still a little drunk. "This is your

~ 97 ~

holier-than-thou alternative to the Kingpin?" He spat on the ground by her feet. "You dirty traitor."

Tavia picked the dirt from her nails with her knife, unfazed. "This is a trial by your peers," she said. "You might want to stop being so volatile. I could lose my temper."

Nolan's laugh was like a gunshot. "Like you scare me."

Except, she needed to do just that if she was going to lead these buskers. Wesley had taught her well what it meant to be feared, and right now the buskers were looking to Tavia to stand in his shoes as a worthy replacement. She couldn't risk not being feared by someone like Nolan, even if it meant she had to become someone worse.

Tavia took a step toward him. "Tell us what you know about Ashwood's plans and maybe you'll get out of this alive."

"You think I know anything about the Kingpin?" Nolan asked. "That's above my pay."

Tavia knelt down and pressed her knife to his neck. She felt the buskers around her smile, heard one lick his lips in the anticipation of a kill. They all wanted revenge for their lives being uprooted and an enemy busker was the perfect avenue for their anger.

"Tell me what you know about the Loj elixir," Tavia said. "How did it find its way onto the streets of Rishiya? Is it anywhere else beyond here and Creije?"

Nolan laughed out a shaking breath. "What's wrong?" he asked. "Creije's best busker afraid of a little magic? From what I've heard, that elixir is a one-way ticket to being on the right side of this war. It's happiness. *Ljoisi uf hemga*, right? It's a bloody suit of armor."

~ 98 ~

Tavia's heart screamed against her chest as her mother's voice echoed in her ears.

Please, ciolo. You have to be strong.

The thought of the same elixir that had poisoned her muma's mind and stolen her from the world being touted as happiness made her blood boil.

The elixir destroyed lives, long before it took minds.

Tavia pressed the tip of the knife harder against Nolan's throat. "It strips you of your free will," she said. "And it's a one-way ticket to losing your sanity."

Can't you see them, ciolo? her mother's memory begged. *My ghosts, Tavia. Can't you hear them screaming?*

"I made a deal with your underboss," Tavia said. "Casim promised to align with us. He told me that your comrades would be here in a few days. Was he lying? Has he been working with Ashwood this whole time?"

Nolan laughed again, and Tavia was beginning to think that it was the worst sound in the realms.

"Casim is a traitor," Nolan said. "And he doesn't see what's going on right under his nose."

"Meaning what?"

"Meaning that I'm not aligning myself with the losing team," Nolan said. "You lot are going to burn. If not by the Kingpin's hand, then you'll get yours in the fire-gates."

Tavia tried to hold her anger in, but it was rising to the surface quicker than she'd thought possible. "How many people in Rishiya have you sold the elixir to? Who gave it to you? Who else has it?"

She wasn't about to let anyone else be driven to madness by mind magic, and if the Loj had gotten ahold of Rishiya, too, then they didn't have time to spare. Tavia had seen what this sort of thing did to people. She had seen the first iterations of the Loj—the *experiments*, Ashwood had called them—disguised as a magic sickness, infecting countless people in the slums of Creije.

She had started this battle because she couldn't bear to see that happen to another family like it had to hers.

"You want me to draw you a map of the supply chain?" Nolan asked. "Why don't you just ask your underboss about it?"

Tavia paled. "What do you know about Wesley?"

"From what I hear, Wesley Thornton Walcott is standing by the Kingpin's side, as loyal as always."

Tavia snarled at him and the knife felt suddenly so light in her hands. "Wesley wouldn't betray us," she said.

He wouldn't betray me, she thought.

Nolan's sneer was unbearably arrogant. "When the time comes, Dante Ashwood and your precious underboss are going to take this realm and kill anyone who gets in their way."

Tavia punched him.

She hadn't even wanted to, but the action was instinctive and before she knew what she was doing she'd raised her fist high in the air and brought it down straight onto Nolan's nose.

His head ricocheted back and hit the forest floor, blood spurting from his hateful face. Tavia's hands shook and she felt the anger lessen inside her, just a little, but not nearly enough.

The buskers laughed and one of them stepped forward and kicked Nolan in the ribs. Then another. One of them bent down to punch him. A fourth stomped on his knee and it was only when Nolan screamed out that Tavia held up her hand.

"Stop," she said.

Though she wasn't sure she wanted them to.

The buskers stepped back.

"You have one chance to save your life," she told Nolan. "And you're really starting to push it."

Nolan shoved himself up from the dirt and clutched at his ribs. He looked newly sobered. "Just kill me and be done with it," he said. "That's what you lot are planning on, no matter what I do."

"Actually, it's not," Tavia said. "You were right before, back in the city, when you said I wouldn't kill you."

The buskers beside her shifted at this revelation.

"But there are things I can do to you that would be far worse than death," she said.

The buskers' smirks returned and Tavia flung her arms out to gesture to them.

"They'd watch and smile while I did it. They'd help and laugh to drown out your screams," she said. "The buskers stand against Dante Ashwood and if you stand with him, then you're not one of us anymore. And I don't think you want to be an enemy of the streets."

For the first time, she saw the defiance in Nolan's eyes lift, and a flash of the fear she had so desperately wanted latched onto his face.

"Tell me about Wesley."

"I don't know much," Nolan said. "There were some whisperings about him and the Kingpin wanting to amass more forces in Tisvgen. It could be bullshit, I don't know."

Tisvgen.

It didn't make sense for Ashwood to take Wesley there, unless Creije was on the verge of destruction.

Unless it was too dangerous of a place to keep such precious cargo.

"And the Loj?" Tavia asked.

"There are groups of Crafters in every city we have," Nolan told her. "They're supplying the buskers across Uskhanya with the elixir. Direct from the Kingpin."

"But Casim—"

"Dante Ashwood isn't stupid," Nolan said, interrupting her. "The only underboss he's ever trusted was yours."

Wesley. She knew it was true. They were only allowed to get so close to Ashwood before because Wesley had been with them. The old man had barely spoken of the others, and when Wesley joked about killing his peers, Ashwood only laughed like he might just approve.

"Ashwood isn't giving the elixir to any of the underbosses," Tavia said. "He's going straight to the streets."

"Rendering Casim and all the rest of them useless," Nolan confirmed. "We don't follow the underbosses like we used to. We get our orders directly from the top now."

"Casim didn't mention being usurped," Tavia said.

"He doesn't know," Nolan told her. "None of them do. The Crafters that gave me the elixir said that if I sold it under Casim's nose, then the Kingpin would reward me in the new world. All the coin, magic, and Cloverye I could want."

It was a small dream to have in a big world, and so Tavia knew what Nolan really wanted—what he'd really betrayed his underboss for—and it wasn't booze or the deception of power. It was what everyone in the realms wanted. Survival. Nolan didn't think Tavia and her side stood a chance.

"How many have you sold?" she asked. "How many elixirs are on the streets of Rishiya?"

"I only sold a handful myself," Nolan said. He wiped blood from his face and onto his arm. "They told me to distribute it out among the other buskers, but the amityguards have been right on my ass, so I haven't had the chance."

Tavia wanted to feel relief at that, but she knew she couldn't. It didn't matter if Nolan had sold only a few elixirs in Rishiya and if no other buskers in the city had their hands on it yet, because buskers across the whole of the realm, from Kythnu to the government city of Yejlath, had backpacks full of the stuff.

The elixir was spreading like an infection and they didn't have a cure.

It wasn't coming: It was here already.

"Whether you kill me or not, you're still going to lose," Nolan said.

Tavia stared down at the bleeding busker.

She put away her knife and got Wesley's gun back out from her belt loop.

The buskers wanted her to kill Nolan; they expected her to. She'd gotten all she needed from him and he was nothing if not a liability. She couldn't trust him to stay here and she couldn't let him back out on the streets now that he knew where their rebellion was.

They have to fear me, she thought. *That's the only way they'll follow me.*

Tavia wasn't good at inspirational speeches like Saxony and

she didn't have that air about her that made people flock to her side like Wesley did. All Tavia had was a prisoner and Wesley's gun.

"I thought your side was all about peace," Nolan said. "Are you really going to kill me here?"

The look in his eyes said that he truly didn't know what Tavia was capable of. And of course he couldn't, because she didn't know either.

Tavia had always thought she was above the buskers and the likes of anyone who patrolled Creije and ruined lives because they wanted to rise to the top. She'd only ever wanted to escape and find a family in her home realm of Volo. But she could see now, how someone could get lost in this maze of power.

How easy it was to forget yourself when so many people had their eyes on you.

"What are you doing?"

Tavia all but jumped out of her skin at the sound of the new voice so close to her ear. She turned with wide eyes to see Karam.

"Gods damn it," Tavia said in a hard voice. "You scared me to death."

She pressed her free hand to her chest to see if her heart was still beating, because she was sure it had stopped.

"You seem pretty alive to me," Karam said.

Tavia gave her a sullen look. "What are you doing out of bed and wandering around at this time of night?"

"I was looking for you."

"That's sweet," Tavia said. "But I'm a little busy right now. Let's talk later."

Karam looked at the bloody Nolan. "Torturing a new prisoner?" she asked.

Tavia cleared her throat and kept her chin high. "Hardly torture," she said. "We were just softening him up a little."

"We," Karam repeated.

She looked around at the couple of dozen buskers who surrounded them in a circle. Karam's glare was palpable and even though the buskers outnumbered her, they looked hesitant to even meet her gaze.

"Go to bed," Karam told them. "I have private matters to discuss with your new leader."

The buskers shuffled a little, perhaps from nerves at whether or not to disobey an order from Creije's best fighter and probably the most deadly person in camp. But also, Tavia suspected, because they weren't quite satisfied with how little blood had been spilled tonight.

They were hungry for war and revenge, and Nolan was the right kind of scumbag to take it out on.

"Do as she says," Tavia told them.

The buskers nodded—a few sighed, some grumbled a little—and then they dispersed, begrudgingly heading back to their beds and to a night filled with dreams instead of death.

Only when they had gone and it was just Tavia, Karam, and the still-bleeding Nolan did Karam speak again.

"I told you to stop being reckless," she said. "First you go into the city and take on a group of buskers alone and now you bring one straight into our camp to torture? What are you thinking?"

"He had information," Tavia said. "And I did what was necessary to get it."

"You sound like Wesley."

"Maybe it's about time one of us did."

"I know that you are frustrated and I am too. I understand that we need to get him back, but this is not the way," Karam said. "Tavia, you need to—"

Karam stopped, and for a moment, Tavia wondered what could possibly make their new moral compass cut off her rant, but then she felt the air shift. Felt the spark of magic ignite in the wind.

Tavia didn't recognize the Crafter in front of them, nor the three women who stood behind him, their eyes almost red in the moonlight with the fire of their magic.

"Can we help you?" Tavia asked.

"My name is Lionus," the man said. "I am a Crafter Liege from the realm of Volo, in the city of Gila. I was asked to come here with my Kin to help your war against Dante Ashwood."

"Gila," Tavia repeated, her voice quiet.

It was the city her mother had grown up in.

A city that would have been Tavia's home in another life.

"Just the four of you?" she said, trying to swallow the heaviness she felt. "Waste of a summons if you ask me."

"We are a dozen," Lionus said. "We heard a scuffle on our way into camp. I told the rest of my Kin to scour the forest in search of your leader while we came to help."

"Well," Tavia said, pocketing her weapon in a show of peace. "No help necessary. We've got it covered."

Lionus looked at her, tilting his head to one side like he was appraising her. Tavia wondered if he knew that she was born from the same land that he was. If he could tell they were of the same people.

It didn't seem likely.

She couldn't see much of a resemblance between herself and the Volen Crafters. Sure, their skin was the same pale white as hers, but staves were spread up their arms in a rainbow of color, from pinks to deep blues, and their clothes were an array of bright oranges and dusty reds—a stark contrast to the blacks and grays that made up much of Tavia's wardrobe. The women wore a single braid in their long hair and even Lionus had one dangling from his beard, while Tavia's black hair cut sharply across her chin, unadorned.

There were so few similarities between her and the people her mother may have once thought of as kindred.

"That boy is a busker," Lionus said, nodding to Nolan. "You should kill him."

"*I'm* a busker," Tavia said. "And since he's my prisoner, we go by my rules. And I get to decide if and when he dies."

Lionus kept his eyes trained on her and his people stiffened beside him, awaiting a command to strike.

"If he escapes, he could alert people to our location," Lionus said.

"She told you that it was not your decision," Karam said. "You should move out of our way."

"Or what?" one of the Crafter women behind Lionus asked.

"Or we will go through you," Karam said.

Tavia discreetly checked how many blades she had up her sleeves.

Lionus smiled. "We did not come here to risk our lives for such stupidity," he said. "The busker dies and that's all there is to it."

Without hesitation, Lionus threw himself toward Tavia while his three Crafters laid assault to Karam.

Tavia had only the briefest second to see Karam block a kick in defense, before Lionus's fist cracked across her jaw.

She kept her ground and dodged his next blow, swinging her leg low to knock him off his feet.

Lionus snarled and thrust his hand out and a spear of ice launched into the air. Tavia dove out of the way just in time for it to miss her heart and graze across her side.

Many Gods damned Crafters, she thought. *So much for helping us.*

Tavia quickly jumped back to her feet.

That was what Karam had taught her, and Tavia wasn't about to let those lessons go to waste.

She heard a crack of thunder in the sky and when she turned to Karam, she saw lightning strike at the ground by her feet. Karam dodged it and kicked her leg out hard enough that one of the Crafter women fell, hitting her head with enough force that she didn't get back up.

Tavia turned to Lionus, who was heading back toward her with a venomous snarl.

"We want to help you," he said. "You should kill your enemies and be done with it."

He thrust his hand out again, but this time Tavia saw the ice coming.

Fool me once.

She swiveled out of its way with seconds to spare and before she was even fully facing Lionus again, she swiped out her knife and watched as it cut through his cheek.

Lionus wiped the blood from his face and pushed her to the ground.

The moment she fell back, Tavia pulled the miniature mirror doll from her jacket. She never let her pockets go empty, after all.

She smeared the blood—Lionus's blood—from her shoulder where he'd pushed her and onto the doll's face.

Then Tavia snapped the left leg of the doll inward.

Lionus let out an ungodly scream.

The sound of blades and thunder disappeared from the air.

The two remaining Crafters ceased their attack on Karam and looked to Tavia with destruction in their eyes.

"You're going to pay for that," one of them said.

Tavia clutched on to her blade.

If this Crafter got one step closer to her, then she would—

A fist cracked against the girl's face with enough force to send her crumpling to the ground with a yell. The blood sprayed from her mouth and onto the soil and she grabbed at her face like it might just fall apart.

"Enough," Karam said. She looked to Tavia. "You are bleeding."

"Yeah, I noticed."

"I thought I taught you not to do that."

Tavia breathed out a laugh. "I'll try harder next time."

"Do we need to start killing each other now?" Karam asked, turning to Lionus as he clasped his leg between both hands. "Is this why you came? To begin a war with us, too?"

Lionus opened his mouth to respond, but the next voice that echoed through the forest was not his.

"No," Saxony said. "And if they know what's good for them, they'll start respecting the way that things work around here."

She was flanked by at least ten of the Rishiyat Kin, as well as Asees and Arjun.

"I might have summoned you, but I'm not going to hesitate to send you right back if you touch any of our people again."

Saxony looked to Lionus, who was still weeping on the ground, holding his broken leg.

Tavia wasn't sure what all the fuss was about. It wasn't like his people couldn't heal him in an instant. It wasn't like she had sliced a blade across his neck.

"We're on the same side," Saxony said. "We called you here to help us fight a great enemy."

"She was going to risk our location by harboring an enemy busker," Lionus said.

At the mention of Nolan, Tavia's eyes searched the forest floor. Nothing.

For the love of—

"Nolan's gone," she said to Karam. "We need to send people out into the forest to find him. *Now.*"

Karam nodded. "I will get the buskers back out of their cozy beds."

Tavia couldn't believe that they'd let Nolan slip out of their hands while they were so busy fighting against each other. It was ridiculous and if Nolan wasn't found, then she was going to use that mirror doll to break Lionus's other leg. Or even his damn neck.

"Are you okay?" Saxony asked her.

Tavia nodded.

"You're bleeding."

"So I'm told," she said.

"I can help heal your wounds."

"No," Tavia said, shuffling away from Saxony's outstretched hand. "I'm fine."

Saxony nodded and cleared her throat, like she was clearing away any awkwardness from the air. She turned back to the Crafters.

"Tavia's buskers will find the missing prisoner," she said. "In the meantime, you should all heal yourselves, and then some of my Kin will show you where you can rest. In the morning, we'll talk strategy. Which, just to be clear, involves killing Ashwood. Not each other."

Tavia smirked.

Saxony looked so much more like herself when she was taking charge, rather than waiting for someone else to give her orders. She looked like a warrior. Like a Liege. Like someone who could lead a band of Crafters from across the world and into victory, without them all turning against each other.

She looked like the person Tavia remembered being friends with and that she so desperately wanted to trust again.

10

Karam

KARAM APPROACHED THE CABIN where Saxony and her grandma were having dinner together. It was the first time they had properly spoken since Saxony went behind her back to summon the Lieges, and Karam knew that she should probably leave them alone to eat, but she had to speak to Saxony before it was too late.

She knocked on the cabin door.

Karam had been putting this choice off for too long, because she was scared to leave Saxony alone in a place where she seemed primed to lose that fire inside of herself. Karam wanted to help Saxony become the leader she knew that she could be, but Saxony was there now. All that was left was Tavia, who Karam had thought needed someone to watch her back, but Nolan's initial capture—and the look on Tavia's face as she held Wesley's gun to his head—told her that Tavia didn't need protecting anymore. She needed an escape from the role she had been forced into.

She needed Wesley.

They all did.

The door opened and Saxony's face brightened when she saw Karam.

When Saxony smiled, even the leaves rustled, like they were giggling alongside her, perfectly synchronized to her happiness.

Saxony's grandma sat at the table behind her, every bit the warrior Karam hoped she would remain when she reached her age. Her hair, braided down to the very edges of her fingertips, was the color of Arjun's sword and gleamed in the same way when the sun hit it just right. Her dark skin matched Saxony's perfectly, though her eyes were not the same guarded brown, but instead shone in the color of stars and fresh clouds.

"Karam," Saxony said. "Did you come to join us for dinner?"

She opened the door wider for Karam to come in and sat back at the table, opposite her grandma.

"Help yourself," Saxony said. "Amja cooked enough for the whole army."

It truly was a feast, with nearly a dozen plates on the table, some sticky with sauce and sweet steam that Karam could smell even from the doorway. It made her mouth water, especially since she had skipped lunch to train with Tavia.

"No, thank you," Karam said.

She was here to talk, not get distracted with such a delicious spread.

"You're quite the dedicated warrior." Saxony's grandma nodded in approval. "Always focused on the task at hand."

Karam smiled, because she didn't trust herself not to say

something stupid. A war ground was not the ideal place to meet Saxony's family, and Karam hadn't had nearly enough time to practice small talk and the right way to make them deem her truly worthy.

"I am glad you are both here," Karam said, lingering by the door. "I have to talk to you and I am not sure if it is something you are going to like."

Though the sad truth was, whether Saxony liked it or not, Karam had to go.

The Loj was spreading, Nolan had escaped, and despite Karam sending their best scouts after him, he'd disappeared into the woods. Even with the Lieges coming from across the four realms to help, and with Tavia's deal with Casim bringing them buskers, they still needed one thing.

They still needed Wesley.

Saxony stopped eating and turned to look up at Karam. "Do I need to stay sitting down for this?" she asked.

"I have been thinking and I have decided that it is time I went to look for Wesley," Karam said.

"Wesley can wait." Saxony waved her spoon, dismissing the idea.

Karam sighed. "He cannot. And it is important that I find him."

"Why?"

"Creije will fall soon if we do nothing," Karam said. "And now that we know that the Loj is spreading to the other cities, the time for delaying the inevitable is over. You know the Crafters and Tavia knows the buskers, but I know how to fight, and to do that properly, we need Wesley. He is the one with the ideas and he will help us in this battle. If Ashwood turns him, then I fear our fight will be lost."

Saxony slammed her spoon suddenly onto the table, sending grains of rice across the floor. She stood and all signs of the smile she'd had just moments ago quickly dispersed.

"Damn it," she said. "Why *you*? I get that Wesley is important, but I'm not trading your safety for his."

"And yet you may need to," her grandma said. "We must not let him be under Dante Ashwood's thrall."

Her voice was stern but gentle, and when she looked to her granddaughter, Saxony brought her hand up to pinch the bridge of her nose, as though just the thought of having Wesley back gave her a headache.

"Since when do you like underbosses?" Saxony asked her. "Amja, I would have thought that you of all people wouldn't want to trust Wesley Thornton Walcott."

"There is a lot you don't know about what I want or what is best," her grandma said. "Which is why you summoned the other Lieges behind my back instead of heeding my warnings."

Saxony thrust her hands into the air. "Will you ever stop being angry about that? I won't apologize for trying to help our people."

"I'm not asking you to apologize. I'm pointing out that you went against the wishes of someone you love to do what is necessary, because you felt it was right. Karam clearly feels the same."

A smile found its way onto Karam's face. If Saxony's grandma thought she was making the right decision, then that must have meant that she'd made a good impression.

"If I do not go, Tavia will," Karam said. "And she will get herself killed doing it. You know how reckless she has become. You have seen how much she has changed. It is as if she is trying to be Wesley because he cannot be here."

Saxony couldn't deny it, because they all had watched Tavia as she tried to wear shoes that never should have been hers to begin with. She wasn't an underboss and she wasn't even really a criminal. Tavia had wanted to save the world, and more and more each day, Karam could see her forgetting that.

"Where will you go?" Saxony asked.

"Tisvgen," Karam said. "Nolan told Tavia he heard something about Wesley being there. And even if he is not, that city lies between us and Creije and the mountains will give me a good vantage point to see Ashwood's hold in the capital."

"You can't go alone," Saxony said. "It's dangerous. Maybe I could—"

"You are needed here," Karam said. "And I will not be alone. I plan to ask Arjun and a few of his Kin to come with me. I will be okay."

"You can't promise that," Saxony said. "I don't want you to leave me."

Those words alone almost broke Karam.

She hadn't told Saxony what she was thinking sooner because of that reason: She didn't want to leave her and she was afraid something would happen to Saxony in her absence. All Karam wanted was to be with her and for them—and their friends and the world—to be safe.

"She is right to leave," her grandma said. "We need the Creijen underboss safe and here with us, ready to do battle."

"*I* need *her*," Saxony said, turning back to Karam. "I need you here, by my side."

Karam wanted very strongly to kiss her in that moment, but it seemed an odd thing to do with Saxony's grandma watching them.

"I owe Wesley my life," Karam said. "Just as you do. We cannot leave him with the Kingpin any longer. His guidance is what we need to win this war."

Saxony still didn't look convinced, and Karam thought that sometimes Saxony forgot that Karam had made her name in the underrealm fighting rings.

"Do not worry so much," Karam said. "I will return and I will bring Wesley back. He might know how to stop the buskers from selling the Loj."

"Tisvgen is dangerous," Saxony said.

"I have lived in this realm for many years and I know what to expect. I can easily navigate across the Shores of the Dead and to the mountains," Karam said.

Saxony sighed in resignation, though Karam could see the doubt still flicker in her eyes. Saxony reached out for Karam's hands.

"You better come back in one piece," she said.

"You know I will."

"And try not to kill the underboss if he isn't in a good mood when you save him," Saxony's grandma said. "He probably hasn't slept much."

They both turned to her, a little surprised.

"You really do want us to save Wesley, don't you?" Saxony asked.

Her grandma nodded. "He is necessary," she said. "And it's time he came back to where he belongs."

"Well, Karam can still punch him if he gets mouthy," Saxony said. "Don't kill him, but make sure to kick his ass if he doesn't at least say thank you."

Karam had no doubt that once Wesley was back, he and Saxony would settle into the same routine of rolling their eyes at anything the other said, while secretly valuing each other's stance on things. They had a lot of forgiving to do, but Wesley had saved Saxony's life and sacrificed himself so she could escape, and that should have earned him absolution.

WHEN THE sun rose the next morning, Karam, Arjun, and Asees had already been training for hours. Karam was glad to finally have a fighting session that didn't end with Tavia trying to teach her all kinds of shifty magic tricks, with a busker's gleam in her eyes as Karam failed to master any one of them.

This was familiar.

This she knew.

She would miss it when she left.

"Time for a break," Asees said in Wrenyi. "I may faint if we continue."

Karam nodded in agreement, wiping the sweat from her brow. She swallowed a gulp of breath that made her chest sting.

"Agreed," she said. "There's only so many times I can beat Arjun to a pulp before it gets boring."

Arjun pointed at her with his sword. "Don't get cocky.

I'm only letting you win so you feel good about yourself. We can't have your bruised ego costing us this war."

"You're bleeding," Karam said.

"You threw a rock at my face!" Arjun protested.

Karam shrugged. "Expect the unexpected."

She slumped onto the log beside Asees.

"You're getting better," she said to the Liege. "Fighting without magic."

"I'm not sure why I need to know how to do that," Asees said.

"You can't rely on one thing to win a battle," Karam said. "Who knows what kind of spells Zekia and Ashwood have created? Perhaps there's one to strip you of your powers or disorient you. Or maybe you just won't have enough time to conjure your gifts."

"You've really thought a lot about people trying to kill me," Asees said, with an amused smile.

"It's mostly about people trying to kill Arjun," Karam said.

He laughed and squeezed himself into the small space between Karam and Asees. "We would've made a great team back in Wrenyal. The three of us against the world."

"You act like we can't still do that." Asees rested her head on his shoulder. "When we go back home, we definitely need to kidnap Karam and take her with us."

"Good luck with that," Karam said. "The way you two punch, I won't even need to try."

Asees let out a loud laugh and Karam closed her eyes and leaned back onto her palms. These rare moments of peace in all the dire things the realms were trying to throw at them needed to be savored. The sound of her friends' laughter and the feel of Arjun's disgusting sweat-slicked arm brushing up against hers, like they were truly inseparable. The sound of his blade picking at the dirt while the trees sang them a lullaby.

"I'm leaving tomorrow," Karam said.

Quick, like snapping a bone back into place.

"Leaving to go where?" Arjun asked.

"Tisvgen," Karam said. "And then maybe Creije."

"You mean you're going to find Wesley, then," Arjun said.

Karam stood and dusted off her palms, soil scattering back to the forest.

"I want you to come with me," she said to her old friend. "I know that together we can bring him back and give our armies the last missing piece they need to win this war."

"It isn't even a question," Arjun said. And then, quickly—perhaps a little too quickly: "And not because I care about the underboss. I just know you'll definitely need my help."

Karam was tempted to start sparring again, if only to knock some sense into him.

"You could at least pretend to ask for my permission," Asees said.

She looked between them both with raised eyebrows, and Karam almost felt guilty for not considering that. She was Arjun's Liege, after all.

"Come with us," Karam said. "Arjun wasn't wrong when he spoke about us making a great team. The three of us against the world? We could do this."

Asees tried to hold back her smile, but Karam could see it. If there was a chance to hurt Ashwood—the man who'd nearly destroyed her Kin—then Karam knew that she would take it.

"I have been working with Saxony and the other Lieges to keep peace and strategize," Asees said. "But I think she has that under control herself now. She is strong."

Karam had always known that.

"I would be honored for you to join me in this," Karam said. "With some of your Kin, too, if possible."

"Ah." A knowing smile dawned on Asees's face. "So you were going to take my second in command and my Crafters, but not me?"

Karam only shrugged. "A few Crafters on my team couldn't hurt."

"It would be nice to stretch our legs," Asees said. "I'm sure the rest of the Kin have been feeling a little trapped in this place."

"We wouldn't need many," Karam said. "And since you and Arjun are Spiritcrafters, the rest we bring should be Energy-crafters and Intuitcrafters. A good mix of gifts will be invaluable for seeing the course ahead and staving off the weather if the mountains in Tisvgen prove unstable."

"Agreed," Asees said. She stood and pulled Arjun to his feet. "We must pick the best of our warriors for this. When did you want to leave?"

"First thing tomorrow morning. The train from Rishiyat station will take us straight to the Shores of the Dead in Tisvgen. From there, we can head to the mountains on foot."

"Wait a moment," Arjun said. "What are the Shores of the Dead?"

"It is a burial ground covering the entire seafront of Tisvgen," Karam explained. "And it will be the quickest way in."

"There better not be spirits roaming the place," Arjun said.

He sheathed his sword. "Do you think half a dozen of us should do it?"

Karam nodded. "A small group is better to go unnoticed."

The last thing they needed was to march half their army into Tisvgen and alert the Kingpin to where they were and what they were doing.

"And the mountains?" Arjun asked. "How perilous are they?"

"The Uskhanyans call the mountain pass the Looming Valley," Karam said. "So take from that what you will."

Arjun sighed, as though he regretted agreeing to the mission already.

"We'll need to amass the most powerful of us," Asees said. "If it's a small group, then we will need the best of us in case we are attacked. Come, let's speak to the Kin."

When Karam next let out a breath, it felt like she was pushing all of the frustrations she had been feeling over the last few weeks out of her. It would be good to finally do something of her own. Tavia had brought the buskers to them, Saxony had brought the Crafters, and now Karam could bring them something too.

Wesley was an asset that, once lost, had been a serious blow to their armies. The buskers were restless without him and Tavia wasn't herself. Even Karam found herself missing Wesley's insights. He had been the one to help shape her into a warrior, after all.

She owed him a lot, and a rescue from Ashwood's clutches seemed like the perfect repayment.

"WAKE UP," a voice said. "You should probably get going if you want to catch the morning train to Tisvgen."

Karam opened her eyes to see Saxony hovering above her, the sun casting a halo through her wonderfully wild hair. Curls flowed in every direction, large ringlets to tight coils.

By the spirits, she was so beautiful.

"Good morning," Karam said.

"Bad morning," Saxony corrected. "You're leaving me. For a *man*."

Karam snorted and stretched out in a yawn among the bedsheets.

"Enjoy this bed while you can," Saxony said, tapping the pillow. "You'll be sleeping on the ground for most of your trip, I bet."

Karam reached up and cupped her face. "The best thing I can do for this war is to bring Wesley back," she said. "We have been over this."

"For once I'm not actually thinking about the best thing for the war," Saxony said. "I'm thinking about the best thing for me, and that's having you by my side."

She picked at the fabric of the bedsheets, biting the corner of her lip like she always did when she was frustrated.

"I know that you have to leave," Saxony said. "But I don't have to like it."

"I would be insulted if you did," Karam said.

"Just don't try to be too much of a hero," Saxony told her. "Make sure you don't put yourselves in danger for Wesley. If he's there, then Ashwood won't be far behind, and you can't engage with the Kingpin or Zekia. It's too risky."

Karam wasn't about to argue with that.

She pulled Saxony toward her and gave her a quick kiss on the lips.

"I promise," she said. "Stop worrying so much."

Saxony only sighed, and Karam felt that in her bones. The sun was rising, but part of her didn't want to get out of this bed. This mission would be the longest time Karam had been away from Saxony since they had first met all those years ago, and she wasn't quite looking forward to the distance.

Still, they could be back within a couple of weeks if they took the floating railway all the way to the Shores of the Dead and then walked through the Looming Valley to Creije. And Karam was fairly certain that it would be worth the missed moments and empty nights.

"Here," Saxony said, pulling off her ring and placing it in Karam's hand.

It was the one she had always worn, since Karam had first met her. A serpent that twisted from her fingers and around her palm, its eyes green as the forest that surrounded them.

"It'll help you find your way home," Saxony said. "Back to me."

Though the two were strangely the same.

"No matter what happens, swear to me that you'll come back okay."

"There is not a person in the four realms who could stop me from returning to you," Karam said. "I swear it."

She pressed her head against Saxony's. "I love you."

"I love you too," she said. "Remember not to die."

"Remember not to kill Tavia while I'm gone," Karam said back.

Saxony laughed against her and Karam closed her eyes, making sure to memorize the sound. When they parted, she pushed a coil of hair from Saxony's forehead.

"Remember that Tavia does not hate you," Karam said. "Remember that you are friends."

Saxony smiled and placed a hand on Karam's cheek. "I'm supposed to be the one worrying about you," she said. "Not the other way around. We'll be okay. *I'll* be okay."

But her voice didn't sound so sure. Even as she pressed her lips against Karam's once more, there was a shakiness there. The uncertainty in her breath and the way she grabbed on to Karam made her feel like it was for some kind of life support. As though Saxony were trying to keep herself from tumbling away.

11

Zekia

THIS IS WHAT BECOMES of us.

Zekia could still hear Ashwood's voice and the words that had haunted her like a promise all those years ago. Even when she squeezed her eyes shut so very tightly and said her prayers to the Many Gods and drank a specially brewed elixir to calm her heart.

Those words were like scripture carved into her bones.

"Creije will be mine," Ashwood said, back straight, hand resting atop his cane like it was both a weapon and a treasure. "We have over half of the districts. It's only a matter of time before the rest of the city is under my control, and my magic is already circulating in the other eight cities of my realm."

On the opposite side of the train, the other Kingpins of the realms stared at Ashwood like they could not quite believe their ears.

The train itself moved in broad circles somewhere in the middle of the Onnela Sea, which Ashwood had told Zekia was neutral ground between them. Or neutral waters. Though Zekia didn't think the other two Kingpins looked very neutral.

Simran of Wrenyal was sitting, arms crossed at his chest, as though he wasn't sure what else to do with them. His outfit was a wonderfully bright mix of color that Zekia thought would look very pretty on her, and a cloth the same blue as the waters outside kept his hair tucked neatly away.

Beside him, Aurelia of Volo leaned against the cabin door, a bright orange braid running down her shoulders. Zekia was still trying to decide whether standing was an act of defiance, to show Ashwood that she would not be seen as lower than him, or if she was just too scared to sit and be caught off guard by an attack.

It was not a very neutral way of thinking.

If Wesley were here, he and Zekia could laugh about their hesitance.

Wesley would whisper something mean about the way Simran's voice shook, or how Aurelia tried her hardest not to blink so she could look fierce. He'd say it in a low and smiling voice and Zekia would have to put her hand over her mouth to keep from laughing. Then maybe Ashwood would look back at them, half-scolding and half-amused himself.

Zekia wished Wesley had come.

She wished he didn't have to sleep so often or heal so slowly.

She wished he understood the terrible world she had seen and how she was just trying to make it better.

"This is insanity," Simran said. "We are shadows and we have become very rich and powerful that way."

"This is about more than riches and power," Ashwood said.

"This is about salvation. A new world of magic, roaming free throughout the four realms."

"We're not innocents," Aurelia said. "We've done horrible things in the name of magic and self-interest, but what you're talking about is treason. Usurping a Doyen? An official world leader? Seizing control of governments and armies? Even if you could manage to topple Fenna Schulze, the citizens would never accept you."

Dante Ashwood did not falter.

He had never faltered.

"That is why I have the Loj," he said.

Aurelia sneered and Zekia had to swallow and squint at the floor to keep from doing something bad.

"Your mind-control elixir is flawed and so is your plan," Aurelia said, pushing herself from the cabin door in frustration. "We will not be a part of this. If you want to destroy your realm for a blood dream, then you can do it without dragging our realms and reputations into it."

Zekia took her eyes off the floor and let them burn into Aurelia.

She did not like her.

Not one bit.

All Aurelia cared about was herself and her ambition. She didn't understand what would happen if they didn't do this.

Zekia stepped forward, biting her bottom lip with a frown.

"You're really mean," she said. Her hands clenched and unclenched at her sides. "I don't like mean people."

She took another step forward and Aurelia's face drained, her mouth parting slightly as she took in an uncertain breath.

Maybe all of her stolen magic could sense the power that Zekia had and maybe it was running scared, leaving its heartless leader to fight alone.

"Now, now," Ashwood said.

Zekia felt his hand on her shoulder, warm and cold at the same time, his shadows squirming loudly by her ears.

Zekia tried not to wince at them. She held her breath so as not to smell the burnt magic they were soaked in. She didn't want Ashwood to know that she was thinking bad things about him.

"My little warrior," Ashwood said. He squeezed her shoulder tightly. "Destined for so much greatness. How proud you make me."

Zekia smiled at that, though she couldn't help but feel it wasn't earned.

That destiny he spoke about was never hers. It was given to her, like a consolation, or a gift meant to soothe her broken heart as Zekia tried her best to live without a mother or a big brother to guide her. Other people got tearful sympathies and tender words. They inherited traits or fancy jewels from their dead parents.

Zekia had inherited an entire people.

She had inherited a fate and suddenly there were grown-ups so much wiser than she was, looking to her for wisdom, pressing the weight of her brother's destiny against her tiny heart.

There would be no more children in the Rishiyat Kin until she fulfilled the role of Liege.

There would be a curse upon them all until she accepted the spirit of her dead brother's magic.

But they didn't understand how hard it was and how loud the voices in her head were when Ashwood wasn't there to quell them. They didn't know what it was like to live in the shadow of a brother born with staves, prophesied to lead them to greatness.

Zekia tried so hard to perfect her magic and quiet its screams, but all it did was lead her straight into the head of a boy just as desperate to prove himself as she was.

Stumbling into Wesley's mind was like a sign, flashing a thousand possibilities across her vision. It sent her Intuitcrafter magic into even more of a tailspin and in every maddening prediction Zekia saw, she also felt with absolute certainty that everything would be okay if Wesley was there.

It was why she'd traveled to Creije to meet him.

And then Dante Ashwood found her.

He opened her eyes to a new way.

He made Zekia realize that there was so much evil ready to swallow the world.

This is what becomes of us.

"You will live to regret waging a war against your Doyen," Aurelia said. "It will be the end of you and perhaps even the end of us."

Zekia shook her head.

Aurelia had it backward. Without this war the realms would burn, but with Ashwood to lead them, they would create a world of light. Zekia and Wesley could help unite people under a time of magic.

Just a little blood, to keep the streets clean of death.

Zekia could *save* everyone else.

And so wasn't it worth it?

Wasn't she good?

Wasn't she deserving of her brother's destiny?

"Is that your final word?" Ashwood asked.

Aurelia looked at him, her chin high enough to hide her uncertain eyes and draw attention from the shaking hands she kept tucked away in the pockets of her dress.

"The underrealm of Volo will never support your claim as Doyen of Uskhanya," Aurelia said. "And I will never gather my buskers and underbosses to help prop up your armies."

Dante Ashwood nodded solemnly. "Then so be it," he said.

Zekia's heart pounded.

He turned to her.

"Little warrior."

She felt him smile.

"Time to fight."

Zekia bowed her head, like the good soldier that she was now.

This is what becomes of us.

Ashwood had whispered it in her ear when they first met, and then in her mind as an ugly, bloody future churned inside of her like a sickness. A vision of how the realms could turn out if they didn't do something to stop it.

It was all she could see and taste and smell, even now, years on. The burnt bodies and slickness of Crafter blood on the ground, the skies raining red and the mad, mad humans—the magic-haters who were so scared of them—smiling as everything crumbled to ash and darkness.

It was all Zekia saw when she closed her eyes, or when she looked into the shadows that surrounded Dante Ashwood.

Dark and ash.

Dark and ash.

Zekia wasn't mad. It was the rest of the realms who had lost their minds. They were mad for not being scared and for not dropping to their knees and begging her and Ashwood to stop it.

Mad, mad, all of them.

"What are you doing?" Aurelia asked, eyeing her.

Zekia swallowed and raised her hand in the air.

Just a little blood. It was what needed to be done.

She looked at Aurelia and when the woman met her gaze, her eyes widened.

"Don't—"

Zekia brought her hand down and the air cut across Aurelia's neck as though it were a knife.

The Kingpin of Volo grabbed at her wound, gargling as the blood spouted from her neck. She stumbled forward and Zekia almost shook her head to scream at her not to come near.

She didn't want to get the blood on her dress. It would stain, like a memory, and she wanted to forget this moment as quickly as possible.

She couldn't step back, though, because Ashwood was there and he was watching and she was his little warrior.

Zekia counted the seconds until Aurelia finally fell to the floor with a horrible thud and stopped making that stomach-churning gurgle sound.

She counted the seconds until Aurelia's eyes went blank and her hands fell from her neck.

The blood was dark and quick.

Simran gulped and it was loud enough to draw Zekia's attention away from the lifeless woman.

"And what of you?" Ashwood asked. "Stand by me, Simran, or I will replace you just like I will be replacing Aurelia. There is not a person in the realms who can stop this war."

Simran kept his eyes on Aurelia's body, and though he opened his mouth to speak, no words came. It took him a few moments to realize this and so he simply nodded, unblinking and unspeaking, watching Aurelia's blood coat the train floor like spilled paint.

"Wonderful," Ashwood said. "Then together we will go down in history as the makers of a new world."

Simran blinked and turned slowly to face Ashwood. To face Zekia. His eyes held a look of fear that turned her heart to lead.

This is what becomes of us.

12

Wesley

WESLEY LOOKED TO THE WINDOW.

He could hear the sounds of the ocean below and feel the breeze from the oncoming rain clouds that circled above the high-rise mausoleum, giving the stately dead a view of the horizon that the sandy graves below couldn't dream of.

This was his window of opportunity.

Literally.

Because Wesley was going to jump out of it.

Just as soon as Zekia came back, which would be in exactly three minutes, like a very predictable and slightly psychopathic clock. Wesley would wait until she untied him—as she always did when she climbed inside his mind, so he wasn't distracted or brought out of the vision by the chafing on his wrists—and once she did that, he'd use his magic to overpower her and leap to freedom.

As far as plans went, it needed fine-tuning, but Wesley

would work on that part after he'd jumped out of the window. All that mattered was that he needed to leave, and despite what he wanted, he couldn't take Zekia with him.

They'd moved him from Creije to the cemetery shores of Tisvgen after Ashwood had made his deal with Simran. Creije was becoming too dangerous of a battleground and so now Wesley had to rethink all the carefully laid exit plans he'd formulated back in his city. These shores were new and strange, but the waters of the Onnela Sea below would prove useful.

Not to mention that Tisvgen was closer to Rishiya, and so closer to Tavia and the others.

Wesley shuffled against the wall.

From the corner, the shadow demon snarled down at him, spit stringing from its ghostly jaws.

"What are you looking at, you giant worm? You're not allowed to kill me."

The demon growled, as though it could actually understand a word of what Wesley had said. For all he knew, it could. Zekia spoke to the demon the same way she spoke to Wesley: with her mind. The Intuitcrafter magic inside of her churning into the demon's brain so her thoughts became its, and there was no way it could dream of disobeying her because she controlled its dreams and everything else.

Wesley knew how that felt.

The demon kept its focus on him and whenever Wesley shuffled, it inched closer or bowed its head to get a better look.

Maybe the mind connection worked both ways and it could see exactly what Wesley was planning to do. Maybe his own

Intuitcrafter powers were backfiring and laying his soul bare.

"Too bad you're a watchdog and not an attack dog now," Wesley said.

The demon stood on its hind legs.

Wesley didn't blink.

He knew the beast couldn't hurt him. Zekia had given her orders and they were circling through the creature's mind over and over and over, like a melody.

The door to the room—to the cell—creaked open and Wesley didn't need to look to know it was her. It was always Zekia and never Ashwood, as though the Kingpin could rarely stand to see his prodigy so weak and useless.

"You look less tired today," Zekia said. "Did you sleep? I couldn't sleep a wink with all those people out there."

By people, she meant the dead.

Wesley turned to her. "It's not like you don't deserve to be haunted a little bit, kid."

Zekia laughed, like Wesley was very naïve and she found it very funny.

"They're not haunting me, silly," she said. "Just letting me know that they're there. Clogging up my head with all the futures they could have had and the things they wanted to be before they died. I don't mind it so much, but the worst of them are the ones who think they should have lived. Like anyone *deserves* to die."

Wesley thought lots of people deserved to die.

Probably both of them included.

"You're not a Spiritcrafter, kid. You can't talk to the dead."

"I didn't say I was talking to them. They're talking to *me*.

Or just existing around me and getting their alternative futures all muddled in my brain. Don't they bother you?"

"No," Wesley said. "But then again, I'm not crazy."

Zekia's smile twitched, but she swallowed whatever emotion she didn't feel like feeling at that moment and walked toward him. Her dress bounced up and down with her steps.

Zekia always wore a white dress, just as she always dressed Wesley in suits—like he was a doll she'd been given and that she cherished as her favorite toy.

"I could teach you," she said.

She knelt down next to him.

"Teach me to be crazy? I'll pass."

Wesley kept his eyes on her hands, waiting for her to snap her fingers and let the silver slivers of her magic trickle around his wrists and loosen his restraints.

But she didn't.

Instead she put her hands on her hips and shook her head admonishingly.

"I could teach you to master your magic like Amja was helping me to do," she said. "When you learn, you can help me and all the other Crafters we've found be safe again and for always. The new realm we're going to build will be so much stronger with you, Wesley. Two Intuitcrafters to lead them would be the best thing they could hope for."

Zekia really did think that by telling Wesley *who* and *what* he was, she'd endear him to her and make him think that they were cut from the same cloth. But telling Wesley he was a Crafter had only reminded him that nobody, not a single soul in the realms, was made of the same dark thing that he was.

He was uniquely Wesley Thornton Walcott and the fact that he had true magic just made him even more of a force to be reckoned with.

It made him think of new ways to bring Dante Ashwood down.

Zekia sighed when Wesley didn't answer.

She tucked her hair behind her ears and then snapped her fingers with a loud huff, like just talking to him was exhausting.

Wesley watched as her magic snaked around his wrists, until he felt a small jolt and the string that bound him dropped to the floor. Almost immediately he felt his magic stir inside of him, nervous and also eager.

It had been starved for so long and, finally, it could sense the time to strike was near.

"Remember how I said you were crazy?"

Zekia nodded. "You say that a lot. It's a little mean."

"Yeah," Wesley said. "Well, it turns out I might be crazier."

And then his hand shot out and Zekia flew backward into the shadow demon. The two of them collided with each other and then the wall, the demon's smoky limbs tangled into Zekia's like some kind of an awful jigsaw.

Zekia made to stand, but Wesley kept his hand firm, pinning her to the floor. He pushed every wish and hope he had inside of him toward her in a tunnel of gray magic.

Just like the one she had tried to use on Saxony back on Ashwood's hidden island.

The one Wesley had jumped in front of that nearly cost him his sanity.

Wesley summoned every single thought he could muster

and launched them at her in a tirade. All of his wants and desires. And then futures, things he hadn't even realized he knew. Possibilities of what he could become and what Zekia could become and what the world could become.

They flowed through him like he was an endless tap for the destinies of the realms.

Wesley's staves grew white-hot on his skin, glowing like beacons in the darkness of the room. His hands shook with the energy of them, but he kept his arm out, bombarding Zekia with visions.

She screamed and clutched at her head and Wesley could see the blood start to trickle from her nose. From her ears.

"Make it stop!" she yelled. "Make it stop, make it stop, make it stop! This isn't what becomes of us. He said it wouldn't be what becomes of us!"

Wesley didn't know what she meant by that.

He didn't even know what he was forcing her to see. The visions flowed through him like a speeding train, too fast for him to catch anything but glimpses, before they crashed into the walls of Zekia's mind.

He couldn't stop.

Many Gods, even if Wesley wanted to, he just *couldn't*.

His magic was free and it refused to be shackled again, even by him.

He could feel the shadow demon screeching in his mind and trying desperately to claw Wesley out, but Wesley kept his thoughts firm, throwing dream after dream into the demon's head until its knees shook and it convulsed to the floor.

Zekia whimpered beside it.

Wesley climbed onto the window ledge.

"Don't," she said.

Zekia's voice was gravelly with desperation.

"Please don't leave me here. I don't want to be alone again."

Wesley swallowed and he couldn't believe that a part of him was even considering what she said.

"Come with me."

Zekia shook her head. "We can't go," she said. "The future can't happen and if we leave, everything falls to dust and ash."

Wesley swore.

He couldn't take her with him.

He couldn't save her.

"I'm sorry, kid," he said.

And then Wesley jumped from the window.

Past the rows of bodies and headstones, into the icy water and down, down, down.

13

Karam

THE SHORES OF THE DEAD were not a ghostly wasteland.

They did not conjure images of restless spirits roaming the sand in search of purpose or revenge, nor did they make Karam clutch at her pehta's pendant like it was an amulet of protection.

It had taken them only a matter of hours to get here via the floating railways, across the threads of the Onnela Sea, which coiled between the cities until finally pitching up onto the sand of Tisvgen. The Shores of the Dead, where people came to grieve or bury their loved ones, looking for solace along the water's edge.

Only, nobody seemed to be looking anymore.

The train had been scarcely filled. With war in Creije, nobody seemed eager to travel, and of the few dozen passengers that had been on the train with Karam and her small group, not a single one had disembarked to Tisvgen with them.

Perhaps they were tired of death.

But the shores gave Karam a peaceful and calming feeling, and the moment she stepped onto the enchanted sands, she felt a quiet in her heart.

The coast was made mostly of white sand filled with glass headstones that glowed under the light of the moon like beacons for travelers. The dead making sure the lost found their way home. A few small monuments were scattered between, child-sized models of the dead, made entirely with coin.

Karam wasn't sure if it was a kind of symbolism to pay their toll to the spiritlands, or if those people just really liked gold.

"We need to get moving," she said in Wrenyi to the others. "The Looming Valley will be at least five days' walk, if we factor in setting up camp along the way. Once we reach the base, if Ashwood's people aren't at the bottom with Wesley, then it'll be perilous and difficult to climb to the peaks to where the outlook is. I'd say another four days."

"He could be at the top?" Arjun asked, incredulous. "He better thank me for all this walking."

"Don't hold your breath," Karam said.

"There's no way to get a train up there?" Asees asked. "I thought Uskhanya had the best railway system in the four realms."

"There are no lines to the Looming Valley," Karam explained. "And if Nolan was wrong and Wesley isn't here in Tisvgen, then the mountain range is the only way to cross into Creije unnoticed. If Wesley isn't here, then he'll be there."

"Five days to the base, another four to climb, and then more time to cross into Creije if needed. Not to mention the time it will take to actually save Wesley once we find him,"

Asees said, with a long sigh. "Now I wish that I had stolen that bottle of Cloverye from Tavia."

"Don't worry," Arjun said. He pulled a glass bottle out from his backpack. "I took care of that."

Karam shook her head. "You two have been spending far too much time with buskers," she said.

Arjun laughed and then looked up to the sky and let out a low whistle.

"Forget about walking for a moment," he said. "By the Indescribable God, would you look at that eyesore?"

He pointed to the skies with his sword.

Karam looked up.

Above them was a mausoleum, unlike any she had seen. It stretched to over fifty floors and she knew it hosted only the richest of the Uskhanyan people, allowing them to stay in their lofty towers and look down at the less fortunate in death, just as they had done in life.

It was her least favorite thing about the shores.

Karam had never been inside the mausoleum tower before. She much preferred the graves on the beach, caressed by the morning waves, the warm sand, and the pink wildflowers that were enchanted to spring up around them.

She thought she would be more at peace being laid to rest there, closer to the earth, rather than trying to reach a hand out to touch the Indescribable God.

Asees turned to the six Crafters of her Kin they had recruited for this mission.

"Come on," she said. "Enough staring at the odd architecture of the Uskhanyans. Karam said we've got a lot of ground to cover and that means no time to soak up the sun or go for a swim with the spirits."

Arjun recoiled like the thought made him shiver.

For a Spiritcrafter, he had a surprisingly odd reaction to ghost stories. Karam was tempted to tease him about it, but she was nice enough to reconsider embarrassing him in front of the Kin.

Asees began to walk and the Crafters followed.

For a moment Karam hung back, taking one last look at the serene shores. Arjun sheathed his sword and they walked in step along the wet sand, toward the grassy verge that overlooked them.

And then Karam stopped.

Her father's pendant grew warm around her neck, and though Karam didn't know why, it made her heartbeat quicken.

"What is it?" Arjun asked.

Karam swallowed and held up a hand to silence him.

Her eyes narrowed as the wind slowly drifted by, in and out of the wildflowers, through Karam's hair and across the moonlit waters.

Such serenity.

Such peace.

Such quiet.

Her father's pendant grew hotter.

Where were the mourners?

Where were the caretakers, sprinkling the sand with trick dust to keep the magic in harmony?

Where were the doves that Tavia had told her soared over the sky like gatekeepers?

"Stop!" Karam yelled.

Asees whipped her head back to face her.

Time slowed and there was a moment—a moment that existed within the grains of sand that housed the dead, between the breaths of wind and the blinking of the stars—when Asees frowned.

A moment when Karam thought that maybe she was just paranoid and there was nothing wrong with a little silence in the world.

The Crafters all looked to her, their backs to the grassy verge and the monstrous things it hid.

Karam's pendant burned against her chest, with the same might as Saxony's fire would have.

Asees parted her lips in a question.

And then the sword appeared.

Through her stomach, straight like an arrow.

For a second, Asees stood there with that same question on her lips. And then in place of the question there was blood. On her lips and her teeth, and when she looked down to see the sword for herself, it disappeared. Pulled back from the other side.

Asees fell to her knees.

Her attacker did not smile or blink or cast a look down at her body.

Karam charged.

She cut and slashed and kicked and stabbed without thinking or seeing. Her vision was filled with fury and fury alone, no space for reality, save for the glimpse of Arjun skidding across the verge and cradling Asees in his arms.

But it was just another moment.

Just another grain of time.

Arjun was screaming, a noise the likes of which Karam had never heard. One she hoped she would never, ever hear again.

His Kin turned back to the verge and from its green depths, an onslaught rose.

Soldiers, more than double their numbers. All with eager snarls on their faces and those same black eyes Asees had when she'd been under the thrall of Ashwood.

The brands of the Loj on their necks looked almost like staves.

An attacker approached Arjun from behind but he leaped from the ground and drove a knife through the man's throat.

"To the death!" Arjun yelled.

The Kin screamed in unison, echoing his cries with swords and magic raised high in the air.

Karam pulled someone's head back by their hair and plunged her knife into their heart.

She ran across the shores, sand splashing up to her thighs, and launched herself into the air until her legs were wrapped around a man's throat and he tried to hit and punch at her calves.

This would be their mourning.

Killing these people would be their solace. It didn't matter if they were outnumbered two to one. These Crafters were already dead.

Karam squeezed tighter, angled her body to the right, and felt the snap of the man's neck.

The beach was alight with magic. It filled the air, so thick that Karam could taste it, almost choke on it. She coughed it up like it was sand. Bright gold swirls of fire and the roll of thunder. Bodies were dropping everywhere.

There was blood all over her and Karam didn't know what was hers and what had been their enemy's.

It didn't matter.

She didn't feel pain, just thirst.

The unholy need to destroy each and every one of these monsters.

The Kingpin knew they would come for Wesley.

His people had been waiting, hidden like hunters in the forest.

Nolan.

Karam would be damned if she died on this beach without making it back to Saxony. She made her way through the army in blood and death.

These infected soldiers could not be saved, the Loj was too far in their veins, and even if they could, Karam would not give them that chance.

Now that Asees was dead, Karam would make each of them pay for it with their souls.

If they still even had souls.

She reached into her pocket and pulled out one of Tavia's trick bags. She threw it at a nearby Crafter and he froze in place, turned to ice on the balmy shores.

Karam threw a knife at him and he shattered into the sand.

These people were not warriors.

They were just the dead waiting to find graves.

She reached for another charm.

Tavia had been trying to teach her how to read them—

to know what they could do and to let their magic flow through her like a melody—but Karam could sense nothing but her own rage and so she just threw the charm high above her and watched it flutter back down like a bird.

And then explode.

Four Crafters flew into the air, crashing through the glass headstones until finally landing back on the shores with a bone-crunching thud.

Dead. Gone.

She ran over to Arjun, who was clutching at his side with one hand and cradling Asees's body with the other. Asees was still, but the blood kept coming. From her mouth and her stomach and by the spirits Karam didn't know how to make it stop.

Arjun put a hand over Asees's wound and closed his eyes, muttering desperately. Some kind of a spell, Karam assumed, and she felt a spark that maybe it was a healing spell and everything would be all right.

Arjun's hands were shaking, alight in the gold magic of their people. His eyes were squeezed shut so tight that his nose wrinkled.

And then Karam turned, just as a man charged at them. His blackened eyes were like that of a wild animal and the mark of the Loj elixir was thick and gleaming on his neck.

He launched a shard of light at Karam and she leaped to avoid it, then swung her foot out and swept the man's legs out from under him.

"We will be saved," he said, pulling out a gun. "We must protect the magic."

Karam did not hesitate.

She cut her knife clean across his neck, before he even had the chance to raise his weapon, pressing her lips together tightly so she didn't have to taste the victory.

"Come on," Arjun said.

He was still focused on Asees, his hands aglow and hovering over the hole in her stomach.

"This has to work," he said. "Come on, Asees. Wake up."

The magic flickered weakly under his palms, like a light trying to stay on in a storm. Only Asees didn't move and the blood didn't crawl from the sand and back into her still body.

Arjun sobbed, the cry of agony so sharp that Karam felt it stab into her heart.

He dropped his hands and the lights went out.

"Please wake up," he said.

He buried his head in Asees's shoulder.

"Arjun," Karam said.

She knelt down beside him and looked at the gash on his side. The sand mingled with the blood, sprinkling across the wound like trick dust. She wondered if he would ever get that out, or if it would embed inside of him forever. Little pieces of the dead shores and their ghostly magic, waiting for the day they would return to this hallowed ground.

"Arjun," Karam said again.

He looked up at her and shook his head. "She can't do this," he said. The tears dripped to his neck. "She can't leave me like this. She can't just go."

Karam reached up an unsteady hand and placed it on his shoulder.

The world around them was so quiet.

"I'm here," she said. "Arjun, it will be okay."

"No."

His voice was a breath in the night.

Arjun shook his head, his tears mixing with the blood on Asees's hand.

"Nothing is okay. She's gone, Karam."

He looked around the beach, at the bodies of his Kin, scattered among the headstones. So many graves.

"They're all gone."

Karam couldn't move.

Even as the tears crawled down her own face, as hot as her rage, she could not speak or move her hand from his shoulder.

She was just still.

Asees was not coming back.

The six of their Kin that Karam had convinced to come here would never return to their families.

Nolan, she thought.

He had led them into a trap. Ashwood's people weren't guarding Wesley. They were waiting, for Karam and whoever else dared to come.

It was an ambush and if Nolan had told Ashwood where they would go looking for Wesley, then that meant he had told Ashwood where to go looking for them.

The forest.

Saxony.

Tavia.

Nobody was safe.

There was a small grunt from behind Karam and she slowly

turned her head to follow the noise. Her limbs felt heavy; everything about the world was off balance.

It took her a few seconds to make sense of it, but the man by her feet, who Karam had sliced across the neck, was still alive.

He was bleeding enough to turn the sand red, but he was still breathing, which was more than she could say for Asees.

Karam hated him for surviving.

How dare he cling to life when Asees could not?

Arjun gently placed Asees's head back to the sand and looked at the man groaning beside them. He wiped a hand across his face to smear away the tears.

"We have to perform an extraction," Arjun said. His voice was as small as a child's. "Before he dies. We must see if he knows anything."

Karam nodded. She said nothing, but squeezed Arjun's shoulder and tried to hold back any more of her own tears.

She would be strong for him.

For her friend, for her brother, for the warrior boy who needed her now more than ever.

Arjun turned the man onto his back and without ceremony or warning, he pressed his hands on either side of the Crafter's temples and began.

Karam had only ever seen an extraction once before, when Saxony had performed it on the consort back in Creije, all those months ago, to find out where Ashwood was hiding.

Saxony had always said extractions were dark magic, because the worst kind of spells were the ones that took over people's minds and sought to ravage their thoughts. It was meant to be agonizing for the victim—if they even survived—and it was meant to bring bad luck to the Crafter who performed it, cursing their entire Kin.

The magic had been outlawed for so long, but these were times of war and they were all already so cursed that it hardly seemed to matter anymore.

Arjun's hand shot out to Karam's, but he kept the other on the man's temple, not breaking the connection.

"He's an Intuitcrafter," Arjun said.

The same as Zekia.

The same as Wesley.

Intuitcrafters could see into all the futures of the world, all the possibilities of what was to come and what had already been.

"He'll die once I break the connection," Arjun said. "But you need to see this."

"You want me to go inside his mind?"

"You must see," Arjun urged, his hand still stretched out. "Give me your hand."

Karam threaded her fingers quickly through his.

The vision did not flow through her. It did not coat her mind like a warm blanket or ease into her sight.

It hit her like a thousand fists.

At first Karam could make out nothing but flashing images and voices so loud that they drilled into her skull. The world was a mess of colors and sound, and no matter how hard Karam tried, she couldn't make sense of it.

She just knew she didn't belong in this place and the place knew it too.

The Crafter's mind wanted her gone and it was going to do whatever it took to expel her.

Arjun squeezed Karam's hand and the world focused, just a little.

She felt a pulling in her stomach, like there was a string wrapped around her insides and someone was yanking it harshly toward them.

Karam closed her eyes.

The pulling grew more violent. She felt her body convulse and the piercing noises got louder and louder.

Then everything went still.

Karam opened her eyes with hesitance, not quite ready to face the world of unending madness and voices screaming in her ears.

But there was nothing.

When she looked to her hand, still clutched tightly in Arjun's, it was alight in the gold of his magic, tethering her to him.

"Look," Arjun said.

He pointed and Karam finally saw.

Wesley stood in the shadows, that familiar half smile on his lips. He seemed taller than Karam remembered and though he was thinner, he still looked very much like Wesley. There was a brand of arrogance and ego to his smile that could never be lost. Tavia was by his side, and in front of them both was Zekia.

Was the Kingpin.

Dante Ashwood was as much a ghost as ever, with his cane clutched in his spindly fingers the only solid part of him. Everything else was shadow and bone.

He placed a hand on Zekia's shoulder.

"My little warrior," he said. "Make me proud."

Zekia nodded.

Karam's eyes widened.

She had Wesley's gun.

Zekia raised the weapon in the air, pointing it straight at Tavia.

"I'm sorry I didn't do this sooner," she said.

And then she pulled the trigger.

Karam yelled out, but the vision broke and she was already being pulled back into reality, flung so hard into the real world that she hit the sand with a painful thud.

Her head felt like it had been cracked in two as the Shores of the Dead flooded into her vision. Karam tried to make sense of what she had just seen, and what was real and what wasn't.

It took her longer than it should have.

So long that it was too late by the time Karam realized the cracking sound hadn't just been the bullet hitting Tavia square in the chest.

Arjun was slumped on the shores in front of her, a bullet in his leg.

Her necklace grew warm again.

Karam turned in a snarl.

And then another shot sounded.

Her body jolted and she felt a burning, unimaginable pain.

Right where her heart was.

Right where she kept Saxony and every promise that she had made.

Karam fell to the sand beside Arjun and let the darkness take her.

14

Wesley

THE FOREST WASN'T HARD to infiltrate.

Wesley was out of practice when it came to being stealthy, but even he had little trouble sneaking past the guard and wandering into the forest like he very much belonged there.

It might have been the Crafter in him, helping him stick to the shadows—or the shadows stick to him—or it might have been because the forest was woefully guarded for a rebellion.

Either way, Wesley was in.

He just wasn't sure why he'd felt the need to sneak past the guards in the first place. He could have easily introduced himself and explained that he was on their side. Even if they hadn't believed him and thought every bruise on his body was some kind of infiltration tactic, the worst they could do was bring him to their leader or try to put him in chains.

It wasn't like he'd never been in chains before.

And it wasn't like he didn't have a good in with their leader.

Perhaps the sneaking was just an old habit, like the not trusting people and the need to prove that he could do whatever he put his mind to.

Maybe he needed it, this small and tiny victory, after being lost for so long.

After swimming for his damn life in water so cold it felt like being shot at a hundred times over.

Wesley strolled through the center of the camp.

It was surrounded by streams that reminded him of Creije. Wesley didn't want to think about it, but it always came to him in the quiet moments.

The home he'd let fall to its knees.

He placed a hand on the trunk of a nearby tree and felt the rough bark beneath his fingers. In an instant, the tree seemed to spring to life, letting out a long exhale, its leaves fluttering in a windswept applause. The forest began to sing, a sweet melody that Wesley was so sure he'd heard before. The branches of each shrub and tree and sapling jerked back and forth in a wave, and Wesley couldn't help but smile.

This forest, evergreen and aglow in ancient magic, felt happy to see him. It welcomed him like an old friend.

This way, it whispered excitedly. *Quickly, come this way.*

The leaves of the trees, veined silver like Wesley's staves, rustled to his left, and Wesley followed them like they were a compass. He wasn't sure where they were leading him or why, but he didn't care. He knew somehow, somewhere deep down, that it was taking him where he needed to go.

The clearing was sparse and at first Wesley thought that he

was alone, but after a few short moments, four figures emerged from the distance.

One was Saxony, talking animatedly to an older woman on her right. The woman sighed, the man next to her shrugged, and then the three of them stopped walking altogether and formed a makeshift circle. They looked like they were arguing about something, but Wesley didn't care enough to try to listen. His focus was pulled toward the fourth person. The girl who had broken away from them and was twirling her knives absentmindedly on a nearby log.

Tavia.

Many Gods, she was right in front of him.

Finally.

Her hair was a little longer now and still a fierce black that swung by her chin. She was dressed in gray, of course, with her sleeves rolled up to perfectly showcase the daggers of her new tattoo. A stave, of sorts. The tattoo of an ally.

Tavia looked older, in the way wisdom and death often shaped a person to be, but at the same time she looked so brand new. The fierceness in her eyes had grown stronger since he'd last seen her, molding her into someone who felt unfamiliar.

She looked over to Saxony with a sigh and then turned to stare into the clearing.

Her eyes fixed onto Wesley's.

Her face paled.

She stood, quick as a cat, lips parted ever so slightly.

She had never looked at him this way, like he had made the day grow brighter, instead of raising the shadows.

Tavia squinted at him, trying to make sense of him being there. Wesley was trying to make sense of her, too. Tavia's eyes were the color of rain clouds and her lips were a thin line that held a perfect cupid's bow when she said his name.

"Wesley."

Her voice carried over to him like a memory.

Tavia was so pretty and Wesley was a little mad at himself for forgetting just how much.

What a mess every hallucination seemed now.

Zekia hadn't even gotten her glare half-right.

"Wesley," she said again, this time louder.

Saxony and the other two people whipped their heads around to face him.

Wesley swallowed. Scrunched his eyes closed in a quick blink.

Things were so bright here and the sun seemed foreign to him after so long in a series of dark rooms.

"Many Gods," Saxony said.

And then Tavia was running toward him, faster than he knew she could be, and her arms were swinging around his neck and clutching on to him as if for life.

Then Wesley was somehow hugging her back, even though he wasn't sure he had told his arms to move. He didn't know they could, he was so tired even blinking hurt, but still his body folded into Tavia's like it was instinct and when he breathed in, he inhaled the scent of her.

By the Many Gods, he had missed that scent.

"Tell me you're not actually here," Tavia said. "Because if this is real, then hugging you is actually quite embarrassing."

"I'm here," Wesley said.

They felt like the first words he had spoken since he'd jumped from that window. Tavia pulled away from him and ducked her head sheepishly.

"I was worried about you," she said.

"Why? It's not like I was kidnapped by a mass murderer."

Tavia's eyes met his. She glared and then she punched him in the shoulder. "You bastard," she said.

Wesley wasn't sure it was possible to miss someone as much as he had missed her.

"Did you win the war without me?" he asked. "Am I too late for the victory dance?"

Tavia looked like she was going to punch him again, but instead she laughed, which Wesley found equally as intimidating.

"Who are your new friends?" he asked, gesturing toward the man and woman who were standing on guard beside Saxony.

The wary way Saxony stared at him, scanning his hands for knives and his eyes for secrets, made Wesley want to smile.

Just like old times.

"Does that glare mean you missed me?" he asked her.

Saxony looked inclined to relax, but she kept her body rigid as if she had a reputation to uphold and being kind to Wesley might interfere with it.

"This is my father, Bastian," Saxony said.

The man by her side stood like a fierce protector, with thick black hair pulled back into braids. He had a beard, which Wesley had never managed to grow himself, and a stern line in the center of his forehead that looked like it could be from frowning or laughing.

"It's nice to meet you," Wesley said.

He held out his hand and Bastian stepped forward to take it.

Wesley would have gone to him, but he was finding it hard enough to stand straight and keep himself from falling over. His body felt depleted and it required all the ego he had to keep anyone from noticing.

The trek from Tisvgen to the Uncharted Forest had not been an easy one, and Wesley had forgotten how average a swimmer he was until he had propelled himself into the Onnela Sea.

He'd also forgotten until now that he still wasn't wearing any shoes, and the moment he remembered his feet began to throb.

"I've heard a lot about you," Bastian said.

Wesley tried to make his voice sound breezy. "I bet none of it was good."

"But all of it was true," Saxony said.

Wesley only shrugged and turned to the old lady. "And you are?"

"This is my amja," Saxony said.

"I'm not expected to call her that, am I?"

Wesley didn't think referring to a lady he barely knew as his grandmother was the right way to go.

"Most people do," the lady said.

"I'm not most people."

"He says that a lot," Tavia said. "You'll get used to the pride. Wesley likes to think he's special."

Saxony's amja looked at him strangely, her eyes soft and white enough that he could almost see his own reflection back in them. Wesley looked away, but then she took his hand in hers.

There was something to the way she looked at him that made Wesley feel unsettled, and when she clasped his hand, the trees hummed softly in the background.

"He is special," Saxony's amja said. "He escaped Dante Ashwood and made his way here in one piece."

Wesley wasn't sure he was in one piece.

"Speaking of the escape," Saxony said. "How did Karam and the others manage to get you out so quickly? Are they getting healed somewhere else in camp?"

Wesley paused. "Karam didn't get me out of anywhere."

"She went to get you," Saxony said slowly, as though perhaps Wesley had misunderstood. "A busker we questioned mentioned you were in Tisvgen and she took Arjun and Asees and a few other Crafters there to save you."

"You mean my old bouncer tried a rescue mission?" Wesley said. "I'm flattered. That would have saved me a trip out of a window."

And that was when any color faded from Saxony's face.

"Are you serious?" she asked. "They left three days ago. If you're here, then where in the fire-gates are they?"

Wesley only shrugged. "I jumped out of a building all by myself and then I just followed the sound of you sighing in my direction. I never saw anyone."

"Maybe they just missed each other," Tavia said to Saxony, placing a reassuring hand on her shoulder.

For some reason, that gesture seemed to make them both stiffen.

"If anyone can take care of herself, then it's Karam," Tavia said. "Besides, she's got a whole gang of Crafters at her back. She'll probably realize Wesley is nowhere to be found, come back here looking all glum at having failed her mission, then see his smirking face and threaten to punch someone."

"You don't know that," Saxony said.

"You don't know anything either," Tavia told her. "So let's give it a few more days before we go panicking. Okay?"

Saxony nodded, but even Wesley could tell that all she wanted to do was run from the forest and to wherever Karam had ventured off to.

To save him.

She'd left this place to go look for him, which shouldn't have surprised Wesley so much, but it did. Arjun, too, who Wesley had made a point of irritating at every moment he could. And Asees? A Liege who once didn't want to give him a speck of power, now agreed that he was an ally worth saving?

Just what kind of topsy-turvy world had Wesley walked into?

"You saved my life on Ashwood's isle," Saxony said. "I never thanked you for that."

A moment of silence passed before Wesley realized that she still wouldn't.

"You're welcome," he said anyway.

"How was Zekia?" Saxony asked. "What happened?"

"You mean aside from the torture?"

Tavia winced and Wesley inwardly cursed himself for revealing that little tidbit in front of her. He didn't want her to think of him as powerless, but he didn't quite know how to hide it.

"She's fine," Wesley said. "I tried to get through to her, but Ashwood has his claws in deep. I don't know if she can see reason. I wanted—"

He broke off.

I wanted to take her with me, he thought. *I wanted to save her.*

"She's a little lost right now," he said.

"I'm not giving up on my sister," Saxony said.

"I didn't ask you to."

Tavia let out an audible sigh, stepping in front of Wesley like some kind of a shield. "Many Gods," she said. "He's been back five minutes."

Saxony's jaw tensed and Wesley looked between them curiously. Something had fractured their bond, and that only made this forest seem more peculiar.

"How about we stop the interview and try asking if he's okay?" Tavia said. "Or if he wants a healer? Or a damn nap? I mean, look at him!"

Wesley wished that they wouldn't.

"I'm fine," he said. "Apparently, I'm a badass Crafter, so I can heal myself. And a nap sounds boring."

The lie was so easy that he hadn't even considered telling the truth.

"How about a new suit and some food though?" Wesley asked. "And what I wouldn't give for a pint of Cloverye."

Tavia laughed. "Sure. I happen to know a great cook."

"If you're talking about yourself, then I'd rather not get food poisoning."

She smacked him on the shoulder and the lights in her eyes danced.

"It's good to have you back," she said.

Wesley smiled at her, best he could.

He'd wanted to get here so badly and resume business as

usual, fall back into the routine and feel as at home with these people as he did in Creije. He thought that once he got here it would be like putting on an old suit.

It had seemed so simple when he stood at the edge of the window with the Onnela Sea and all the dead of Tisvgen calling out to him from below. Surely the torture was the hard part. Surely being back with people he trusted was easy.

Except that wasn't true.

Wesley couldn't let his guard down here any more than he could with Zekia, because these people needed him to be okay and if they knew how weak he felt, then they wouldn't rely on him.

If he wasn't strong, then he was no use to anyone.

"Are you sure you're okay?" Tavia asked, searching Wesley's eyes for all the things he hid.

Wesley swallowed and kept the smile strong on his face.

"I'm always okay," he said.

15

Tavia

IT WAS RAINING IN RISHIYA and Tavia sat with her legs hanging from the tree house edge. The Uncharted Forest was beautiful and when the water hit the leaves just right, the entire city looked like it was made of stars, deep green leaves glistening and tree roots stretching across the muddy sky to stow their thirst.

Wesley had just finished up in his shower and was currently trying on the new suit Tavia had gotten him from one of the buskers in camp. She'd been prepared to trade her knife for it, but it turned out that being a leader meant free gifts as a perk. Besides, when the guy had heard it was for Wesley, he'd all but stripped off in the middle of the clearing.

Tavia unscrewed the cap from the bottle of Cloverye and placed it on the floor beside her, next to a single glass.

"This is a little tight around the shoulders," Wesley called from the spot in the corner where he was changing behind a makeshift curtain.

"Must be from all those bulging muscles you have," Tavia said sarcastically.

"Must be," Wesley said back. "I did see you noticing earlier."

Tavia took a drink to keep from killing him, but she was surprised when she brought the bottle to her lips and realized that she was somehow smiling. She'd missed this. She'd missed *him*, from the warm husk of his voice to his irritating sense of humor.

"I was going to come for you," Tavia said. "As soon as I found out where you might be. But then Karam left and the buskers were so uneasy."

"I'm glad you didn't," Wesley said. "It was too dangerous and you—"

"Excuse me," Tavia interrupted. She slammed the bottle down hard enough that a puddle spilled out onto the floor. "I've been leading a horde of buskers while you were gone. I can handle myself."

"I just meant that it wouldn't have been worth the risk," Wesley said.

She heard the sound of the curtain drawing back.

What he'd meant to imply was that putting herself in unnecessary danger would have been stupid. What he'd actually said—what Tavia had heard coating his words—was that he didn't think he mattered enough for her to try.

He didn't think he was worth saving.

She thought back to when she'd seen him in the clearing, shirt torn and his feet bloodied with dirt.

She'd had to try so hard to keep from crying.

"You're worth the risk, Wesley," Tavia said.

She turned to him, finally, dressed in the best suit she could find. It fit him snugly and though, yes, it was a little too tight around the shoulders, if he hadn't said it, she wouldn't have noticed. He looked like he belonged in that suit. He looked like himself in it.

Except for the bruises.

Except for the bags under his eyes.

Except for the way he smiled, like he didn't mean it at all.

Tavia hated Ashwood and Zekia more than anything in that moment.

"You should let Saxony heal you," she said.

"I can heal myself."

"You shouldn't need to."

Wesley didn't answer. He just sighed and adjusted his cuff links, as he always did when he was trying to distract his mind.

"I have something for you," Tavia said.

She slid the bone gun onto the floor beside the bottle of Cloverye.

It had been the only thing of Wesley's she'd had to keep her mind calm and her heart alive, but now that he was back, she could feel the old gun calling to its owner, begging to go home.

When Wesley saw it, his smile turned, far more genuine than the one he'd given her just seconds before. It was the smile he'd had when they were kids running from the amityguards with possibility in their pockets, and the smile he'd given her when they got rooms opposite each other in the busker dorms, and the smile she'd savored when they created their first crystal ball together.

It was her favorite thing in the world.

"Damn, I missed this thing," he said.

Wesley took the gun from the ground and sat beside her. His feet dangled next to hers, close enough that they could touch if they were ever so careless.

"I hope you took good care of it," he said.

He examined the bones that made up the weapon, checking for scuffs and scratches.

"If there's a mark on here anywhere, then you're cleaning it off."

"Your precious little murder weapon is fine," Tavia said. "I'm glad to see your priorities are still in check."

Wesley shrugged and placed the gun into the inner pocket of his suit jacket, right where his heart was.

"Do you think Karam is okay?" Tavia asked. "Saxony looked really worried earlier."

"Aren't you?"

"She's good at fighting her way out of trouble," Tavia said.

Only, she was still just as worried as Saxony was. Karam could fight, sure, but that didn't mean that she could fight anything Ashwood threw at her. It didn't mean she was invincible, and Tavia cursed herself for thinking otherwise. She'd always seen Karam as unstoppable, unkillable, but that was a lie and now that she wasn't here, Tavia couldn't stop thinking about how she'd let that lie comfort her too often.

She hoped desperately that Karam would come storming back into camp, angry that Wesley had escaped before she'd had a chance to rescue him.

"There are a lot more people here than I thought there would be," Wesley said.

He peered over the edge to look down at the camp below, brimming with buskers and Crafters.

"Yeah." Tavia took the bottle from Wesley and downed another swig. "Saxony contacted all the Lieges in the four realms and a bunch of them agreed to send us more Crafters. It's not much, but including Saxony's and Asees's Kins, we have eighty Crafters already. When the others come, it should bump that up to a hundred and fifty or so."

"And the buskers?" Wesley asked.

"A little deal I made with Casim," she said. "We've got fifty of his buskers and he's negotiating with the other underbosses of Uskhanya to send us their forces too. So that gives us ninety altogether so far, with more possibly on the way."

Wesley looked vaguely impressed.

"I used your name to threaten him, by the way," Tavia said. She passed the bottle back over to Wesley, neither of them bothering to use the glass. "Hope you don't mind."

"Go for it," Wesley said. "I'm glad my name still strikes fear in the hearts of my cowardly colleagues."

"Yeah," she said. "Underbosses really are all chickenshits."

Wesley laughed and the sound jittered amid the rain, like it was a storm in itself.

"What was it like?" Tavia asked him.

He looked at her in questioning.

"Where you were," she said, and then, softer, "What happened to you?"

Wesley stiffened, and she knew that she shouldn't have asked. If he'd wanted her to know, then he would have told her. But the thing was, Wesley had a habit of never telling people things

~ 169 ~

that would make him look weak. He had a habit of being too stubborn for his own good. It was why Tavia had wanted to get him a suit, to make him not just look more like himself, but to feel comfortable enough to relax a little. If he was relaxed, maybe she could get through to him.

She wanted Wesley to know that it was okay for him not to be okay.

"What did they do to you?" she asked.

"It wasn't about me," Wesley said. "It was about her."

"Zekia?"

"She's just a scared kid," he said. "Ashwood is in her head and he has her thinking that this war is the only way she'll ever be safe. She thinks that she's protecting me and the rest of our people. I think that she's afraid of what he might do if she starts to doubt him."

"You're wrong," Tavia said.

She didn't think Zekia was just a kid, following orders because she was too afraid not to. That *kid* had tried to kill them on the Kingpin's isle and then she'd stolen Wesley—the only family Tavia had left—and did Many Gods knew what to him.

She wasn't a child, she was a monster.

"She's had it rough," Wesley said.

"Well, excuse me if I don't feel sorry for her," Tavia said. "We've all had it rough, but when someone tries to kill the people that I care about, it kind of dampens my sympathy."

"She wouldn't have killed me," Wesley said.

"Just her own sister, then?"

Wesley didn't seem to have an answer for that, so he sighed

instead. "You seemed to be the one who has a problem with Saxony," he said.

"That's nothing."

"If it's nothing, then get over it already."

Tavia narrowed her eyes. "Yeah, I'll take advice on holding grudges from you," she said.

Gods, how had she forgotten how easily he got under her skin? Wesley could make Tavia mad in a moment and she wondered how in the fire-gates she'd actually *missed* it.

He was infuriating.

"How was Ashwood?" she asked, trying to distract the part of herself that wanted to argue with him.

Wesley barely mustered a shrug. "Mostly it was just me and Zekia and the shadow demons she got to rough me up when she got tired of me kicking her out of my head."

His expression was blank and his tone was far too apathetic, like Wesley was talking about it happening to someone else, or like he didn't care that it had happened to him.

Tavia cared.

She hadn't seen a shadow demon before, but she'd heard enough stories to know that she never wanted to. They were the worst creatures in the four realms. They were death made visible and so Tavia couldn't stop herself from grimacing at the mere mention of them.

Wesley saw it—he saw everything, even if he wasn't looking at her—and so quickly he righted himself, adjusting those cuff links and putting on the smirk she hated.

"I didn't see Ashwood much," he said. "He probably thought that it was best to let Zekia wear me down. The lesser of two evils and all that. Plus he was busy destroying our city."

"Is Creije really ready to fall?" Tavia asked.

Wesley nodded.

The rain soaked down Tavia's legs.

She couldn't stomach the thought.

"If we lose our home," she said. "Then I . . ."

She trailed off, because she didn't have an end to that sentence. If Creije was gone, then Tavia didn't know what she would do.

"We won't lose it," Wesley said. "Ashwood might be good at being a murderous dictator, but I'm not so bad at it myself."

"Trust you to make being a sociopath a competition," Tavia said. "What if Creije is too far gone to save already? What if we don't live to bring it back?"

"*Skeht*, Tavia," he swore. "Can you try being a little more positive?"

"I'm just saying," she said. "It's not like we're invincible."

"You're so morbid," he scolded. "Trust me, it's going to be fine. There isn't a world where I'd ever let anyone hurt you. There isn't a future that exists where you're not okay. So drink your damn Cloverye and quit being such a huge downer on my first night."

Tavia almost laughed, but as she looked at him the sound got caught in her throat. She'd just noticed, suddenly, without reason, how much browner Wesley's eyes looked in the wake of lightning.

There isn't a world where I'd ever let anyone hurt you.

Tavia's breath disappeared somewhere deep in her chest as Wesley kept his gaze locked on hers, his face newly serious.

Wesley's hand was sitting idly on the ground between them, and Tavia didn't give herself the time to second-guess before she placed hers overtop.

"I'm so glad that you're here," she said.

Only, she didn't know what to say next. Tavia had thought about the moment when she saw Wesley again, what she'd give to make it happen and what she'd do once it did, but now that he was here she forgot about every scenario she'd thought of.

She forgot everything but how beautiful he looked.

"Tavia," he said.

Her name was magic on his lips, a spell that pulled her inward.

She wanted to kiss him.

She'd wanted to for years, really, but she'd never dared to let herself think it before. Now, though, after knowing what the world would be like without Wesley by her side, it was all Tavia *could* think about. She wanted to feel him pressed against her. Feel his smile on her neck. She was hungry for him, like the trees hungered for the rain and the stars hungered for the night.

They had never spoken about the thing that existed between them, as broken and complicated as it had become, and Tavia wasn't sure what words she could say to put it back together in all the perfect ways.

What if she ruined it somehow?

"I missed you," Wesley said.

Lightning cracked across the sky.

"Me too," she said.

Wesley's hand was warm under hers and he turned it so that their fingers locked together. He squeezed her hand tightly.

"No matter what happens, I'm not going to leave you again," Wesley said.

Tavia shivered as the rain soaked through to her toes.

She didn't speak, for fear her voice might not sound like her own. For fear that if she started, she might not be able to control everything that came spilling out.

"Do you know why I love Creije so much?" Wesley asked.

Tavia shook her head. "Good booze?" she guessed, gesturing to the Cloverye.

"Creije is the city that showed me magic and wonder," he said. "It's the city that shaped my soul. But most of all, it's the city that gave me you."

Tavia's throat was painfully dry.

"If we don't die, then you're going to really regret embarrassing yourself with that speech," she said.

She laughed nervously, but Wesley's face didn't change.

He brought his thumb to her mouth and swiped a raindrop from her lip. "I've never regretted any moment with you," he said.

She hadn't either, even the bad ones that Tavia had once thought would be so easy to throw away. Now she wanted to cling to each of them.

Wesley didn't kiss her, but he did keep his hand tangled in hers, and after a few breaths, after they stared at each other for so long that Tavia could see her reflection in his dark eyes, Wesley turned to the ledge and looked back out at the army below.

They sat there like that, in the quiet of the forest, with the wet rain trailing down their legs and the bottle sitting between them, and their hands tied together. Neither of them spoke again and neither of them needed to. Tavia hadn't known what the right words to say were, but Wesley always did, and he'd said them when she wasn't brave enough to.

For the first time, Tavia felt like things would be okay.

She felt like the world wasn't ending after all.

16

Zekia

ZEKIA WAS VERY GOOD at being invisible.

She was also very good at being alone, even in rooms of people. Even when those rooms and those people were in her own mind.

Wesley was gone, again.

He had left her with Ashwood, again.

And this time, he had hated her enough to drill into her mind while doing it.

He'd left holes there, where she was sure there wasn't space left to leave any more, and now Zekia felt the shiver of emptiness in her bones.

He didn't understand that none of this was a choice.

She'd tried to tell him about the future and how it would be worth it in the end. Every death and every bad thing would make way for the light, because Zekia was saving the world.

She was saving everyone.

She was *good*.

And once they were done in Creije and Tisvgen, they could travel to Rishiya and begin the next phase. That was where the resistance was, waiting to be liberated to Ashwood's new realm.

Where Zekia's Kin was.

Where her family was.

Where Wesley was probably waiting for her to save him again.

He doesn't want to be saved, her mind chided. *Not by you.*

Zekia tried to push her thoughts aside, but they were stronger than her. Probably because there was hardly anything left of her anymore. No family. No Wesley. Even her visions had turned against her, only ever feeling like nails in her skull when they came.

Without her Kin to help steady her powers, what should have come to Zekia as wisdom was now always an army of futures that seemed like they were attacking her, fighting for space in her head, and they wouldn't stop until Zekia had disappeared and all that was left was a shell, filled with their wicked deaths.

Even having Ashwood's Crafters by her side didn't help. Zekia needed her Kin. She needed a blood connection to settle her spirit.

It had been worse since Wesley left. Zekia felt more unbalanced than ever. Visions were a funny thing. They were never certain, almost always perilous, and they sent Zekia into a tailspin that made her forget who she was and why she was.

This one was no different.

Or it was different, because it was worse. Because it was the first one in so long that was clear.

Zekia dropped to the floor as the images flashed in her mind. Her mother was a goddess.

She had bronzed eyes and freckles that sparkled like glitter in the sun. Her hair was a bundle of tight curls, just short enough to touch the very tips of her ears and though she wore a dress the same deep and galactic purple as the Loj—though her smile was warm and her eyes were kind, and the staves against her black skin looked like pretty pictures—she was a fighter.

Zekia could tell just by looking at her. She wasn't sure how or what it was exactly, but a part of Vea Akintola looked ready for war.

She'd grown up on stories of her mother, and even a few scattered photos, but those did no justice, and stories were often prone to lies. People liked to remember the dead the way they weren't. They liked to take the best parts of them and pretend that was all there was.

Zekia had grown up being told that her mother was perfect and she'd grown up knowing it wasn't true. Now, seeing her as clear as a shadow moon, Zekia could understand how the lies got mixed with the truth.

Her mother was not perfect, but she was glorious.

She carried a child in her arms who Zekia knew was her brother, though she'd rarely heard about Malik besides what a great leader he was destined to be. All the stories about her brother were about what he could have been, or should have been, but rarely what he was.

Malik was supposed to save them.

Malik was supposed to be Liege.

Malik was supposed to change the world.

And instead they got stuck with her.

Zekia's brother was tiny and that struck her as odd, since he would have been older than her if he were still alive. But now she was looking at him, a baby, and she was suddenly the older sibling. It felt like an enormous responsibility, even if it was to a dead boy.

Vea carried Malik into a small shed.

Zekia watched.

Vea held him up in the air and sobbed.

Zekia watched.

Amja drew strange symbols on the floor, her hands shaking the entire time.

Zekia watched.

And then Malik cried and the shed was engulfed in black flame and everyone screamed and the forest withered and all the while Zekia watched.

She wanted to look away, or even blink. But you couldn't blink if the thing in front of you was actually inside of your mind.

You could only watch.

Only listen.

Only wish that it would stop.

The flames seemed endless and Zekia wasn't sure how long she would have to stare as her mother and brother died, but soon minutes passed and the black smoke faded, as did the forest, and from it Wesley Thornton Walcott appeared.

A phoenix from the ashes.

The smoke morphed into his face and he was standing in front of her, with his bone gun pointed at Dante Ashwood, while a song chanted in the distance.

Time will be carried in strange hands,
across the realms and through stranger lands.
What is done will be undone,
a battle lost is a battle won.
When midnight rings on a child's betrayal,
every success is doomed to fail.

It repeated over and over until Zekia started mumbling the words to herself, humming the tune like she had known it her whole life. It played for so long that when it finally stopped, abruptly and without warning, Zekia kept singing, thinking that it might start up again.

But it didn't.

And Wesley still stood there, pointing his gun, like he was frozen in time. A clock chimed somewhere and only then did Wesley blink, as though it had sprung him back to life.

Dante Ashwood, made of magic and the kind of dreams you remembered vividly one moment and forgot the next, smiled.

"My boy," he said.

"Not anymore," Wesley said.

He fired the shot and Ashwood exploded into a flurry of shadows that flew away like bats. They screeched and screeched as they fled toward the shadow moon.

And the sun burst through.

The darkness faded and the light broke and all around Wesley, silver soaked the streets.

Magic dust. Staves inked on the stone under people's feet. Painted on buildings and thrown between jugglers like balls, while a crowd clapped and laughed and sang.

A world of magic.

A world of peace.

Zekia let out a breath like it was her first as the vision faded and she was plunged back into the real world.

She gasped in the air and clutched at her throat, the blood from her nose dripping down to her chin.

She wiped it away with shaking hands.

Her demon nudged at her legs, but Zekia could not move to calm the beast, nor reach into its mind to tell it to just *go away*.

It didn't make sense.

Wesley—*her* Wesley—destroying the man who was meant to make the world better, and creating something even more glorious in its place.

Zekia pressed a hand to her head to try to stamp out the future, but it still sang in her mind like a song she'd never forget the tune to. Like the ghostly vision that Ashwood had shown her, only for some reason Zekia felt this one in her heart and in her spirit.

It soothed her, and that was the most confusing part of all.

When Dante Ashwood walked through the door to her room, Zekia pulled herself to her feet and quickly brushed off her dress. It had dust marks from the floor and it wasn't quite white anymore and she didn't want him to be angry about that.

"What is it, my little warrior?" he asked.

He crossed the room and reached out a hand to her bloody face.

"Was it a vision?" he asked. "What did you see?"

Zekia pushed the possibility of a new future out of her mind, where he couldn't find it.

"I didn't see anything new," she said. "More of that scary world we have to stop." She looked up at him. "We will stop it, won't we?"

Dante Ashwood nodded and kept his hand on her face, stroking her cheek like she was his favorite thing.

"Of course we will," he said. "Together, we will change everything. But first, we must talk about your family."

Zekia stared at the dirt on the edges of her dress.

The walls of her mind were closing in again and if she didn't concentrate hard enough, then she knew she'd forget what she had just seen. She knew she'd forget everything that mattered.

Zekia was so tired of forgetting.

She was tired of her mind being such a lonely place.

She smiled up at Dante Ashwood and, in the perilous corners of her mind—where she kept the memories of Saxony and Amja and her father, where she kept the hearts of her Kin and the fragile pieces of her childhood she couldn't quite let go—Zekia called out to Wesley.

Please, she said. *Please don't leave me here again.*

17

Karam

KARAM FELL ONTO THE SAND.

It only hurt for a moment—less than a moment—and it was not the kind of pain that mattered. It was like banging her knee on a table, or stepping on something sharp.

Quick, dull, and then gone.

When the bullet went through her chest, Karam didn't feel much at all. Just the sand, wet on her face.

Still, her only thought was this: I'm going to die. I think I'm really going to die. And she had the idea that she should say something, her final words, but she couldn't think of anything to say and when she tried to move her jaw to speak, all that came was breath.

"If magic won't kill you, then maybe this will," the Crafter said, stepping closer to her.

Karam tried to move to kick his legs out from under him, or charge at him, or do something, but her body felt so heavy.

The world felt heavy and the more Karam tried to keep her eyes open, the more everything blurred.

She wiggled her toes, to check that she could still do that at least. Then she thought about praying to the Indescribable God, but all she wanted to do was curse it.

She hadn't done everything she'd wanted to yet, had she?

Could she hold on if the spirits tried to take her?

This wasn't her time. This wasn't how it was supposed to happen.

And yet.

And yet.

"Long live the Kingpin," the Crafter said.

He raised the gun again.

Karam waited for the warm light to reach her eyes and for the spirits to cross over into this world to ferry her back into theirs.

They didn't come.

They didn't need to.

A sword cut through the Crafter, from shoulder to torso, slicing him nearly clean in half. He fell to the beach without a scream or a gasp, just the sound of a thump in the sand.

Karam caught a final glimpse of Arjun, sword held high, before her eyes got too heavy to keep open.

"Karam," Arjun said. "Don't do this to me."

She could hear his voice break, but she couldn't see him.

She could only see Saxony's face, Saxony's smile, and Saxony's freckles.

Just Saxony, laughing.

Saxony, pulling her beautiful hair back from her face.

Saxony making her promise to come back alive.

"Karam!"

KARAM SHOT up and reached instinctively for her knife, but the clearing where she and Arjun had set up camp was quiet.

She touched a hand to her heart. It was beating normally, fine, as though death hadn't come looking for her.

"Bad dream?" Arjun asked.

He sat up from the ground where he had been sleeping beside her.

"I'm okay," she said.

Arjun didn't look convinced, but Karam was too tired for convincing.

"How is it?" Arjun asked, gesturing to her chest.

The place the bullet had gone in.

Where Karam's hand still pressed against her heartbeat.

"You healed it fine," she said. "As though it never happened."

But it had happened.

Too much had happened.

"We should leave when the sun comes up," Karam said. "We've spent too long here."

Here being the Barren Woods of Tisvgen, where Arjun had taken her to heal the rest of her wound. It was a short walk from the Shores of the Dead, and the only shelter they had. It had been three days now—two of which Arjun had spent finishing off the healing on Karam's wound and his own—plus this one, where all Karam wanted to do was go back to Rishiya.

If Nolan had sent them here to be killed, then who knew what he had sent back to Rishiya to kill their army? Karam couldn't let anyone else die, not after everything.

Not after Asees.

"We can't use the railways," Arjun said. "I haven't seen any trains when I've gone back to the shores to scout. They're not coming here anymore."

They both knew what that meant: Something had happened or was happening out in the world. Dante Ashwood's hold must have been growing and when Karam finally faced Saxony and Tavia again, what would she have to help them? This mission she had been so sure of had brought them nothing but pain.

She hadn't found Wesley. She'd only lost Asees and the six other Crafters from the Grankan Kin they had recruited.

Karam had wanted to prove she could do some good in this war, and all she had done was lose them more soldiers.

"We're never going back," Arjun said.

"Don't say that."

"We're stuck here."

"We're not. There has to be a way back."

"A way back? Neither of us can swim!" Arjun yelled. "And even if we could, it's miles and miles across the waters. There are no trains, do you hear me? There is *nothing* between us and Rishiya. We can't go back. We're trapped here and we'll die here, just like Asees and the others."

He threw the blankets off of himself and stood. Karam wasn't sure what she could do but stand by his side. There wasn't anything she could say to make it better.

"I don't know what to do," Arjun said, burying his face in his hands. "They're all still on the beach. She's still . . ."

He dropped off and shook his head, collapsing down beside the small fire they had lit before they drifted off to sleep.

The bodies of his Kin were still scattered across the Shores of the Dead. Karam and Arjun hadn't had the time to give them a proper funeral, and apparently nobody was coming to Tisvgen anymore.

"That's what we'll do first, then," Karam said. "We'll send their spirits off well, so that they may join the Indescribable God. After that, we'll figure out the rest."

Arjun nodded. "Okay," he said, and that was all he said.

Even as they gathered what little supplies they had left, rolling up their blankets into their bags and hooking knives to their belts and swords to their shoulder straps, Arjun stayed quiet.

It was only just before they left that he gathered the small barrel of rainwater and turned to her. "Swear that we'll avenge them," he said.

"I swear it," she promised him.

And then Karam watched as Arjun threw water over the fire and the light turned to ash.

***

IN WRENYAL, when a person died, their body was turned to flame and thrown into sacred water, so that their spirit could be free to escape this world and travel on to the next to join the Indescribable God.

The Onnela Sea wasn't divine water, but it was water nonetheless and it was the thing that circled this realm before joining on to the mighty ocean that led to Wrenyi. If Karam thought about it that way, then it seemed better, as though the ashes of their friends might just find their way back home to their own realm.

They had gathered the bodies of their fallen soldiers and placed them into a circle, where Karam and Arjun now stood in the center. Karam tried not to look at their faces, but she couldn't help it. Asees looked calm, not like she was sleeping, but like she was taking in the beauty of the shores and the smell of the ocean salt.

"Let us pray," Arjun said.

The spell took a few minutes. Arjun couldn't conjure flame from nowhere like Saxony could and so he had to call upon the spirits to grant him the element.

Karam held his hand until the spell took hold, and together they watched the Shores of the Dead burn.

The bodies of Arjun's Kin were alight in beautiful yellow flame, so close to the gold of their staves. As the fire grew, so did the wind, and Karam could see Arjun focus his powers to mold the breeze. It swirled around the flames until finally the fire diminished and ash circled in the air.

Arjun kept a tight hold on Karam's hand.

"Go in peace," he said. "Be with the spirits and with our god, and look down on us in love, knowing we are warm and we are safe."

"Go in peace," Karam echoed.

The ashes of the Kin danced together and swept toward the water. They hovered for a moment and Karam knew that Arjun was hesitating.

She squeezed his hand.

"Let them rest," she said.

Arjun took in a breath and the ashes slowly fell into the sea.

Karam looked into the distance, hoping there would be answers somewhere on the shores. She wanted to think of something perfect to say to him or something perfect to do to take his mind off of everything. She wanted—

Karam paused.

She didn't see answers, but she could see *something* on the part of the shore where the forest that had hid them met the sea.

"Are those boats?" she asked.

Arjun turned to follow her stare. "Are *what* boats? Those floating dots?"

"They're boats," Karam said, firmer this time.

She could see the outline of their frames and the way they bobbed on the small carcass of wood they were tied to.

"You've got eyes like an eagle," Arjun said.

Karam didn't answer, she just ran. She ran over the wet sand so fast that her thighs began to ache and the sound of Arjun calling her name as he chased after her faded, as the wind blew so strongly in her ears.

She ran for miles.

For what felt like an hour.

And then she reached them and she saw that she was right.

There were four rowboats pitched to a small pier that was barely the length of an old oak tree. The wood looked a little rotten, but she couldn't see any holes in the frames and the oars were still intact.

"Are you training for some kind of athletic competition?" Arjun asked.

He was breathless and when Karam turned to face him, Arjun's hands were pressed against his knees as he bent over to gulp in the air.

"This is how we get back," Karam said. "This is how we cross to Rishiya without the railways."

"They're boats," Arjun said, as if Karam hadn't noticed. "You want to cross to another city in those?"

She nodded.

"Karam, we don't know how to row."

"We don't need to."

"They're *row*boats," Arjun said. "And I don't even think these old things could handle the task."

He stepped toward them and knocked one lightly with his foot.

"It would be two days' journey at least."

"You're a Spiritcrafter," Karam said to him. "With the help of your magic, you can harness the wind to propel us onward. We could do it in half the time and with half the effort."

Arjun's frown softened as he thought this over. Spiritcrafters could channel the weather, and if Arjun could help them move a train through the perilous waters of Ejm Voten, where nobody dared cross, and toward Dante Ashwood's hidden isle, then he could push a rowboat over to the next city.

He looked to Karam, and for the first time in days, Arjun smiled.

"We're not stuck here," Karam said to him. "We're going back."

18

Wesley

WESLEY STOOD IN THE center of the tree house and peered down at the forest below, alight in green and the dim yellow glow of the lanterns. He could hear the trees singing, like a lullaby in the night.

"Enjoying the view?" Tavia asked. "You said you wanted updates, but if you just feel like sightseeing, let us know."

Wesley gave her a sullen look. "Take it away," he said, and gestured to the magical fire in the center of the room, where Saxony was currently warming her hands. "What have the new busker boss and Crafter Liege been up to while I was away?"

"I've stolen enough magic from the Rishiyat buskers to fuel our people," Tavia said. "And now that we have Casim's buskers with us, all that's left is to wait for him to convince the other underbosses to help. Though now that you're back, you could probably do a better job at rallying them."

"And you?" Wesley asked, looking to Saxony.

She stood and sighed, to let him know that she didn't like the thought of reporting to him.

"Tavia already told you that I summoned Crafter Lieges from across the realms," Saxony said. "Most have already made their way here."

"And when the others come, are they all going to be happy about you being Head Liege of all Lieges?" Wesley asked. "We need a united magical army for this to work."

Saxony cleared her throat. "I'm not a Liege," she said, and the way she looked down at the floor told Wesley that it wasn't a choice she'd made for herself. "My amja is taking over Zekia's duties for now."

"Bullshit."

Saxony's head shot up. "Excuse me?"

"You have the experience," Wesley said. "You fought against Ashwood and you took the initiative to summon the other Crafters. Why are you taking orders from anyone else?"

"Because that's the way it is."

"Until you say otherwise."

Saxony scoffed, like Wesley couldn't possibly understand their ways. And she was right. Wesley didn't get how someone like Saxony, who had fire burning in her veins and the scars of war on her fingertips, could step down and let someone else make her decisions for her.

"So what parts of Uskhanya have you set up bases in to protect?" Wesley asked. "What did the Doyen say about all of this when you spoke to her about an alliance?"

The almost chastised looks on their faces made Wesley want to go back into Zekia's hold. At least she and Ashwood had a plan.

"You did speak to the Doyen, didn't you?" he asked, already knowing he wouldn't like the answer.

"We can't just send a bat to a world leader," Tavia said. "And we've been busy. We've been—"

"Sitting around sniping at each other?" Wesley asked.

Tavia gave him a familiar *I'm going to punch you* kind of a look. "What was your contribution to the war effort these last few weeks?"

"I didn't die," Wesley said. "And since you so clearly need me around, I'd say that I did you a favor by staying alive."

Tavia didn't argue with that, which made a change.

"We need to speak to Doyen Fenna Schulze and align with her forces," Wesley said. "While you were building an army, did none of you think about the army that was already out there? The entire military force of Uskhanya could be on our side right now."

"Yeah," Saxony said, rolling her eyes. "Because what the officials want in the fight against magic is a bunch of Crafters and crooks."

"Except that I already negotiated that deal."

It seemed like a lifetime ago when Wesley was back in the amity precinct with Tavia, negotiating Saxony's release with the Vice Doyen. Agreeing to kill the Kingpin in exchange for becoming the Kingpin. It didn't seem possible that only a few months had passed, rather than years.

Wesley pictured himself then, feet kicked up on the table and his suit not pressed with blood, feeling like nothing in the world could hurt him.

"Vice Doyen Armin Krause gave us permission to go after

the Kingpin and said that we'd have Schulze's backing," Wesley reminded them. "Since the Kingpin isn't dead, as far as I'm concerned that deal still stands. It's about time we collected."

"You really think she'll join forces with us?" Tavia asked.

"I don't think she has a choice."

None of them did now.

It was kill or be killed, just like the streets had been when Wesley was coming up. Though now those shadowed streets had spread their arms and the entire realm was at risk of having to look over their shoulder every second, or fear that doing or saying one wrong thing could cost them their lives. That doing or saying nothing could cost them worse.

Wesley had done a lot of bad in his life, but he didn't want to be part of a legacy of suffering. He didn't want his name remembered beside Dante Ashwood's.

If nothing else, Wesley wanted to make sure his city survived.

Wesley whistled the old tune that every person—Crafter, busker, or the ordinary—was taught as a child. The melody to call a *delg* bat from their haunt. There were at least a dozen in the Uncharted Forest—Wesley had seen them hanging from the trees by the curved river—and so it took only a minute before one flew in from the window and landed straight in his palm.

Wesley stroked the blackened creature and it cooed in his hands, flapping its night wings and nibbling at his finger.

"Find Fenna Schulze," Wesley told the bat. "And tell her that the underboss of Creije wants a meeting. I have an army of magic that I'm willing to align with her forces. If we join together, we can finally end Ashwood's reign and stop the Loj elixir from spreading."

The bat chirped in response and leaped from Wesley's hand. It was fast and it only took a matter of seconds for him to lose sight of it altogether. Wesley wasn't sure where the bat was heading; he didn't know exactly where Schulze was, but the creature would find her. *Delg* bats were magical things, feeding off of psychic energy. They could find anyone, anywhere, even at the edges of the realms. Some people said that if the bat was ancient enough and loyal enough to its master, it could even cross into the afterlife to ferry messages to the dead.

So somewhere like the Halls of Government in Yejlath shouldn't be a problem.

"The Doyen should get the bat within a day," Wesley said. "And after that we—Damn it!"

Wesley yelled out in pain.

A sudden sharpness pierced through his mind like a hundred needles, stabbing and stabbing.

He grabbed at his temples, teeth grinding together.

"*Skeht!*" he cursed.

"Wesley!" Tavia said, running over to him.

But then Saxony started screaming too.

There was a darkness in Wesley's mind, clouding his vision until the real world blurred and he could only focus on the images in his head. The shadows squirmed through his mind like worms looking to take root.

It felt like it had when Zekia tried to claw through his mind, only this time Wesley didn't sense the hesitation he'd felt from her, or the conflict as she watched him cry out.

All he felt now was darkness.

Then from that darkness, a cloud of fog descended.

Saxony gasped out and the fire in the room died like a gust of wind had blown violently through it.

Dante Ashwood's face appeared inside of Wesley's mind.

"Hello, my children," he said.

Wesley winced at the sound of his voice, like nails scraping into him.

"Many Gods," Saxony cried out, her voice strained. "He's inside my head."

She was clutching at her skull, squeezing her eyes shut tightly as if to try to push Ashwood out. But it was no use.

"Today, I come to you not just as a leader, but as a beacon."

"Make it stop!" Saxony yelled.

She fell to her knees and something inside of Wesley lurched. He wanted to walk over to her, but the pain rooted him to the spot. He felt like if he tried to move, he might collapse as well.

"What is it?" Tavia asked. "What's going on?"

She couldn't hear him.

Wesley's head pounded as he tried to keep the Kingpin's voice at bay, but all that practice defending his mind meant nothing now.

In the forest below, he could hear the screams of their camp.

Wesley looked out of the window and saw the chaos. People on their knees like Saxony, hands over their ears and clutching at their temples, while others around them looked on in horror.

The Crafters.

The Kingpin was speaking only to the Crafters.

"Today is a day of great joy and progress," Ashwood said.

"It is a day to rejoice and finally unite the realm of Uskhanya."

Wesley winced and his knees trembled with the pain of keeping himself upright while his head spun so violently, but he'd be damned if he knelt down to Dante Ashwood.

He hadn't done it when the shadow demon sank its teeth into him and he wouldn't do it now.

Not here. Not like this.

"I have taken hold of the capital of our great realm," Ashwood said. "Creije is now mine."

Many Gods.

Wesley couldn't believe what he was hearing.

The last district in Creije had fallen.

It didn't seem possible.

"Wesley, what's going on?" Tavia asked.

"It's Ashwood," he said. Even speaking felt painful, with the walls in his mind trying so hard to block the Kingpin out. "He's taken Creije."

He looked to Tavia, jaw clenched.

"It's gone," he said. "Our home is gone."

Though perhaps *gone* wasn't the right word. Ashwood hadn't destroyed Creije, he'd just destroyed everything it stood for. He'd just stolen the streets from the dreamers and taken the city Wesley had built on his back, and fed it to wolves.

Tavia's lips parted and her eyes almost instantly filled with tears. She slipped her hand into Wesley's and squeezed it tightly, tethering him to the ground so he didn't crumple.

Wesley looked at the tattoos that danced up his arms: the streets of Creije painted on him so he'd always remember his home and fight to keep it.

Only, everything Wesley had made now belonged to Ashwood.

Maybe it always had.

"It is with joy that I make this announcement," Ashwood said. "I, Dante Ashwood, a man born on the streets of this great capital, a man who lived through the war and has seen the wonders of the future, will usher us into greatness."

Ashwood's pale lips tilted to a smile and Wesley could feel every moment of his twisted delight.

"As the new leader of Creije, I summon any and all Crafters of the realm to my capital, where they will be welcomed and respected," he said. "I put an end to bans on black magic, declaring all charms legal in this city. And I officially recognize anyone who challenges my authority as an enemy of change. Including the so-called Doyen Fenna Schulze. This is a city of magic and it will be your city of respite."

"He's declaring war on Schulze," Wesley said.

He felt the blood drip from his nose and then the scratch as Tavia used her sleeve to wipe it away. It was taking everything he had not to let Ashwood's voice consume him completely.

"I can't keep him out," Saxony said, her palms flat against the floor as she keeled over. "It's too loud."

"The first step to eliminating these enemies is to begin at home," Ashwood said. "I will conquer the rest of this realm, starting with the government city of Yejlath. My forces are already making their way there, but I know I must prove that I'm willing to start over. To enact change and punish those who once sought to harm you. I must prove that you are safe with me and that I'll protect you from this realm and everyone in it. Including my own people."

There was a flicker as Ashwood waved his shadow arm, and then the vision of him exploded into eight separate clouds of screaming and blood.

Wesley's breath lodged in his throat as he saw the familiar faces.

Ilaria. Stelios. Felix. Luca. Chiara. Greta. Enori.

All of them dying in front of him.

"It's the underbosses of Uskhanya," Wesley told Tavia. "Ashwood is killing them all for the Crafters to see."

Then Casim's face flashed in the eighth cloud and Wesley's stomach lurched as he realized that meant Ashwood's people were in Rishiya. That they were so, so close.

They cut through the underbosses one by one, knives at their throats and swords through their hearts. The blood splattered outward and Wesley blinked and stumbled, as though it might spill from the projection and rain down on them all.

Tavia caught his arm to steady him.

"Sacrifices are necessary for change," Ashwood said. "I know that you think they were going to help you by sending you more buskers, but these are the vermin responsible for your shackles. These are the criminals who use your magic for profit. They are your enemies."

The clouds disappeared and the vision in Wesley's mind refocused on Ashwood's ghostly face once again.

Tavia shuffled closer to him, her hand dangling by his, eyes searching the forest as if something in the wind was calling to her.

Wesley could hear it too.

He could hear the trees, no longer singing.

But screaming.

Whenever Wesley's hand twitched against Tavia's, the leaves of the forest hissed in warning. The branches smacked together.

They were not alone.

They were not safe.

Run, the trees said. *You have to run.*

"You must make a choice now," Ashwood said. "Come to me in good faith, or die as traitors."

Wesley kept ahold of Tavia's hand.

And then, as sudden as a storm that had brewed in silence, an army appeared. Below the tree house, where Wesley watched the Crafters cry in pain and the rest of their people surrounding them unable to help, a new enemy blinked into existence.

First bones, then veins and skin and hair.

Teeth that glistened in the sun like monsters finally free to walk the day.

The invisibility charm they had harnessed shattered and they licked their hungry lips. Wesley could see the mark of the Loj on some of them, their eyes like broken stars. But the others, the ones who looked the most hungry and hateful, gave off a familiar wave of magic and blind devotion.

Crafters.

Soldiers.

Dante Ashwood's willing followers.

"This is a new realm," Ashwood said, his voice barely a murmur as their enemies descended. "And we shall build it together."

19

Tavia

TAVIA DUCKED AS A ball of fire flew straight at her head.

"How did they find us?" she yelled as Wesley grabbed her hand and pulled her toward the door.

"It doesn't matter," he said over the screams. "They're here now."

He threw open the door and barreled through, Tavia and Saxony following behind.

She knew he was lying, though, because it definitely mattered and they were definitely all thinking the same thing: *Zekia*.

Saxony's sister had betrayed them, again.

She had finally told the Kingpin where her family was.

They ran down the tree house steps, skipping two or three at a time, until finally they crashed onto the mud.

Tavia looked around the forest, at the chaos that was descending.

Blood stained the warning leaves and her allies were tripping over bodies as they made to run toward, or from, their enemies. They threw magic at each other in a deafening roar, with lights of blinding white and blue flashing across Tavia's vision like some kind of deadly rainbow.

"I have to find Amja and my father!" Saxony yelled, running for the center of camp.

Tavia lost sight of her in moments and then a bolt of lightning, conjured from a clear sky, headed toward her.

Tavia and Wesley dove out of the way, and she landed with a heavy thud in the soil. She cursed at the row of bruises she knew would appear down her legs by tomorrow.

If she lived until tomorrow.

Tavia pushed herself to her feet and grabbed two of the knives from her belt. A Crafter surged toward her and Tavia flung her arm out, slicing the knife across his neck.

One down. Only a hundred left to go, she thought, throwing a punch at another.

He took it to the nose and while he was busy clutching at his face, Tavia took the opportunity to jam her knife into his chest.

But stabbing someone wasn't always easy. It wasn't like slicing a loaf of bread. It was hard and gristly and Tavia winced as she desperately tried to pull the knife back out, only for the blade to get stuck somewhere in the man's chest.

She sighed, and left that knife behind. She had plenty more.

Beside her, Wesley was taking on three Crafters, slamming his fist into the face of one, and his magic into the others. She made to help him, but a beam of light shot out toward her from behind a distant tree.

Tavia barely dodged it in time.

She swore, loudly, hoping that was the last time she was thrown to the ground, because her ego—and her bruised ass—couldn't handle much more.

"For the love of the Many Gods," Tavia said, glaring at the sky. "Could you cut me a break?"

"You're praying right now?" Wesley asked, appearing suddenly by her side like a ghost.

He pulled Tavia to her feet.

"Want to splash some blessed water on our enemies, too?"

Tavia ignored him and threw one of her knives at a nearby attacker. It landed straight in the center of his forehead and the way that Wesley's eyebrows shot up was almost comical.

"Where did you learn to do that?" he asked.

Tavia shrugged, like she wasn't extremely impressed with her own aim.

"Karam," she said, as casually as she could muster.

Wesley let out a low whistle. "I'm not sure whether to be scared or turned on."

Tavia elbowed him in the stomach, harder than she'd intended, and Wesley let out a low grunt.

"Turned on it is," he mumbled as Tavia ran toward a group of Crafters she could see surrounding Saxony.

There were six of them hurling balls of energy at her like they were stones. Saxony snarled, her Energycrafter shield shuddering with the force of their power.

Tavia could see her skin begin to take on a red hue as her fire magic grew inside of her, set to spill out like a volcano and send these bastards back to the fire-gates.

Tavia kicked one of them from behind, which was a cheat's

move but she really didn't care. Her foot jabbed into the back of his knee and he went down like a shot. Before he had time to turn and react, Tavia stabbed her knife into his spine.

Saxony's shield splintered.

There was blood covering her side and spreading from her ribs. Tavia gasped, but as she started to run to her, Saxony let out an almighty yell and the flame burst out of her like spikes, impaling the five remaining Crafters.

They crumpled to the ground and the fire spread across their bodies until they dissolved to ash.

"Damn it," Saxony said. "One of them pierced my shield."

Tavia stepped through the cinders with a wince.

"You're lucky it was just one," she said.

She held out a hand and hauled Saxony to her feet. Her palms felt like pure fire, but Tavia didn't pull away. She kept her grip firm and steady, helping Saxony to regain her balance as she pressed a hand to her bleeding ribs.

"Are you okay?" Tavia asked.

Her skin felt like it was blistering.

Saxony clutched her ribs.

"Go and help the others," she said. "I'll be fine in a minute."

Tavia shook her head.

"I'm not leaving you to bleed out," she said, gripping on to Saxony's arm a little tighter. "Let me help you."

She had a good reason to be angry with Saxony. *Many* good reasons, in fact, but Tavia wasn't going to abandon her on a battlefield.

"I appreciate the heroics, but I can heal this myself in a few minutes," Saxony said. "Go and help somebody who needs it."

Tavia looked between Saxony and the bloodbath surrounding them.

"You sure?" she asked.

"I am," Saxony said, pushing her away. "Go!"

So Tavia did.

She ran without aim, punching and kicking. Slicing her knives across throats and jamming them into people's stomachs like Karam had shown her.

She wasn't sure how all of this blood would ever wash from her hands.

And then she spotted a group of enemy soldiers, circling like vultures around someone, and suddenly she wasn't so worried about shedding too much blood.

Nolan.

That son of a bitch, she thought.

He and his friends were advancing on Saxony's father.

Tavia ran toward them, reaching into her pocket and flinging out the first charm she thought would be of any use. It was a simple wind charm, but it sent them flying backward onto the ground with a loud crash.

"Are you okay?" Tavia asked Bastian, her eyes quickly scanning him for any wounds.

Bastian nodded and let out a shaken breath. "You have strong magic."

"I wish I could take credit, but I stole most of it."

Bastian laughed and put a hand on her shoulder. "Thank you," he said.

"Nice trick," Nolan said, dusting himself off. "But it'll be your last."

In front of him like a barrier, five thugs looked at her like hungry beasts.

"At least you get to go out with a bang," Nolan said. "Creije's best busker defeated by Rishiya's best. It's kind of poetic."

"Read better poetry," Tavia said.

Nolan ignored her and from his pocket he pulled out a small round object that looked a little like a fortune orb, save for the fact that it was not made of glass—or the watery kind of magic that looked like glass—but instead from some kind of stone.

It was bright blue, with pinpoints of white freckled around the polished smooth surface. It looked old and dangerous, the way most magic often did, and perched atop its perfectly rounded tip was a thin fuse.

"What's that?" Tavia asked.

Nolan twirled it in his hand like a prize. "I call it a Star Egg," he said. "You stole a bunch of them from me back in Rishiya. Or don't you remember?"

Tavia remembered.

"Luckily, I had a couple in my private stash," he said. "But I'll be looking to get back everything you took from me soon enough."

A lot of the magic Tavia had stolen was already distributed among the buskers, but the rest—the things kept aside for training, or the few rare cases where she couldn't figure out the nature of the charm—had been cataloged and stored for safekeeping.

She was glad Nolan hadn't found that store and reclaimed his mysterious treasures yet.

"Want to see what it does?" Nolan asked.

She really didn't.

Tavia flung out a charm and the marble beelined for the buskers trying to protect Nolan. It burst into a hundred tiny insects that swarmed around three of them, biting and stinging without relent.

They yelled, waving their hands through the air to keep the creatures at bay. But by the time they parted to let Tavia get to Nolan, it was too late.

He had pulled a lighter from his pocket and lit the fuse of the Star Egg.

Nolan took a worrying step back and said nothing before throwing a shield over himself.

The Star Egg exploded in a loud whistle, shooting sparks up into the sky like a lightning bolt in reverse. They were gold and glistening and when they hit the clouds, they screamed and then scattered across the night like rain, readying to pour down on the camp.

Quickly, Tavia pulled a shield charm from her own pocket and cast it overhead. Whatever crap magic Nolan had loaded into that device, she didn't want it getting anywhere near her or Bastian.

The sparks hissed angrily over the shield, but for a good twenty feet in any direction of her, the ground sizzled and smoked. People fell to the ground, blisters burning on their skin as they screamed and screamed for the pain to stop.

They were dying. Dozens of people. Including Nolan's friends who she'd taken down with the insect charm.

Many Gods.

The Star Egg was like nothing Tavia had ever seen. What had looked like a glorious explosion in the sky was now washing down like deadly poison, melting people's skin to the bone, while Nolan looked on with a smug smile.

"Now that's a shame," Nolan said. "I put a perfectly good acid charm inside of that thing and you didn't even die."

Tavia swallowed as the light subsided and her shield began to crumble.

"Guess I'll just have to gut you instead," Nolan said.

Tavia cursed and readied to show Nolan that he didn't know who he was dealing with.

"There's a busker trying to kill you," a voice whispered in her ear.

Tavia jumped at the sound of Wesley, suddenly beside her.

"Are *you* trying to kill me?" she asked, hand pressed to her chest.

Wesley didn't answer, but his eyes narrowed toward Nolan.

"I don't appreciate you attacking my best busker."

"*You're* the underboss of Creije," Nolan said. "I've been wanting to meet you."

"Why? You got a death wish or something?" Wesley asked.

Nolan smirked. "You're not so tough," he said. "The infamous Wesley Thornton Walcott, come to save the—"

Wesley pulled out his gun and shot Nolan straight in the head, before he had the chance to finish.

His aim hadn't suffered one bit in the months of captivity.

Nolan's body fell to the ground.

"Definitely had a death wish," Wesley said.

"By all that is holy," Bastian said, with a gasp.

"I've never been called holy before." Wesley holstered his gun. "Godly, maybe."

He turned to Tavia, his eyes scanning over her bruised arms and the scratches she knew were marked across her face.

He reached out and pressed a hand to her cheek, and Tavia nearly froze with the shock of his touch. Warm hands pressed against her skin, in a way that was more tender than she could bear.

"I was going to take care of him," Tavia said. "Nolan was *my* problem to solve."

Wesley dropped his hand back to his side.

Tavia felt the cold absence of his touch.

She wasn't trying to sound ungrateful, but Tavia had been the one to let Nolan escape and it was her fault he'd been able to come back here and hurt people.

She'd wanted to deal with him herself, like she hadn't been able to before.

"I'll let you kill the next one, if you really want," Wesley said, like a peace offering. "I didn't realize you'd become so bloodthirsty."

Tavia rolled her eyes. "Just stop talking and start saving people," she said.

"Yes," Bastian said eagerly. "We must help the others."

Wesley cast a glance to Saxony's father and nodded.

"We'll help them," he said. "You stay here and find shelter."

Bastian looked offended. "I shall help to protect my people."

"You shall get yourself killed trying," Wesley said, in a blustering mimic of Bastian's voice. "So stay here and stay alive. If you die, your daughter will blame me. So for my sake, try not to get stabbed or shot."

"Or hit by charms," Tavia added.

Wesley took his gun back out of the holster, reloading.

"Come on." He grabbed Tavia's hand and she felt that old warmth return. "Let's play heroes."

20

Saxony

IN THE CENTER OF the forest where Saxony's family and her Kin had made their home for decades was a damn tornado.

Saxony didn't know which of their enemies had conjured it, but she hadn't exactly been given training on how to quell magical storms.

"Need a hand?" Wesley asked.

Saxony's teeth gritted under the strain. "I can't keep it at bay."

Her hands were held up into the air, creating a force field around the beastly thing, but her entire body shook with the power of it.

Her feet skidded back against the soil as it pushed her away, refusing to bow down to her powers.

"Where are your Spiritcrafters?" Tavia asked.

They were the only ones who had dominion over the weather and nature's spirit, and Tavia was right to think that if one of the Kingpin's Spiritcrafters had conjured this, then they'd need a Crafter with the same specialty to stop it.

Unfortunately, that wasn't on the cards right now.

"People are a little preoccupied," Saxony said.

Every person in the camp was fighting for their lives, and for all they knew, every Spiritcrafter on their side had already lost theirs. Some kind of acid charm had rained down from the sky on the other side of camp, and by Saxony's count, at least two dozen people had died from that magic alone.

"Then I suppose it's up to us," Tavia said.

Saxony turned away from the tornado to raise an eyebrow at her. "You got a charm in there that can make nature bow to your whim?"

"No," Wesley said. "But I just might have something."

He stepped beside Saxony and took in a breath, like he was really going to regret this next part.

"This time I want a *thank you*," he said.

Saxony wasn't quite sure what he meant, since she'd definitely thanked him for saving her life that *one* time, and it wasn't like she hadn't helped him out before.

Sure, she still owed him a life debt, but trust Wesley to be thinking of debts at a time like this.

Wesley raised his hands in a parallel of Saxony's and pushed.

Intuitcrafters didn't have force fields or control of the weather. They couldn't bind their enemies or command nature, but it seemed like Wesley didn't need to. He was a force of nature himself.

Not that Saxony would ever say something like that to his face.

As soon as Wesley thrust his arms out, the tornado winced, shuddering backward like it had been slapped. Saxony pushed forward with her own force field and with the weight of both of their magics working together, the beast began to truly tremble.

Saxony whipped her head over to Wesley and couldn't help but smile at him, maybe for the first time. There was something about this moment—about them combining their powers—that made her feel at peace, even with a Gods-damned tornado at their feet. Wesley's Crafter magic synced up to hers so easily that it made Saxony wonder if maybe, just maybe, the Many Gods had wanted them to be a team all along.

Wesley muttered something low and musical under his breath, and Saxony didn't realize it was a spell until the trees of the forest began to coo in response.

She had never seen them act that way before.

They rocked back and forth, over and over, until they created their own kind of power source—a wind tunnel that crashed against the tornado and sent it crouching to the ground.

Wesley's smile was like a weapon and Saxony couldn't take her eyes off of him, not least because Wesley was glowing. Not in a weird flowery way that made Saxony's bones shudder to consider—he was very literally glowing.

The staves that crisscrossed up Wesley's arms, in between the slits of his tattoos, were alight, and shining, silver swirls that looked like stars trailed up his dark skin and toward his neck, mingling with the lines of the city he had tattooed over himself.

The storm didn't stand a chance against them both.

The tornado wilted under their magic, Saxony's force field and the weight of power Wesley was funneling, the two of them like an oddly perfect magical duo.

Crafters were always best when casting as a team; that was why they made Kins, after all.

"We need to press just a little harder," Saxony said. "I can feel it dying."

"Way ahead of you."

Wesley thrust his hands out farther and thick black fire pooled from his fingertips, slowly at first, like shadows retreating from the dawn, but then it sprung to life and reached for the tornado.

It was like hands, burning and scratching and clawing.

Fire ready to devour the storm whole.

The base of the tornado turned to soot and the wind screamed, but the fire didn't cease. It flowed from Wesley's hands, such a pure and familiar black that Saxony almost lost her concentration.

She had seen fire like that before.

Just once, as a child.

The sight of it nearly brought her to her knees, seeing those flames in reality when she'd spent years only ever seeing them in her nightmares. Her heart thumped loudly and she tried to shut the memories out.

The last time she had seen her mother and her baby brother, before those flames swallowed them whole.

Saxony squeezed her fists together, her concentration on the tornado wavering. Though thankfully it didn't matter, because under the flames it had crumbled to dust.

The fire slithered quickly back to Wesley's fingers like an obedient servant.

"Where did you learn that?" Saxony asked him. "Who taught you that?"

Wesley only smirked back at her, blissfully unaware. "I don't know," he said. "Guess I'm just full of tricks."

Tavia stepped beside Wesley and let out a whistle to echo the one he had given her earlier. "Nice moves," she said. "Looks like you've got a taste for being the hero."

Wesley's smile was unrivaled. "It's pretty easy." He picked up her knife from the ground and handed it back to her. "We should do it more often."

Tavia twisted the knife in her hands, grinning like the world owed her one. "Nah," she said. "Sounds boring."

Saxony caught her breath back, shaking her head as the shock of seeing that fire again started to subside, only to be replaced with a new ache. Seeing Tavia and Wesley together like that reminded her of Karam. Of the other half of her, that was out there somewhere. Saxony had half-expected Karam to show up in the height of battle, frowning at how easily the rest of them were ambushed, before saving everyone.

But she hadn't.

Karam was still gone and there was no sign she'd be back anytime soon.

"You really did it," her amja said, marveling at the scene. "You both saved us."

Amja stared between Saxony and Wesley, like together they were a marvel, or an oddity, and then she scanned the staves up Wesley's arms—as though she were translating the language of magic that marked him—and smiled, warmer than any smile she'd given Saxony since they'd come back.

Around them the battle settled, and though Saxony didn't want to begin counting the bodies, it looked like they had won. They were diminished, but not defeated, and that was all that mattered.

The Kingpin had tried to stamp them out like ants, but he had failed.

They'd make sure he kept failing.

21

Saxony

WHILE EVERYONE ELSE WAS getting ready to leave the Uncharted Forest, Saxony was getting ready for something far more important.

The rest of the camp packed what they could, gathering supplies as they prepared to head to Wesley's safe house. He'd said that it belonged to the old underboss of Creije, who had ruled the city before Wesley took the reins. According to Wesley, he had a few scattered throughout Uskhanya, just in case. It seemed the last thing underbosses did was trust people, and so they were going to flee to the small estate, on the edge of the ivy towns, just big enough to house their army.

But before then, Saxony needed answers.

She needed the truth from the people she had never expected to lie to her in the first place.

"Saxony," Amja said. She placed a pair of boots into a bag. "Are you ready to go?"

"I need to talk to you first."

Her father shook his head. "Saxony, you must pack your things. The others are waiting. Wesley said—"

"Wesley is what I want to talk to you about."

Amja kept her eyes focused on the bag and slowly placed a vest inside. "Oh?"

Oh.

It was the smallest word, but it made the biggest difference. It said a thousand things and the one that stuck with Saxony most was that it said her amja had been lying to her about something.

"The magic that Wesley conjured to deal with the tornado was familiar," Saxony said. She squeezed her fists together to try to keep her voice steady. "I've seen it before."

They were the same flames that had killed her mother and her baby brother. The memory was like a shard of glass in her eye as it replayed over and over, the same nightmare Saxony had for years, only now she could see it when she was awake, too.

The black embers devouring her family. It had been over a decade since Saxony had seen that magic. In all of her years, she had never known anything like it again. Until now.

"I know you recognized it too," Saxony said. "I saw the way you looked at Wesley afterward."

Amja sat back onto the bed. "What are you asking us?"

"For the truth," Saxony said. "What happened to my mother and Malik? What is that magic?"

Saxony couldn't figure out the look on Amja's face, but at the very least she was looking at her, unlike her father, who stared at the ground and nothing else.

"You're keeping something from me," Saxony said. "And I won't just ignore it. I'm tired of lies and secrets."

Amja nodded.

Her father swallowed.

The silence that gathered around them was strange, and made Saxony almost want to turn and walk away from the conversation, since it clearly wasn't going to lead to anything good.

Nobody started a conversation with silence if it was going to be good.

What if Wesley was somehow connected to her family's death?

There would be no going back from that.

"Your mother was a Spiritcrafter," Bastian said. "And she suffered for it every day."

He took Saxony's hands in his and they were so large that she almost felt like a child again as he knelt in front of her.

"Like you, Vea was powerful," he said. "And sometimes the ghosts of the world were all too real. Their memories would haunt her and stay for weeks at a time. They were violent and desperate, and she couldn't shut them out. It wasn't a tap she could turn on and off, but a river that flowed endlessly into her mind. She could never drown out the noise of their sorrow."

Saxony's hands shook in her father's grip.

Weren't the living supposed to immortalize the dead in overly happy memories? When people were gone, they were supposed to be thought of as invincible and without flaws, as those who were left behind rewrote their histories wherever necessary. So every memory Saxony had of her mother was of a warrior, unfathomable in her grace and unbreakable in her spirit.

Try as she did to think back, Saxony couldn't recall a single moment of her mother's tears, or when her smile faltered and her hugs weren't warm and long.

Through the eyes of a child, Vea Akintola had been perfect, and even though Saxony couldn't have known otherwise—even though her mother had clearly hidden it from her for a reason, because it wasn't a child's responsibility to know such things—Saxony felt guilty for it.

"She'd disappear for weeks," Bastian said. "And once, when you were very young, she was gone for months. The forest gave people peace, but for her the quiet meant that the dead screamed louder. She always fled to cities, where the noise could overthrow them, and I also think her heart craved the adventure."

"She loved you very much," Amja said.

She looked to Bastian with a smile, warmer than Saxony had ever seen them share. They enjoyed antagonizing each other like it was a sport, but the tender way Amja looked at her father now told Saxony that she loved him as a son. That perhaps he wasn't her blood, but he was still her family.

"What happened?" Saxony asked.

Amja's sigh was deep. "Though Vea loved your father, his spirit was tied to the trees and hers to the wind. When she came back after those long months, she came back pregnant."

Saxony's lips parted, but she couldn't find the breath to gasp or the words to demand it was a lie.

"That baby was Malik," Amja said.

Saxony didn't know what to say to that, and though she thought that she should have been sad or even angry with her mother, the first thought that came to her mind was: *That's why Father doesn't like to hear Malik's name.* Not because his son died, but because he never had a son to begin with.

She knew it was a horrible thought, because as far she remembered, Bastian had always been kind to her brother. He'd always played with him and hugged him, and never liked to scold him even when he was being a little brat. Still, she couldn't help but think it.

"You know Malik was destined for greatness," Amja said. "He was supposed to be our Liege, but there was a darkness inside of him."

"A darkness," Saxony repeated. "He was just a baby."

"And we couldn't wait to see the man he would grow into," Amja said. "But then an Intuitcrafter saw in a vision that he would bring about war and death if he was raised by magic."

Saxony didn't think laughing was the appropriate reaction, but how else was she supposed to handle the sincerity with which her amja spoke? A vision, one in thousands, had scared her that much?

"It can't be worse than the war and death we're facing now," Saxony said. "It was just one Crafter's vision."

"I thought the same, until another saw it," Amja said. "Both of them saw that future and only that future. It wasn't just one in a hundred scenarios, Saxony. It was the only future they saw, in a hundred different ways. And so we made a choice."

Saxony shot up.

She wasn't prepared to hear this.

She wasn't ready to know what they had done.

And yet—

~ 221 ~

"Did you kill him?" she asked.

"Many Gods, no," Bastian said. "He was a child, Saxony."

"But we knew we had to do something," Amja said. "And so we decided to hide his powers and send him far away. We swore the two Intuitcrafters to secrecy and they carried it to their graves."

Saxony's breath didn't just catch, but disappeared altogether.

"You used death magic to hide him," she said in a whisper. "A blood spell."

The darkest of all Crafter magic was the kind that required a sacrifice.

It was outlawed among every Kin in the four realms. It could hide a Crafter's magic from everyone, including themselves, but performing something so ungodly came with a price: a curse over the entire Kin that would never end.

Saxony's mother hadn't just died in a fire. She had sacrificed her life to hide Malik from the world. Saxony thought back to that black flame, burning through the tree house. How her mother didn't try to run and she didn't scream; she just let it take her. Saxony always thought she'd remembered that part wrong, but she hadn't.

She thought about how that same black fire that had destroyed her family had poured from Wesley's fingers when they were attacked.

How the trees in this beloved forest had sung when Wesley appeared and rustled their leaves in joy whenever he made a joke, like they were laughing alongside him.

How his staves were such a bright silver against his dark skin, just like hers. Just like the rest of her Kin.

"Many Gods," Saxony said.

It couldn't be true. It just couldn't.

"Wesley?" she asked.

Amja and her father didn't need to nod for Saxony to know she was right.

That was how he was able to perform a spell at the consort's headquarters all those months ago in Creije. How he was able to take on Arjun, a Crafter who had trained his whole life, without breaking a sweat. How he'd nearly killed Ashwood.

Malik was a magical prodigy after all.

"I would have tried to find another way if I knew what Vea was planning," Bastian said. "But I think she knew it was the only choice."

"I don't understand," Saxony said. "You sent Malik—"

She paused.

She couldn't say Wesley's name.

"You sent him to *Creije*?"

"It wasn't a magical mecca then," Amja said. "It was just a dreamer's paradise, and the Intuitcrafters said that of all the futures they saw, the ones that had Malik in Creije felt the most hopeful. They said being there would grow his heart. We had allies there who we knew and trusted. The Liege of the Creijen Kin took him in."

The Liege.

The Creijen Kin was small, that's what Theodora had said when Saxony and Asees summoned her. *Their old Liege and his entire family were killed by buskers twelve years ago.*

Twelve years ago, when Wesley had become a busker.

The floor felt unstable beneath Saxony's feet, like it was

made from wet soil instead of wood and Saxony was preparing to sink into it.

"They promised to keep Malik safe from all magic to stop that future from coming true. They stopped practicing to protect him."

"And he became an underboss," Saxony said bitterly. "He grew up as an orphan on the streets, until Ashwood groomed him to be a killer. That's the future that gave him the most hope? Zekia and I could have had a brother! Being with us could have saved him because we would have *loved* him. You stole that."

"Zekia wouldn't—"

"You shouldn't even say her name," Saxony snapped at her amja, angrier than she had ever been in her life.

Amja blinked back the surprise of it.

"Because of you, Zekia grew up with the weight of a Kin on her shoulders," Saxony said. "You destroyed her future."

"We couldn't tell anyone the truth about Malik," Amja said. "We didn't know if the Kin would accept our choice."

"So you lied and let them thrust his destiny onto my little sister? Because of what you did, she was driven into Ashwood's arms, just like Wesley."

As soon as Saxony spoke the words, something in her mind clicked.

That was the reason that Zekia had been able to stumble into Wesley's mind and forge a connection in the first place. Not just because they shared the same specialty, but because they shared the same blood. And that was why Zekia and Ashwood hadn't been able to use the Loj elixir on Wesley while they held him captive.

A Crafter couldn't be swayed by their own magic.

My magic is your magic, my blood is your blood.

Zekia had told Saxony once that the only reason she was able to overcome the Loj was because they were sisters. Saxony shared Zekia's blood and so that made her immune to her sister's elixir.

Wesley was the same.

His sister, *their* sister, had no magical hold over him.

"You shouldn't have kept this from me," Saxony said. "I spent years by Wesley's side. I could have done something to prevent all the death Ashwood brought. If Malik, Zekia, and I were together, we could have stopped him as a team."

Amja went to grab her hand again, but Saxony stepped back, disgusted.

"You told me to kill him," she said.

She wanted to be sick.

"Back in Granka when we were first trying to recruit Asees, you told me that the underboss of Creije had to die, no matter what."

"Saxony—"

"You should feel ashamed of yourself, standing in place as Liege of this Kin," Saxony said. "You're not worthy of it."

Her amja hadn't just lied, but she'd cursed their entire Kin with dark magic.

That was the reason no children had been born to them since. It wasn't because they were waiting for their rightful Liege. It was because they had been damned by the magic and lies of Saxony's family.

"Everything that's happened is your fault," Saxony said.

She turned from them, but Amja stepped quickly in front of her, face desperate and frown deep enough to look like a wound.

"Where are you going?" she asked.

"I'm going to speak to my brother."

Amja grabbed hold of Saxony's shoulders. "You can't tell him yet," she said. "He isn't ready."

"I'm not going to turn my back on him like you did and I'm not going to lie to my family like you did."

"Please, listen to me," Amja begged.

"I'm done listening to the two of you."

Saxony snatched herself from Amja's grasp and ran from the room. She didn't care what they thought or what two Intuitcrafters thought. The future wasn't set and she had already wasted years that could have been spent by Malik's side.

Saxony might have lost her mother, but she could still save her sister *and* her brother.

She could still have her family.

22

Wesley

"YOU SAID YOU WANTED to talk, so talk," he told Saxony. "I've got to help Tavia and the buskers move the magic so we can get out of this place before Ashwood sends another ambush."

Saxony only stared at him, her eyes running up and down the length of Wesley's arms, taking in his staves and his scars and the way they blended into his tattoo of Creije almost too perfectly. Like those parts of him had always been intertwined. A city of wonder and a boy of magic.

"You might want to sit down," Saxony said.

"I'm fine standing."

Wesley didn't like the way she looked at him.

He didn't trust how worried her eyes were.

Saxony had never looked worried for him before.

"Are you going to try to kill me again?" Wesley asked. "Because I thought we'd moved past that stage of our relationship, and fighting for my life is going to make me super late for packing."

Saxony crossed her arms over her chest and frowned at him. "You make everything so difficult," she said. "Before, too, but especially now."

Wesley didn't know what had changed, but he knew he had a habit of pissing people off—especially Saxony—and so he just shrugged.

"I promised myself once that I'd do whatever it took to save the people I love," Saxony said. "I think now that means going against everything I thought was right."

"Are you talking about Karam?" Wesley asked.

It made sense that she'd be worried. It had been nearly a week since anyone had heard from his old bodyguard, and Wesley could only imagine what he'd be feeling if it were Tavia who was gone and him who was thinking the worst. Still, if Saxony was considering sending troops out to find Karam, then he needed to shut down that idea fast. They couldn't afford to lose any more people.

"You might want to send out a search party for her, but that's not the smart play."

"I wasn't talking about Karam," Saxony said. "She's a survivor and she'll find her way back to me. I know she will."

"Then Zekia?" Wesley asked. "If you're doubting whether we can get her back, I'm telling you that I can get through to her."

Whatever Zekia had done, it had been Wesley's fault. At least partly. And it didn't matter what the kid said to him, or even what she did to him, because Wesley knew what it was like to stand beside the Kingpin and feel infinite.

To feel like his way was the only way to not get swallowed by the shadows of the realm.

He could save her, like he should've done all those years ago.

He could fix that mistake and give Saxony her family back.

"I'm not just talking about Zekia," she said. "I'm talking about being honest with the people I care about. And that includes you."

The shock must have shown on Wesley's face, because Saxony's eyes went suddenly wide and her entire face wrinkled.

"Not like that," she said quickly. "That's disturbing. I meant like family."

Wesley found that thought equally disturbing.

"Just because we haven't killed each other, it hardly makes us family," he said.

Though really Wesley supposed that family, or friends, were the only people he didn't kill. And Saxony, however irritating she chose to be, was a part of that.

Saxony didn't say anything as she stepped a few paces closer to him, and it was only when they were near enough for Wesley to notice how many freckles she had that he took a sudden step back.

"What are you doing?" he asked.

Saxony's smile was sad.

"Being honest for once," she said. "Malik."

Malik.

Wesley had heard that name before. Somewhere, in the hollows of his mind, where only the darkest creatures lurked, it called to him.

Wesley took another step back.

"What did you just call me?"

"Malik," she said again.

Wesley didn't know why, but he winced.

"I thought my little brother was dead," Saxony told him. "But he's not. He's here."

She reached out for him, but Wesley jerked his shoulder back.

"I don't know what you're talking about."

But Saxony didn't stop.

"Years ago, my amja performed a spell, sacrificing our mother's life to send you away," she said. "They were worried about some prophecy and they punished you for it."

"Are you drunk?" he asked.

"I'm sorry," she said. "For everything. But it's going to be okay now."

It was a fool's promise to make, but something about the way her voice smoothed out on the words made Wesley shift. The room felt small. Smaller than the cells he'd been locked up in with Zekia's shadow demon.

"Malik," she said. "You're my b—"

Wesley didn't wait to hear what she had to say before he pushed past her and all but leaped from the room. He didn't stop until he was back out in the forest, taking in a gulping breath of the leafy winds.

But it didn't make a difference and that name still called out to him.

Malik.

Tavia was on the forest floor, legs folded, a dozen charms spread by her bare toes. She looked wild and beautiful in the moonlight and Wesley wanted to call to her but he couldn't find his voice.

He could only hear that name, over and over in his mind.

Unlocking something, awakening something that wanted to stay sleeping.

Malik.

Saxony yelled after him and when Wesley spun back to her suddenly, she was with her amja and her father.

"Wesley?" Tavia asked.

He could hear her footsteps behind him on the grass as she approached.

"What's going on?"

Wesley shook his head and held out a hand to stop her from coming closer.

"Don't be afraid of this," Saxony said.

Wesley felt fire at his fingertips.

"I'm never afraid," he said.

"Can someone explain to me what's going on?" Tavia asked.

"I've finally found Malik," Saxony said.

"Your *brother*?"

"I'm not her brother," Wesley snarled. "I have a family and they may not have loved me, but they were mine and they could still be out there."

"They're not," Saxony's amja said. "I promise you that they are gone."

Wesley couldn't stand the sound of the old woman's voice in that moment. He hated that one by one they were trying to unravel his past. It might not have been perfect, but it was *his*. His childhood, his memories, and they had no right to try to change them.

"The Thornton Walcotts were murdered twelve years ago,"

Saxony said. "Ashwood likes his buskers to be orphans."

"Bullshit," Wesley said. "He didn't know I had a family when he took me in."

"There's not much that beast doesn't know," Saxony's amja said. "And believe me when I tell you that the way your guardians were killed was nothing short of beastly."

Wesley never had much love for his family, because they'd never had much love for him, and he was a big proponent in giving as good as you got. He barely remembered their faces, but the thought of them being dead, and not just by the magic sickness or some rogue accident, but by very deliberate hands, made him feel dirty.

Like Wesley was just a pawn, an object, passed from their hands to Ashwood's.

"It's lies," Wesley said. "I would remember."

"We took your memories with your magic," Saxony's amja said. "Look at your scars, my dear one."

Wesley touched the skin under his cuff links. The burns he carried with him, hidden partly by the tattoos of his city and, now, his staves.

"They're from my father," he said.

"They're from your magic," Saxony said. "The fire you used to burn the tornado was the same fire I saw when our mother died."

"*Our* mother?" Wesley said, like the thought was a curse.

And it was, wasn't it?

What they were telling him was trying to erase all that he was. All he had worked to become.

"We could only quell your powers," Saxony's amja said. "Vea

sacrificed her life to try to get rid of it, but your magic fought so hard to stay that in the end we could only hide it and pray that you'd never find it again."

"Why would you do that?"

"There was a prophecy," Saxony said. "A prediction that you'd bring about a war if you had magic. They got scared and they got stupid."

"I'm trying to stop a war," Wesley said. "I'm trying to help people."

"I know that. That's why I'm telling you this. I trust you."

Wesley shook his head and stumbled back, right into Tavia. Her hands touched his shoulder, but for the first time ever the feel of her didn't calm him. It didn't erase the awful feeling in his heart.

"The Thornton Walcotts tried to keep you safe from magic," Saxony's amja said. "They feared your destiny just as we did."

The Thornton Walcotts had done a lot of things to Wesley, but keeping him safe wasn't one of them. He didn't remember much and what he did remember he always pretended to forget, living his life as though it had only started when he became a busker.

It wasn't a lie. The time before that hadn't been a life at all.

His father had seen to it that the only things Wesley had or knew were the ones he had turned rotten before handing over.

Wesley never felt safe in that house. Feeling safe was dangerous, his father had always said, and he'd branded those lessons into Wesley's mind and onto his body so that he'd never forget them. Saxony said his scars were from a fire and even if that were true, even if some of them weren't from his father, he remembered all the ones that were.

He'd been so desperate to leave that he'd gone to Ashwood willingly, rather than waiting to be recruited like all the other buskers. And when the magic sickness swept Creije, Wesley hadn't worried about the family he'd left behind.

He hadn't mourned for their deaths.

He'd been grateful for them.

He'd grown up as a prisoner and his guards had never afforded him any kind of love. In the most twisted way, Dante Ashwood became the loving father Wesley never had.

And now they were telling him that all of that, every hateful thing in Wesley's memories that he'd tried to scrape out, was because of some prophecy?

"Please."

Saxony held out her hand for his and Wesley realized that she was crying. He wasn't sure when she'd started, but she didn't look like she'd ever stop.

"Please," Saxony said again. "Let me help you."

Wesley didn't want her help.

He rarely accepted help from anyone, because that was a surefire way to show weakness, and weakness got people killed in this realm.

"If what you're saying is true and you all think I'm such a monster," Wesley said, "then maybe I should start acting like one."

"As opposed to before when you were a saint?" Tavia asked.

Wesley glared at her.

Though a part of him wanted nothing more than to take her hand and run away from this place.

"You're saying that my mother killed herself to keep me from the world," Wesley said.

That was how much of a bastard he was.

That was how much his mother had hated him.

"She should have done a better job."

Wesley's hands shook by his sides, not with anger or frustration, but with magic. It hummed through him, rattling his bones and rising up to the surface of his skin so that a layer of shadow clung to him like morning mist.

He couldn't control it.

He couldn't stop it.

"Vea was trying to keep you safe," Saxony's amja said.

Her eyes were on his hands and Wesley wanted to shove them behind his back and hide the fact that he wasn't in control. This was his *grandmother* and she was scared of him.

They all were.

"Vea loved you so much that she cursed our Kin," Saxony's amja said. "A child has not been born here since she performed that spell. Because of what we did and the magical laws we broke, the Many Gods may never bless us with another. Once you were gone, everything went wrong."

"I didn't go anywhere," Wesley said. "You threw me out."

Saxony's amja sighed and the first thing Wesley thought was that nobody had ever sighed at him like that before. Like they were simultaneously disappointed in him and in themselves.

"Visions are a tricky thing," she said. "They can even be self-fulfilling. Maybe we misunderstood it. Maybe we made a mistake, but we just wanted to protect you."

"Or maybe I'm a lost cause," Wesley said.

"Quit saying shit like that."

Tavia's face was stern as she stepped in front of him, and it was only then that the fire on Wesley's skin quelled. She was too close and his magic was screaming in desperation.

It scared him, and Wesley had never been truly scared before.

Tavia stood barely a breath away, her eyes locking onto his.

It was odd, that Wesley's family had feared him so much that even as a child they sent him away, that even now they looked at him with apprehension, and that Wesley himself had somehow come to fear what he was capable of.

But not Tavia.

She didn't look like she was afraid of anything.

He should have kissed her that day he came back, with the rain soaking them both and her eyes open with possibility. She'd wanted him to, he knew it, and he hadn't had the guts.

He hadn't felt like he was worthy of it.

"I abandoned Zekia," Wesley said. "Twice now."

Tavia didn't step away from him.

"I killed the old underboss to take his place. I did Ashwood's dirty work for years."

"I don't care about who you were or what you did," Tavia said. "I know who you are. And it doesn't matter if you're Saxony's family, because you were my family first."

She took Wesley's hands from behind his back and the shadows inside him retreated, fading into the air like they feared hurting her.

His magic calmed.

"I've already lost so much," Tavia said. "I couldn't take it if I lost you too."

Wesley blinked.

That was all it took.

Tavia was quick and he had forgotten just how much until her free hand went to her pocket and was suddenly in front of him, filled with magic dust.

Wesley blinked and she took that second to blow the dust in his face.

In a weird way, he felt proud that she'd gotten the upper hand—that the student had, in some way, become the master.

Tavia squeezed his hand tighter in hers and Wesley tried to pull away, because he knew he was about to keel over and he didn't want to take her down with him. Still, Tavia kept her hold strong and her eyes piercing.

"Just relax," she said.

Wesley did.

He closed his eyes and felt the night smile.

IT WAS dream dust Tavia had thrown. Wesley knew that much and he welcomed the thought of sleep. The waking world had become far more bizarre than the dream world could ever be.

When Wesley opened his eyes again, he was still in the Uncharted Forest, only Tavia and the others were gone and in their place there was a woman with firewood eyes and a smile to kill and soothe. She had Saxony's freckles and the same pointed jaw as Zekia, and wore a green dress that flowed behind her like a cape.

"You're finally home," the woman said.

Vea Akintola.

His mother.

Wesley had a mother.

"My boy," she said.

Wesley relished how different those words sounded in her voice. Ashwood loved to call him that when he was being his most terrible.

My boy, I will make you the world.

My boy, you have never doubted me before.

My boy, be very, very careful.

The words were possessive on his shadow lips, as though Wesley belonged to him. His favorite toy. His most treasured lapdog.

They were a claim.

But when Vea spoke them, with delicacy and a soft smile as warm as Creijen summer, Wesley felt newly cherished.

My boy.

A way of telling him that he wasn't alone anymore.

"Is this real?" Wesley asked.

Vea nodded.

"How can I be sure?"

"Spiritcrafters can connect with the dead," she said. "I was one, but I didn't handle it so well. You've got a hold on your power in a way I never did. Then again, you were born with staves, so I shouldn't be surprised that you're a quick learner."

"I'm not a Spiritcrafter. I'm an Intuitcrafter."

"Magic works in strange ways," Vea said. "Yes, every Crafter has a specialty. But sometimes, every so often, gifts are inherited. Sometimes, the rules get to be broken, just a little."

"Either that, or I'm high on dream dust," Wesley said.

Vea laughed and Wesley thought it was strange that he could miss a sound he'd never even heard until now.

"I think the Many Gods wanted us to talk," Vea said. "We're vessels for their will."

Wesley grimaced.

A vessel was just a fancy word for a pawn and he had quite enough of being the product of someone else's plans.

"I don't believe in the Many Gods," he said. "It's just a good curse word to throw around."

Vea shrugged, like she'd expected him to say that.

"You've grown so much since I last saw you. Are you happy with it?"

It was not the growing she meant, Wesley quickly realized, but who he had grown into. Wesley didn't want to reply, a little because he thought Vea already knew the answer. But also because Wesley wasn't sure whether or not *he* did.

Yes, Wesley was happy that he'd grown into someone who could protect himself, but that had only been possible because his family had abandoned him.

He was happy to have built himself a home, but now Ashwood had destroyed that.

He was happy to have shared a childhood alongside Tavia, but he didn't know what their future would be.

Besides, Wesley was less concerned about himself and more curious about Vea and whether or not she was happy with all he had become. He'd never wanted to impress anyone before, Tavia aside, but he felt the urge more strongly than ever now.

Did Vea fear him, like the others?

Was she angry at all he had done?

"Are your sisters well?" Vea asked.

His sisters.

Wesley had sisters.

Zekia. *Saxony*.

He thought for a moment about that and about what might have happened if they'd grown up together. Saxony was older and Wesley might've tried desperately to impress her, while she taught him magic tricks and ruffled his hair like he was some kind of welcome annoyance.

And Zekia.

Many Gods, then there was Zekia.

Would Wesley have looked out for his baby sister and teased her and chided her and fought anyone who hurt her?

He didn't have the chance to know, because that world didn't exist and in this one Wesley had sisters, but he had betrayed them instead of protecting them.

One hated him.

The other was driven to madness because of him.

"They're alive," Wesley said. "I don't know how they are. I've never asked."

"That's not very brotherly."

"You'll soon learn I'm not all that familial."

Vea's laugh was like a music box and Wesley wanted to bottle the sound and take it back with him to the real world for safekeeping. It was the saddest thing that Vea was dead and nobody would hear that laugh ever again.

"You've become a bit of a liar," she said, the smile still light on her lips. "Luckily you're still kind. Even if it's deep down."

She paused.

And then—

"Deep, *deep* down," she said.

Wesley scoffed a laugh.

Vea held out a hand and he walked forward, so that her palm pressed against his cheek, cupping his face. This close, Wesley could see his eyes in her eyes and his curiosity in her furrowed brows.

"Promise me one thing," Vea said. "Promise not to forget when you go back."

Wesley put his hand over hers. "I won't forget you."

"Not me," Vea said. "You."

It was a strange request.

"I know who I am," Wesley said.

Though he wasn't sure if that was true anymore. He wasn't sure if it had ever been true.

"Not who you are," Vea said. "Remember who you could be. Remember that only you get to decide such things. You made a home and somehow you also made a family. You are not the sum of your past. You are the decisions in your future."

She smiled at him one last time and then without warning the wind breezed by and she disappeared along with it.

Wesley sighed, closed his eyes, and let the world flood back.

23

Tavia

THERE WERE SOME MOMENTS that lived up to the dream of
what they could be and some that fell into the depths
of what they never were. Some moments were too weighted
and others too easily dismissed.

Tavia had always thought people took moments for
granted, even before they happened, trying to guess what
they were supposed to be and then discarding them when
they became something else. Moments that were fleeting
and moments that were stretched to the boundaries of
time.

The moment Wesley came back to the forest was one of
those and Tavia was too scared it would end in some kind
of strange hallucination to bother being disappointed that
she hadn't brought him back herself. She hadn't been the
one to save him from Ashwood and she hadn't been the one
to find him in the maze of the world.

Instead, Wesley had to seek her out, to save himself the way he'd always done.

Tavia hated that.

She wanted Wesley to be able to rely on her. She'd promised him, back when they visited the sins of their past, that they would conquer their demons together. And instead she'd left him to the wildest monsters the night held.

She wouldn't make that mistake again.

When Wesley's eyes closed, Tavia guided him as gently to the ground as she could. Though he was heavy and she was tired, she was impressed that she kept him steady enough so he didn't crack his head on the ground.

"What did you do to him?" Saxony asked.

"Dream dust," Tavia said. "I figured he needed a time-out. His magic looked like it was ready to get out of hand."

Saxony nodded, and together with Bastian they heaved Wesley inside and laid him down on a bed. Tavia wondered what he was dreaming about, but more than that she wondered what they were going to do when he woke up.

"So Wesley's your brother," she said.

Saxony burst into a laugh and put her head in her hands. "Yeah."

"Did Karam know?"

"*I* didn't even know until an hour ago."

Saxony glared over to Bastian and her amja, both of whom glared back, albeit sheepishly.

"You're not related to anyone else, are you?" Tavia asked. "I'm not your wacky second cousin or anything?"

Saxony's frown dissipated. "You wish."

Though Tavia really didn't, because now being related to Saxony meant being related to Wesley and that was just—

"Do you think he'll hate me when he wakes up?" Saxony asked.

"No more than before," Tavia said.

Saxony punched her not so lightly on the arm. "That's not comforting."

Tavia shrugged and sat down on the bed beside Wesley.

Saxony didn't follow, but leaned against a nearby wall and looked down at him with guarded eyes. Tavia wasn't sure if they were guarding against Wesley, or against anyone else who might try to come inside the room. Or even Saxony's amja and Bastian, who stood by the door like they were wary of stepping not only closer to Wesley but closer to Saxony.

I'm really not interested in your family drama, Wesley had said to Saxony all those months ago, when he'd first recruited her to help take Ashwood down and she'd asked for him to save her sister in return. It was ironic to think about that now.

Wesley stirred and Tavia inched her body a little closer to his, so that when he opened his eyes, he saw her before he saw the puzzle of a lost family.

He shifted a little and then his eyes fluttered open.

"Good dream?" Tavia asked.

Wesley frowned and looked around the room.

"It's weird to watch people sleep," he said.

"It's weird that you're related to my best friend," she countered.

Wesley shuffled upward. "Everyone needs to stop looking at me like I'm a time bomb."

"It's probably just a habit," Tavia said. "You're kind of a wildfire on the best of days."

"What did you dream about?" Saxony asked.

"My mother."

His mother.

Not Saxony's.

He didn't seem quite ready to put the two together and Tavia couldn't blame him. Mothers were complicated, especially when they weren't around anymore. She knew the pain of losing her parents, but the pain of never knowing them at all was different, and she couldn't imagine the confusion Wesley must have felt knowing those missing parts of his life couldn't be replaced.

"She said I was powerful enough to be in charge of my own future and that my magic was special."

"And yet I knocked you out," Tavia said. "Win for me."

Wesley shot her a look that told her he'd very much like it if she never brought that up again.

"How are you feeling?" Tavia asked.

"Fine."

"I sent you to sleep because you looked like you were about to lose control of your magic," she said. "Are you in control now?"

"Yes," he said.

"Promise?" Tavia held her palm out for a handshake.

Wesley didn't take it, but he nodded. "I promise."

Tavia eyed him with suspicion. "If I turn my back, you're not going to shoot my best friend?"

"Why, did you forget to take my gun away?"

She hadn't forgotten and Tavia knew that Wesley could surely already feel the cold absence of the bone gun against his hip.

"Can you forgive us?" Saxony's amja asked. "Can you still fight by our side in this war?"

Wesley looked like he wasn't too sure about the forgiveness part, but Tavia knew he'd never turn down a good fight.

"You're fighting by my side," Wesley said. "There's a difference. This was always my battle against Ashwood and for my city."

Typical Wesley. Tavia didn't doubt that if he had his cuff links, he would have been polishing them haughtily right now.

"You will come back to us because of her influence," Saxony's amja said.

She looked at Tavia.

"You are *sulfjgi*. Just as I suspected."

Tavia's eyes widened and she jumped up from the bed, as far from Wesley as she could.

"Hang on a second," she said. "Nobody is anybody's *soul mate*."

"You have the string of destiny between you. Magic and death, sorrow and joy, all of it perfectly aligned to bring you together. Creije was supposed to grow Malik's heart and because of you, it did."

Tavia looked over to Wesley with a snort. "I don't think so," she said. "I mean, for starters, his bow ties are woeful. He collects them and—"

"The girl who only owns black is questioning my fashion sense?" Wesley asked. "Now I know that I've hit rock bottom."

"I'll hit you with an actual rock if you don't shut up."

Tavia glared at him, but her focus shifted down to his lips and *damn it* if she didn't stop thinking about that almost-kiss, she might hit herself with a rock too.

"You should be proud, not scared," Saxony's amja said. "Everything, from Vea's death to your own mother's death, was part of a design to bring you together."

Now that pissed Tavia off.

She believed in a lot of things, but to suggest that her mother had died for Wesley's future, or for anything other than Ashwood's sick plan to perfect his mind magic, was an insult to her memory. And to make out like all the pain Tavia had gone through was for some guy to get his happy ending was an insult to all the hard graft she'd done to get to where she was and survive through everything she had.

She wasn't just a string in someone else's destiny.

If Saxony's amja thought for one second—

"Don't bring her mother into this," Wesley said. "The Many Gods didn't conspire to ruin Tavia's life just so I'd fall in love with her. Nothing is that simple."

Tavia's breath caught on the word *love*.

Wesley had never said that to her before.

Did he mean it, or was it just an example to poke fun at what Saxony's amja was saying? If he meant it, then why hadn't he kissed her back in the tree house when he promised to always protect her?

"Love is a choice," Saxony's amja said. "You're destined to simply impact. Two forces striking to create a wave of change."

"Well, this wave isn't going to have anyone else try to control her life," Tavia said. "Thanks, but no thanks."

"I think your Kin should have learned better about believing in destiny by now," Wesley said. "We need to stop basing everything on fate and start using our heads."

"I second that," Saxony said, with a bitter glare. "The last time you put stock in destiny you took my brother and my mother from me."

Her amja looked rightly chastened again.

"So what now?" Tavia asked.

"Now we get our fingers out of our asses and think of a real plan to take down Ashwood," Wesley said. "If we're together, then he doesn't stand a chance."

Those words were more of a comfort to Tavia than she had expected. So much had gone wrong, hearing Wesley's faith made her own come back.

Tavia smiled and let out a satisfied exhale. It felt like she had been holding her breath for so long, biding time and worrying about what to do and how to do it. She had a cause but not a direction, a mission but not a way to achieve it, but with Wesley here, every missing thing came back into focus.

Though Tavia wasn't sure if anyone would dare to call them heroes, when Wesley was by her side, she felt young and unending. She felt magic, not just in her pocket or in the air, but in her heart.

Family was strange that way. It had an uncanny knack for leveling out the world and bringing order to the chaos. Wesley was Saxony's family, but he was hers, too, and now they were going to take on the world.

She felt sorry for anyone who stood in their way.

24

Zekia

YOU HAVE TO TRUST ME, KID. You have to be brave.

Zekia looked into the mirror and smiled, hoping Wesley could see.

She hadn't thought he would ever speak to her again, let alone puncture her mind like this. But hearing his voice was a relief to her heart, and she was glad he hadn't abandoned her after all.

That he hadn't left her alone again.

I'm sorry, Wesley said, reading her mind like always. *I didn't want to go without you.*

"But you did anyway."

Don't be selfish with my company, he said. *You know I'm a very popular guy.*

Zekia snorted and scrunched her nose up at the mirror. She didn't think anyone could hate Wesley, but she'd bet a lot of people wanted to punch him.

Hey, he said. *I heard that.*

Zekia turned away from the mirror to hide her smile.

She had missed him so much—too much—and now that he'd been able to steal time to speak to her, she could finally share everything she had seen in that vision. In the beautiful future of what could happen if Wesley took power. And the wicked truth of the world if he didn't.

She had been so confused, all this time. She had been so lost, all this time.

But, finally, there was light ahead. A hope for a future that meant she could stop being so scared. That meant she could finally rest.

"How's Tavia?" Zekia asked him. "And my sister and my father and Amja?"

They're all fine, he said. *They're worried about you.*

"Did Amja make you that bone broth yet?" Zekia asked. "Isn't it so bad?"

Wesley stayed quiet for a moment. *We need to talk about the forest, kid.*

Zekia stepped away from the mirror completely.

She didn't want Wesley to see the look on her face now.

"I didn't tell him," she said. "I swear that I didn't. He made me promise that when the time was right that I would, but the time never felt right. And he said that he wouldn't go looking for them and that he'd give everyone the chance to join us by themselves. He *promised*."

I know, Wesley said.

Zekia's heart jumped.

"You believe me?"

I believe you. I'm willing to bet it was all down to that bastard Nolan.

"I had a vision," Zekia said.

She had to tell Wesley the truth. He'd know what to do. They could think of a new plan together, or find a way to tell Dante Ashwood that his world wasn't worth fighting for. If they chose peace instead, if Ashwood stopped fighting, then everything would be okay.

"I saw you kill him," Zekia said. "And the world went bright again."

Ashwood? Wesley asked. *Kid, I appreciate the faith, but there are a thousand futures out there and you can't tell which ones are solid. Trust me, I know better than anyone that we shouldn't be putting stock in visions.*

Zekia kept her eyes focused on her hands and tried not to fidget too much.

Wesley didn't understand. He hadn't seen it.

"This one was different," she said. "The shadows went away and the magic was everywhere and it was so pretty. Everyone felt so happy."

Zekia swiped the tears from her eyes.

"I don't know who to trust," she said. "And I can't trust myself, because before I saw a future where Ashwood was leader and things were good. And now I see the opposite and I don't know what to do. You know what to do, though, don't you? You always know."

The only thing I know is that people deserve a choice, Wesley said. *We can't decide their futures for them, based on a vision or anything else. You have to know that, kid. You have to* understand *that.*

Only, she didn't understand.

Zekia was supposed to be a Liege and Lieges had to make the hard choices and lead people. They had to decide what was best, even if nobody could see the wisdom of it. All Zekia wanted was for magic to be safe and not to destroy her brother's legacy by letting the Crafters down.

But she'd done all of that anyway.

I can only protect you if you let me, Wesley said. *But I can't save you from yourself.*

It wasn't herself that she needed saving from, though. It was everyone else.

It was the visions that snuck into Zekia's mind like a thief and stole everything that made sense and replaced it with fear and death.

She had been asleep ever since and she didn't know how to wake up again.

She didn't know if she even deserved to.

25

Karam

THE FOREST WAS DECIMATED.

The tree house that Saxony had kissed Karam good night in had fallen from its stoop and the tree that housed it—best at ferrying messages from one side of the camp to another—was burned to cinders.

There was barely anything left of the place Saxony and the Rishiyat Kin once called home. The Uncharted Forest was gutted and all that was left in its ashes were bodies. It looked like the Shores of the Dead that Karam and Arjun had left behind, desperate to find hope back in these woods.

"It's all gone," Arjun said. "The weapons and the magic. Do you think it was a raid? It must have been Ashwood and that bastard busker Nolan. They split us up so they could attack us when we were most vulnerable. Everyone is gone and we're all that's—"

"Check the bodies," Karam said. "Check who they are."

Check if they are anybody we care for, she thought.

She wouldn't consider the worst until she'd seen it for herself.

So they thumbed through the dead and with each body Karam turned over, or those whose faces were bloody enough that she had to go by their clothing to see whether they were busker or Crafter, she prayed that she wouldn't see anybody she loved.

There were some Rishiyat Crafters and a few of the buskers Karam recognized from their camp, but she couldn't find Saxony, or Tavia, or anyone in Saxony's family. She couldn't see her friends and when Karam sat on a charred log that looked like it had been part of a building once, she let out a long exhale.

They were alive, somewhere out there.

She shouldn't have wanted to smile, surrounded by so many bodies—so many of someone else's loved ones who didn't make it—but Karam had already lost so much that she thought she was owed this small spark of hope.

"What do we do now?" Arjun asked. "We came all this way and they're gone."

"Saxony wouldn't have fled this place without me," Karam said, certain. "She would have left a sign somewhere to hint at where they were going."

"Signs can be read by anyone," Arjun argued, unconvinced. "They wouldn't have risked that."

"Then it would have to be something only I know," Karam said. "A thing only I would be able to follow."

"Karam—"

"Stop it," she said. "We're not losing anyone else."

Arjun pressed his lips together and nodded.

Asees was gone and six of Arjun's friends had died with her. Karam and Arjun had been too late to save them, but they weren't too late to save the others. Whatever had happened here, their army had survived, and that meant there was a chance of redemption for Karam.

She could still live up to the legacy of the Rekhi d'Rihsni her family had formed to save magic.

She could still help them win this war.

She could still save Tavia from that awful future she had seen.

Nobody else Karam loved was going to die.

"Think," Karam said to Arjun. "What would only we see? What here would mean something to only us?"

Arjun picked up a piece of ashen wood. "Maybe they wanted to leave something and didn't have the chance," he said. "If they had to run from this attack, then they couldn't have stayed around to leave signs and clues. There wasn't time."

"Saxony would have found a way," Karam said.

If there was one thing in this world she still had faith in, then it was Saxony; it was the woman she loved and her inability to give up on somebody she cared about. Saxony wouldn't have abandoned Karam, any more than Karam would have fled this forest without her, or a way for them to find each other again.

Love didn't bow to time and neither did Saxony.

"You're glowing," Arjun said.

Karam wrinkled her nose. "What did you just say to me?"

"You're glowing," he said again.

Her nose stayed wrinkled. "I told you to think, not to be weird."

"No," Arjun said, sighing. "I mean you're really glowing."

He stretched out his arm and took Karam's hand in his,

holding it up to her face for her to see. The ring that Saxony had given her was alight. The green eyes of the serpent whose body coiled around her fingers and all the way up to her pulse were indeed glowing, just like Arjun had said.

"What is that?" he asked.

Karam didn't know what it was, but she felt a comfort when she looked into its eyes. It made her feel inexplicably warm, as though there was a voice somewhere inside of it, familiar but not enough so that she could put her finger on it, telling Karam it would all be okay.

"Saxony gave it to me before we left," she said.

"It's a strange present," Arjun said, examining the snake. "Whatever happened to flowers?"

Karam didn't reply; she just kept staring at the serpent, wondering what it was trying to tell her with those fire eyes. She didn't have to wonder for long, because once Karam had blocked out Arjun and kept her focus on the creature curled around her finger, the snake began to whisper to her.

This way, it said. *Out of the forest and into the ivy.*

"Do you hear that?" Karam asked.

Arjun frowned. "What am I supposed to hear?"

This way, the snake said again. *She is waiting.*

Karam turned around, just in case the voice was coming from somewhere else, but the moment she did, the snake's eyes fell dark.

"It stopped glowing," Arjun said.

She looked back at him. The eyes of the creature lit up again.

Arjun stepped back. "What *is* it?" he asked. "It's looking straight at me."

"No," Karam said. "Not at you."

She stretched out her arm and walked forward, past Arjun and farther into the clearing. All the while, the snake's eyes grew brighter.

"I think it's a compass of sorts," Karam said. "It's going to lead us out of the forest."

"To where?" Arjun asked, following behind her.

Karam didn't know where to, but she knew *who* to. Saxony could have given her a weapon of some sort, a protection charm to keep with her or something to curse any enemies Karam came across. But she hadn't done any of that. Instead, Saxony had given her this ring, and it had to be for a reason.

It'll help you find your way home, Saxony had said. *Back to me.*

Karam's smile grew.

The ring wasn't just a compass; it was a map, it was a beacon, it was a way for them to finally find what they were looking for.

"Where is it going to take us?" Arjun asked.

"To Saxony," she said.

And that was all she needed to know.

26

Saxony

THE IVY TOWNS WERE BEAUTIFUL and sweeping, with vines dripping from the walls among the fresh lavender buds and dahlia spheres that inked the rooftops like a second shield. The ground was as green as any of the trees in the forest, and though there was something so wild and untethered about this part of the city—where the rich and the righteous resided—it was also refined in its curved architecture and broad streets.

Saxony felt somewhat out of place, hidden among the swells of the city as a soldier readying for war. She longed for the scent of the forest and the echo of its trees, but they couldn't go back there. Not now that it had been compromised.

"This place is so different from the forest," Amja said, like she had read Saxony's mind. "I miss the whispers of the trees already."

"It doesn't matter what any of us miss," Saxony said. "The forest is gone."

She hadn't meant to sound so harsh, but Saxony couldn't seem to keep the edge out of her voice when she spoke to her amja.

"It's my fault," Tavia said. "If I hadn't let Nolan escape, none of this would have happened."

"I thought you were supposed to apologize when you did kill someone, not when you didn't," Wesley said.

"Funny," Tavia said, but she was looking at Saxony.

Her eyes were almost pleading with Saxony's for forgiveness, as if there was anything to forgive. Tavia wasn't to blame for the Uncharted Forest. It wasn't her job to take responsibility for everything that went wrong in the world.

"It might not have been him," Saxony said.

She didn't want to think it, but how could she not? Dante Ashwood knew about the Uncharted Forest and with Zekia by his side, she'd be a fool not to consider that her sister might have told him. Though Tavia seemed sure it was Nolan, Saxony couldn't quell the doubts in her mind. Her Kin had been hiding there for decades without suspicion and yet their attackers knew the weakest parts of their defenses.

Zekia had betrayed her so many times now. Saxony couldn't trust that she hadn't done it again.

It made her wonder whether her sister was truly lost.

"It wasn't Zekia," Wesley said.

"How could you possibly know that?" Saxony asked.

"Because she told me."

"She told you," Saxony repeated.

Wesley looked reluctant to say more, as if admitting any kind of connection between him and Zekia would be acknowledging the connection that he and Saxony now shared.

"Think of it as using her own tricks against her," he said.

"Mind magic is a two-way street and once a lock's been broken, it's not hard to walk through the door."

If Wesley was suggesting what Saxony thought he was, then that seemed dangerous. He'd only known about his powers for a few weeks, whereas Zekia had been learning to craft since she was a child. If Wesley wanted to try to invade her mind from here, it would take work, and Saxony worried about just how much.

She looked at him, into those black eyes that still unsettled her. It happened sometimes with magic poisoning, or when Intuitcrafters spent too long inside a person's mind, which was a roundabout way of saying that Zekia had drained all of the color from Wesley's eyes when she tortured him.

Saxony felt too much shame to know what to say.

She should have done more to stop Zekia from taking him. She should have tried harder to save him and worked with Tavia to bring him home.

But she hadn't. She'd left her brother to rot.

Saxony already owed Wesley her life and now she had yet another debt to him that she couldn't repay. Another mistake she couldn't take back.

"Mind magic is tricky," Saxony said. "You could hurt yourself."

Wesley looked insulted at the thought of himself not being invincible. "It's not tricky with her," he said. "I don't even need to try much when it comes to Zekia."

"Yes," Amja said. "Your connection is strong, both in your minds and in your blood."

Wesley shifted a little, probably because of the unblinking way Amja stared at him.

He adjusted his lapels.

"Point being, I can make her see sense. We just need to hold out."

And by hold out, he meant *hide out* in this safe house with a weakened army and little hope for more recruits. They had lost dozens in the fight, and now that the other underbosses had been killed, there would be no reinforcements from their buskers.

The Kingpin had seen to that. He'd slaughtered their soldiers before they'd even had time to recruit them.

"What we need now are ideas on how to deal with Ashwood," Wesley said. "Fenna Schulze has agreed to discuss an alliance. Now that Ashwood's forces are closing in on the government city, she welcomed my bat."

"So we need to have a plan to present to her," Tavia said.

Wesley nodded. "Any ideas on a way we could halt the spread of the Loj?"

"You should speak to my amja about that." Saxony folded her arms across her chest. "She's the one with all the plans."

Like the plans to have Saxony kill her own brother.

"And you're the one who enjoys doing whatever you like with no regard for my wisdom," Amja said.

"At least I'm not a liar."

"Well, not right *now*." Tavia leaned back against the wall with her eyebrows raised. "But your track record is a little shady."

Saxony turned to glare at her. "Says the girl who runs off to rob buskers by herself without consulting anyone and nearly gets herself killed."

"Yeah, well, you're the one who—"

"Enough!"

Wesley slammed his hands down on the table.

"We need to present a plan to the Doyen, and right now the only thing I have to show her is a bunch of people feeling sorry for themselves."

He rubbed his temples like they were giving him a headache.

Saxony had rarely felt so chastened, even by her amja, who made a sport out of guilting her.

"I just meant that my amja is the Liege," she said. "So you should speak to her."

"I'm speaking to you."

"My amja is—"

"Not you," Wesley finished.

He looked over to Saxony's amja, who was watching the whole affair with still eyes and a look on her face that Saxony rarely saw: curiosity. Interest.

As a child, Amja was the person who Saxony saw as most certain in her life, most unwavering and, if she was being honest, unwilling to compromise, but now her grandmother looked at Wesley like he might just stand a chance at being heard.

"I'm not trying to offend you," he said. "But Saxony has great power and she led the Crafters back when we first went against Ashwood. It's because of her that the other Lieges from Kins across the realms have joined with us. She can unite people in a way that I don't think you're capable of."

"You think I'm not capable of leading my people?" Amja asked.

"I think you're too scarred by the past to see the future clearly," Wesley said.

Amja blinked and her eyebrows furrowed together ever so slightly, and for some reason that made a sudden panic shoot through Saxony.

He'd offended her.

"Wesley," Saxony said.

It was one thing for her to insult her amja, but another thing entirely to hear someone else do it.

"You need to respect how things work," Saxony said. "You're way out of line."

"No." Amja's voice was soft as the breeze. "He isn't. He has wisdom."

"Wisdom," Saxony repeated.

"I can see what he has seen in you," Amja said. "I have seen your bravery and your determination, Saxony. And most of all, your ability to look past what others want and see what is needed for the realms."

"You just said you were angry that I went behind your back and summoned the other Lieges," Saxony said.

Amja shook her head and stepped toward Saxony, taking her hands in hers. "I'm not angry with you," she said. "I'm angry with myself for refusing to listen."

She stroked Saxony's cheek.

"My dear child," she said. "This is your path. Your judgment gave us an army of Crafters and Lieges who helped protect us in the forest. And your power, your fierceness, helped quell the tornado and the magic that tried to attack us."

Saxony's heart drummed fiercely against her chest, but she tried to stifle it, not daring to let her hopes get too high.

"Are you saying that you want me to be Liege?" Saxony asked.

She had to be certain.

She had to make sure she was hearing right.

Amja smiled, squeezing Saxony's hands. "I'm saying that you already are. You have been acting as one since you arrived in the forest and I have stupidly been getting in the way of that."

When Saxony breathed next, it was like all of the tension in her relaxed.

This felt *right*, like it had felt when she spun spells by Wesley's side to take down that tornado. Becoming Liege was Malik's destiny, and then they thought it was Zekia's, but maybe it was nobody's fate at all. Maybe it was something you had to earn, or something you discovered inside of yourself.

Maybe that was why their Kin had been cursed for so many years; they weren't waiting for Zekia to fulfil her destiny. They were waiting for the right person to decide their destiny for themselves.

And Saxony had decided a long time ago that this was what she wanted. She just hadn't expected everyone else to want it too.

THE WALLS of the garden trees cast shadows on the winter-dulled grass as they gathered their army in the large courtyard at the back of the estate. One hundred and fifty Crafters and nearly a hundred buskers all crowded around Saxony, Tavia, and Wesley.

They waited for the news.

It hadn't been Saxony's idea to round them up, but Wesley thought it would boost morale to let them know about her new position as Liege. *The Crafters already trust you*, he'd said. *And the buskers know you well, so it could help to unite them.*

"We've called you here to let you know about a change of leadership," Saxony said. "I'll be taking over as Liege of the Rishiyat Kin and will be in charge of overseeing all the Crafters in our army from now on."

She waited for anyone to protest, but the Crafters seemed pleased by the decision, most looking like it hadn't made much of an impact at all. As though Saxony was just confirming what they already knew and wanted.

"How does that affect us?" a busker called from the crowd. "Just another Crafter asserting her authority while we all get picked off one by one."

"Nobody is getting picked off," Saxony said.

"Says you!" he yelled. "The Crafters attacked us back in the forest and we lost some good people."

"Good people is a bit of a stretch," Lionus—the Liege from Gila who had attacked Tavia—said. "And let's not forget that there were buskers in that raid too. None of you can be trusted to stay loyal."

"Bite me," the busker said.

The crowd around him cheered.

Saxony could feel their anger growing.

"We've lost so much more than any of the Crafters," another busker chimed in. "Our underbosses were all slaughtered. If they're electing new leaders, then we should too."

"You've got to be kidding me," Tavia muttered.

But the buskers didn't look like they were backing down. They looked incensed.

"The other eight cities need leaders now more than ever," he said. "And we've got some real good men here who can take the reins."

"Did he just say *men*?" Tavia asked.

She looked at Saxony and Wesley in turn.

"I heard that, didn't I? He said *men*."

Saxony let out a sharp breath.

"No offense," the busker said. "But the Kingpin is conquering Uskhanya while a woman is in charge, so that clearly shows—"

"If he finishes that sentence, can I kill him?" Tavia asked.

"No," Saxony said, at the same time as Wesley said, "Sure."

"Look," Saxony said to them all. "In case you didn't notice, I'm a Crafter and your business exploits my people. So let's just focus on one problem at a time. The biggest one being, killing Ashwood."

"Walcott," another of the buskers said. "You're on our side, aren't you?"

"I'm on my side," Wesley said. "Which is the winning side."

"We need to be ready to fight the Crafters, not share a camp with them," the busker said. "Tavia, surely you see it? You haven't trusted Saxony from the start."

Saxony felt like she had been slapped upon hearing those words. Sure, she and Tavia hadn't been best pals these past few weeks, but that didn't erase years of having each other's backs.

Tavia's nose wrinkled. "Don't lump me into the same category as you. I might be a busker, but you and I aren't the same."

The busker scoffed. "You're cozying up to them because you're scared," he said. "Creije's best busker is a Crafter-lover now? After everything they've done to us?"

For the first time Saxony saw the bored expression lift from Wesley's face. His back straightened.

Tavia took in a deep breath, like she was trying hard not to reach for her own knives. "I think I missed that last part," she said. "Could you repeat it? Something about calling me a coward, which couldn't be true unless you had a death wish."

"Look," the busker said. "I just think—"

Wesley tutted loudly from beside Tavia.

"Who told you that you could think?" he said.

He righted his suit, sleeves pulled down and cuff links perfectly perpendicular.

Wesley did many things well, but looking like he was about to kill someone without getting a speck of blood on himself was up there with the best.

"We're not picking out underbosses and we're done turning on each other," Wesley said. "The Doyen will meet us here in a couple of days and if all goes well, then we'll have her forces from Uskhanya's armies to tag-team with. Their numbers, their weapons, our smarts and our magic. Once that happens, Ashwood is dead."

Saxony looked at Wesley, and he stiffened like he could sense her gaze and thought maybe it was judgment.

It wasn't. If anything, she was proud.

Wesley had changed from an underboss into a real leader.

"We're a team now," Saxony said, backing him up. "We need to stop thinking of ourselves as Crafters and buskers and start seeing ourselves as one force."

"I'll start braiding the friendship bracelets," Wesley said.

"Good," Saxony told him. "I like purple."

Wesley smirked in place of laughing.

This was the feeling she had been craving: the feeling of being a team again. Wesley had a way of uniting people, but it wasn't just that. Saxony had begun this mission to avenge her people and unite her family. With Wesley by her side, leading one army while she led another, Saxony was doing just that.

All that was missing was Karam. Saxony pushed down the pain that threatened to spill from her and out into the world. She tried to forget, for just a second, about the danger Karam and the others could be in, but it was getting harder every day.

"Does this make me the new future Kingpin?" Wesley asked. "Because the last time I went for that gig, I got kidnapped and tortured."

"You're not a Kingpin," Saxony said. "You're a true leader and you have a reputation they can trust."

"My reputation is built on the fact that people *can't* trust me."

"I trust you," Saxony told him.

Even Wesley, master of lies, couldn't hide the surprise from his face at the thought of that.

Thing was, it was never truly Wesley that Saxony didn't trust, but the thing that lived inside of him. The demon she knew clawed at his mind for control. There were two sides to Wesley Thornton Walcott, and Saxony's problem was that she never knew which side she was going to get. The uncertainty was what had always scared her, but times changed. Wesley wasn't just an underboss, he was her brother, and he had earned her trust so many times over.

"Did we miss the meeting?" someone called from behind her. Saxony's lips parted at the familiar lilt of those words.

She almost didn't want to turn around, in case she was wrong and her mind was playing tricks on her, but she couldn't help herself.

Please, Saxony thought. *Many Gods, let it be true.*

And when she finally turned, Saxony saw exactly what she'd wished for: Karam stood with Arjun by her side, alive.

"It was a little hard to find, but I do like the new house," Karam said.

"Karam!"

Saxony's heart almost broke free from her chest as she ran toward Karam. She didn't want to waste a second and she didn't care who was watching as she dove into her warrior's arms.

All that mattered was Karam.

All that mattered was that she was finally back.

27

Karam

SAXONY STOOD LIKE SUNSHINE on top of a snow-coated mountain, her mouth parted perfectly in the shape of Karam's name. The surprise on her face was like an explosion. Sudden and disarming. Saxony ran toward her and the force of her hug when they connected felt like a train.

"You're alive!" she said.

"Not for long if you keep squeezing me like this," Karam said.

Saxony dropped her arms to her sides, and then quickly raised them to Karam's cheeks and kissed her.

"I thought you died."

"She's got more lives than any of us," Tavia said, appearing by her side with a smile. "You know you're bleeding, right? You look like crap."

Karam had missed her eloquence, but she sacrificed a reply in favor of turning to glare at Wesley, who was inexplicably standing in front of her.

"You are supposed to be a prisoner."

"Sorry to disappoint you," he said. "But I didn't fancy being your damsel. I don't need to be saved."

"Your tune never changes does it, underboss?" Arjun asked. "You never need to be saved."

Wesley shrugged. "I'm a lone wolf," he said, and just about all of them turned to look at him with raised eyebrows.

"What happened in the forest?" Karam asked. "We came back and you were not there."

"Ashwood found our camp," Tavia said.

"Nolan?" Karam asked. "We were ambushed too."

"Divide and conquer," Wesley said. "It's not a bad plan. How did you find us?"

"With this."

Karam held up the ring and Saxony grinned.

"I knew you'd find your way back to me," she said.

"Magical compass aside, what happened on the beach?" Tavia asked. "Where are the others? Where's Asees?"

It was then that Karam became acutely aware that she'd been trying not to cry for days. That Arjun, standing like a warrior beside her, was taking slow and shaking breaths.

Saxony's eyes narrowed.

"Everyone else get back inside and give us some privacy," she called over her shoulder.

The rest of the army was still gathered around them with open ears and prying eyes. With a grumble, the strangers, those who were not *family* in the same way that the rest of them were, shuffled inside. Karam was thankful. She could not handle an audience at this moment.

Saxony looked between her and Arjun.

"What is it?" she asked.

"Our group was attacked by Ashwood's men as soon as we reached Tisvgen," Arjun said.

"I was being held there," Wesley said. "They moved me from Creije a couple of days before I escaped. There were hardly any Crafters there, though. Just me, Zekia, and maybe a handful of others."

"Which means that Nolan did tip Ashwood off," Karam said. "There were so many of them on the beach by the time we arrived. Too many."

She swallowed.

"Asees is dead," she said, so Arjun wouldn't have to.

Her voice was quiet, but not in an uncertain way. It was quiet in an angry, bitter way she hadn't felt since her pehta died. Quiet in the same way the skies were as they changed color into a silent black, while the storm and the lightning and the hail brewed inside.

She was quiet in the same way death often was.

"Everyone is dead."

Wesley's eyes flickered. "Because you came for me."

Karam pictured Asees's broken body, bloody on the beach, and tried to keep herself from crumbling at the pain.

"It was not because of you," Arjun said. "I know you think that the realms revolve around you, underboss. But this was the Kingpin, and I will not let you take Asees's death from his hands. Or her justice from mine."

Karam sucked in a breath.

Justice. She dismissed the notion. It was revenge they needed. *Blood.*

"I will take over as Liege of my Kin," Arjun said.

His voice was too small for his stature.

There would be only a handful of his people left.

"Of course," Saxony said. "I'm leading the Rishiyat Crafters now and will work with you to head up the magical army. I promise that we'll make Ashwood pay."

She placed a hand on Arjun's broad shoulder.

"Are either of you injured?" Saxony asked. "Karam?"

By the spirits, the way that girl said her name made everything in Karam shake. Feel weak and strong at the same time. She wanted nothing more than to kiss her. Between the not-dying and the rowing between cities, it had been far too many days of not kissing Saxony.

But it was taking all of her strength not to cry and so she stayed focused on that instead.

"Do you two need to be healed?" Saxony asked again.

"I am fine," Arjun said. He moved forward, hand on his sword. "And I am ready for battle."

"Whoa there, soldier."

Wesley pushed past Saxony and Tavia to place two firm hands on Arjun's chest to hold him back.

"The war is taking a break right now," Wesley said. "And so should you. I get wanting to smash everything, but you're not going to be much use to anyone unless you get some rest."

Arjun's jaw shook.

Don't cry, Karam thought selfishly. *I couldn't bear it if you cried again, Arjun.*

"I'll show you to a comfortable room and we can get you cleaned up," Wesley said.

Those words were such a surprise to Karam that when Arjun accepted with a curt nod and the two walked back inside the estate, she could only blink in surprise.

Perhaps what Arjun needed wasn't a friend who shared in his pain, but someone who could let him grieve alone.

"You need some rest too," Saxony said, holding on tightly to Karam's hand.

"Yeah," Tavia said. "I wasn't kidding when I said you looked like crap."

Karam tried for a laugh, but she was aching too much, both inside and out.

"Actually, I need a moment to speak to Tavia alone," Karam said.

"Tavia?" Saxony asked. "Really?"

"Yeah," Tavia said. "Me?"

Karam nodded. "It is important."

"Okay," Saxony said, though Karam could tell she was confused.

Karam wanted nothing more than to fall asleep in her arms and to tell her how much she had missed her, but Tavia needed to know about the vision Karam had seen first, and telling someone they were going to die required privacy.

"I'll help Wesley take care of Arjun," Saxony said. "We'll fill you in on everything that's happened later."

She kissed Karam's cheek softly and followed after the others, until Karam was left alone with a baffled Tavia.

"I have to tell you something," Karam said. "Arjun used an

extraction on one of our attackers and it showed us a vision."

She wasn't sure how to phrase the next part with any kind of tact. So she simply looked at Tavia and said, "Zekia is going to kill you."

Tavia took a moment to stare blankly and then swallowed and said, "Kill me? Are you sure?"

Karam nodded.

"When?"

She was taking it better than Karam had expected.

"I do not know," Karam said. "We were on a bridge somewhere. I think it might have been in Creije."

"What a homecoming," Tavia said.

She bit her lip, as though she didn't know what else to do.

"I am sorry," Karam said.

What else could she say? She could promise to keep Tavia safe, but those words would sound so hollow right now.

"Don't tell Wesley."

"What?"

"Don't tell him," Tavia said again. "He thinks he can get through to Zekia and if he finds out about this, then he'll stop trying. We can't let him do that."

"And he will lock you up in a room made of cushions," Karam agreed. "He will not let you go anywhere near Ashwood or Zekia."

"Exactly," Tavia said. "Which is why he can't know."

"Understood. But when Saxony finds out—"

"You can't tell her, either."

"I am not lying to Saxony," Karam said.

Tavia's eyes were firm. "Yes, you are," she said. "You know as

~ 275 ~

well as I do that she can never find out. That's why you asked to speak to me alone."

Karam couldn't deny the truth.

They didn't know how Wesley would react with Tavia's life on the line, and as much as Karam hated to admit it, Saxony couldn't be trusted when it came to her sister. She had a history of refusing to see the worst in Zekia, and if it came down to her sister's life or her friend's, Karam wasn't sure who Saxony would choose.

Saxony couldn't face the harsh truth that Zekia might not be worth saving.

It would be up to Karam to do what needed to be done, before Tavia's life was sacrificed. It was her job as one of the sole surviving descendants of the Rekhi d'Rihsni. Saving Crafters and the world had to be more important than saving just one person.

I will protect my friends, Karam thought. *No matter what.*

"Okay," Karam said. "We keep this between us and Arjun."

She clutched the pendant, tied tightly around her neck.

This was the way for her to redeem herself for the mission gone wrong. She would respect Tavia's wishes and do whatever it took to make sure that vision never came true.

Karam would not give their enemies any more chances.

If it came down to Tavia or Zekia, then she knew what she'd have to do.

And she wouldn't hesitate.

28

Tavia

TAVIA TWIRLED HER KNIFE and thought about death.

She'd lived each day knowing every one might be her last. That was the price that came with being a busker: pockets full of magic and uncertain futures. She thought she'd be prepared to die when the day came, but that was when it was a *maybe* or a *what-if* and not when it was a vision her friend had seen, clear as day.

Now that Tavia *knew* she was going to die, she wasn't ready. She didn't want to go.

She didn't want to leave Wesley when it seemed like they were finally on the cusp of being something.

"We have one day left until Schulze gets here. She is taking time out from defending Yejlath from being the next city to fall," Wesley said. "And I haven't heard a good idea yet."

Tavia licked her dry lips and tried to push the thought of dying from her mind. They had a war to win and if she was going down, then she'd make sure everyone she cared about was safe first.

"Who knew it wouldn't be easy coming up with a plan to defeat an army of mind-controlled killers?" she asked.

Wesley gave her the side-eye and rolled up his shirtsleeves. "In case you didn't notice, we have an army too. And it's not like we've ever actually been in a fair fight before."

Tavia shrugged in response, because she knew Wesley had a point but she never wanted to admit it when it happened.

If Arjun were here, he would have called Wesley out on never playing fair, but what Arjun needed now wasn't more strategy and planning. It was time to mourn before he was forced to face more death.

"Weird how all that's standing between Dante Ashwood and success are us misfits," Tavia said. "We're in for a ride."

She hadn't meant it to be comforting, but oddly, after she said it she felt a little more ease creep into her heart. After so long with so many people intercepting their makeshift crew, coming and going and living and dying, it felt almost nostalgic to have just the four of them in a room again. Plotting like old times, readying to finish the battle they had started together.

It took Tavia back to the train journey, when they had first fled Creije and headed for Karam's homeland of Granka. Just her, Wesley, Saxony, and Karam, interrupted rarely by odd buskers who'd count the hours for them, or look at Wesley like they wanted desperately for him to give them an order. Tell them how to piss properly or chew with their mouths closed. Just waiting for any kind of direction from a fearless leader they had learned to rely on. But despite those interruptions, it had still just been the four of them.

They had begun this journey together and now they would end it that way.

As a crew, except that they rarely agreed on anything.

As a team, except that they rarely trusted each other.

As a family, except that sometimes they hated each other.

Actually, Tavia supposed that made the family part even more accurate.

"Ashwood is in Yejlath because conquering the Halls of Government is a surefire way to cement his hold on the realm," Saxony said. "So Schulze will want to make that a priority before anything else."

"Ashwood will expect us to come at him in Yejlath," Wesley said.

Saxony turned to him. "You don't know that," she said. "You just want to be right all the time."

Wesley smirked. "Does that mean you're admitting that you're wrong all the time?"

Saxony threw her hands in the air and Tavia was half-surprised when fire didn't erupt from them and head straight for Wesley's face. She was showing a new restraint now that she knew Wesley was her blood. Saxony cared about him—she couldn't help it—and Tavia understood that. Wesley had a way of making you feel for him, against all odds, in the face of all the bad he might have done. There was just something magnetic about him that made you want to keep him by your side.

Tavia had been longing for some alone time with him ever

since he'd gotten back, so they could talk about the moment in the tree house when he had wiped the rain from her lips and looked at her like she was the only person he saw.

But war had a funny habit of getting in the way.

"Whatever we do, we need to have a way to take down the Loj-crazed army," Tavia said.

"Zekia is still our best bet," Wesley said.

Zekia. Wesley wouldn't have had such blind faith in her if he knew what Tavia knew, or if he had seen the future Karam had seen.

Still Tavia nodded. "If she comes to our side, do you think she can cure everyone of the Loj and put an end to this?"

"I hate to break it to you," Saxony said, "but she can't just whip up a cure in the heat of battle and disperse it to the thousands Ashwood has enthralled."

"And what if she does not join us?" Karam asked. "What if your sister cannot be saved?"

She emphasized *your sister*, as though she still couldn't quite believe Wesley was related to Saxony and Zekia. Tavia couldn't either, but the reminder that they were related made her think.

It almost gave her an idea.

"She's your *sister*," Tavia said, mirroring Karam's emphasis.

They all looked to Tavia and she felt her heart begin to race as the idea sprang up in her mind, so obvious, she couldn't believe none of them had considered it yet.

"Yes," Wesley said, shuffling a little uncomfortably. "I appreciate the update."

"She's your *family*."

"Yes," he said again. "You can stop now."

"You're her *Kin*."

"Are you on something?" Saxony asked her. "Did you break into a secret stash of Cloverye and not spread the love around?"

"You're her *blood*," Tavia said. "Both of you."

"I think you're right," Wesley said to Saxony. "She's definitely been at my stash."

"Shut up," Tavia said. "I'm onto something."

She paced the length of the room, her hand fiddling with a blade to keep her thoughts steady.

"You both have immunity from the Loj elixir because Zekia does." Tavia tapped the knife on her palm. "A Crafter can't be enthralled by their own magic. That's why Saxony was able to fight against it when she attacked me back in Creije."

"And then recover so quickly," Karam said.

"Exactly!" Tavia pointed the knife at her. "And why they couldn't use it to turn Wesley when they kept him captive. So if the immunity is in their blood, then couldn't the cure be in it too?"

"You think that we could create an antidote without Zekia," Wesley said. "With our own blood." He turned to Saxony. "Would that work?"

Saxony blew out a breath and leaned against the wall with a frown. "I'm not sure," she said. "It would mean creating an elixir of our own, infused with our blood. Nobody has ever tried something like that before."

"But theoretically, it's possible," Tavia said. "You could do it?"

Saxony shrugged. "Theoretically, we could do anything. We're Crafters. Miracles are kind of our thing."

"So we make our army immune by using your blood," Tavia said. "Stop Ashwood and Zekia from trying to turn our own people against us during the fight. And then when the battle is over, if Zekia still isn't on our side, we can use it to cure the others that aren't with Ashwood willingly."

"She'll be on our side," Wesley said, a little more sternly than Tavia had expected.

Tavia bit down on her lip, harder than needed. Wesley frowned.

"She tried to kill Saxony once before," Tavia said. "None of us are different."

She turned away from Wesley, before he could see the look on her face, but Karam was watching her too. Tavia cleared her throat and tried to focus anywhere but on Karam's hardened stare.

Zekia will try to kill me whether I make eye contact with Karam or not, Tavia thought.

Many Gods, she wanted more than anything to tell Wesley. Now more than ever she needed to hear him say that things would be okay, but revealing that possible future would mean him turning his back on his new family for her. Tavia knew what it meant to lose family, and she wouldn't be the reason that Wesley threw his away.

"So now we have an idea for a cure, we just need a way into Yejlath," Tavia said.

"That's the easy part," Wesley said. "Yejlath is a central city, so it's bordered on all sides."

"Meaning we could access it on foot through Tisvgen," Tavia said, with a slow nod. "Or—"

"Creije," Wesley said. "We go at it from Creije."

He had a look of determination in his eye that Tavia knew was never a good thing.

"I don't think that's the best idea," Saxony said. "Creije has been entirely conquered by Ashwood. It'll be heavily guarded. He won't want to lose that stronghold."

Wesley did not budge. "That's why we need to take it back. We can split our forces, so half go to Yejlath and the other half stay on in Creije to take the city back."

"But Creije will be full of Ashwood's soldiers."

Wesley looked overly irritated by Saxony's interruption. "Creije is our home," he said. "So we have an advantage that Ashwood and his army will never have. I know every street in that city like the back of my hand. Every turn and nook and where every shadow falls. I could navigate my way through Creije blindfolded, with a million enemy soldiers, and still never be caught."

Tavia didn't doubt it and she knew in her heart of hearts that she could do the same. Creije was home to them all, in some way. Tavia's family may not have come from there, but she was made in that city. She was shaped and she knew it just as well as it knew her.

"Okay," Saxony said. "There's still just one problem."

"Of course you have a problem," Wesley said.

Saxony turned to him, hands on her hips like a scolding parent. "*You* can get through Creije blindfolded. And, Many Gods, maybe the three of us could too. We could run through the shadows unseen. We could *become* shadows. But that's four people, not an army."

The three of them looked at each other in silence, their frowns a mirror, and the exasperation in the air like a wave of darkness dimming any light they saw in their plan.

Thankfully, Tavia wasn't so easily swayed.

"Time," she said. "We could use time to sneak everyone into the city."

"Like *bang*, one moment we're here and the next we're in the future, on Ashwood's doorstep?" Wesley asked.

Saxony shook her head. "Time doesn't work that way. You can't just skip over it like it's not there."

"But you can pause it." Tavia's smile was low. "Like we did with Wesley's explosive barrels back on Ashwood's hidden island."

Saxony's head whipped to face her and a wide grin spread across her lips.

Her grin mirrored Wesley's so alarmingly that Tavia almost blinked. Many Gods, the similarities between them were so blinding that she felt a little ashamed not to have noticed before. How the lines of their faces curved in the same way and their eyes narrowed in equally frightening measure and when they were both at their most dastardly, their smiles set fire to the skies.

"We can pause everyone but us," Saxony said. "Make our army immune just like we did before."

"Do you think Schulze will go for it?" Tavia asked. "It'll mean using Crafter magic, and we all know how much the Doyen hates that."

"She'll go for anything that keeps her in power," Wesley said.

Good priorities, Tavia thought.

She'd be happy when it was over so she could keep clear of any future political battles and the arrogant little bastards who wanted to argue over who got to rule the world.

"Then the four of us can easily sneak into Creije and head for the bridge that divides the city," Tavia said. "Detonate the time barrels from there, giving half our army the chance to cross into Yejlath unseen and the other half the upper hand when they attack Ashwood's forces in Creije."

"But we'd need something lighter than barrels," Wesley said. "It'd take at least a dozen to cover the length of the city, and that's too much for the four of us to carry."

"The Star Egg!" Tavia said.

She knew that bastard Nolan would come in handy somehow.

"It's a dispersion device. All we need to do is load a bunch of them up with the time magic, then set them off and watch them rain down on the entire city."

"Freezing Creije and giving our army the chance to walk through as the rest of the city is at a standstill," Wesley said.

Many Gods, Tavia enjoyed plotting alongside him like this.

She enjoyed a good fight every now and again—and this fight would definitely be good when she got to knock Dante Ashwood off of his pedestal—but talking tricks and planning alongside Wesley was always half the fun.

"Do you think the eggs can cover the whole city?" Karam asked.

Saxony nodded. "I can amp their range with a simple booster spell."

Tavia twirled her knife in her hand like it was a prize.

"Well then," she said, the blade glinting with her eyes. "It looks like we finally have a plan to present to the Doyen."

This battle had begun in Creije, on the streets that had forged them all in fire and moonlight. One way or another, they were going to end this war, and they would do it there.

Where it all started.

Home.

29

Wesley

THE ESTATE SAT ON a small hill at the edge of the ivy towns, with the Onnela Sea crashing against the rocks below. Wesley looked down at the water and thought back to that window in Tisvgen.

Before he'd jumped from it, the sea had beckoned him in, and when Wesley hit the water, it didn't hurt like he had expected. It didn't scrape his skin or cut into his heart. He'd melded into it, the waves rolling over him like warm hands, welcoming him in. In those moments he stayed under the surface, he felt like everything might just work out.

It had all been so clear. He'd had such clarity, as he got pulled farther down and felt the water in his lungs. Wesley knew that as soon as he broke the surface he would feel new again, and once he found Tavia the realms would steady themselves and he would go back to being Wesley Thornton Walcott.

Nobody's puppet and nobody's fool.

So why was everyone looking at him like he was crazy?

"That is the suit you are choosing to wear to meet a Doyen?" Arjun asked.

He sat at the rounded table with the others, only two seats empty: one for Wesley and one for Schulze. Arjun would be leading the ground forces that accompanied the Doyen to Yejlath, so he needed to be present for the meeting, but he didn't need to be criticizing Wesley's fashion sense.

"This is a nice suit," Wesley said, at which point Arjun snorted a laugh loud enough to sound like a sneeze.

Wesley wasn't quite sure what the problem was and why everyone seemed to have such an aversion to bow ties and purple velvet. He thought it was rather fitting, since purple meant royalty and meeting a Doyen was as close as anyone in the new world could get. Besides, it made far more of an impression than the large four-bladed sword that Arjun had strapped around his shoulder.

"The day I take fashion advice from you is the day I really do go insane," Wesley said.

"You are already insane, underboss."

"Says the man carrying his sword to a diplomatic meeting."

Arjun adjusted the strap that kept the blade close to his back. "It was a gift," he said.

And the unspoken words that hung on the end of that sentence were so clearly *from Asees*. Wesley could tell by the way Arjun hadn't let the sword out of his sight since he'd returned. The warrior had always been a bit too attached to the weapon, but even Wesley had noticed the extra care he took when sharpening or polishing the blade. How he wore it day and night, no matter the occasion.

This was grief, a kind Wesley had never experienced. A kind he hoped he'd never have to.

"Just try not to decapitate Schulze before she signs over her army to us," he said. "I think it would make a bad impression."

"You really think she'll go for an alliance?" Tavia asked, slouching back in her chair to kick her feet up on the table. "Your oh-so-charming bow tie aside, she's still meeting with a bunch of buskers and Crafters. Considering all of her anti-black-magic campaigning, I'd think the last thing she'd want to do is team up with people like us."

Wesley adjusted his bow tie. Played with the newly polished cuff links on his sleeves. He hadn't felt so anxious in a while, or so desperate to hide any doubts in his eyes.

"You'd be surprised what people agree to when their life is on the line," he said.

"Like meeting an underboss and a busker who she would've thrown in jail just a few months ago," Saxony said, with a pointed glance at Tavia.

"Or a group of Crafters, when Ashwood's army is littered with them," Tavia shot back.

Wesley wasn't in the mood for more of their sniping and he definitely wasn't in the mood to ask either of them about their problems. But Doyen Fenna Schulze had to see them as a united front, because trusting an underboss and his new Crafter friends was one thing, but trusting a fractured army who couldn't even seem to trust each other was even riskier. It was something only somebody very stupid would do.

And Schulze wasn't stupid.

"For the love of the Many Gods and my patience," Wesley

said, looking between Tavia and Saxony. "Would you two sort out your issues?"

"I don't have issues," Tavia said. "I'm just—"

"Pissed that Saxony tried to double-cross us back in Creije," Wesley finished. "I wasn't exactly happy about it at the time either, but she was trying to kill me, not you. And it wasn't her fault that Ashwood intercepted her *delg* bats or that Zekia took me captive."

Tavia started to argue, because that was what she was best at, but it was Saxony who spoke first.

"I never wanted any of that to happen," she said. "But I can't spend the rest of my life saying sorry."

"You're just as bad," Wesley told her. "You need to stop second-guessing every choice Tavia makes. You're a Liege now, but you're not a wise old warrior. You both have the same experience, especially when it comes to getting on my damn nerves. So kiss and make up already."

Wesley tugged on his lapels, trying to contain his frustration. He'd survived being tortured for weeks and he still forced his chin up. If he could pretend everything was okay, then the least everyone else could do was follow his example.

"I have been trying to fix them for a while now," Karam said. "But they both enjoy the sound of their own voices. I suppose they learned that from you."

Wesley touched his chest, affronted.

Tavia cast a glance at Saxony. "I'm not going to say Wesley is right, because I'd *never* say that. But I know that not everything that goes wrong is your fault," she said. "And I haven't exactly been the best company."

"You're a busker," Saxony said, with a playful smile. "You can't help but be annoying."

Tavia narrowed her eyes, but she didn't seem to be offended. Barbs and insults were a language she understood, the same as Wesley. Growing up on the streets of Creije, being vulnerable often got you killed. Being a bastard often saved your life. And so it was easier to joke than it was to bare your soul to someone.

It was easier to be hated than loved.

Wesley knew that better than anyone.

"Great," he said. "Now let's present a united front and try to convince Schulze that she can trust us."

Saxony folded her arms across her chest and reclined back in her chair, to signal how much of a pain in the ass she was about to be. "She should be convincing us to trust her, after all her government has done to fail Crafters."

"She's a politician," Tavia said. "They're basically crooks in their own right."

"So we'll have something in common, then," Wesley said. "That should help us join together to stop anyone else from being killed. We are all agreed that dying would be bad, right?"

It was supposed to be a joke, but the mood in the room turned even more somber and Karam stole a glance at Tavia that Wesley did not like. Especially since Tavia then looked pointedly away, in a direction that had no chance of meeting Karam's stare.

Wesley only liked secrets when he was the one uncovering them. And he especially hated secrets when it came to Tavia.

"Yeah," Tavia said. "Dying would suck."

She smiled at Wesley, in the lying way he'd taught her to

when they were kids and she needed to get one over on the old underboss.

"Thankfully we're all pretty good at cheating death," she said.

It was true, since every person in the room had survived when the odds were against them at least a handful of times. Karam and Arjun just a few days before. They might not have been great at a lot of things, but there was something to be said for a group of outcasts who refused to let life slip through their fingers.

There was a knock then and by the time Wesley turned, the double doors had been pushed open and a group of at least a dozen amityguards filled the room. They surrounded the small circle that Wesley and the others had made, their dark green uniforms pressed and cleared of even the smallest specks of dirt.

The faces of the men were freshly shaven, the women's hair pulled back into tight ponytails, and each of their belts with a single gun to the left and a host of magic in perfectly organized pouches across the rest of the loops. The Uskhanyan insignia was on their breast pockets and when Fenna Schulze entered the room, they pressed their palms flat against it—against their hearts—and dipped their heads in a show of fealty.

"Wesley Thornton Walcott," Schulze said. "Former underboss of Creije."

"Fenna Schulze," he said back. "Former Doyen of the realm."

Schulze didn't afford him a smile, but she did reach out her hand for Wesley to shake and he took it with slow and careful consideration. He was more than aware of the eyes of the amityguards, watching his every move for even a twitch of his fingers.

"I'm still the Doyen," Schulze said.

"For now. But we all know Ashwood has other plans."

Schulze sighed and took one of the two empty seats at the table. Wesley took the other, directly across from her.

Fenna Schulze had led Uskhanya to greatness since her election, working to secure better trade and clean up the streets of the realm from the darkest magics. She'd given rehabilitation to addicts and created banks where people could hand in illegal charms without fear of prosecution. She'd done a lot to help people feel safe from the underrealm again.

And she looked all the worse for it.

Not surprisingly, Schulze looked haggard and far more anxious than she did on the posters and graffiti drawn across the capital with slogans like *Schulze for a better realm*, scrawled by her angled jaw. Now, her short red hair was pushed haphazardly away from her face and her serpent-green eyes were lined with sleepless circles.

This woman was the leader of the realm, the elected Doyen, and she looked very much like she needed a drink.

Thankfully, Wesley already had a bottle of Cloverye in the center of the table.

"I assume it isn't poisoned," Schulze said, gesturing to the bottle.

"It's not," Wesley said.

He leaned over to grab the bottle and pushed it beside Schulze's empty glass.

"Of course," Schulze said, pouring out a drink for herself.

"Poison is too clean and you do like to make a mess of things."

Still, she looked at the bottle and then at Wesley expectantly, and it was only when he poured his own drink and took a sip that Schulze finally let her lips touch the glass.

"I appreciate you agreeing to meet us," Wesley said. "It's not every day that an underboss gets to see a Doyen in the flesh."

"Your bat was too interesting to turn down. Though do be warned that I have taken precautions for my safety and if I don't check in with my people every ten minutes, then they have permission to burn this estate to the ground," Schulze said. "You're surrounded with quick-fire charms."

Wesley hadn't expected any less.

"Then I guess I should talk fast," he said. "Starting with the fact that Ashwood is on a mission to rule Uskhanya in your place."

Schulze took another, much larger, sip of her drink. "And he's already taken my capital," she said. "And Tisvgen, where our dead can now no longer rest in peace. Now he is in my government city and I have had to be evacuated from my home. There's no way back into Yejlath and a bulk of my forces are trapped inside, trying to defend it from those monsters while I'm unable to help."

"That's why we're proposing an alliance," Wesley said. "So we can kill Ashwood together."

"Kill him," Schulze repeated. She slammed her glass down on the table, hard enough that Wesley was surprised when it didn't shatter. "Is that a joke?"

"Was it funny?"

Schulze eyed Wesley with as much suspicion as anyone had done. He was used to it. He'd built a reputation making sure that was the first thing people did: worried about what he was capable of and whether or not they could trust him with their lives. Fenna Schulze couldn't be blamed. Her entire career was built on the idea that Wesley and anyone like him was a danger to the realm.

She was the most prominent politician in a place where Wesley was one of the most prominent bad guys.

"My people are dying," Schulze said. "And you want me to join with Crafters and crooks. Can you understand why that would not be my first decision?"

Wesley could. Just like he thought Schulze should understand that joining with the woman who wanted to tear down his empire was not his preferred course of action. Unfortunately, none of them had the luxury of options anymore.

War stole a lot from people, but more than anything it stole their choices and their freedom to dictate their own fate.

"You don't need to be scared of us," Tavia said. "Only of what could happen if we don't learn to work together."

Schulze looked close to laughing. "Ah yes," she said. "Please, busker, tell me how the black magic you peddle to feed people's addictions isn't dangerous."

"Now hang on a minute," Saxony said.

"And you, Crafter." Schulze turned to her with a disbelieving sigh. "When so many of your people willingly slaughter mine by Dante Ashwood's side. Will you also preach about how trustworthy you are?"

This was not going well, but Wesley knew these were things that needed to be said if the air between them was ever going to be clear.

"Or you?" Schulze asked Karam. "Protector of the most dangerous man in Creije and fighter in the deadly underrealm rings. A killer for sport, aren't you?"

Karam's eyes did not flinch. "I am a descendant of the Rekhi d'Rihsni," she said. "My family were warriors and protectors of justice."

"They were protectors of magic," Schulze said.

"Magic is what fuels this world," Karam said. "You may hate dark magic, but light magic keeps your trains running and your waters clear and your amityguards armed to protect people."

"It also helps keep your reelection campaign relevant," Tavia said.

Schulze leaned back in her chair, so similarly to the way Tavia and Saxony were slouched that Wesley briefly remembered none of them were born politicians or underbosses with the weight of realms of their shoulders. They were all just people, trying to do what they thought was best. And maybe that was what Wesley needed to do in order to win Schulze's trust: remind her of what was best for the realm.

"Dante Ashwood took my city," Wesley said. "And now he's going to take your realm. I made a deal with your Vice Doyen to stop him and I'd like to follow through on that."

"Armin Krause was a great man," Schulze said. "He was smart and he was curious that your friend survived after being injected with the magic sickness. That curiosity got him killed."

"Magic sickness is a farce," Tavia said, her back straightening. "It was caused by Ashwood's experiments to create his Loj elixir. All of those people died for nothing."

Her voice was as sharp as her knives and Wesley knew she

was thinking about her mother, one of Ashwood's earliest experiments. Wesley may have left his family in search of another life, but Tavia didn't have a choice. Her mother was stolen from her. Her chance at a different kind of life was ripped away.

Ashwood thought of himself as a god, choosing who lived and died. Choosing whose life to ruin on a whim.

"We'll make sure nobody else dies because of that monster and his sick desires to destroy all the good in the world," Tavia said. "And we're willing to sacrifice our own lives to do it. Are you even willing to sacrifice your pride?"

Wesley frowned. He knew Tavia was in pain, they all were, but he didn't think predicting and planning their own deaths was going to help. There wasn't a plan, or any kind of future, where Tavia didn't make it out of this alive.

The thought wasn't something he would even entertain.

"Armin trusted Creije's notorious underboss and his best busker to get the job done," Schulze said. "Was he right? Can you really end this war?"

Wesley nodded. "With your help. If we're going to take Ashwood on, then we need everyone. Soldiers from your militia. Buskers from my streets. Crafters from across the realms. We've already ticked two of those boxes. The third rests on you."

Schulze tipped back her Cloverye and finished the glass in a large gulp, like she still couldn't quite believe she was in this moment, having this conversation. Or the fact that she knew there was no other way out of this war. Wesley saw the twitch on her face. She was desperate and he could work with desperate.

"We have around two hundred and fifty people," Wesley said.

"Ashwood has double that," Schulze said.

"But combined with your forces we outnumber him."

"Except that his forces are mostly Crafters. Do you have a plan to deal with them and save Yejlath from their magic?"

"Actually, we do," Wesley said. "I'll lead a small team into Creije, at which point we activate magic to freeze Ashwood's forces in the city, locking them in a moment of time. At that point, our army will head in. Half will go to Yejlath to defend the city from falling, led by you and Arjun over here." Wesley nodded at the sword-wielding Crafter. "The other half will stay in Creije, led by me, and start taking out Ashwood's incapacitated forces, regaining the capital."

"A double-pronged attack," Schulze said with interest. "We would come at Dante Ashwood from all sides?"

"Exactly," Wesley said. "He won't know what part to defend."

"But he still has the elixir," Schulze said. "Even if we defeat his forces once, he could make more."

"It seems my people are coming up with all the plans."

Wesley said it like it was real hard work and he took no pleasure in it at all. Only, he took great pleasure in his team being brilliant.

"We have a potential cure for the Loj," he said. "It'll protect our armies during battle and give the rest of the realms immunity in the future to stop this from ever happening again."

Even a politician as well-practiced in deception as Schulze couldn't hide her intrigue. Wesley and the others were offering her everything she needed to get her realm back and keep it.

The cure was still in the works, but Saxony was confident

she could perfect it in a couple of days, especially with an entire legion of Crafters at her side helping, and Wesley was sure that when they finished, it would be a success.

It had his blood, after all, and what could be stronger than that?

"I'm impressed with all that you've done," Schulze admitted. "It seems that Armin was right to align with you. And I don't say that lightly."

"Does that mean we have a deal?" Wesley asked.

He held out his hand for Schulze to take.

"I accept your alliance, underboss," she said. She shook his hand and the sunlight filtered stronger through the window. "When do we advance?"

For the first time since the Doyen had walked into the room, Wesley let out a long breath of relief and clasped his hands on the table.

They had an army.

They had a plan.

Now all they needed was Dante Ashwood's head on a platter.

30

Tavia

"THAT IS NOT HOW you play Clover Cards," Tavia said, throwing her hand down on the table.

"It's how *I* play," Wesley said.

"Yeah, well, you're an idiot. And a cheat."

Wesley scooped up Tavia's cards and shuffled them into the rest of the deck.

The estate was quiet with the night, but while the rest of their army slept and rested their bones, Tavia and Wesley sat in the gardens with the moon hovering like a streetlamp above them.

This was the last night they had before they headed into battle and she'd wanted them to spend it together, like old times.

The air was balmy but there were rare moments when the wind picked up speed and ruffled the playing cards like feathers, like the night was breathing out a sigh of relief that it didn't have to be alone. The darkness had Tavia and Wesley for company.

When Tavia won a hand, the wind clicked the nearby tree branches together in a steady clap.

When Wesley won, the trees themselves swayed so rhythmically that they created a low whistle, the leaves stirring in a rustled cheer.

Tavia didn't think it was fair for plants to play favorites, especially when Wesley was so clearly a cheat, but apparently the trees liked it most when he played dirty.

"Want another game, or are you tired of losing already?" Wesley asked.

Tavia shot him a rude gesture. "It's three all," she said. "That's not losing, that's a draw."

Wesley shrugged. "Whatever helps to stroke your ego."

Tavia glared at him and snatched the deck back. "I'll shuffle. That way you can't palm the cards or fix your hand."

"So little trust in me."

Wesley put a hand to his chest, like he was entirely offended.

"Never trust an underboss," Tavia said, dealing him his hand. "The only thing they're good for is screwing people over."

Wesley nodded, like she had a point. "That's me," he said. The air shifted swiftly with his breath.

"Born a bastard. Destined to be a crook."

Tavia paused mid-deal.

She hated the way his voice changed so abruptly when he said that. She'd only meant it to be a joke, but the resigned smile Wesley gave, casual and accepting, like that was his past and his future and he had no escape, made her want to scream.

It was she who had no choice.

Karam had seen it. Arjun had seen it.

Tavia was going to die by the end of this war, and if that happened, she didn't want Wesley to spend the rest of his life feeling sorry for himself.

"Don't talk shit," Tavia said, laying the final card on the table.

Wesley quirked a brow. The moon pounded down, reflecting the unwavering black in his eyes that Tavia still couldn't get used to.

"Don't look so serious," he said.

"Don't be such an idiot, then," Tavia countered. "None of us were born crooks. Ashwood made bastards out of us all."

"Yet you turned out okay," Wesley said.

Tavia nearly laughed.

"I'm not okay."

She didn't realize how true those words were until she said them.

They'd come out like a reflex, something to say so Wesley didn't get the last word or convince himself he was the only awful person in the realms. But by the Many Gods, Tavia felt those words crawl across her skin like insects, biting down hard.

She wasn't okay.

She hadn't been okay for a long time.

Not since her mother died and not since Wesley had been taken from her.

And now, with the knowledge that his little sister was going to kill her. It was just another thing piling up on the unsteady walls she had built around herself, and with each new brick an old one crumbled.

Tavia had always said she didn't believe in fate or destiny. They were just excuses for people who didn't have the conviction to make their own choices. And yet here she was, with her life on the line, and she didn't know what she could do to stop it. She couldn't tell Wesley and take his focus from the war and to her own life, which she knew that he would in an instant.

She could only wait to die.

"I'm not okay," Tavia said again, picking up her cards and trying to keep her focus intently on them. "And maybe I'm not turned out yet."

"I hope that isn't true," Wesley said. "I hope this is who you are forever."

Tavia glanced back at him, and she wanted so badly in that moment to tell him everything, but the way Wesley looked at her, like she was so shiny and new, like there was a light in her that never dimmed, trapped the words in her throat.

He hadn't looked at her like that since that time in the tree house. At least not without turning away or making some kind of quip.

"I'm sorry that I couldn't save you from Ashwood," Tavia said. "I'm sorry you had to deal with all of that on your own."

Wesley painted an easy smile on his face. "Quit apologizing," he said. "It was just another day at the office."

Tavia threw down her cards and stood up from the table with a disbelieving sigh.

"Stop messing around," she said. "Can't you be serious for once? You could have died."

Wesley rolled his eyes, as though that was the most dramatic thing he had heard all day. "I don't die," he said.

It only made her angrier.

Wesley was stupid to believe that Ashwood's twisted obsession with him made him indispensable. He was reckless and arrogant enough that someday someone was going to kill him and he wouldn't even see it coming until the bullet landed between his eyes.

Wesley Thornton Walcott was not invincible.

He was just a boy.

"You're ruining this for me," Tavia said to him. "This is the last night we have before we head into battle and all you can do is be a cocky little git."

Wesley stood up and buttoned his suit jacket. "Are you done being mad at me?" he asked. "Or should I go to bed and let you be dramatic on your own?"

Many Gods, Tavia wanted to punch him in the face.

"You think this is dramatic?" she said. "You're the one who left me in the middle of a self-imploding island. One moment you were there and then suddenly you were just *gone*. You ran off with Zekia and I didn't know if you were dead or alive, or if you were ever coming back. That was dramatic."

"It wasn't my first choice of strategies," Wesley said. "And like I told you before, I don't die. Haven't you heard that demons have nine lives? Or is that cats?"

Tavia didn't hesitate to lean over and push him.

Hard.

Harder, even, than she had meant to.

Wesley stumbled back a few steps.

"*Hey*," he said, dusting off his suit jacket. "What's wrong with you?"

Tavia wasn't sure how to answer that. There were so many things wrong with the world, but he was the only thing that made sense—the only part of her life that seemed *right* anymore—and she was about to lose all of that.

Just as she was close to having everything she wanted—friends, a family, and Wesley—it was going to be stripped away from her.

"Stop making jokes and pretending like this is all a game," she said. "I'm scared. Don't you get that? I'm scared and I need you to tell me things are going to be okay."

When Wesley frowned, a dimple appeared in the center of his brow that Tavia found so unreasonably distracting that she had to look away.

He stepped closer to her, his breath heavy, like he could read every thought going through her mind. When he swallowed, Tavia felt the sound in her bones, and when he lifted his hand to her chin, so her eyes met his again, she felt like every part of her was suddenly primed to fracture.

You're going to die, she thought. *You're going to die without ever telling him how you feel.*

"What's wrong?" Wesley asked.

"You're an idiot," she said. "That's always what's wrong. You're an idiot and I need you to . . . I just *need* you."

Tavia tried to steady her shaking hands. Her shaking everything.

"I need you," she said again.

It only took a breath, a tiny space within the seconds, for Wesley to grab her with enough force to send them both hurtling back into a nearby tree trunk. Tavia took in a quick breath and then Wesley's lips were on hers, hands knotted in her hair, pulling her closer to him so that every inch of their bodies was touching.

Suddenly Tavia couldn't think about anything else.

Not the war or Ashwood or the realms hanging on the line.

Not the fact that she was going to die and this would be the first and last time she ever kissed Wesley.

Tavia couldn't focus on anything past the burning inside of her. Kissing Wesley helped put the fire out and then ignite it all over.

She ripped off his suit jacket and slid her hands across his chest, under the thin layer of his shirt. He was skinnier than she remembered and it broke something inside of her to think about why. The months of torture he'd endured alone and in the dark.

Wesley pulled away for a moment to push her hair from her eyes, revealing the high arc of her cheekbones. "Tavia, I—"

But she didn't listen. Couldn't listen.

She needed him. More than words. More than anything.

How had she gone her entire life without kissing him?

Tavia pulled Wesley's head back to hers, sucking on his bottom lip, and Wesley pressed harder against her. Tavia traced the lines of his stomach and Wesley made a beautiful, wretched sound in the back of his throat that reverberated through her.

He moved his hands lower, sliding her up against the bark of the tree. Tavia hitched her legs around his waist so their bodies curved into each other.

She pulled away, breathless, panting as Wesley trailed kisses along her collarbone. Tavia cupped one arm around the back of his neck, pulling the small locks of hair and twisting them between her fingers.

His teeth skimmed Tavia's neck and she knotted the collar of his shirt in her fist, before crashing her mouth back onto his.

She was hungry for him.

She felt like she had been hungry for years without ever admitting to it. But months apart, and then seeing him again, bruised and beaten but *alive*, had changed everything.

Tavia ran her teeth across Wesley's lip. He tasted like oranges and bonfire smoke. Bitter and sweet as his tongue glided over hers.

Every inch of her was exploding.

"Wait," Wesley said. "I have to tell you something first."

He was shaking.

Tavia opened her eyes to his, glassy and near black, fluttering in a blink with every breath. He looked at her like he was trying to hold something back and it was so, so close to being let out.

Tavia touched her lips to his again, delicate, trying to swallow the yearning that seeped into her veins.

She didn't know she could want someone so much, but if this was it—if this was her last chance to be with him—then Tavia was done holding back. She was done pretending.

Her legs were still wrapped around Wesley and she could feel every twitch of his bones and the thump of his heart against hers.

She pressed her hand to the back of his neck and Wesley's breath turned ragged.

"Gods." Wesley swallowed. "Tavia, just stop for one second."

It was like a plea.

Tavia broke away, untangling herself from him just as

suddenly as they had collided, a weight of disappointment inside her heart.

It wasn't enough.

There just wasn't enough time in the world anymore.

Her legs slid slowly down Wesley's body and when her feet met the ground, the world felt tilted and shaken.

She didn't think she could keep standing if Wesley's hands weren't pressed firmly against her shoulders, like he was trying so desperately to keep himself from her.

Tavia wished he wouldn't try so hard.

"What is it?" she asked.

Wesley pressed his forehead to hers, breath as uneven as the world felt. He kissed her again, but it was short and quick and it left Tavia's lips dry and aching.

"I've loved you since we were kids," he said.

When Tavia looked into his eyes this time, she saw color. Rimming the pools of black that had engulfed his irises was a small circle of brown. It was thin, and against the moonlight she had to squint to discern the colors, but it was there. The same brown as the tree bark.

"I love you," Wesley said again.

Tavia thought hearing those words would make her happy, but she only wanted to cry. She'd been waiting so long for him to say them and now that he had, it was too late.

She couldn't be with him anymore, no matter how desperately she wanted it.

"I love you too," she said.

Wesley smiled and bit by bit, piece by piece, she was coming undone.

"I just wanted us to say it," he said. "Just once, just in case."

"We're not going to die," Tavia told him. "Everything will be okay."

It was the worst lie she had ever told.

"Is that a promise?" Wesley asked, that old smile tugging at his lips.

Tavia tried not to break promises often. It seemed like a bad habit most buskers picked up and she prided herself on not being like most buskers. But promising Wesley they'd both make it out of this war in one piece, when she knew that her future was already sealed, felt like the only way to make sure he went ahead with his plans. To make sure he focused on Ashwood, instead of her. To make sure he didn't turn his back on his family.

He can't know, she thought.

Tavia held on to Wesley's hand. This was the boy who she'd survived the streets of Creije with. Who'd become her friend, when she had none, and her family, when she had none. Who meant so much more to her than anyone could.

Tavia looked into Wesley's eyes.

"I promise," she said. "It's all going to be okay."

Tavia kissed him again, slow and endless, a kiss wild with possibility. Like if she wished hard enough, the night would never end and the sun might never rise and they could just stay locked in that moment, and that promise, forever.

31

Wesley

TAVIA'S HAIR SPREAD ACROSS the pillow as she played with the mirror doll.

Wesley watched her.

He'd been unable to take his eyes off of her for the past few hours, but now that she had the mirror doll he definitely couldn't stop staring. They were his least favorite kind of magic and though Wesley dealt in many things that were deadly and devious, he found nothing quite as eerie as a puppet for somebody's life.

They varied from maker to maker, but the dolls were consistently dreadful. Made from buttons and badly stitched thread, or tree bark and twine, they began as a jigsaw person, barely formed and off-kilter, their black-spot eyes ready to change with the flick of a charm.

Only then did they become person-like, their form dislocating from the makeshift to the harrowing reality, tree bark turning to rotten skin and patches of hair growing from the twine, their button eyes hollowed out to mummified pits and jagged nails sprung from their new fingertips. Once blooded, they transformed into corpse-like versions of their victim.

For now, Tavia held a puppet.

Soon, she would hold a body.

Tavia stroked her hand over the doll's head tenderly, like it was some kind of a pet.

"You know, that's really creepy," Wesley said. "Why do you keep that thing by your bed?"

"Oh, relax." Tavia waved him off. "It's not like it's linked to anyone yet."

"I think that makes it worse."

An absent vessel, a body without a soul, a puppet without a master, waiting for Tavia to shape it into whoever she wanted.

Wesley didn't know what Crafter had thought up such a thing, but he was glad that whoever they were was long gone.

"Seriously, put that thing away," he said.

He reached over the covers to grab it from her, but Tavia jerked it away.

"Worried I'll slip some of your blood over its smile?" she asked.

Wesley scoffed, but the way she looked over at him, amused, unsteadied his heart.

Tavia nudged him with her elbow, grin dangerous, and Many Gods, it made Wesley want to kiss her again. Truthfully, he never wanted to stop kissing her now, or to get out of this bed, but that didn't seem like the best plan with death on their doorstep.

Or perhaps it was.

Perhaps, Wesley should test the theory, just in case.

"I wanted to talk to you about something," he said.

No, not talk.

Kiss.

Kiss first, and then ask if she still planned to run to Volo when the battle was over, like she'd always dreamed of. They hadn't had the chance to talk about it yet and Wesley didn't want to push his luck.

He hoped Tavia would help him rebuild Creije. He wanted them to stay in the city they had grown up in so they could continue growing there together. But just because things had changed between them, it didn't mean Tavia had changed her mind about what she wanted for her future.

"It's about what we're going to do after we kill Ashwood," Wesley said.

Tavia put down the mirror doll and turned to him. "Let's not talk about after," she said. "Let's just focus on now."

She reached over and curled her hand around the back of Wesley's neck, pulling him to her. His lips locked onto hers and with Tavia's free hand she squeezed his, like she was pressing some of her strength into him.

Wesley pulled the bedsheets backs over their heads and Tavia laughed loudly. Gods, he couldn't get enough of that laugh.

And then there was a knock and Wesley paused.

He pulled the sheets back down and looked to the door.

"Are you expecting company?" he asked.

Tavia shook her head. "You get it," she said, stretching. "I'm comfortable."

Wesley rolled his eyes and reluctantly pushed himself up from the bed, throwing on the suit trousers that were slung over the chair.

"Whoever it is, just kill them and come back to bed," Tavia called over to him.

Wesley smirked and opened the door, ready to do just that. Until he saw Saxony's amja standing on the other side.

Wesley cursed to himself.

That family had woeful timing.

"I'm not interrupting, am I?" she asked.

Yes, Wesley thought.

Out loud, he said, "No, it's fine."

"Can we talk? It's important."

Wesley cleared his throat, suddenly aware he wasn't wearing a shirt. "Sure." He crossed his arms over his chest. "Just give me a second."

He quickly closed the door and shot Tavia an apologetic look, but she was grinning.

"Did your amja just interrupt us for a quiet little talk with her grandson?" she asked. "Because that's hilarious. All we need now is for your sister to come in wanting to borrow a cup of sugar."

"I'm failing to see the humor in all of this," Wesley said, grabbing his shirt from the floor. "I won't be long, I promise."

"It's fine, go." Tavia stretched out farther amongst the covers, burying her face in the pillow. "I'll be glad for the space, if I'm being honest."

"Funny," Wesley said. "But don't get too used to it."

Tavia wiggled her eyebrows and Wesley wanted nothing

more than to jump back into bed with her. Unfortunately, family came with responsibilities.

He just wished those responsibilities ended after sundown.

Wesley turned back to open the door.

"Is everything okay?" he asked Saxony's amja.

His amja.

She was Wesley's too now, and he needed to at least try to get used to it.

Wesley shuffled out into the hallway and closed the door softly behind him.

"I'm sorry to disturb you," Amja said. "I'm sure you want to spend this night doing something other than speaking to me. It's just that we haven't had the chance to talk about everything that has happened."

"You didn't need to come and speak to me," Wesley said, clearing his throat to counteract the tense atmosphere. It was odd how unsettled he felt, being alone with this strange woman who shouldn't have been strange to him at all. "I'm not sure there's much for us to say."

"I disagree," Amja said. "I want you to know that I'm sorry for all I've done to wrong you, but I'm here for you now, Malik. As I always should have been."

Wesley couldn't help but wince at the use of his old name. It didn't feel like his—the life that Malik had before Creije didn't feel like his—and though the Uncharted Forest had carried a sense of home while Wesley was there, it still wasn't quite Creije enough for him.

Wesley knew who he was and who he wasn't.

And he wasn't Malik Akintola.

He had been once, a lifetime ago, but not now. Despite the fact that he could see that Saxony and Amja so desperately wanted him to return to that boy, Wesley knew it wasn't possible.

He could do a great many things, but not that.

There wasn't enough magic in him for that miracle.

"I will do my best to watch out for you," Amja said. "Like a real family would."

Wesley swallowed. He didn't know how to react to that.

Nobody had ever promised to watch out for him before.

"I've never much liked families," he said, leaning against the wall as indifferently as he could. "Bad experience and all."

"That's fair," Amja said. "I've not had the best experience with grandsons."

Wesley couldn't help but laugh at that.

"You mean that time you cursed your entire Kin to send your illegitimate grandchild across the realm to live with strangers?"

Amja let out a large sigh. "Yes. Though you could have said it with less of an attitude."

"Sorry," Wesley said, with a shrug. "I'm from Creije. Attitude is a requirement for survival."

"Tact, then."

"What's that?"

Amja shook her head, though there was the spirit of a smile on her stern mouth. "We need to speak about your future, Malik."

Wesley wished she would stop calling him that. He wished everyone would stop trying to mold him into who they wanted him to be, because he finally liked who he was.

"I already know my future," Wesley said.

It was behind that door and in the city they would travel to tomorrow.

"What about your destiny?" Amja asked. "You were supposed to be our Liege."

"Saxony is your Liege and she's earned it."

"And you should rule by her side once this war is all over," Amja said. "That's who you are."

Except it wasn't. So many people thought they knew Wesley, when he had been careful to spend a lifetime making sure the exact opposite was true.

"You might see me as a prodigy for your Kin," he said. "But when this is all over, I'm going to stay in Creije, because that's where I know I belong."

"Vea didn't intend for you to stay there forever," Amja said. "She sacrificed her life to keep you safe, hoping one day you'd return to us. You can't know what it's like to care for somebody that much. To a love person so much that you would give up the world for them."

But Wesley did know.

He'd known for a while.

"Does that busker girl mean more to you than your family?" Amja asked.

Wesley's jaw ticked.

"Watch yourself," he said. "Tavia *is* my family."

Amja sighed again. "Perhaps I'm selfish wanting to keep you after this is over," she said. "I just don't want to lose my grandson so soon after getting him back. My dream would be for you and your sisters to be by my side forever."

"I'll get Zekia back," Wesley said. "I swear it."

"And then you'll leave."

Wesley hated the softness in her voice. This woman who had lived through wars and led a Kin, and Wesley was somehow making her feel fragile.

"I'm sorry that I can't give you what you want," Wesley said. "But that's not what's important right now."

"Then what is?" Amja asked. "What do *you* want, Malik?"

Wesley ran his hand across his wrist, over his scars and up the lines of his tattoos, meeting the first of his staves. So many parts of his life now intertwined across his skin.

A past forgotten, a present lived, a future promised.

"What do you need?" Amja asked him.

Wesley's fingers traced over the stave and he breathed, like he was breathing in the magic.

"To win," he said.

Wesley would end the battle for Uskhanya and for Creije.

He would return home and fight like never before, with an army that loved him and an army that hated him.

He would win this war.

He could win back his home and have the life with Tavia that he'd always thought was out of reach. Nothing was going to stop him.

32

Zekia

DANTE ASHWOOD, LEADER OF USKHANYA'S magical nexus and capital city of Creije, was sipping Cloverye. He let Zekia have some, mostly because she was bored and he didn't seem much for conversation in the late hours of midmorning. Ashwood was like a moon flower, blooming best at night when the shadows and the darkened skies came out to play.

While he sipped his Cloverye and the glass disappeared beneath his cloudy lips, Zekia toyed with the core of an apple.

They brought her out in a rash whenever she ate them, but she liked the taste, and scratching away at her skin almost felt like she was scratching away all of the evil things inside of her, like the fruit was bringing the rotten parts to the surface and Zekia could scrub them into nothingness.

"There's still much to do," Dante Ashwood said. "So much left to conquer, even after Yejlath falls."

Zekia nibbled at the apple core.

"Your once Kin, for example," Ashwood said. "Your once family ran and escaped like the treacherous rats they are. They couldn't face us and our vision for this great realm."

Zekia put down the apple core and scratched at the rash on her hand.

"You said you wouldn't hurt them. You promised that we'd wait until I was ready. That busker Nolan—"

"Gave me what you couldn't, little warrior." Ashwood shook his head and placed his Cloverye in the center of the table. "You and Wesley are starting to disappoint me."

Zekia looked to the floor and kept scratching, but the more she did, the more a voice scratched at the back of her mind. As though Wesley, upon hearing his name through the winds of the world, had come to say his piece.

Zekia, he whispered.

His voice touched at the back of her mind, like he was tapping against a door.

Zekia opened her thoughts to him.

"Let me tell you a story," Ashwood said. "About a little boy who grew up on the streets of Creije, long before you were ever born."

He wiped a hand across the surface of the table, smudging the dust between his forefinger and thumb.

"He was raised by a doting mother, who only wanted what was best for him, but she was too poor and too sick to be of any real use. She couldn't take care of the boy or give him what he needed."

Ashwood circled the table, running a hand along the back of Zekia's chair. She stiffened in response.

Zekia, Wesley whispered again.

To Wesley, she said, *Hello! There you are! You didn't forget about me.* And smiled into the very corners of her mind.

"The little boy was fascinated by magic and one day he met a busker who promised him wonders," Ashwood said. "He begged the crooked fellow to give him something to help his mother. Then the busker pulled out a vial, bright as the sun, and told the boy it was the secret to happiness. And so the boy ran home as fast as he could and poured the elixir into his mother's soup and watched her drink it. He waited for the moment it would fix all of their problems."

Ashwood paused with a long sigh.

"The elixir did not fix anything," he said. "It only made the boy's mother sicker, until one day she died. The busker had called it happiness, but it was the destroyer of happiness."

Zekia had never heard this story before, but it echoed with familiarity. Ashwood had named her elixir the Loj because of *ljoisi uf hemga*—the light of happiness. She had never questioned why he'd chosen that name, but it made sense now.

Zekia had finally given him what nobody else had been able to.

It's not your fault, kid, Wesley said. *Don't listen to him. Listen to me. Listen to my voice.*

Zekia bit down on her lip.

"Before the boy's mother died, she told him a secret," Ashwood said. "She told him his father's name with her dying breath. Magnus Robertsson."

The old Realm Doyen. Zekia knew the name just as anyone in Uskhanya did.

"He knew he was my father and he didn't care. He turned his back on his family just like he turned his back on the realm. He tried to erase my destiny."

"But leaders aren't chosen by blood," Zekia said. "They're elected."

She knew the words were dangerous as soon as she spoke them, because good little warriors knew when to stay quiet.

Ashwood spun Zekia's chair around and slammed his palms on the armrests. When he leaned in, close enough that she could smell the ash on his breath, he said, "My story isn't finished yet."

It's okay, kid, Wesley said. *I'm going to get you out.*

There is no out, she whispered back. *There never was.*

Ashwood righted himself and adjusted his suit in a way Zekia had seen Wesley do so many times.

"After my mother died, I set out to find my father and confront him," he said. "I vowed to become a man he could never ignore. That's why I found that busker who gave me the elixir and killed him. Why I approached the then-underboss of Creije with his head as a trophy and earned my place in the ranks. Back then the underrealm was barely organized and poorly maintained, but I had vision. I saw the opportunity to be great and eventually I took charge of the magical trade and became the first ever Kingpin."

He looked to Zekia.

"When the War of Ages broke out across the realms and the Crafters revolted, my eyes were open to the way the world should be," Ashwood said. "But by then it was too late. Still, the Many Gods did grant me one favor. Can you guess what it was?"

He continued circling the table until he settled in front of Zekia again and placed a hand on her small shoulder.

"I met my father on the battlefield. I saw the Realm Doyen of Uskhanya, surrounded by death. It was a sign from the Many Gods that my path was true. And so I approached that man, under the light of a shadow moon, the magic of my Crafters embedded into me. I told him who I was. I watched his face change. And before he had the chance to speak, I gutted him."

Zekia's hand still itched from the apple, but she was too scared to move to scratch it.

"You see, leaders are *born* and family must sometimes be sacrificed for the greater good. You know that my vision for the realms will have Crafters take back the world from the weak. I will have magic be worshipped like the gift from the Many Gods that it is."

He placed a hand on Zekia's cheek and it was cold, cold, cold.

"I will keep our family safe, little warrior."

Your family is with me, Wesley said. *We're still in Rishiya and we haven't given up on you.*

I don't have a family, Zekia told him. *I don't have anything anymore.*

Yes, you do, he said. *You have me, kid.*

Wesley had never referred to Zekia as family before, no matter how hard she tried and how good she was. If something had happened in Rishiya to change that, then Zekia felt very sad that she had not been there for it. She felt a little left out that half of her—the old, with Amja and Saxony and their father—was mixing with the new. With Wesley. All without her.

"You still believe in our future, don't you?" Ashwood asked.

You never told me your name back when we first crawled into each other's minds, Wesley said. *I guess I never told you mine, either.*

Zekia frowned and then righted her brow quickly before Ashwood saw. She knew Wesley's name, just like everyone this side of Uskhanya did. Only, she also knew his favorite color and his worst nightmares. She knew him well enough that sometimes it seemed like he was a character in a story she had created, each line and curve of his mind a reflection of her own imagination.

Wesley Thornton Walcott, she said to him, uttering a name she knew so many people had whimpered right before their death.

"It's because of you that we were able to achieve so much," Ashwood said. "Because of you, I can take the realm that is rightfully mine and carve our new world from the blood of those who challenge me."

Zekia felt Wesley shake his head inside of her mind and the action jolted her enough that her own head threatened to sway.

Malik, he said. *My name is Malik Akintola.*

Zekia dug her hands into fists to keep from screaming.

Malik.

The digging wasn't an effective technique, because her hands started to shake so much, and then bleed from her nails, that she had to shove them quickly behind her back.

You need to listen to me, Wesley said. *I can only protect you if you let me, remember?*

Zekia swallowed.

Malik, she said. *MalikMalikMalikMalik.*

Her big brother wasn't gone and a part of her wasn't even

surprised. She had sensed it, maybe, all along, and perhaps that was where the desperate urge to please Wesley and make him a part of her new family had come from.

This was the boy whose destiny she had stolen. Whose future had been thrust upon her before she was even old enough to know his face.

"Little warrior," Ashwood said. "You still trust me, don't you?"

MalikMalikMalik.

"I trust you," Zekia said.

Ashwood smiled, but she wasn't speaking to him. She was speaking to her brother, whispering in her mind and watching over her even now. She was speaking to the boy who would make the world okay again, just like she had seen in that vision.

Malik would fix it all.

Malik would fix her.

"Good," Ashwood said. "Because I need you more than ever."

I have to ask you something, Wesley said. *I have to ask you to make a choice.*

Zekia hadn't made a real choice in a long time. She wasn't sure that she still knew how. Somewhere the realms had gone off-kilter and no matter how often she tried to steady them, or pull all the fragments together to create a new and level line, nothing was quite like before.

Zekia didn't trust her decisions or her thoughts, or even her magic.

"If it comes down to it and we can't bring Wesley to our side, then we'll need to kill him," Ashwood said. "He can't be a weapon for our enemies. You know that, don't you? You must be prepared to do what's needed."

Is that what you want? Wesley asked. *Or will you join us?*

I want it to be over, Zekia said. *Please, just let it be over.*

I can't promise that, Wesley said. *Not until you give me your answer.*

Zekia closed her eyes and pictured her brother's face.

She pictured her visions, side by side: the world she had seen that Wesley could bring, filled with so much light. And the world that Ashwood had shown her he could create, with Crafters no longer afraid.

Just a little blood and they had already spilled so much.

Wouldn't it be wasted to stop now?

Would that make all of those deaths mean nothing?

"Little warrior," Ashwood said. "Will you do this for me?"

Kid, her brother whispered. *Will you join us?*

33

Saxony

CREIJE WAS A CITY dulled by death.

What was once a dazzling dreamscape of colorful buildings and air sweet with the tang of magic had now been devastated by battle. It was not that the buildings had fallen, or that the streams of the floating railways didn't still curve in and out of the city like paintings, looking at once sharp as knives and delicate as spiderwebs.

On the surface, it was still the city Saxony remembered calling home, but she was well-practiced in seeing beyond the facade of things, and truth was, to anyone who had named Creije theirs and been witness to the undeniable spell of the city, it was barely an echo.

The street art was chipped and debris-covered, the trick dust once embedded into the cobblestone had faded to a bare glint, and the Steady Mountains that overlooked it all appeared newly ashen.

Even the moonlight, which usually shadowed the most winding of streets to hide the secrets of the city, and cast a bewildering glow on the most beautiful of crevices, kept itself unnervingly consistent: shining equally on each edge.

Gone were the tricks of light and the need for second takes.

This new moon allowed every part of Creije to be seen in the exact same way.

Saxony looked over to Wesley and Tavia, and though she saw the reflection of home in their eyes, she also saw how their breath hitched in unison and they kept themselves close to each other's side. Like they needed the familiarity of each other in the face of this scarring reality.

They had both noticed the difference in the city just as Saxony had, and they were equally as pained by it.

Perhaps more so.

Saxony had fallen in love with Creije over time, instead of at first glance like so many people did. Like she had done with Karam.

But Wesley was different.

She knew that he had fallen in love with Creije in a single moment. He talked about it often enough: how it was the blink of an eye and the click of a finger, forever tying him to the city and the ruin it held.

Quick as the death of innocence, she'd overheard him say to Tavia once.

"Where to now?" Saxony asked.

They were in the city outskirts, where only those who had lived in Creije forever—whose families had been born and died there—or those who had come for a dream and found desolation roamed.

Well, them and Tavia.

Tavia, who fled to the outskirts and as far from High Town and the busker dormitories as she could, to hold her morality close and keep Wesley at a distance. Neither of which had really worked, in Saxony's opinion.

Her old flat was just a few streets away and Saxony recalled the many times they had both stumbled back there, drunk as the fire-gates, and she'd spent the night dozing on Tavia's sofa and trying to drown out the sound of her snoring in the other room.

"Which way?" Saxony asked again.

She didn't ask because she didn't know, but because it seemed necessary to try to fill the mourning silence.

"The alley behind the amity precinct," Wesley finally said.

Saxony almost sighed in the relief his voice brought. He didn't sound broken, but then again, Wesley was an expert at hiding anything he didn't want people to see, especially when those things were as complicated as emotions.

"It's the closest shelter before we hit the bridge," Wesley said. He looked to Tavia.

"Got the little explosive eggs ready?"

She patted her backpack, which held six of Nolan's Star Eggs.

"Check," Tavia said. "Ready to go boom."

Saxony looked to Karam. "Got your fists ready?" she asked.

"Check," Karam said, with a narrow smile.

They swerved through the streets together, jumping from shadow to shadow like ghosts, moving between the various

Crafters and buskers, or even the Loj-infected. Tourists, once wide-eyed, who were now far more empty-eyed. Who had been forced into battle, or gotten trapped in the city during the fight and been found and forced to drink the Loj elixir. Their eyes like ash and their necks marked like cattle.

Saxony and the others navigated through them so easily that it made her realize how much she had not only grown to love Creije, but to know it.

Like the back of my hand, Wesley had said.

Like mine, too, she thought now.

Returning to Rishiya and the Uncharted Forest felt like returning home after so long in Creije, but now returning to Creije after so long in Rishiya, that felt like home too.

Another side of Saxony: the side that held on to her brother so tightly.

She pushed herself up against a wall, back to the brick, and walked step by step in the pieces of the path that the moonlight didn't quite touch.

Up ahead, there was music coming from the amity precinct.

A group of seven guards sat outside on old wooden chairs, clapping and laughing in low, cold tones. They had a music box on the ground by their feet, enchanted to play the kind of beat Saxony had only ever heard at the Crook when the drinks started to dry up and the sun was readying to rise.

"Look at him move," one of the amityguards said. "We've got ourselves quite a show, haven't we, lads?"

It was only then that Saxony noticed one of the seven guards was not a guard at all, but a man. A civilian. Dressed in what looked like nightwear, with long brown hair down to his shoulders and bruises swatched everywhere across his milky skin.

He was dancing madly, erratically. In a way that could only be charmed.

The guards clapped and cheered him on and the man, who sobbed and winced while he moved in beat with the music, kept going.

Saxony looked to his feet. Bare and bleeding.

She flinched and it was almost as though that action jolted the spell because the man suddenly collapsed onto the street.

Beside Saxony, Wesley let out a breath.

Straightened his cuff links.

Relaxed his tightened jaw.

He had broken the magic somehow. Cast a spell in the time it took for Saxony to blink and assess the situation. She hadn't even heard him utter the words or felt his power travel through the air.

Wesley's magic was like a ghost, roaming through the world undetected, seen only when it wanted to be. After so long lost, it had gotten quite good at hiding.

One of the guards jumped to his feet, knocking over the chair he had been lounging on so that it clattered to the ground. The noise would have once vanished in the musicality of Creije, but with the eerie silence that now blanketed the streets, it seemed as loud as a gunshot.

"Who said you could stop?" the guard spat.

The dancing man looked up at him from the ground, lips trembling. They were torturing him, in the middle of the night and the middle of the street. In full view of anyone who dared to look.

"What in the fire-gates do they think they're doing?" Saxony whispered.

"Having the time of their lives, apparently," Wesley said.

He studied the amityguards with a blank expression, no mirror of the outrage Saxony felt and no sign of pride at having saved the man. But Saxony could see his eyes narrow as he took in the scene, evaluating every moment and weighing up what he should do next.

"We have to stop them," Saxony said, making the choice for him. "Those guards are damn *rieshles*!"

"No," Tavia said. "They're not."

She had the same look as Wesley, a little placid as she watched the bleeding man beg for his life.

How could Tavia think that they weren't assholes?

They were going to drive that man to his death.

"Are you out of your mind?" Saxony asked. "Look at them."

"She means that they're not guards," Wesley said. "Look again."

Saxony did.

And then she cursed herself.

Tavia and Wesley were right.

It would take a certain kind of amityguard, who had fought against dark magic under Fenna Schulze, and worked to keep Creije as a thriving tourist hot spot safe from the underrealm scum, to then switch sides and work for the Kingpin. Saxony suspected that most of those who hadn't been killed had refused—and then been killed—and the only ones that remained were those who were already on the take.

The rest were replaced by more of Ashwood's people.

The six in front of her didn't even wear proper uniforms. They were the right color and the belts were filled with the right weapons and magic, but the Uskhanyan insignia had been torn from the breast pockets and the sleeves were bloodstained. Probably by the original guards whose uniforms they had repurposed.

There were no real amityguards anymore.

Just soldiers.

Just Crafters in uniform, or longtime victims of the Loj with the mark on their neck now as deep as a scar.

"Get up and dance!" the guard screamed down at the man.

Wesley cleared his throat, quiet enough that the guards didn't hear over the roar of their music. Loud enough that it told Saxony they weren't sticking around to find out how this ended.

"Come on," Wesley said. "We need to go."

"We're not going to save him?"

"First we save the city."

Saxony shook her head and turned to Tavia for backup, but her friend's face only held an apologetic grimace.

"This is Creije," Tavia said, in a small whisper. "People die all the time. We have bigger enemies to deal with and we can't risk getting caught. We're supposed to be invisible, remember?"

Saxony couldn't quite believe what she was hearing. She expected it from Wesley. After all, he'd had to survive as an underboss in Creije and that meant doing things nobody else wanted to, but Tavia had never left an innocent person behind to suffer. She hadn't even wanted to sell magic on the streets half of the time and she blamed herself whenever she did and somebody got hurt because of it.

Saxony looked over to Karam, in a last-ditch effort to rally some support, but before she had even fully turned to her, Saxony knew it was a lost cause. Karam was nothing if not practical in the face of battle.

"We cannot risk engaging them in case something goes wrong," Karam said. "They are distracted now. They will not see us cross the bridge. And with that music, they will not hear us until it is too late."

Saxony looked over her shoulder and back to the man. "But—"

"We save that man by saving my city," Wesley said. "Now come on."

He headed for the next side street, Tavia following him without hesitation. Karam shrugged, squeezed Saxony's hand, and then ran after them.

With an aching regret deep inside of her, Saxony did the same.

They made their way toward the bridge that separated the two halves of Creije. The outskirts from High Town. The amity precinct from the magic markets.

The bridge was a grand spectacle, pure white with swirling arches and engraved beams that dipped into the water. The suspension chains were a glacier blue that matched the Steady Mountains, and each of the grandiose towers it bore was roofed by the Uskhanyan flag. From a distance it looked a little like a monument.

"We need to float up to the top of the center tower and set

off the Star Eggs from there," Wesley said. "Smack bang in the middle of the city."

"To the top," Tavia said. She looked up at the central tower. "Of that thing?"

She swallowed, loudly, and it was then that Saxony remembered how scared of heights her friend was.

"Don't look so worried," Saxony said, slinging her arm over Tavia's shoulders. "If the magic flops and you fall to your doom, it'll be a quick death."

Tavia glared and shrugged her arm off, at which point Saxony laughed.

"Do we have enough hover charms for that?" Tavia asked.

Wesley snorted. "We don't need hover charms," he said. "You have two Crafters."

"I thought that Crafters could not fly," Karam said.

"We can't," Saxony said. "This is more of a dramatic hop."

"A hundred and fifty feet in the air?" Tavia asked, with wide eyes.

"Don't be ridiculous," Wesley said. "It's more like one twenty."

Tavia gave him the finger, but Wesley only rolled his suit sleeves up, unfazed.

"Hold on tight to your backpack," he said.

"Sure, because the explosives breaking would be so terrible for everyone." Tavia cast one last look up at the towers. "Never mind my neck."

Wesley consulted his wristwatch. "Your neck won't stop time and allow our army to get into the city unnoticed. Let's go."

He held out his hand for Tavia's and she took it quicker than Saxony expected. She wasn't sure when they'd climbed the invisible barrier that had been keeping them apart for years, caught between furtive glances and stolen seconds, but Saxony could see the change in them now. For once, Tavia didn't hesitate to take Wesley's hand or seem at all unnerved by it, and neither of them tried their best to avoid looking at each other anymore.

That's good, she thought. *Better late than never.*

Saxony threaded her hand into Karam's and then took Tavia's, too. It seemed to be the safer option than trying to hold Wesley's and ignoring the awkwardness that might bring.

With the four of them hand in hand, Saxony and Wesley jumped.

The wind whirled across Saxony's ankles, blowing her hair wildly into her face, sucking her clothes tight to her stomach. It took little time to reach the top, but Saxony still marveled at the view as they soared above the city they were trying to save.

She didn't need to look at Tavia to know that her friend's eyes were squeezed tightly shut.

In less than a minute they were at the top of the central tower, their feet slamming into the observation balcony. Tavia all but collapsed onto the ground the minute they made contact.

"Oh, sweet safety," she said, lying flat on her back with a deep sigh. "Praise the person who invented ground."

Saxony snorted.

"How did you grow to become the best busker this city has to offer?" Karam asked.

From the ground, Tavia glared. "We don't usually conduct magic shows from the stars."

Wesley set up the six Star Eggs at the opposite end of the balcony, lining them in a neat row like they were charms on display, rather than deadly devices that would preserve Creije in a moment.

"We're ready," he said. "Let's get this show started."

Karam pulled Tavia from the ground as Saxony made her way over to Wesley.

"You sure this will work?" she asked him.

"I'm always sure," he said. "And if not, it'll still work out."

"You might have nine lives," Tavia said, saddling up beside them. "But the rest of us were only blessed with one."

Wesley laughed.

Saxony clicked her fingers.

Her fire magic sprouted at the base of each of the fuses that twirled from the Star Eggs, hissing its way to the top.

They took a step back.

Moments later it began.

The explosives hit the sky like lightning, cracking across the face of the moon. It broke the night in pieces, cascades of color raining across the city in a mirror of the Everglow. As though the phenomenon had broken free of its abiding nature and exploded into new being.

The lights cast patterns over the stars—blossoming flower petals and cutting spears like the knives Tavia kept in her waistband and on her boots.

"Just look at it," Wesley said. "Best view in the city."

The fire display illuminated every crevice Creije held and Saxony's brother looked enthralled with each new bang of light.

It struck Saxony then how much Wesley was like their mother. The Uncharted Forest, however much it loved him and craved his return, was never his home. It was too wild to contain him, just as it had been too wild to keep Vea's heart at peace.

"I almost forgot how beautiful this place was," Wesley said.

"No," Saxony said. "You didn't."

Wesley looked over to her and there was a trace of a smile on his lips. She couldn't remember the last time he had smiled at her. She couldn't remember if he had *ever* smiled at her like that—Many Gods knew she'd probably never smiled at him—but seeing it now made her feel so sad and so happy all at once.

Happy that her brother was alive.

Sad that she had spent years wishing he wasn't.

Saxony turned back to the explosions, still filling the sky with light and color. It took a while, but when they were finally done painting the sky in glory, they faded to rain and a swirl of hues trickled down and over the city.

It coated Creije like a liquid rainbow, puddling in the streets and slicking over rooftops.

It ran across Saxony's dark skin and then dripped off and onto her shoes, and though she felt a little light-headed, and her heartbeat seemed to quicken—which could have been from the sheer beauty—it had no lasting effects.

At least, not on her.

Not on Karam or Wesley or Tavia.

But for the rest of Creije, time stood still.

The city meandered to a halt and the wind froze midair and the footsteps sank into the ground and the music caught in the space between worlds.

The people stopped moving.

The moonlight stopped glistening.

There was just Saxony. Just her brother and her lover and her friend, standing over the city they loved, preserved in a stolen infinity. It was only the waters around them that continued to glisten and move with unbreakable fluidity.

They joined hands once more and descended from the tower, making their way back onto the center of the bridge path.

"Let's never do that again," Tavia said, once they landed. "I'm all for a good light show, but the flying I could do without."

Her hand was still locked in Wesley's and neither of them made to let go.

"Arjun and Schulze should have a clear path to Yejlath now," Wesley said. "And the rest of our forces can start taking back Creije."

He looked proud, but more than that Wesley looked relieved, as though he hadn't expected their plan to go so smoothly. They weren't used to winning when it came to Ashwood.

"Up ahead," Karam said.

She pointed over the bridge, to the river that led out into the winds of the other Uskhanyan cities.

For a moment Saxony thought it was strange that Arjun and Schulze would approach with their half of the army from the river, rather than through the outskirts as they had planned. She wondered where they had commandeered the small train from and who was navigating, but when she saw the train fully, she knew that it wasn't Arjun and her Kin or the Doyen inside.

The train was an obstinate black, with just a single carriage small enough to carry a handful of people, not an army. It glided through the waterways as though time was not pinned in place. It docked just under the bridge, stopping in the center of the river, and a small hatch opened up on the roof.

A figure drifted out, made of darkness.

And then following him, a small girl climbing the ladder to the top.

They stood on the roof of the train and looked up at Saxony and the others.

Dante Ashwood, who looked like death incarnate.

Zekia, who looked so small from the bridge's slope.

"Hello, sister," Zekia said.

She smiled up at Wesley.

"Hello, brother."

Saxony was surprised at how happy her sister looked to see them both, and how happy she felt to see her sister again. They had spent too long apart, and now that Saxony had found one half of her family, she wanted the other half back more desperately than she could say.

"Zekia," she said. "How are you here?"

"You froze Creije, but not the waters that bind the cities," Ashwood answered in her place. "Time cannot touch those."

"You can see your light show all the way from Yejlath," Zekia said. "It's very pretty. We were already on the train, so I missed most of it, but the flowers were nice."

"Already on the train?" Saxony asked.

Ashwood laughed, like she was just some silly little child.

"Did you really think I would not know?"

He looked up at Wesley, whose hand was still precariously entwined in Tavia's.

Saxony saw the moment Ashwood's eyes met his.

"My boy always finds his way home."

34

Karam

"SHALL WE MAKE THIS QUICK?" Ashwood asked, as he and Zekia ascendend onto the bridge. "Or slow?"

Karam stepped closer to Tavia, keeping her eye on Zekia.

"It will be quick," Karam said. "Just like the quickness with which our armies are slaughtering yours."

"Ah yes," Ashwood said.

He did not look afraid, or surprised by what Karam had thought would be a revelation.

"I have to admit, using magic to freeze my forces in Creije was a smart move. I imagine your treacherous little army is making its way through the city now?"

"Not just in Creije," Wesley said. "Fenna Schulze is crossing over to Yejlath with half of our forces. They're not going to let the government city fall."

Ashwood flinched a little upon hearing the Doyen's name, as though that, rather than all Wesley had done before to bring him down, was the true betrayal. The Kingpin recovered quickly, though, and replaced his slight frown with a wicked smile.

And then he clapped.

Not slow and tense, but loud and erratic, bubbling with laughter as he did so. His shoulders shook with glee.

"Bravo, Wesley," Ashwood said, delighted. "You really are a wonder. So many great plans inside of that head. It's a shame that you waste it all."

"He has a lot of potential," Zekia agreed.

Karam didn't like the way she stared between Wesley and Tavia.

"Your armies will fall," Karam said.

When she spoke, Zekia's eyes shot to her, taking her attention from Tavia.

Ashwood shook his head. "Every soldier I have can be replaced," he said. "Can you say the same?"

Karam couldn't.

Each loss she had felt was a blow, and Asees's death had nearly been the thing to kill her spirit. If she lost someone else—if she lost Tavia to that awful future she had seen—then Karam would never forgive herself for it.

"I don't need an army to deal with you four," Ashwood said. "You're just children who must be disciplined."

"Why don't you quit talking and try to kill us?" Wesley asked. "And then I can take back my sister."

Karam could see Zekia's lips shaking and how her hand flinched to move forward, as though to reach out, maybe, and grab on to Wesley, like a child clinging to her favorite toy.

Or, Karam supposed, a little girl clinging to her big brother.

But it was too late for that now. It was too late for Zekia.

Ashwood inclined to face Wesley, his shadows shifting to reveal the point of a smile on his narrow face.

"She was never yours," he said. "She was always mine."

Zekia brought a hand to the back of her neck, like she was rubbing away old strings.

"Don't forget, kid. You get to choose," Wesley said to her. "I trust you."

Zekia sighed.

At him. At herself.

She looked at him with those same graveyard eyes that Wesley had, took in a breath, and said—

"That's dangerous."

No sooner did the words float from her lips than a burst of lightning exploded from the sky and snapped at Tavia's feet. Without thinking, Karam shoved her out of the way and the two of them toppled to the ground in a heap.

Ashwood clapped his hands again, applauding Tavia's near death.

Karam scrambled to her feet and pulled Tavia up with her, but Zekia was already sending another shot of lightning her way. Karam pushed Tavia again, but the busker's ankle caught and when she crashed to the ground for a second time, Tavia's head bounced against the pavement.

There was blood in her mouth.

She's going to kill her, Karam thought.

This was the moment she and Arjun had seen in that vision.

This was the bridge that Tavia was going to die on.

"Yes," Ashwood cheered. "My little warrior, you are a wonder."

Karam half-expected Saxony's sister to be laughing maniacally beside him, but Zekia stood still, with an odd crease in the center of her tiny brows. She did not look happy to see Tavia's blood painted across the bridge.

Wesley and Saxony ran over and while Wesley lifted Tavia from the ground, Saxony cast a wall of protection in front of them.

Karam pulled out her knives.

She wouldn't let this happen.

"Don't do this," Wesley said. "Don't turn your back on your family."

"I'm not," Zekia said. "I know who my real family is."

Whatever side Zekia was on, she would have family. Ashwood had plagued her thoughts and twisted her mind so that she saw him as a father she would gladly choose over her sister and her brother.

"Gods damn it, kid," Wesley said. "Don't be an idiot!"

"Wesley," Ashwood said.

His voice filled with something close to love.

"Don't be rude. You're standing in the way of our new world."

"A new world," Zekia repeated.

Her voice was smaller than Karam remembered.

"I've seen the world and—"

"I have seen things too," Karam said. "And unlike you, I will not let them come to pass."

She threw her knife at Zekia.

It sailed past Ashwood, nearly clipping his shadow ear as

it twisted into the air and landed straight in Zekia's shoulder.

She fell back and Ashwood yelled with such force that the beams of the bridge clanged and shook.

Saxony started to run toward her sister, and Karam realized at the last minute that it wasn't to help Zekia to her feet, but to keep her perpetually on her ass.

Magic against magic.

Tavia fell into Karam, who just barely held her footing, as the bridge shook with Ashwood's anger. But Wesley seemed unmoved, unfazed, as though even the possibility of the bridge crumbling could not shake him.

Karam twisted her extra knives in her hands.

"You two take Ashwood," she said. "Saxony and I will handle Zekia."

Anything she could do to keep the girl occupied.

"Karam," Tavia said.

She could see the fear on her friend's face.

"I will handle it," Karam told her. *I will keep you safe*, she thought. "Just finish what we started."

Wesley and Tavia nodded, and Karam wasted no time in running toward Saxony and her sister, who were flinging magic at each other.

"Saxony!" Karam called out in warning.

Zekia lifted up a hand and a cable from the bridge snapped, flicking toward Saxony in a whip. It missed her somehow, but the bridge teetered with the force of it, dropping closer to the waters below.

Karam gritted her teeth and tackled Zekia to the ground.

She pressed a knife to the young girl's throat.

Saxony would never forgive her if she did this.

Tavia wouldn't survive if she didn't.

"You can't do that!" Zekia said.

She flung her hand out and Karam was lifted off of her and thrown backward.

"You don't understand," Zekia said, pushing herself up. "You don't know what's going to happen."

She tried to walk toward them, but Saxony thrust her hand out, her entire palm engulfed in bright yellow flame.

"Get back!" she said. "I mean it, Zekia. Don't make me do this."

Saxony's voice splintered on her plea and it broke Karam's heart to hear it.

"I don't want to hurt you," Zekia said. "We're not going to do this."

"Yes, we are," Karam told her.

She stood and adopted her fighting stance, steadying any doubt in her bones.

"I'm doing what I have to," Zekia said.

"So am I," Karam said.

Karam was supposed to be a protector, she was supposed to be honoring her family's legacy.

And she couldn't do that if Zekia lived.

35

Tavia

There he was, finally.

Dante Ashwood, standing in front of Tavia and Wesley.

The man who had poisoned the poorest people in Creije with his dirty elixir long before this war, creating the magic sickness in a bid to be all-powerful.

The man who had destroyed Tavia's home.

The man who had made her into an orphan.

Don't cry, ciolo, the memory of her mother's voice whispered.

"Two against one," Tavia said. "I don't hate those odds."

Ashwood's shadows shook with his laughter. "Just like a busker to be so cocky. I wonder if you'd feel the same if my boy came back to my side?"

Wesley straightened beside Tavia and she hated, truly hated, how the Kingpin's words still had such a hold on him.

I know who you are, she thought, hoping that somehow he could hear. *I love you and nothing can change it.*

Then, miraculously, as though Wesley really could read her mind, he squeezed Tavia's hand in his and she felt her heartbeat steady.

"You're not going to make me into your little lapdog again," Wesley said.

"You were never my lapdog," Ashwood told him. "You were my family."

Wesley's jaw tightened, but it was only for a second, and then the rigidness was replaced by a smile, so quick that Tavia was sure only she had caught it.

It was one of her greatest talents—seeing the parts of Wesley that nobody else could.

"I already have a family," Wesley said.

He threw his hand out and black smoke curled from his fingertips, just like it had back in the forest. The flames were fast, sliding across the bridge and toward the Kingpin without mercy.

Hope shot into Tavia's heart.

She had seen Wesley use those flames to decimate a tornado.

She knew the power he had and maybe, just maybe—

Ashwood held up his hand as if to say *stop* and a barrier of light slid in front of him.

Wesley's flames hissed against it, like it had burned them. They retreated and then faded into smoke.

His magic couldn't get through.

Wesley tried again, slinging both arms forward and hurling a tunnel of images toward the Kingpin.

Tavia recognized the magic.

It was the same magic Zekia had used back on Ashwood's island to try to attack her sister.

The magic Wesley had jumped in front of to save her, weakening him enough for Zekia to take him away.

Wesley had learned a few tricks.

He pressed harder and the cyclone of illusions raced toward Ashwood, only to rebound off his shield like they had been hit. The images splintered across the bridge, breaking apart and fading into the cement.

Ashwood only laughed.

Nothing Wesley threw at him could penetrate the old man's magic.

Dante Ashwood had been alive for more than a century, and years spent with dark, stolen magic had morphed him into something that wasn't quite human anymore.

Something that might not have been killable.

Tavia turned.

Across the way, Zekia dodged Karam's knife and then lifted her into the air, slinging her back into Saxony. The two slid across the bridge, but then Zekia clenched her fists and they stopped just short of slamming into the metal beams.

Tavia saw the young girl wince.

She looked nothing like the ruthless assassin Tavia remembered, willing to do whatever it took and kill whoever it took to please Ashwood.

She was holding back.

Why was she holding back?

It didn't matter.

Ashwood was their priority now and Tavia would deal with Zekia when it came to it.

"You can't beat me, boy."

"Watch me," Wesley said.

His arms were wide as he gathered a sphere of magic, bright enough to look like a Crafter moon, and then threw it toward Ashwood.

It cracked as soon as it hit the shield, the ball splintering across the bridge into shiny moonlight shards.

And then Tavia saw it.

The gap in Ashwood's defense.

Zekia was supposed to be taking care of Saxony and Karam, and the Kingpin was staring straight at Wesley, so why would he need to watch his back?

Rookie mistake, Tavia thought.

She slid her knife slowly out of her pocket and inched forward.

She could do this.

Dante Ashwood was not going to kill her. Karam had seen the future and Tavia knew how she died. It wasn't by his hand.

Before she could talk herself out of it, Tavia ran forward, faster than she had ever run. She saw the moment Ashwood caught her out of the corner of his eye, but by then it was too late. She was close enough. She twisted behind him, lifted her arm high in the air, and brought the knife down into his back.

Ashwood grunted and turned slowly to face her.

He reached up, lips thin, and pulled the knife from his back.

And then threw it over the bridge.

No, Tavia thought, watching it tumble. *No, no, no.*

Ashwood's smile stretched across his face and he moved his finger from side to side, admonishingly.

It wasn't a mistake.

Ashwood hadn't left a gap in his shield because he'd slipped up; he'd done it because he didn't care who tried to hurt him. He wasn't afraid of them.

Wesley's magic still pressed against his shield.

"Tavia!" Wesley yelled. "Run!"

She stumbled backward.

Her mother's face flashed in her mind.

Don't be scared. It'll all be okay.

Tavia couldn't remember if those were the last words she had spoken before she died—before Ashwood's dirty magic had driven her to death—but they were one of the few she could remember and they still haunted her.

Ashwood tapped his cane on the bridge and the sound reverberated into the wind.

Wesley made to move for Tavia, but Ashwood was quicker than him and he flung his hand out, knocking Wesley backward, far enough that Tavia lost sight of him.

His bone gun landed on the bridge where he had been just moments before.

The smoke poured from Dante Ashwood like it was water, pooling around his feet and winding in and out of his mouth, through his eyes, between his long fingertips.

"Coralina's little girl, ready to take me on once more," he said.

He raised his hand and Tavia lurched backward.

Through the air, through the wind.

It felt like she was being pulled from the inside out, her every organ tugged backward, her skin threatening to tear from her bones if she didn't follow.

Tavia hit the side of the bridge, hard.

She fell against the metal column with a clang and then slumped onto the ground. She knew she needed to get up, but when she tried to lean on her palm to push herself off the ground, her arm collapsed beneath her.

It hurt like the fire-gates.

Still, Tavia pushed herself to standing, ignoring the blinding pain up her arm.

She slumped against the bridge beam, cold metal pressing onto her skin and through the tears in her clothing.

Ashwood's lips quirked.

"Such hunger to live." He stepped closer and the breeze blew by in a deathly croon. "I'll enjoy taking you apart, piece by piece."

He won't kill me, Tavia thought again. *It's Zekia who kills me. It's Zekia. It's Zekia.*

The mirror doll hitched in the back of her trousers called to her, begging for blood.

Tavia cursed at her knife, sinking slowly to the bottom of the waters where Ashwood had thrown it.

Still, she had one last dagger left.

She pulled it from her sleeve and flung it at Ashwood, but the knife caught midair and with a flick of the Kingpin's wrist it sailed back toward her.

Tavia ducked in barely enough time.

She couldn't kill Ashwood. She could only delay him.

And if that was all she could do, then she'd do it well.

She reached for her belt loop and pulled out the first marble she felt.

Cutting charm.

She threw it toward Ashwood and it split into a thousand pieces in the air, glistening daggers of glass heading straight for his cloaked face.

Ashwood waved a hand. Bored, almost lazy.

The shards fell to dust before her eyes.

"So much potential," he said. "All of it wasted."

Ashwood crossed the gap between them in a blink and grabbed Tavia by the shoulders.

His nails dug into her like knives of his own.

"At the very least, your mother died without a fuss," he said.

Tavia spat on the ground by his feet.

"After I kill you, nothing will stop my boy from coming back to me."

Tavia looked at Wesley's bone gun on the bridge floor and steeled herself.

Ashwood was close enough to whisper in her ear, cold breath making the hairs on the back of her neck stand on end.

"Wesley and I will create a new world together."

Tavia flung her head forward.

The tip of her skull cracked against a part of Ashwood's face that wasn't made from shadow and magic.

He growled and stumbled backward and Tavia propelled herself forward, moving past him and skidding across the rough concrete of the bridge.

It burned against her skin, so much so that she felt like she'd grazed herself to the bone.

She grabbed Wesley's gun, felt the familiar weight of it in her hands. The comfort it had brought for those weeks when she didn't know if he was dead or alive.

She aimed. Dante Ashwood's blood-red lips tilted upward.

"I like the old world just fine," Tavia said.

And then she pulled the trigger.

36

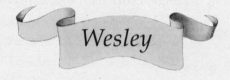
Wesley

THE BULLET WENT THROUGH Ashwood's neck and hit the bridge column behind him with a loud clang.

Wesley winced and stood, rubbing his head as Ashwood gurgled and clutched at his neck, letting out a strangled kind of cry.

Wesley ran for Tavia.

It wasn't enough. That couldn't kill him.

Wesley needed to get to her before Ashwood did.

Ashwood swiped his hand through the air again.

Wesley flew backward. Tavia flew backward.

They tumbled through the air together with frightening speed and Wesley caught a glimpse of Tavia crashing against the barrier before his head hit the beam and he catapulted over the side railing.

Wesley had just enough time to gather his magic and stop himself from falling into the watery depths.

He floated below the bridge, his magic jutting in and out as the pain in his head started to throb. He felt dizzy with it, the realms blurring and then struggling to refocus again.

He'd hit the beam hard enough that he could feel blood on him, but he couldn't tell which part of his face it was coming from. Everywhere hurt, like thousands of tiny needles puncturing his cheeks and the cracks in his lips.

Wesley reached up a shaking hand and grabbed the railing.

The moment his fingers curled around it, his magic let out a sigh of relief as though it thought that meant it could rest for a moment.

Wesley sucked in a breath as he dangled from the bridge, one hand gripping the railing and the other floundering in the air.

He wasn't sure he had the strength to pull himself up.

"Give me your hand," Tavia said, appearing in front of him.

She flung her arm over the railing.

The sight of her was like a miracle in itself.

Wesley called on every ounce of strength he had to reach up for her. He called on his magic to quell the spinning in his head and halt the blood he could feel trickling down his neck.

Come on, he said. *We can do this.*

He stretched up.

"Just a little closer," Tavia urged.

There was a tingling in Wesley's hands, like a newfound power surging straight to his fingertips as hers dangled so close to his, and with a mighty yell Wesley lurched up and grabbed on to Tavia.

She clasped both hands around his arm and pulled him desperately until he was back over the railing.

Wesley collapsed over the top and onto the bridge, beside Tavia, both of them gasping for air.

"Idiots," Ashwood said.

He sneered down at the bullet that had pierced him and kicked it across the ground.

It was soaked with his gray blood. The blood of tainted magic, acquired through years of stolen power. Wesley could see it.

See it, but not get to it.

Son of a bitch, Wesley thought, pushing himself back up once more.

They needed that bullet, that blood, if the final part of their plan was going to work.

"You will pay for that," Ashwood said.

He strode toward them and Wesley pushed himself in front of Tavia.

Ashwood laughed. "You're powerful, my boy. But I am ancient."

He raised his arm, as if he was going to wipe them from the world.

"Wait."

It was Zekia who spoke.

She was no longer battling Karam and Saxony. In fact, the three of them were watching onward with startled expressions, as though the sound of Tavia's gunshot and the sight of Wesley dangling over a bridge had pulled them away from each other and back to the real enemy.

Wesley narrowed his eyes and looked to Zekia.

His head still pounded.

You can help, he thought.

All they needed was a minute. Just a minute to grab that bullet and then—

"Kid," Wesley said out loud. "This is your chance."

The bullet, he whispered in her mind. *We need the bullet Tavia shot Ashwood with.*

"You can help your family," Wesley said.

"She *is* helping her family," Ashwood said. "I'm her family."

When he stared at Zekia, it was almost as a challenge.

"I'll do it," Zekia said.

Wesley's sigh was like a gust of wind as he watched his little sister step to Ashwood's side.

"Tavia is Wesley's favorite," she said.

Ashwood's impatience was palpable. "And?"

Zekia stared at Tavia, and Wesley wasn't sure he liked where this was going.

"He's always leaving me for her. So I should be the one to take care of her."

"No!" Karam yelled, lurching forward.

But Ashwood held out his hand and both Karam and Saxony came to a sudden stop. Wesley could see them struggling, but it was like their feet were rooted to the bridge.

Ashwood spread his arms toward Tavia, like she was a prize. "By all means, little warrior. Show me where your loyalty lies."

"Kid—"

"Stop talking!" Zekia yelled. "I have to concentrate and I can't do it if you won't stop talking."

Her lips trembled, eyes unblinking and unfocused as she stared at Wesley with so much fear that he almost trembled alongside her.

He looked at the bullet across the way, by the barriers of the bridge.

So damn far.

Please, kid, Wesley called out to his sister. *Get Tavia the bullet.*

But Zekia wasn't listening.

She held out her hand and Wesley's bone gun was suddenly clasped in her tiny fingers. In the very corner of his eye, he saw Tavia pat her belt loop, to see if she could still feel the cold bone against her back.

Nothing.

Wesley knew it before she did.

Zekia was holding the gun he had used to kill his old underboss and take his place.

The gun that Tavia had held on to while the Kingpin kept him as prisoner.

The gun made from bone and blood, on which Wesley had built an entire empire.

The gun he wanted to use in a perfect display of irony to bring Ashwood to his knees.

"My little warrior," Ashwood said, placing a hand on Zekia's shoulder. "Make me proud."

She nodded.

The bullet, Wesley tried again. *Kid—*

"I'm sorry I didn't do this sooner," Zekia said.

She squeezed the trigger and in an instant, Wesley's world broke into a million pieces.

The gunshot was like an explosion and in the time it took for Wesley to blink, for his heart to pound furiously in his chest—just once, like a dying scream—Tavia stumbled back.

Her hand went to her chest.

There was blood. So much blood. On her hands and dripping from her mouth.

In the distance, he thought he heard Saxony cry out.

Karam screamed in grief.

"Wesley," Tavia said in a gasp.

This isn't happening, he thought. *This can't be happening.*

Wesley blinked and for the first time he saw the world truly ending.

If she died, then there was no going back. If he lost Tavia, then nothing mattered. Not magic and not time and not winning this war.

Tavia hit the ground, hard enough that it sounded like another gunshot.

She reached out a shaking hand toward him. One last attempt at a lifeline.

Wesley didn't move.

Couldn't move.

Couldn't breathe or think straight.

It's not real. It's not real. Please don't let it be real.

And then her arm fell and her eyes closed and Tavia's breath stuttered to a final stop.

37

Saxony

SAXONY SAW HER FALL.

The bullet hit Tavia and the time it took for her to tumble to the ground stretched between the seconds.

The Kingpin's glee broke her concentration, releasing Saxony from the spell that pinned her in place. Yet she still couldn't move.

In a moment, in a single gunshot, the truest friend she had was gone.

And her sister had been the one to do it.

Tavia was sprawled across the ground behind Ashwood and Zekia, covered in too much blood for Saxony to bear looking at.

She was still and pale and Saxony's gut wrenched.

It was like being kicked in the stomach over and over, until she could barely pant out a breath.

Tavia was gone.

Wesley knelt beside her, unblinking, almost frozen.

There was no fury in him, just despair.

"No," Saxony said in a whisper. "She's not . . ."

She swallowed, like she was swallowing words too terrible to speak, and buried her head in Karam's shoulder.

"I am so sorry," Karam said. "I thought I could stop it."

"What are you talking about?"

Karam pulled away and steadied Saxony's shoulders with her hands.

"I am sorry," she said again. "But we still have to finish this. We have to fight for her and all of the others."

Saxony didn't know how much fight she had left in her. That bullet hadn't just taken her best friend, but it had taken her sister from her too, because there was no redemption for Zekia now, and there was no way Saxony could ever look at her sister the same way again.

Saxony couldn't save her.

"Forgive me," Karam said.

And then she ran for Ashwood.

She swung her fists wildly, but it was of little use. All the training Karam had clawed from the world wasn't enough.

Karam kicked out.

Ashwood caught her leg and pushed her to the ground.

She flipped herself back up in an instant and swung again, but Ashwood snatched her arm, like her speed was no match for him.

Karam's knees buckled under his strength.

"You have no power here," he growled, low and impatient.

Saxony's teeth ground together.

First he took her sister, then he killed Asees, and then Tavia.

She wouldn't let him take Karam.

She wouldn't let him take anyone else.

"I'll show you power," Saxony snarled. "Karam, move!"

Karam swiped out her legs, catching Ashwood at the ankle.

He seethed and dropped her arm, giving the warrior a moment to dive out of the way.

As soon as Karam was clear, Saxony thrust her hands toward the Kingpin.

The arrows of fire darted from each of her fingertips, the force of expelling them nearly throwing Saxony off balance. She was summoning all the magic she had inside of her and it engulfed the air so much that the heat from the ground started to burn even her.

A wave of fire, almost tidal, flew toward Ashwood.

But the Kingpin threw up his hand and the fire collided against a new invisible wall, sizzling.

"I'll show you what real magic can do," he said.

Ashwood pushed forward and Saxony's fire turned to ice, melting into a body of water that spilled over the sides of the bridge.

He clicked his fingers, and whether it was necessary or for dramatic effect Saxony didn't know, but she felt the air grow uneasy and then disappear completely.

She couldn't breathe.

Many Gods, she couldn't breathe.

Saxony clutched at her throat as Ashwood pulled the very air from her lungs.

Zekia took a step toward her, but with one deadly, daring look from Ashwood, she stopped in place.

"Stay where you are," he said. "I'll kill her myself."

Saxony wondered if after he'd finished with her, Ashwood would leave anyone behind to mourn her, or if he would decimate the world. There was a moment where all the hope she had gathered over the weeks disappeared and all she could do was focus on her breath and ponder which one would be the last.

And then she noticed it.

A flicker moving in the air in front of her, like it was just in the corner of Saxony's eye where she couldn't quite focus. Nobody else seemed to catch it and the harder Saxony looked, the harder it was to see.

But it was there.

Some kind of a ripple.

Something impossible, where Tavia's body was supposed to be.

Hope.

38

Tavia

BEING DEAD SUCKED. Thankfully, those kinds of things weren't always permanent.

Tavia patted herself down, touching her chest where the blood had been moments ago.

She wasn't dead.

Why wasn't she dead?

I had to make it look real, a voice in her head whispered. *I'm really sorry if I scared you.*

Zekia.

Tavia searched the bridge until her eyes settled on the young girl, who was trying her best to look anywhere else but at Tavia.

Get to the bullet, Zekia said. *Wesley told me you needed it. You have the time now. He thinks you're dead.*

By he, she meant Ashwood, but all that came to Tavia's mind was Wesley.

He was knelt beside the false image of her that Zekia had

conjured. There were tears staining his eyes, trembling at the corners like they were too afraid to drop.

She'd never seen his face like that before.

She never, ever wanted to again.

She made to move toward him.

The bullet, Zekia urged. *Go now!*

Tavia bit her lip and looked back to Zekia.

She was risking her life to help them and it occurred to Tavia then that the future Karam had seen wasn't of Tavia dying; it was of the world thinking she had.

Zekia was as good a planner as her brother.

Thank you, Tavia whispered inside of her mind, hoping Zekia could hear.

She took a tentative step forward.

Ashwood's back was to her, which was just what Tavia needed.

Karam was on the ground by Ashwood's feet, his hand clutched around her wrist. Her arm shook as she tried to push him off, but Ashwood persisted.

Saxony's face was one of pure rage.

"I'll show you power," she said.

And then her hands set ablaze and the ground around her lit up with pools of fire.

Tavia could feel the heat from where she was and when Saxony threw her hands out, Tavia ducked and placed her hands over her head on instinct.

The fire shot toward the Kingpin.

Only Wesley didn't move.

He stayed kneeling by Tavia's body, staring at the illusion of her like there wasn't a war just a few feet from where he was.

Tavia wanted to scream that she was alive, and that everything was okay, but this was the moment she needed.

The distraction of Saxony's fire would give her time.

She walked slowly away from Wesley, toward the bullet that had pierced through Ashwood and was lying on the bridge. Her movements were careful, in case the illusion shattered. Magic was a fragile thing and Tavia couldn't risk being seen.

Especially when Zekia had killed her so convincingly.

A little too convincingly, Tavia thought.

Because though she didn't feel the pain of the bullet, there was a small glitch, maybe ten seconds or so, when she'd seen the blood on herself and the look on Wesley's face as he'd seen it too. The few fractures of time when the illusion propelled into the world and Zekia forgot to omit Tavia from it.

For a moment, Tavia thought she was going to die.

The bullet was squashed and wrinkled and when Tavia picked it up, it was still a little warm. The blood that coated the gold metal was an almost black shade of red.

Tavia clasped it with a busker's smile.

Ashwood still had his back to her, his magic clutched tightly around Saxony's neck.

Her friend was gasping for breath.

Tavia narrowed her eyes and set Dante Ashwood in her sights.

With hands quick enough to earn her reputation as Creije's best busker, she reached into the back of her trouser pocket for the mirror doll and wiped the bullet, riddled with Ashwood's blood, onto its body.

The change was instant.

The doll's head snapped back and its body shook as it shed its makeshift form and mutated into something other, growing flesh in place of fabric, hair stringing from its ghostly scalp.

Its face was muddled and incomplete, just as Ashwood's was. Eyes that were a faded black and lips that were smudged across its deathly face. The only thing human about it was the heartbeat, the breath that escaped its tiny mouth, and the way it shuddered under Tavia's touch.

Ashwood whipped around to face her and Tavia caught the moment his shadows jolted and his thin frame stiffened.

Saxony gasped, Zekia smiled, and Tavia swore that Karam looked close to rolling her eyes.

And Wesley, who blinked as the pretend Tavia's image faded and he looked up to see the real thing standing over him, swallowed loud enough for it to sound like a crack of thunder.

He said her name, just once, in utter disbelief, voice splintering on the sound. And then he was by her side and she thought maybe he was going to kiss her in the middle of this battle until she heard Ashwood hiss, and they both turned to see his graying teeth bared.

"Impossible," he said at the sight of Tavia alive. "You—"

Tavia snapped the doll's leg backward.

Ashwood fell to a knee, clutching on to his cane to keep himself upright.

Up ahead, the skies growled with his anger.

"Foolish child," he said from the ground. He was staring at Zekia. "How dare you betray me like this?"

His hand cut into the air and suddenly Zekia was on the ground, screaming.

Her body twisted, like he was snapping her bones apart.

"I will make you pay. I will make you regret the day you were—"

He paused and let out a choked sound.

Tavia squeezed the neck of the doll tightly.

See how you like it, she thought.

Ashwood pulled his hand from the air and brought it to his own throat and Zekia let out a gasp of relief as the Kingpin's magic ripped from her.

They watched, all of them, as Ashwood gasped for breath, choking on nothing at all.

He looked up as Tavia pinched the neck of the doll and Wesley, standing by her side where he belonged, watched on.

"My boy," Ashwood said in a breathless stammer. "Help me."

Wesley's face remained plain.

"He's not your boy," Tavia said. "And nobody's going to help you now."

39

Karam

Karam could not see the Kingpin's face, but she could sense his growing fear as he looked from the mirror doll to Tavia to Wesley. To the two crooks that his legacy had created, who were now ready to undo him.

Tavia had managed to blood the doll after all.

And they had Zekia to thank.

Karam had been so sure the vision was real and she had been so sure Tavia's death was final, and all of it had been an illusion.

If they lived through this, Karam planned to have strong words with the Indescribable God on how to be a bit clearer with its plans for the future.

"Your mirror doll won't destroy me," Ashwood said. "I cannot be killed."

"Then I guess that I'll have fun trying," Tavia said. "I've always loved a good fight."

"Be careful what you wish for," Ashwood sneered.

His smile basically hissed.

"Wekne ohg vjs."

The words howled like a storm as they slid out of his mouth.

Karam recognized the words. It was a summoning, all too familiar.

Awaken and feast.

On cue, a bang as loud as the Star Eggs sounded from underneath the bridge.

"Here is the fight you wished for," Ashwood said. "If I can't kill you, then they will."

The water below rippled and then parted ever so slightly, giving breath to the cruel life that hid beneath. There was a screech, like the sound the night made before the sun tore it down, and then from the depths of the Creijen waters, six ungodly creatures scurried out.

Shadow demons.

These were the things Karam had fought alongside Arjun and, even before that, in the rings of the underrealm. She had seen them clawing at men's necks and faces, drinking their blood like *fimpir* bats.

"In the name of spirits," Karam said, staring in horror.

And the demons, like they had heard her gasp, turned their shadow heads from the waters that birthed them and growled up at her. It took only seconds for them to leap up onto the bridge.

Karam swallowed and the demons barked back.

Spit stretched like string between their teeth and their bones bulged from their half-shadowed bodies. One dug its claws into the bridge and scraped a line through the ground like it was a throat.

"Cast a light," Karam called out, to Saxony or Wesley or whoever could manage it first. "It will make them cower."

But Saxony was at her sister's side, tending to Zekia, who was still curled on the ground, sobbing in pain from whatever it was the Kingpin had tried to do to her.

Tavia was beside them, clutching on to the mirror doll to keep Ashwood at bay.

And Wesley just stared.

He blinked, staring at the demons in total horror.

"Wesley," Tavia said. "Cast a light!"

Zekia winced up at her brother. "It's my fault," she croaked. "Please don't be afraid."

Saxony's jaw tensed and it was then that Karam knew Wesley was scared, perhaps for the first time in his life.

These demons had tortured him under Zekia's control. They had ripped into him and not only torn the flesh from his bones, but it seemed they had gotten their claws into something else.

Something deeper.

Something far inside his mind.

And the creature could sense it as much as Karam could, because five of the six galloped toward Wesley and the others.

"Use your shield to keep them away!" Karam yelled to Saxony.

But she didn't need to, for her love was already casting a protection over the four of them as all of the demons tried their attack.

They bit and clawed and scraped at the barrier, trying desperately to get in and feast on their flesh.

All except for one.

A single shadow demon kept its focus on Karam, circling her.

It seemed to smile when it saw she was not planning on running under the protection of the shield.

Karam had taken these creatures on before, in the fighting rings and on the Kingpin's isle.

She could do it again.

Karam grabbed a blade and ran at the demon, sliding along the ground and slicing across its belly.

The creature howled, thick blood like ink spraying across her face.

But the wound wasn't as big as it should have been, and Karam had only caught half flesh, while the rest was all shadow.

The demon turned to hiss at her.

Karam flipped back to her feet and struck out with her knife again, but she was met with only claws. The shadow demon raised its talons in the air and swiped out, scratching across her chest. She jumped back and the creature pounced, knocking her over.

It was on top of her, its spit and blood coating her face.

Quickly, Karam brought the hilt of her blade up through its neck and into its skull. The demon's head trembled uncertainly, as though it was trying to shake the blade.

And then Karam reached up through its shadow body and took ahold of its spine.

She grabbed, squeezed, and then snapped it violently in half.

The demon screeched and fell back in a quiver.

Karam knew she hadn't killed it—not even she was capable of such a feat—and sooner or later the pieces of darkness that made up the creature would merge back together.

But for now it was gone.

For now, she was alive.

One down, five to go.

She turned back to her friends to see the five remaining shadow demons were still clawing against Saxony's shield and it was barely keeping them at bay.

Karam ran for her friends and the demons that surrounded them, catching Saxony's wince as her shield began to dwindle.

The shadow demons hungered for flesh.

One of them ripped its hand through Saxony's magic and grabbed ahold of Wesley's ankle, pulling half of his body from Saxony's protection.

It tore at Wesley's leg, teeth showing no signs of letting up.

He yelled out in pain, while the others tried desperately to pull him back inside the barrier.

Karam felt a burning in her chest.

No, not in her chest. *On* her chest.

She looked down and her father's pendant was aglow against her heart, burning into her just like it had done that day on the shores of Tisvgen.

Then, it had warned her of the danger they were in. Now, it felt like something different entirely.

It felt like faith.

Like her father's spirit whispering to her.

My daughter, it said. *Do not lose hope.*

Karam touched a hand to the pendant and felt her father's light.

She felt the force of the Rekhi d'Rihsni.

This was her family's legacy: to protect the Crafters and

bring peace to the realms. Her grandparents had died for it. And Karam would see to it that their dream for the future was fulfilled.

For the first time, Wesley truly needed her help and she wouldn't let him down, like she had almost let Tavia down.

"The light!" Karam yelled out to Saxony. "Cast a light."

Saxony held out her other hand and a small yellow orb began to glow in her palm.

It was dimmer than Karam would have liked, but juggling to keep the shield up alongside this new magic must have been draining her.

Still, it was bright enough for the demons to recoil. They flinched back as the light burned their bodies, barking and growling like they were screaming at Saxony to stop.

But the demon with the hold on Wesley's leg didn't move away or tear its teeth from its new meal. It persisted, gnawing at the space below Wesley's knee like Saxony's light meant nothing to it. Even as her magic burned the bones of its ankle to ash, it refused to let go.

Ashwood, still kneeling on the floor as Tavia continued to squeeze the mirror doll as hard as she could, was yelling.

Yelling at the demon.

"Don't stop!" he screamed. "Make them pay!"

He's controlling them, Karam thought.

The creature would risk being burned by the light of Saxony's magic if it meant obeying its master. It was up to Karam to save Wesley. She was supposed to be his bodyguard after all.

Karam reached for the pouch on her belt. Trick bags weren't

her weapon of choice, but Tavia had taught her how to read charms for a purpose and Karam was not about to waste those lessons.

The small marble felt like melting glass in her hands.

Splinter charm, she thought.

Karam threw the marble and it hit the shadow demon square in the tallest spike of its spine.

It went still and then it shattered into smoky pieces by Wesley's feet.

"Are you okay?" Karam asked.

Tavia pressed her hands on his wound, keeping the blood in, and Wesley leaned against her shoulder, like he found relief from the pain in her touch.

"Nice work," Wesley said to Karam. "We might make a busker of you yet."

She grimaced at the insult. She would have punched him for suggesting it if she didn't think he had been hurt enough.

"I was doing my job," she said.

Wesley clutched at his leg. "Remind me to give you a raise."

She checked the others for injuries, but they seemed fine, except for Zekia, who still squeezed her eyes shut in agony.

Whatever the Kingpin had done to her, it was too painful for her to even move now.

"I can't keep this light going by myself forever," Saxony said.

Wesley clenched his teeth together and held his hand out, trying to conjure a light of his own to keep the remaining demons at bay, but it was as dim as Saxony's and Karam could still see the fear in his eyes.

"It's okay," Tavia said, like she could see it too.

She folded her hand into Wesley's, like together they might just be unstoppable.

To Karam's surprise, his light grew a little brighter.

Karam smiled.

They could do this.

She kept hold of her blade and the four of them faced the four demons just like they had faced every enemy they had: together.

40

Zekia

ZEKIA PULLED HERSELF to her feet, blood trickling down to her toes.

It felt as though Ashwood had pulled her apart from the inside. And maybe he had. Maybe he'd done it a long time ago and she was only now feeling the pain.

It had been a while since she'd been this weak, but also a while since she'd been this strong: this clear on who she was and what she needed to do.

The world was a scary place, but she had a family and all they wanted was to protect her from it.

From herself.

Zekia had forgotten that once, but not now.

Karam yelled something and plunged her knife into a demon's side.

It barely faltered.

The second licked its lips, teeth bared, and Tavia gripped tightly to her charm pouches.

They would be no use.

Magic rarely was, because these demons were made from magic and the dark matter left behind by the most beastly spells. They crawled up from the space between magic and reality. If Crafters were creatures of the Many Gods, then shadow demons were born from the things that came before the Gods. From pure evil.

And evil was a hard thing to kill.

"Here, boys," she said.

The demons turned their heads to her, Zekia's voice like a familiar bell in their minds.

She let out a low whistle and they jumped up, retracting their claws, backing away from Zekia's family.

"Stay!" Ashwood yelled.

The demons flinched at their master's voice, but their focus stayed on Zekia. They recognized her—the girl who had been their kin—and in a way they craved her.

Craved her familiarity.

Craved her flesh.

The demons slithered toward Zekia, wary of what power she might still hold over them.

Not one to miss an opening, Tavia crouched back down to Wesley's side and sprinkled some kind of trick dust over his injured leg.

Zekia breathed in a calming sigh and looked back to the shadow demons. They hissed at her wavering focus. They sensed the new weakness in her body and perhaps even her new loyalties.

They felt Ashwood's influence.

Zekia could feel it too—his mind trying to invade theirs and his voice trying to yell over hers.

Stay calm, she told the creatures.

Kill her, Ashwood screamed.

Zekia wanted to be strong. Now more than ever she wanted to be strong, but Ashwood's voice was louder and Zekia couldn't hold them.

The demons growled.

And then they galloped toward her, arms like ragged nails and spines cracking with the impact of their speed.

Zekia closed her eyes and reached back into her mind.

It used to be as easy as breathing to control these creatures, but the new clarity she had, lifting the fog inside of herself, had cast a darkness on her connection with them.

How could she form a bond with death when she was so disgusted by it?

She heard their calls.

Their growling and the low rumble as half of them—the half made from shadow—caught in the air and broke the breeze.

Stay, she thought.

Enough.

And it was enough.

She'd had enough of all this darkness inside of her.

It needed to stop.

It needed

to

just

stop.

Zekia opened her eyes and the demons crouched before

her feet. She was in their minds again, though unlike before, she was not one with them.

She was not their kin, but their master.

"Sit. Down," Zekia said.

They cowered reluctantly with the strength of her voice, pressing themselves into the floor.

She had once thought they couldn't be killed, because magic could not be killed, but she had seen that there were many ways to destroy something—to butcher it beyond compare—and perhaps magic could not be conquered entirely, but she was starting to believe that evil could.

This evil, so tainted in misery, could be killed by a strength of good just as pure. Zekia could do one final act of good, not for forgiveness, because that was not hers to ask for. But because it was the right thing to do. The only thing that would save her family from the monsters she had helped to create.

"This is not what I made you for," Ashwood said. "This is not what you are supposed to do."

But he was wrong.

This *was* what Zekia was made for, what she was always destined to do.

Save her Kin.

Take Malik's destiny to be a great Liege and do good with it.

Inside of Zekia, her powers rose like a heartbeat, pounding on the surface of her skin.

They wanted to help.

They wanted redemption.

They wanted to be free.

And so, finally, she let them go.

The magic exploded from her and swept over the shadow demons in a blast of glorious yellow light.

Zekia was a sun.

She was the daybreak.

And darkness had no place here.

The demons shook and roared, but it only took moments for them to fade, like the night faded from the sky.

The warmth of her powers stayed with her, just for a moment afterward, and she felt them tinkering with her bones and putting her insides back in place.

Healing her, as a gift for her sacrifice.

And then they disappeared.

Zekia fell to the ground, newly empty.

Newly healed.

Just *new*.

Her magic was gone and she felt like a weight had been lifted from her. She also felt dizzy and like she might just faint if she closed her eyes, but the lightness in her heart was welcome.

This was her true destiny.

This was what she needed: to be free of all the pain her magic had brought.

To use it for good and to finally free herself.

Zekia had spent too long being scared and letting that fear take over, until she became all the things she never wanted to be.

Zekia closed her eyes.

She was good.

And she would not be scared again.

41

Wesley

TAVIA, SAXONY, AND EVEN KARAM—who just a few minutes before had considered Wesley's youngest sister their worst enemy—ran to Zekia's side like she was a precious thing they had to keep from breaking.

Thing was, Zekia had broken a long time ago. Wesley had seen to that.

He felt the moment her magic vanished into the air, like those powers were as connected to him as they were to his little sister.

He felt the shame of her having to make that sacrifice because of something he had started.

Tavia squeezed the mirror doll tight enough in her shaking hands that Dante Ashwood couldn't even make the noise of a scream.

He just mimed the action: the gasping and the grasping.

The snarl as his demons disappeared from the world.

Wesley held out his hand for the doll.

Tavia gave it to him without question, because of all people, Tavia knew Wesley best, and she knew that this was something he had to do.

The mirror doll felt light as air in his hands.

Wesley twisted its arm, hard enough that the corpse-like creature cried out, its deathly mouth twisting in pain.

Ashwood mirrored the noise and his arm flung behind his back, bone jutting from the shadows.

"You do not want to do this," Ashwood wheezed.

Wesley's magic laughed beneath his skin.

Yes, it said. *Yes, we do.*

There were many things Wesley didn't want, like to watch Tavia bleed out on the side of the bridge. That was still too real, still too much to even think about. And he didn't want to have shadow demons rip at his flesh again. Or have his sister sacrifice her magic to save him. He didn't want his city destroyed.

But if there was one thing Wesley did want, then it was to kill Dante Ashwood.

Tavia pulled a small syringe from her pocket.

"I have an idea on how we can finish this," she said to him.

"What?" Wesley asked.

"This is time serum," she said, holding up the syringe. "Nolan tried to sell it to me once, saying it could undo the years for a while. Like I was some old crone."

Of course.

Magic to undo a person, turning back time on their body. Making them young again, for few hours or even a day, erasing all that they were, for what they used to be.

They couldn't kill this version of the Kingpin, with all his magic and darkness, but maybe they could kill another, earlier, version.

"You're brilliant," Wesley said.

Tavia frowned. "Don't sound so surprised."

"Let me do it."

Wesley had to be the one to end this and they both knew it. Tavia handed him the serum.

Wesley looked down at it.

At his cuff links, dirt-smeared and crooked. To the scars they sat misshapen atop. The scars he had gotten from his mother, who had sacrificed everything she had to ensure he would not fulfill some ominous future.

And then Wesley heard it, somewhere in the back of his mind, a memory turning to a song.

A prophecy cooing in his ear like a lullaby.

Time will be carried in strange hands,
across the realms and through stranger lands.
What is done will be undone,
a battle lost is a battle won.
When midnight rings on a child's betrayal,
your every success is doomed to fail.

His magic had been trying to tell him for months, back when it burst from the fortune orb he had helped Tavia build, when it finally reunited with him in Granka, and now, as he stood before his father.

Wesley wasn't going to end the world.

He was going to save it.

The syringe of time swelled in bright blue waves.

Ashwood swallowed.

"You can't kill me," he said. "You're my boy. My flesh. It's why I've never taken your life, even after you've constantly disappointed me. Don't you see, Wesley?"

Ashwood's voice was quick and pleading.

He was desperate, trying for any way to survive.

"Family does not give up on each other," Ashwood said. "And I've always wanted my son to be great."

"Don't listen to him," Saxony said. "He's just trying to get inside of your head. Malik . . . Wesley. Please just—"

Wesley held up his hand to stop her. "Enough," he said.

It was the awful truth he never wanted to face.

Wesley thought that hearing those words spoken out loud would send him off-kilter somehow, making him doubt all that he was and imbuing him with some kind of misplaced loyalty to the Kingpin.

But it didn't.

It didn't matter whether it was a lie or if he and Ashwood were blood. Either way, the Kingpin had always been his father. He had raised Wesley and taught him everything he knew and a few things he wished he'd someday forget. He was kinder to him than Wesley's other father had been and he had shaped Wesley into the man he was today.

Blood or not, Dante Ashwood was always going to be a part of him.

And Wesley surprised himself with how much he just didn't care.

"You don't get to claim him," Tavia said. "Wesley is his own person and he gets to choose his family."

Wesley looked up at her, no longer blood-soaked, the illusion faded to give way to the wonderful cherry bark of her eyes.

She gave him a hard smile and Wesley's heart jarred.

She was right: Wesley had chosen his family long before he found them.

"I'm pretty much related to everyone nowadays," Wesley said to Ashwood. "You're really not that special."

He stabbed the syringe directly into the heart of the doll.

Ashwood screamed.

The doll screamed.

The world screamed.

His body shook and convulsed, head twisting from side to side. His broken arm snapped back into place and the shadows around him blinked and staggered, like they were struggling to keep ahold of him.

Wesley's eyes widened as he watched his once-Kingpin writhe and blur, the different sides to his face screaming away from each other and then catapulting back together.

Time was not just catching up with him, but erasing him altogether. Pulling the magic from Ashwood's bones, reversing all that he had gleaned from years of enslavement and murder.

The years rewound inside of him.

It was undoing him.

It was sucking the power from him.

Ashwood fell onto his knees, his shadows gone, his cane broken by his feet.

And his face.

Human.

Plain for all to see.

Dante Ashwood's face was not haggard, but rewound to give him a youthful and unaffected glow, marked only by a few pinked scars. He didn't look much older than Wesley, with long dark hair that brushed past his chin. His skin was pulled tight across his face, pale as the ocean's crust, with eyes the color of a serpent's skin and a look of hate spread to the very corners of his curled lips.

Dante Ashwood, Kingpin of Uskhanya, destroyer of cities, was human.

He was just a man.

And Wesley had a lot of practice killing men.

Wesley's gun was on the ground, where Zekia had dropped it after her illusion, and though Wesley couldn't get to it with his leg still so jacked up, he knew he didn't need to move to reach for it.

His magic surged, eager.

Yes, it said. *That, we can do.*

Wesley looked at the bone gun, licked his lips, and then watched it disappear from the ground and reappear in his own hand.

The familiar hilt, the slick way it fit to his palm, like it had been made for Wesley and nobody else.

Tavia locked her fingers between Wesley's, and the warmth of her, the familiar scratch of her scars and calluses, steadied his heart.

He gripped the gun in his free hand.

"Wesley," Ashwood said.

Fatherly. Perhaps pleading.

"You're my son."

The wind whistled in Wesley's ears as he aimed the gun.

The clock tower that headed the Crook chimed.

Midnight.

"Yeah," Wesley said. "I know."

He fired the shot, straight through Ashwood's newly human heart.

His father fell to the ground.

Ashwood's eyes were wide, his hands still, his lips bloody and quivering.

His darkness, finally, fading from the world.

42

Tavia

He was gone.

Dante Ashwood slumped on the ground, bullet through the heart Tavia was sure he didn't have. He didn't move or get back up in some death-defying display of magic. He just lay there, with his eyes as wide as could be, staring straight at Wesley.

Finally, it was over.

"Holy shit," Tavia said.

Wesley put his gun back in the holster. "Eloquent as ever."

"I know you guys had a complicated relationship and I should probably say something comforting or poignant," Tavia said. "But holy shit."

She couldn't help but smile, which was probably inappropriate with someone who may have been Wesley's father lying dead by their feet. Still, she smiled, because they had just saved the world and she was owed the feeling of happiness that rose in her chest.

They had avenged her mother and everyone else who had died from the magic sickness and who had lost themselves and their loved ones because of the Loj. They had stopped a war. They had kept their city from ruin.

You see, ciolo. I told you that it would all be okay.

Her mother's voice blew through her mind like the wind and for once Tavia didn't want to cry or shut it out. She wanted to savor it and she wanted to laugh.

I know, she told her mother. *And I wish you were here to see it.*

Tavia squeezed Wesley's hand.

He turned to look at her, deep brown eyes and a half smile that she felt in her bones. He was still wearing those damn cuff links and though the bow tie was gone—strange, considering this was *definitely* an odd day—his shirt was buttoned to the collar in true Wesley style. Almost pristine, if not for the blood splatters, which she kindly chose to ignore.

Wesley reached out and placed his hand on Tavia's cheek, like he still couldn't quite believe she was standing in front of him, rather than bleeding out on the ground.

"Don't ever scare me like that again," he said.

"I was just keeping you on your toes," Tavia teased. "And in my defense, it wasn't *my* plan. You have your sister to thank for—"

"Never again," he said.

When he kissed her, it was soft and delicate, like he was afraid she might break, or that this living Tavia was the illusion and if he kissed her too hard then she'd fade away. So Tavia brought her hands around his neck and pressed him harder against her, letting him know that he didn't need to be careful with her.

She was real.

She was here.

And she wasn't going anywhere.

She felt Wesley smile under her lips and the world went newly quiet. He had the power to make her heart slow, like he was pulling all the bad from the world and all the worry from her body.

And then somebody cleared their throat and they quickly broke apart.

Tavia turned to face her friends, her cheeks warm.

She'd almost forgotten they were there and that she and Wesley weren't the only two people in the world.

Saxony was tending to Zekia, pulling her sister to her feet and trying to avoid eye contact with Tavia, but Karam didn't have that problem as she collected her fallen knives from the ground and stared at Tavia with her patented glare.

They all looked like they'd rather not have seen Tavia and Wesley kissing.

"So we're alive," Tavia said to them, in case they didn't already know.

"Yeah," Saxony said. "And some of us are enjoying it a little too much."

Though she was smiling, and Tavia hadn't thought about how much she missed Saxony smiling at her until then.

"Want to celebrate with me?" she asked.

"I've seen the way you celebrate," Saxony said. "I'll pass."

But Tavia was already running toward her and she practically tackled Saxony into a hug. Her old friend arched her neck to raise her eyebrows at how Tavia was clinging to her like some kind of weird animal.

"Many Gods," Saxony said. "Let me breathe, will you?"

Tavia loosened her grip, just enough for Saxony to take a breath, and then she squeezed her back into a tight hug once more.

"Okay, you win," Saxony said, laughing. "I surrender."

Tavia broke away, grinning, and Saxony ruffled her hair. Tavia turned to Karam and her warrior friend took two steps back.

"If you hug me, I will stab you," she said.

Tavia weighed this up in her mind for a moment, but decided it was worth it. She swung her arms around Karam and though she heard her friend let out a long groan, her hands still wrapped around Tavia's back and squeezed. Just once, brief and strong.

"You're the world's worst hugger," Tavia whispered in her ear.

Karam pushed her away with a frown. "Now I stab you. That was the deal."

"We should check on the army," Wesley said. "See if Arjun and Schulze are still alive."

"You care about Arjun?" Karam asked.

"No," Wesley said, all too quickly. "I just want to make sure he protected the Doyen. I need Schulze alive for our deal on new magic rules going forward."

"Can we also get me a healer?" Zekia asked. Then, her voice a little smaller as they all turned to look at her: "If anyone still wants me healed. My magic did most of it, but I feel a little odd. I could try myself if nobody wants to."

Tavia felt a pang of sympathy for her would-be murderer.

Zekia was the youngest of them and she had sacrificed the most in a lot of ways, and now she looked as though she didn't know if she had anything left.

With Ashwood gone, she seemed unsure whether the family she still had would take her back.

Wesley sighed and limped over to Zekia so that he could place a hand on her head. The trick dust Tavia had sprinkled on his leg was good at easing the pain temporarily and even stopping the bleeding, but it hadn't healed him.

Just like his sister, Wesley would need true magic for that.

"You're kind of an idiot, kid," Wesley said to Zekia.

Tavia knew that was Wesley's way of saying that he cared and there was no way he was going to accept anyone not jumping at the chance to help his sister.

Saxony took Zekia's hand in hers. "Come on, little sister," she said. "Let's go home."

Heading down from the bridge and onto the shores that separated Creije from the rest of the Uskhanyan cities, Tavia wasn't sure what to expect.

But it sure wasn't Arjun and Doyen Fenna Schulz, followed by dozens of their soldiers, climbing out of a small train, similar to the one the Kingpin had slithered out of.

"Aren't you all supposed to be in Yejlath?" Wesley asked.

The Doyen's back straightened. "Yes, well. We defeated Ashwood's people there. With the help of your Crafters and buskers we . . . Well, it was a fair fight," she said, as though she hated to admit it. "We came back with a few of our people to see what had become of Ashwood and if you had been able to uphold your end of the bargain."

"Consider it upheld," Wesley said.

"Great, now you will brag about it until the end of days," Arjun said.

Tavia couldn't hold back her smile at the sound of his stubborn voice.

"It's good that you're not dead," she told him.

Arjun scoffed, in that haughty and unsmiling way that only he could make endearing. "Grankans do not give up easily," he said. "We are warriors. We are champions and we—"

"You bored them all to death, didn't you?" Wesley asked. "Be straight with us. That's how you won, isn't it?"

"Don't be so mean," Tavia said. "I'm sure that he bored some of them into surrender. Give the guy credit where credit's due."

Arjun's eyes narrowed. "I cannot wait to go back to Wrenyal and never have to deal with you two again."

Tavia touched a hand to her chest. "You're saying you won't miss us? After all the training sessions and late-night bonding?"

"Late night," Wesley repeated, his eyebrows raised. "How late exactly?"

Tavia wrinkled her nose, just as Karam stepped forward and held out her hand for her childhood friend.

Arjun sheathed his sword and threaded his fingers through hers.

"Are you okay?" he asked her.

She nodded. "Asees is avenged," she said. "We have gotten justice for them all."

Everyone in Arjun's Kin who had been killed or manipulated by the Kingpin.

Everyone in the realms who had died so Ashwood could have more power.

They couldn't undo it, but maybe they could make the pain a little easier to swallow.

"She would be proud," Arjun said.

He gripped his hands tighter around Karam's and then pulled her into a hug. Tavia couldn't help but notice that Karam was hugging Arjun far more nicely than she'd hugged her. She saw Karam's back lift in a sigh of relief as she clung to her friend and let go of all the worry about possibly having lost anyone else.

They were all safe.

"So now what?" Tavia asked.

"We discuss what happens next," Wesley said, looking at the Doyen.

He was already adjusting his suit sleeves and was attempting to make himself look more imposing than his disheveled presence allowed. He took in a breath, like he was preparing himself to either throw a punch or take one.

"Our deal is still on, I assume?"

"There is a lot to discuss," Schulze said.

Tavia shoved her hands into her pockets.

She knew that meant they would have to go to Yejlath, and she hated Yejlath. It was so *uppity* and the last thing she wanted after fighting a war was to go to the Halls of Government and talk politics with a Doyen. She wanted a damn bath and a good meal and an undisturbed night's sleep.

It was the least they were all owed.

But she knew that Ashwood still had Crafters and buskers spread across the realms and it was their job to come to an agreement on next steps. Those who were enthralled by the Loj would now be free to get their minds back, and those who followed him willingly would now be aimless without a true leader.

They would surrender to the army Tavia and the others had built.

They would surrender to the armies that the other Realm Doyens would undoubtedly bring into Uskhanya to help ferry peace.

And if they didn't, Tavia and her friends would be right there, waiting.

43

Saxony

THE CITY OF YEJLATH felt like a ghost city, despite the fact that it was crawling with soldiers. Ashwood had only taken a small part of his army to Creije and the rest had been here, in the government city, where Schulze's people had bested them.

The people not dead were already imprisoned and Schulze's soldiers patrolled the cobbled streets for any enemies they had missed, but even with the sparse groups of everyday people meandering across the roads, Saxony couldn't help but think Yejlath looked rather sad.

The Halls of Government were well guarded, and earlier, when Saxony, Tavia, and Karam had walked toward the collection of grandiose buildings, Saxony noticed how pristine they still looked, even after the bloody battle that had taken place on their steps just days before.

They were painted an even cream, arching in high bulbous statues, with grand gold doors and cobblestoned pathways.

But with no people and no echo of the music that usually flowed from the windows—remnants of the enchanted government orchestra instruments that played endless symphonies from dusk until dawn—they had a dead quality to them that made Saxony's jaw go tight.

Ashwood had sucked the spirit from this realm and it would take time to call it back.

Saxony shuffled among the crowd.

Karam, Tavia, and Zekia were lined up alongside her, as rows of the realm communicators—who usually spread gossip faster than news—waited among the public in anticipation for the talk to begin.

It would be the first time the Doyen had made an official appearance and an official announcement since the war had ended, and Saxony was eager to hear exactly what it was she had to say after days spent in discussion with Wesley.

Schulze hadn't let the rest of them be a part of the talks. It was a sacred and serious discussion, she'd said, between her and the underboss, who could represent the buskers and the Crafters.

After all, Wesley belonged to both.

"I wish they'd hurry up," Tavia said. "I need to pee."

"Then pee here," Karam said. "It is not like anyone expects buskers to have manners."

"Is that why you brought knives?" Tavia asked. "Because you're so well mannered?"

"They argue a lot, huh?" Zekia asked.

She was standing on her tiptoes so that she could whisper in Saxony's ear.

"You don't know the half of it," Saxony said.

She smiled at her sister, and when Zekia laughed, a peace fell into Saxony's heart.

She couldn't believe her little sister was laughing at her side again.

The crowd rumbled, murmurs growing as Fenna Schulze finally walked out onto the stage, followed by over a dozen armed guards and Wesley Thornton Walcott. He stood next to the podium as Schulze cleared her throat and readied to address the realm.

"I am here today not just as your Doyen, but as a citizen of this realm," she said. "As many of you know, just days ago the Kingpin known as Dante Ashwood was killed, as part of a joint effort between our forces and volunteers from buskers and Crafters across the realm."

The audience stirred at the mention of Crafters.

Saxony's people were supposed to be the bad guys, after all.

"Because of these noble efforts, we were able to end the war that threatened our peace and our freedom," Schulze continued. "And with thanks to our allies, we were also able to develop a cure for Dante Ashwood's mind-control elixir. This has already been made available across Creije and Yejlath, and will be distributed to the other cities in the realm within the coming days."

Saxony had been the one to create more of the cure she had fashioned from her family's blood, teaching other Crafters how to do the same and imbuing it with duplication magic so that it could spread more seamlessly across the realm.

It was still a work in progress, but thanks to her, the magic factories where love elixirs and all manner of legal and overpriced magic were usually concocted were now able to produce and reproduce the elixir faster than ever.

She didn't expect any personal thanks, but a little nod wouldn't have gone amiss.

"Those infected with the Loj will be given clemency," Schulze said. "They will be cured and given the chance at a second life, closely monitored by amityguards for a limited time. Those not marked with the Loj, who followed Dante Ashwood because they shared his vision, will be found, arrested, and will face trial. We do not take their crimes lightly."

Schulze said the last part like she was still addressing an army, rather than a crowd of civilians and communicators. She looked like a warrior instead of a politician.

"Now I must talk to you about the continued alliance we plan to have with both the buskers and the Crafters, all of whom were essential in helping us to secure this victory," she said.

At that point, Wesley moved forward, his shoulder brushing not so lightly against the Doyen's as he leaned into the speaker.

"That's where I come in," he said, adjusting his tie.

With a tight jaw, Schulze stepped aside to give Wesley the full platform, which he looked all too pleased by.

"Dante Ashwood is dead and you won't be surprised to know that *I'm* the one who killed him," Wesley said.

A few of the crowd sucked in a breath, but most kept their mouths firmly shut.

Which was probably the smart course to take.

Only one spoke up—

"Will you be vying to take his place?" a woman asked. "You were the underboss of Creije, weren't you?"

Saxony resisted the urge to let her magic rise up to the surface. After all Wesley had done, after *saving the realms*, they still thought he was the same as the Kingpin. That he was just another underboss on a power trip.

"Alleged underboss," Wesley said. "And nobody is taking Ashwood's place. The time of black magic dealing in Uskhanya is over, just like the time for fearing magic is over. All magic sold on the streets will be legal, with more charms available than before, and buskers trading within the law. And, it also must be said, Crafters who feared being hunted or used for magical profit will now be free to live their lives as anyone else might. They do not have to be afraid and they do not have to hide."

Saxony swallowed.

Karam threaded their hands together.

A free world, where Saxony and her family—where all of her people—could have a real life, with no hiding and no secrets. They could leave the Uncharted Forest and explore what the rest of the realms had to offer, without being scared that leaving their homes would mean never being able to return.

"We will have a world where everyone is equal and magic can be dealt safely," Wesley said. "Of course, there will be bans on dangerous charms, but as a whole we need to learn to respect magic instead of fear it. Just like we must learn to respect Crafters. It was only because of magic that we were able to stop Dante Ashwood."

Schulze cleared her throat, like the truth of that made her more uncomfortable than anything.

"We need to unite," Wesley said. "Civilians, amityguards, buskers, and Crafters. It's the only way for peace."

His eyes scanned the crowd, the look on his face similar to the one he wore as an underboss, except this time there was a new authority to it, not rooted in ego or the desire to be the best, but the need to keep as many people safe as he could.

To protect Creije as he had always done.

Saxony never thought that she'd feel proud of Wesley Thornton Walcott, but looking at him now, standing in front of a microphone as the realms watched on, a Doyen by his side, that was exactly what she felt.

He didn't want to take over the magic trade; he wanted to make sure there wasn't a trade that could harm their people. Just magic, some good, some not so good, but all of it available and none of it made to keep Crafters in shackles.

"This is the beginning of a new realm," Wesley said. "And a fresh start for us all."

He held out his hand for the Doyen to shake, a formality that was so desperately needed in these times.

Schulze looked down at Wesley's hand, and with only the smallest of frowns did she clasp it in her own.

Saxony let out a long breath, and for once it wasn't a sigh or a preparation for scary futures to come.

It was relief.

It was hope.

Doyen Schulze was willing to make a deal to give Crafters the chance at a normal life. Finally, more than fifty years after the War of Ages had ended, their realm and her people could begin to heal.

This was the future Saxony had always wanted. It was the reason she had come to Creije: to avenge her family by killing Ashwood, to free her people by changing the laws and attitudes toward magic, and to unite the people she loved.

She had done all of that now, and with her sister at her side and her brother onstage shaking hands with a Doyen, Saxony felt her heart lift.

This was everything she had ever dreamed of. And so finally she could stop dreaming and start living.

44

Wesley

SAXONY, KARAM, AND ZEKIA were seated on the grass by the riverbank, where the next train to Rishiya waited. Most of their army had congregated inside, except for those who wished to stay in Creije. Or those who planned on getting the first train they could out of Uskhanya entirely.

"Is Tavia here?" Wesley asked.

Saxony looked at him with a raised eyebrow, untangling her hand from Karam's. "I'm sorry, is our company not good enough for the underboss of Creije?"

Wesley shrugged, his smile tipping upward.

"She is by the Crook," Karam said. "Where else would a busker be?"

That sounded like Tavia.

Wesley sat down on the grass beside Zekia, resigned to the fact that his suit was ruined.

"How's our Doyen?" Saxony asked.

"Busy," Wesley said. "Who knew reshaping the world was so much work?"

It had been a week since Dante Ashwood had been killed. After they had addressed the realms from the Halls of Government, they had traveled back into Creije to begin reopening the capital city's most notorious and inspiring landmarks. The museum, the library, and, of course, the bars would soon follow. The Crook would be the first of them to open its doors and wet its glasses with Cloverye for the nervous patrons, helping to ease everyone back into the routine of daily life.

But despite all that, it would be at least another few weeks until their armies would be able to properly scour Uskhanya and find the strays of Ashwood's people. Not to mention that there were bound to be hundreds of innocents scattered around the realm, in need of saving and curing. Wesley couldn't see himself getting a break anytime soon.

"Are you excited?" Zekia asked.

Wesley turned to her with a curious expression and lounged back onto the palms of his hands. "About what?"

"Being in charge," she said.

"I'm always in charge," he said. "I'm just excited to be home."

Saxony looked down at the grass. "I almost forgot that you'd be staying."

Impossibly, Wesley had too.

He had been so busy helping to amass enough prisoners to fill the Halls of Government to bursting, and enough victims of the Loj to fill the Grand Infirmary and keep their healers occupied for the foreseeable future, that he had forgotten that he didn't need to leave Creije again.

"I need to stay to get a proper drink," Wesley said. "It's a good thing that Ashwood didn't destroy my bar."

Karam couldn't help but laugh, but Saxony didn't mirror her smile in the slightest.

"You could come with us," she said, in a voice soft enough to make Wesley shuffle. "The Rishiyat Kin would love to have you home."

Home.

Only, Wesley was already home. Rishiya was his past, but Creije was his present and his future.

"I don't think they need me around," Wesley said. "Not with their new Liege taking the reins."

Wesley nudged her with his shoulder.

"Zekia and I agree that it's your destiny," Wesley said. "Don't we, kid?"

"Yep," Zekia said. "I'm going to dream and relax and have Amja tell me stories."

Saxony smiled, but Wesley could see he hadn't given her the answer she wanted.

"Do you think the Kin will be mad when I go back?" Zekia asked.

She looked up at him with worried eyes, her chin nuzzled into his shoulder.

"What if they hate me now?"

"If you want advice on redemption, then you're talking to the wrong sibling." He ruffled her hair and Zekia pulled away from him to smooth it back out. "You've seen a thousand futures, kid. At least one of them had to have been on your side."

Saxony let out a disbelieving laugh. "Look at you, the wise old man."

Wesley frowned at the word *old*, but thought the *wise* part was enough of a compliment to let it slide.

"Just take care of her," he said, pushing himself up from the grass.

He needed to find Tavia. It had been hours since he'd last seen her.

Saxony, Karam, and Zekia stood too, and there was an awkward moment where Wesley thought Karam might hug him, but instead she merely stepped forward and clapped him on the shoulder.

"You fought well," she said. "Even if I fought better."

Wesley would take that goodbye.

He'd miss his favorite fighter. Despite everything, Karam and he had been in each other's lives for years, and that meant he couldn't think of anyone who he'd rather have accompany his sisters back to Rishiya. There wasn't a person in the realms he trusted more to guard them. And to love them.

"I'll see you around," Wesley said to her. "Look after those two, okay?"

Karam gave him a rare smile.

"Of course," she said. "I will go with them back to Rishiya and watch over them."

That was good enough for Wesley. Knowing Karam would be watching over his family meant that he knew they would always be safe.

"You'll be okay here?" Saxony asked.

"I'm always okay," Wesley said.

Saxony said nothing in return, but she pulled him into a tight hug that threw Wesley for a loop. He was not a hugger, but he'd also never been a brother before, so he guessed things changed. He wrapped his arms around Saxony and felt the moment she sighed against his shoulder.

"See you soon, little brother," she said, pulling away.

Wesley sucked in a breath. "Let's stick with first names," he said. "See you around, Saxony."

She put her hand on his cheek and it was then that Wesley realized for the first time just how much taller she was than him. And how suddenly he was not only a big brother, but that he had a big sister, too.

For the first time, he had someone to look up to and rely on. Someone whose job it was to have his back.

"Stay safe, Wesley," she said.

"Sounds boring."

Saxony rolled her eyes. "Stay boring, then."

Wesley grinned. "Never."

45

Tavia

THE CROOK STILL STOOD, and aside from a few scrapes and bruises to the old clock tower, it looked as beautiful as ever.

"You'll miss the train," Wesley said, half-joking. "I think the next one to Volo is coming soon."

He strolled over to her, and though Tavia didn't turn to see him, she felt the moment he was by her side. Wesley made the air around him charged, both with magic and something else that Tavia couldn't explain, but that she could feel in her very bones.

"You're going to need a reopening party for this place," Tavia said. "If you're finished saving the world, that is."

"There's a lot to take care of now that I'm a big hero," Wesley said. "Including throwing some great parties."

Tavia all but snorted. "A few free shots and some bottles of Cloverye and people will be lining up around the corner again. A place for the hopeless to lift their spirits."

"I hope so," Wesley said. "It's strange to have this place so empty."

She felt it too.

The streets weren't bustling or electrified by the laughter and wonder of tourists, and the Crook wasn't thumping with music and magic tricks. It felt like the heart of the city had wilted somewhat, but Tavia knew that it would flower again.

Creije had always been a place for the dreamers, where the lost were found and the lonely realized the world could be a comforting place. That in a city that didn't close its eyes or turn off its lights, there really wasn't a place to feel like you were on your own.

It wasn't just a city, it was a family.

A family of wanderers looking to find their next adventure.

There was no way that Creije wouldn't return to its former glory, especially with Tavia and Wesley there to fight for it.

"So," Wesley said. "Volo. When are we going?"

We.

Tavia hadn't known that such a small word could feel so big. So wonderful.

"Volo was always the plan," she said.

She couldn't help but enjoy the way Wesley sighed at the words. The last thing he wanted to do was leave Creije, but it had been Tavia's wish, for too many years to remember. She had spent endless nights dreaming of the day she'd see the paper lanterns during the celebration of the Lonely Goddess's sacrifice. She wished for the chance to walk down the streets her mother had as a child and find a home there, and perhaps a family, too. That was all she had ever wanted: a place to belong with people she loved and who would love her back without agenda or motive.

What a shame it had taken her so many years to realize that she didn't need to travel across the realms to find something she already had.

Everything Tavia needed and everything she wanted was right here in Uskhanya.

In Creije.

"But I think the trip will have to wait," she said.

"The trip," Wesley repeated.

He cleared his throat and she could feel the nerves radiating off of him.

Wesley was never nervous.

At least, he never showed that he was.

This new vulnerability, or inability to pull his facade properly over his face, was rather endearing.

"Wasn't it supposed to be the final destination where you laid down your roots?" he asked. "I was readying for a life of commuting between realms. Long-distance *delg* bats or something."

"You want me to leave all this?" Tavia spread her arms wide. "Not a chance. My family in Volo can wait."

She turned to face him.

His suit didn't quite fit right. Borrowed, probably, since his stash in Creije had been destroyed and the tailors weren't yet open again. There was a scuff mark on the tie that was decidedly *un*-Wesley, but underneath it all were the tattoos and the scars. The calloused skin and the eyes that bored into her soul, even on the days where she tried to convince herself that she hated him.

Truth be told, Tavia had never once hated Wesley.

Truth be told, she could not remember a time when she didn't love him.

"It's the family that I have right here that needs me," she said.

Wesley raised an eyebrow. "What about traveling the realms?"

Tavia smiled. "There will be plenty of time to do that after we help rebuild them."

She took Wesley's hand in hers. Skin against skin. Scars against scars. They had grown up together and though there were many years behind them, she knew there were so many more in front of them now.

She looked at their hands, so precariously entwined.

Tavia didn't have the words to tell Wesley what she felt for him in that moment, and so she simply kissed him instead. Soft, brief, his lips warm against hers and their hands never once breaking apart.

She pulled slowly away from him, savoring each breath.

"One day I'll explore Volo and anywhere else my heart takes me," she said. "But I won't be away from home for too long."

They had so many memories to come and so much magic left to craft. They would rebuild their city—their home—and cast charms into the air and tricks onto the streets, reveling in the wonder that it brought.

They would light up the realms together, one adventure at a time.

Tavia pressed her forehead to Wesley's. "Can't have you getting into trouble while I'm gone."

She felt him laugh against her. "People keep saying that," Wesley said. "But trouble is fun."

"I know."

Tavia pulled away so she could see the full glory of his smile.

"That's why I'm staying," she said. "You can't have all the fun without me."

The End

Also by Alexandra Christo

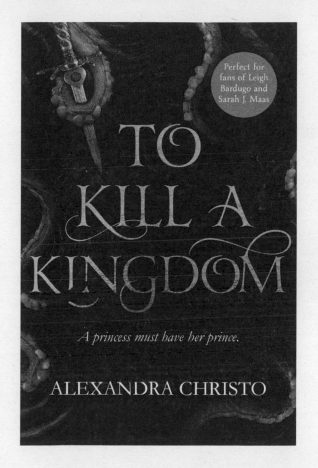

Turn the page to read an extract.

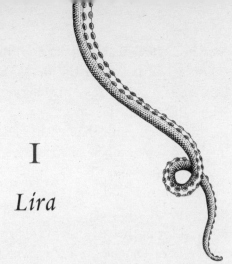

I

Lira

I HAVE A HEART for every year I've been alive.

There are seventeen hidden in the sand of my bedroom. Every so often, I claw through the shingle, just to check they're still there. Buried deep and bloody. I count each of them, so I can be sure none were stolen in the night. It's not such an odd fear to have. Hearts are power, and if there's one thing my kind craves more than the ocean, it's power.

I've heard things: tales of lost hearts and harpooned women stapled to the ocean bed as punishment for their treachery. Left to suffer until their blood becomes salt and they dissolve to sea foam. These are the women who take the human bounty of their kin. Mermaids more fish than flesh, with an upper body to match the decadent scales of their fins.

Unlike sirens, mermaids have stretched blue husks and limbs in place of hair, with a jawlessness that lets their mouths stretch to the size of small boats and swallow sharks whole. Their deep-blue flesh is dotted with fins that spread up their arms and spines. Fish and human both, with the beauty of neither.

They have the capacity to be deadly, like all monsters, but where sirens seduce and kill, mermaids remain fascinated by humans. They steal trinkets and follow ships in hopes that treasure will fall from the decks. Sometimes they save the lives of sailors and take nothing but charms in return. And when they steal the hearts we keep, it isn't for power. It's because they think that if they eat enough of them, they might become human themselves.

I hate mermaids.

My hair snakes down my back, as red as my left eye – and only my left, of course, because the right eye of every siren is the color of the sea they were born into. For me, that's the great sea of Diávolos, with waters of apple and sapphire. A selection of each so it manages to be neither. In that ocean lies the sea kingdom of Keto.

It's a well-known fact that sirens are beautiful, but the bloodline of Keto is royal and with that comes its own beauty. A magnificence forged in salt water and regality. We have eyelashes born from iceberg shavings and lips painted with the blood of sailors. It's a wonder we even need our song to steal hearts.

"Which will you take, cousin?" Kahlia asks in *Psáriin*.

She sits beside me on the rock and stares at the ship in the distance. Her scales are deep auburn and her blond hair barely reaches her breasts, which are covered by a braid of orange seaweed.

"You're ridiculous," I tell her. "You know which."

The ship ploughs idly along the calm waters of Adékaros, one of the many human kingdoms I've vowed to rid of a prince. It's smaller than most and made from scarlet wood that represents the colors of their country.

Humans enjoy flaunting their treasures for the world, but it only makes them targets for creatures like Kahlia and me, who can easily spot a royal ship. After all, it's the only one in the fleet with the painted wood and tiger flag. The only vessel on which the Adékarosin prince ever sails.

Easy prey for those in the mood to hunt.

The sun weighs on my back. Its heat presses against my neck and causes my hair to stick to my wet skin. I ache for the ice of the sea, so sharp with cold that it feels like glorious knives in the slits between my bones.

"It's a shame," says Kahlia. "When I was spying on him, it was like looking at an angel. He has such a pretty face."

"His heart will be prettier."

Kahlia breaks into a wild smile. "It's been an age since your last kill, Lira," she teases. "Are you sure you're not out of practice?"

"A year is hardly an age."

"It depends who's counting."

I sigh. "Then tell me who that is so I can kill them and be done with this conversation."

Kahlia's grin is ungodly. The kind reserved for moments when I am at my most dreadful, because that's the trait sirens are supposed to value most. Our awfulness is treasured. Friendship and kinship taught to be as foreign as land. Loyalty reserved only for the Sea Queen.

"You are a little heartless today, aren't you?"

"Never," I say. "There are seventeen under my bed."

Kahlia shakes the water from her hair. "So many princes you've tasted."

She says it as though it's something to be proud of, but that's because Kahlia is young and has taken only two hearts of her own. None of them royalty. That's my specialty, my territory. Some of Kahlia's reverence is for that. The wonder of whether the lips of a prince taste different from those of any other human. I can't say, for princes are all I've ever tasted.

Ever since our goddess, Keto, was killed by the humans, it's become custom to steal a heart each year, in the month of our birth. It's a celebration of the life Keto gave to us and a tribute of revenge for the life the humans took from her. When I was too young to hunt, my mother did it for me, as is tradition. And she always gave me princes. Some as young as I was. Others old and furrowed, or middle children who never had a chance at ruling. The king of Armonía, for instance, once had six sons, and for my first few birthdays, my mother brought me one each year.

When I was eventually old enough to venture out on my own, it hadn't occurred to me to forgo royalty and target sailors like the rest of my kind did, or even hunt the princes who would one day assume their thrones. I'm nothing if not a loyal follower of my mother's traditions.

"Did you bring your shell?" I ask.

Kahlia scoops her hair out of the way to show the orange seashell looped around her neck. A similar one just a few shades bloodier dangles from my own throat. It doesn't look like much, but it's the easiest way for us to communicate. If we hold them to our ears, we can hear the sound of the ocean and the song of the Keto underwater palace we call home. For Kahlia, it can act as a map to the sea of Diávolos if we're separated. We're a long way from our kingdom, and it took nearly a week to swim here. Since Kahlia is fourteen, she tends to stay close to the palace, but I was the one to decide that should change, and as the princess, my whims are as good as law.

"We won't get separated," Kahlia says.

Normally, I wouldn't mind if one of my cousins were stranded in a foreign ocean. As a whole, they're a tedious and predictable bunch, with little ambition or imagination.

Ever since my aunt died, they've become nothing more than adoring lackeys for my mother. Which is ridiculous, because the Sea Queen is not there to be adored. She's there to be feared.

"Remember to pick just one," I instruct. "Don't lose your focus."

Kahlia nods. "Which one?" she asks. "Or will it sing to me when I'm there?"

"We'll be the only ones singing," I say. "It'll enchant them all, but if you lay your focus on one, they'll fall in love with you so resolutely that even as they drown, they'll scream of nothing but your beauty."

"Normally the enchantment is broken when they start to die," Kahlia says.

"Because you focus on them all, and so, deep down, they know that none of them are your heart's desire. The trick is to want them as much as they want you."

"But they're disgusting," says Kahlia, though it doesn't sound like she believes it so much as she wants me to think that she does. "How can we be expected to desire them?"

"Because you're not just dealing with sailors now. You're dealing with royalty, and with royalty comes power. Power is *always* desirable."

"Royalty?" Kahlia gapes. "I thought . . ."

She trails off. What she thought was that princes were mine and I didn't share. That's not untrue, but where there are princes, there are kings and queens, and I've never had much use for either of those. Rulers are easily deposed. It's the princes who hold the allure. In their youth. In the allegiance of their people. In the promise of the leader they could one day become. They are the next generation of rulers, and by killing them, I kill the future. Just as my mother taught me.

I take Kahlia's hand. "You can have the queen. I've no interest in the past."

Kahlia's eyes are alight. The right holds the same sapphire of the Diávolos Sea I know well, but the left, a creamy yellow that barely stands out from the white, sparkles with a rare glee. If she steals a royal heart for her fifteenth, it'll be sure to earn her clemency from my mother's perpetual rage.

"And you'll take the prince," says Kahlia. "The one with the pretty face."

"His face makes no difference." I drop her hand. "It's his heart I'm after."

"So many hearts." Her voice is angelic. "You'll soon run out of room to bury them all."

I lick my lips. "Maybe," I say. "But a princess must have her prince."

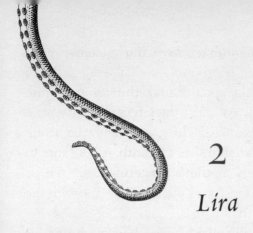

2

Lira

THE SHIP FEELS ROUGH under the spines of my fingers. The wood is splintered, paint cracking and peeling over the body. It cuts the water in a way that is too jagged. Like a blunt knife, pressing and tearing until it slices through. There is rot in places and the stench makes my nose wrinkle.

It is a poor prince's ship.

Not all royals are alike. Some are furnished in fine clothes, unbearably heavy jewels so large that they drown twice as fast. Others are sparsely dressed, with only one or two rings and bronze crowns painted gold. Not that it matters to me. A prince is a prince, after all.

Kahlia keeps to my side, and we swim with the ship while it tears through the sea. It's a steady speed and one we easily match. This is the agonizing wait, as humans become prey. Some time passes before the prince finally steps onto the deck and casts his eye at the ocean. He can't see us. We're far too close and swim far too fast. Through the ship's wake, Kahlia looks to me and her eyes beg the question. With a smile as good as any nod, I return my cousin's stare.

We emerge from the froth and part our lips.

We sing in perfect unison in the language of Midas, the

most common human tongue and one each siren knows well. Not that the words matter. It's the music that seduces them. Our voices echo into the sky and roll back through the wind. We sing as though there is an entire chorus of us, and as the haunting melody ricochets and climbs, it swirls into the hearts of the crew until finally the ship slows to a stop.

"Do you hear it, Mother?" asks the prince. His voice is high and dreamlike.

The queen stands next to him on the deck. "I don't think . . ."

Her voice falters as the melody strokes her into submission. It's a command, and every human has come to a stop, bodies frozen as their eyes search the seas. I set my focus on the prince and sing more softly. Within moments his eyes fall to mine.

"Gods," he says. "It's you."

He smiles and from his left eye slips a single tear.

I stop singing and my voice turns to a gentle hum.

"My love," the prince says, "I've found you at last."

He grips the ratlines and peers far over the edge, his chest flat against the wood, one hand reaching out to touch me. He's dressed in a beige shirt, the strings loose at his chest, sleeves torn and slightly moth-bitten. His crown is thin gold leaf that looks as though it could break if he moves too quickly. He looks desolate and poor.

But then there is his face.

Soft and round, with skin like varnished wood and eyes a penetrating shade darker. His hair swings and coils tightly on his head, a beautiful mess of loops and spirals. Kahlia was right; he's angelic. Magnificent, even. His heart will make a fine trophy.

"You are so beautiful," says the queen, staring down at Kahlia with reverence. "I'm unsure how I've ever considered another."

Kahlia's smile is primordial as she reaches out to the queen, beckoning her to the ocean.

I turn back to the prince, who is frantically stretching out his hand to me. "My love," he pleads. "Come aboard."

I shake my head and continue to hum. The wind groans with the lullaby of my voice.

"I'll come to you then!" he shouts, as though it was ever a choice.

With a gleeful smile, he flings himself into the ocean, and with the splash of his body comes a second, which I know to be the queen, throwing herself to my cousin's mercy. The sounds of their falls awaken something in the crew, and in an instant they are screaming.

They lean over the ship's edge, fifty of them clinging to ropes and wood, watching the spectacle below with horror. But none dare throw themselves overboard to save their sovereigns. I can smell their fear, mixed with the confusion that comes from the sudden absence of our song.

I meet the eyes of my prince and stroke his soft, angelic skin. Gently, with one hand on his cheek and another resting on the thin bones of his shoulder, I kiss him. And as my lips taste his, I pull him under.

The kiss breaks once we are far enough down. My song has long since ended, but the prince stays enamored. Even as the water fills his lungs and his mouth opens in a gasp, he keeps his eyes on me with a glorious look of infatuation.

As he drowns, he touches his fingers to his lips.

Beside me, Kahlia's queen thrashes. She clutches at her throat and bats my cousin away. Angrily, Kahlia clings to her ankle and keeps her deep below the surface, the queen's face a sneer as she tries to escape. It's futile. A siren's hold is a vice.

I stroke my dying prince. My birthday is not for two weeks.

This trip was a gift for Kahlia: to hold the heart of royalty in her hands and name it her fifteenth. It's not supposed to be for me to steal a heart a fortnight early, breaking our most sacred rule. Yet there's a prince dying slowly in front of me. Brown skin and lips blue with ocean. Hair flowing behind him like black seaweed. Something about his purity reminds me of my very first kill. The young boy who helped my mother turn me into the beast I am now.

Such a pretty face, I think.

I run a thumb over the poor prince's lip, savoring his peaceful expression. And then I let out a shriek like no other. The kind of noise that butchers bones and claws through skin. A noise to make my mother proud.

In one move, I plunge my fist into the prince's chest and pull out his heart.

ACKNOWLEDGMENTS

YOU'VE REACHED THE END! Now this is the part where you get to read about all the people I love (or the ones who bribed me into putting their names in here).

First off, I have to thank my parents. Literally, have to. They're forcing me. Help! (Kidding.) Mum, Dad, you guys are more than I could ever have wished for. I'm so happy to have you by my side, championing me whatever I do.

To the rest of my family, who are far too big to name, and far too wonderful for words. And, of course, to Nick, because although times will change, these acknowledgments never will. I love you. You're not getting in my book.

To Daniel, who insists I named a character after him before we even met. Who makes me laugh every day and who still gives me first-date butterflies, even now. You're my favorite person. Even if you are the world's slowest reader.

Thank you to all my friends in the publishing world and outside of it. To Leanne and Becca, as always, for being the best of friends. To Sasha Alsberg, Sarah Glenn Marsh, N.J. Simmonds, Brigid Kemmerer, Melinda Salisbury, Rebecca Kuang, and

Tricia Levenseller. And to Siiri, for always bouncing into my life when I need a smile!

And, gosh, all the people who made this book possible!

Emmanuelle, thank you for being the best agent a writer could ask for, and a great friend to boot. Your championing of all my stories, and all the possibilities they could hold, makes me believe anything is possible. And to Whitney, for helping to bring those words to people and countries I'd never have dreamed of.

To all of the people at Macmillan and Feiwel & Friends who have helped make magic a reality. To Holly, for being a rock-star editor and helping me find the story I wanted to tell. To Morgan, for being the best publicist and always throwing exciting things my way. To Liz and Yehrin for creating a masterpiece of a cover! To Kaitlin, Jessica, and Starr, and to everyone else on the team who played a part in making this book, this series, great. I appreciate you all so much!

To everyone at Bonnier Books and Hot Key Books, my fellow UK crew! You guys are the best and I'm so grateful for all of your hard work, your vision, and your endless enthusiasm for all the stories I throw your way. Thank you, thank you, thank you. To Fliss, to Carla, to Lizz, to Isobel, to every single person who has brought so much laughter and positivity to this whole experience! And to Tina, who I hope to get to work with again someday.

Of course, how could I finish with anything else but a thanks to YOU. Dear reader. Dear friend. Dear person who picked this book up, cracked its pages, and dove straight in, headfirst, ready to be swallowed by adventure.

I created this world for you. I hope you loved it.

I hope it helped you find the magic you have inside of yourself.

Thank you for choosing a Hot Key book.

If you want to know more about our authors
and what we publish, you can find us online.

You can start at our website

www.hotkeybooks.com

And you can also find us on:

We hope to see you soon!